BOWL OF HEAVEN

BOWL OF HEAVEN

GREGORY BENFORD

AND

LARRY NIVEN

TOR®

A TOM DOHERTY ASSOCIATES BOOK

NEW YORK

BOWL OF HEAVEN

Copyright © 2012 by Gregory Benford and Larry Niven

All rights reserved.

Illustrations on pages 7 and 71 by Don Davis

Design by Mary A. Wirth

A Tor Book
Published by Tom Doherty Associates, LLC
175 Fifth Avenue
New York, NY 10010

Tor® is a registered trademark of Tom Doherty Associates, LLC.

ISBN 978-0-7653-2841-0

Printed in the United States of America

Cast of Characters

Cliff Kammash—biologist
Mayra Wickramsingh—pilot, with Beth team
Abduss Wickramsingh—engineer, with Beth team
Glory—the planet of destination
Captain Redwing
SunSeeker—the ramship
Beth Marble—biologist
Eros—the first drop ship
Fred Ojama—geologist, with Beth team
Aybe—engineer, with Cliff team
Howard Blaire—engineer, with Cliff team
Terrence Gould—with Cliff team
Irma Michaelson—plant biologist, with Cliff team
Tananareve Bailey—with Beth team
Lau Pin—engineer, with Beth team

CAPTAIN REDWING HAS FOUR CREW ABOARD *SUNSEEKER*

Jampudvipa, shortened to Jam—an Indian bridge officer
Ayaan Ali—Arab woman navigator/pilot
Clare Conway—copilot
Karl Lebanon—general technology officer

ASTRONOMER FOLK

Memor—Attendant Astute Astronomer
Asenath—Wisdom Chief
Ikahaja—Ecosystem Savant
Omanah—Ecosystem Packmistress
Ramanuji—Biology Savant
Kanamatha—Biology Packmistress
Thaji—Judge Savant
(The Adopted, those aliens already encountered and integrated into
    the Bowl, will have further names used in Volume 2.)

Folk Terms

TransLanguage
Long Records
Late Invaders
Undermind
Serf-Ones
the Builders
Third Variety (Astronomer variety)
Astronauts (Astronomer variety)

Bowl of Heaven

PROLOGUE

Here about the beach I wander'd, nourishing a youth sublime
With the fairy tales of science, and the long result of Time

—TENNYSON, "Locksley Hall"

THE LAST PARTY

Cliff turned from the people he was saying good-bye to and looked out at the world he would never see again.

The party roared on behind him. Laughter, shouts, hammering hard music. The laughter was a touch ragged, the music too loud, a forced edge to it all, and an electric zest fueled a murmur of anticipating talk. They had said good-bye already to relatives on Earth. Now, *SunSeeker*'s crew and passengers had to say farewell forever to the starship construction teams, the training echelons, the embodied political and economic forces that were about to launch them out into a vastness beyond experience.

The view was razor sharp, but it was of course a screen, adjusted to subtract the station's centrifugal gyre. So Earth held steady and he could see the tiny silver motes of flung packages headed toward the *SunSeeker* complex. They trailed back toward the flingers on Luna, and another line of specks pointed toward the fatter dots of manufacturing complexes in higher orbits. A dingy new asteroid was gliding in on its decade-long journey. Already, silvery bee swarms of robo-factories accompanied it, hollowing out its stony core for a smelter colony. Glass-skinned biofactories waited for the work crews that would pounce on the asteroid prey, their liquid riches hiding behind fogged domes for sunlight to awaken them.

It struck him how much like artworks machines seemed in space. Here they suffered no constraints of gravity, and so looked like contorted abstracts of Euclidean geometries, cubes and ellipsoids and blunt cylinders that made mobiles without wires, moving with glacial grace against the faint jewels of brimming starlight.

Within the geostationary orbit, he could not see distinct satellites, even after he hit the magnification command and the screen narrowed in. Here, the busy swarm held luxury hotels for ancients now well over two centuries old. Religious colonies were more common but rather Spartan, and ships flitted like dappled radiance everywhere in the incessant sprawl of commerce. The solid Earth swam in a countless froth of tending machines.

He leaned sideways and caught the sheen of the Fresnel lens at the L1 point, a gauzy circle seen nearly on edge from here. It hung between Earth and the sun, deflecting sunlight from the still rather overheated planet. Adjusting patches twinkled in slow splendor.

"Y'know, it'll all be fixed up fine by the time we even wake up." Beth's soft words came from behind him.

Cliff turned and his eyes brightened. "But we'll be this same age."

She blinked and grinned and kissed him back. "Hard not to love an optimist."

"If I didn't think we'll wake up, I wouldn't go."

She wore a sheath dress that definitely wouldn't be going to Glory. It clung to her lithe body, wrapped close around her neck, and anchored at amber bracelets on her wrists. Her

right showed bare skin colored like chardonnay as the dress
polarized, giving him quick glances of flesh. The silky dress
had variable opacity and hue she could tune with the bracelets, he guessed. He hoped this show was for him. People
nearby were making a great show of not noticing. Just as most
ignored the profusion of plunging necklines, built-in push-up
bras, spangles, feathers, slits, and peekaboos. Plus codpieces
on some of the guys, muscle shirts, the hawk hats that made a
man look like a predator.

"A lot of overt signaling tonight, isn't there?" Beth said
dryly.

Not his style. "Bravado, smells like." So he simply took
her in his arms and kissed her. That was the usual best move,
he had learned early on, especially if he could not think of
something witty. Her green eyes blinked. Everyone continued not noticing. He wouldn't see most of them ever again,
after all.

This thought got underlined when a banner rolled across
the room's suspension ceiling. It was from the assembly teams
who for years had worked with the crew, outfitting and running *SunSeeker*.

HOPE YOU ENJOYED GIVING US THE BUSINESS

AS MUCH AS WE ENJOYED TAKING YOU FOR A RIDE

Terry and Fred came by on their way to the bar, laughing
at the banner. "Funny," Terry said. "We're going on to Glory,
and tomorrow they'll be back at work on the next ramscoop.
But they're celebrating harder than we are."

"Yeah," Fred said. "Odd. They're as glad to see us leave as
we are to go."

Terry said, "We're all scarce types. All the psychers say so.
Why wouldn't anyone grab a chance at a whole new, fresh
world?"

"Instead of staying here to fix the one we screwed up?"

Cliff asked. An old issue for them all, but it still clung to him.

Beth shrugged. "We finesse climate, or climate finesses us."

"It's good practice," Terry said. "The previous generations terraformed Earth first. Now it's our turn with a whole new planet."

A tray crawled past; you couldn't use float trays in low-spin gravity. The tray was piled with exotic dishes and surrounded by diners who would not be eating this well for centuries to come. Fred joined them, then Terry, edging into the crowd with minimal courtesy.

"My, my," Beth said warmly. "Ummm . . . maybe we should leave now?"

Cliff looked out over the crowd. Some Earth bureaucrat had on a leash a dog that closely resembled a breakfast pastry with hair. The dog was lapping up someone else's vomit. Three others were laughing at the sight. Apparently most of the party was having a better time than he was.

No matter. This was surely the last time he would see most of them—the crews who had built *SunSeeker*, the endless bureaucrats who at least pretended to add to the effort, the psychers and endless engineers and trial-run crews who would never see another sun. . . . He grimaced and relished the passing moment. All moments were passing, of course. Some, more so. "My heart is full but my glass is empty."

She gave him a rueful nod. "We won't get booze on *Sun-Seeker*."

"In flight? Cap'n Redwing would frown."

"He seems more the 'throw 'em into leg irons' type."

Her laughing-eyed remark told them both that they needed celebration. It helped ward off the doubts, fears, and . . . an emotion he had no name for. *So be it.*

They stood with arms around each other's waist and watched Earth's wheeling, silent majesty. Into the rim of their view swam *SunSeeker*, looking much like a lean and hungry shark.

Yes, a shark waiting to swim in the ocean of night. The large mouth was the magnetic funnel, waiting to be turned on, furl outward, and begin the slow acceleration out of the solar system. That scoop would yawn and first dive close to the sun, swallowing great gouts of the solar wind as start-up fuel. Behind the head complex curved the hoop of the control deck, its ruby glow alive with workers. Cliff watched tiny figures in their worker pods putting finishing touches on the long, rotating cylinder of the habitat and cryostorage sandwiched between the supplies storage vaults. Then came the wrinkled, cottonball-white, cybersmart radiators that sheathed the drive system. Its cylindrically spaced vents gave in to the fat fusion chambers, big ribbed barrels that fed the final thruster nozzles. Wrapped around these in a saddle truss were the big yellow fuel pods that would feed the beast as it accelerated into the deep dark, then fall away. From there on, it would glide through the centuries inside a magnetic sheath, safe from the proton sleet ahead. *SunSeeker* was a shark for eating away at light-years.

They had all ridden her out into the Oort cloud, tried the engines, found the flaws that the previous fourteen ships had tested. Ran the AI systems, found the errors in rivets and reason, made better. In the first few generations of interstellar craft, every new ship was an experiment. Each learned from the last, the engineers and scientists did their work, and a better ship emerged. Directed evolution on the fast track.

Now they were ready for the true deeps. Deep space meant deep time, all fleeting and, soon enough, all gone.

"Beautiful, isn't it?" a man's voice said from behind them.

It was Karl, the lanky head flight engineer. He had an arm around Mei Ling and seemed a bit bleary and red faced. From a snog-fog burst, Cliff guessed. Mei Ling just seemed extraordinarily joyful, eyes glistening.

Beth said, casting a sideways glance, "Yes—and we're counting on you to keep her happy."

"Oh yes, I will," Karl said, not getting the double entendre. "She's a great ship."

Mei Ling got it, arched an eyebrow, and nodded. "Saying good-bye to the world, are we? How do you think they'll think of us by the time we arrive?"

Beth said, "I'd like to be remembered as the world's oldest woman."

They all laughed. Mei Ling asked Cliff, "Hard to say farewell to it all, isn't it? You've been over here at the view most of the evening."

She had always been quick to read people, he recalled. She would understand that he needed merriment now. That they all did. "Um, yeah. I guess I'm a man of the world; my trouble is I'm trying to find which world."

They all nodded soberly. Then with a quick, darting grin, Karl showed off his newest trick. In the low centrifugal grav, he poured a dark red wine by letting it fall from the bottle, then cutting off the right amount with a dinner knife before it hit the glass. Three quick slices, Mei Ling rushed some glasses into place, and done. "Impressive!" Beth said. They drank.

"Got some news," Karl said. "Those grav waves near Glory? No signal in them. Just noise."

"How does that help us?" Beth asked. Cliff could tell from her expression that Karl was not her sort, but Karl would never know.

"It means there's not some supercivilization on Glory, for one thing."

"We already knew there are no electromagnetic signals," Mei Ling said.

"Well, sure," Karl said. "But maybe really advanced societies don't bother with primitive—"

"Hey, this is a party!" Beth said brightly. Karl took the hint. He shrugged and led Mei Ling away. She had some trouble walking.

"Cruel, you are," Cliff said.

"Hey, we won't see him for centuries."

"But it will seem like next week."

"So they say. What do you think about the grav waves?"

Just then a Section head broke in, using a microphone to get above the party noise, which was still rising. "We just got a launch congratulations from Alpha Centauri, folks! They wish you good speed."

Some hand clapping, then the party buzz came back even stronger. "Nice gesture," Beth said. "They had to send that over four years ago."

Tananareve Bailey spoke behind him. "It probably came in a year back and they've been saving it." Cliff hadn't noticed her approach. She was more covered up than most of the women, but gorgeous, an explosion of browns and orange against black face and arms. She stood with Howard Blaire, once a zookeeper and something of a bodybuilding enthusiast.

Beth nodded. "Once we're in flight, the delay times will mean we're talking to different generations. Spooky. But you were saying about the grav waves—?"

Howard twisted his mouth, trying to recall. "Look, *Sun-Seeker* was nearly built before LIGO 22 picked up those waves. It took all the time we were out on our field trials to verify the detection. More time to see if there was anything in it—and apparently there isn't. No signal, just some noisy spectrum. No, we're going to Glory because a biosphere is there. One of the Astros told me these grav waves probably come from just accidental superposition. A good chance there's some pair of orbiting black holes far across the galaxy, but the Glory system is in the way—"

"That's what I think, too," a familiar voice said. They turned to find a red-faced Fred, back again, obviously a bit the worse for wear. "Can't get good resolution on the source area, and Glory's over in one corner of a degree-wide patch in the sky. The grav waves could be from anywhere in there, even in another galaxy."

Beth looked at Cliff and gave him her covert rolled-eye look, saying, "I'm a bio type, myself."

Fred was a trifle intense, or "focused" as the psychers put it. Some found him hard to take, but he had solved a major technical problem in systems tech, which cut him some slack with Cliff. All crew had to have overlapping abilities, but for some like Fred, breadth was their main qualification. Of course, Fred was oblivious to all these nuances. He gestured at the screen. "Hard not to look at it—beauty and importance combined. The *Mona Lisa* of planets."

Beth murmured approval and he went on, talking faster. "Even now, I mean—hundreds of bio worlds with atmospheric signatures, but no better's been seen anywhere."

Irma Michaelson passed by without her husband in tow, her head turning quickly at Fred's remark. "You mean the new Forward probe data?"

"Uh, no—"

"Forward Number Five just checked in," Irma said. "Still pretty far out, can't get surface maps or anything. Plenty of clouds, got a smidge view of an ocean. Shows the atmospheric thermo pretty well, I hear. We got the tightbeam relay just in time! We might need to do some atmosphere work to make it comfy."

Beth asked, "What kind?"

"They say we may need more CO_2. Glory's a tad light on greenhouse gases," Fred said so fast, he could barely get the words out. "Surface temperatures are more like Canada. The tropics there are like our mid-temperate zones."

Now that we've terraformed Earth back to nearly twencen levels, Cliff thought, *here comes another whole world. . . .*

He shook this off and listened to Fred, who was hurtling on bright-eyed with, "Once we learn how to suck carbon out of air really well, we can make a climate that will be better than what we were born into. Maybe better than humans ever had it."

By this time, he was lecturing to a smaller audience. He gave them a crooked smile, as if to acknowledge this, and walked off into the crowd, which was getting predictably more noisy.

"A lot of anxious energy humming through here," Beth said.

"An emotional bath," Cliff said dreamily, and nodded at Earth. "The big issue down there is our ever-smarter machines demanding back wages. What's retirement look like for a multicapillary DNA sequencer?"

Beth laughed, her eyes dancing. "I got a must-answer from SSC, asking what actor would best portray me in the series about us."

"At least we won't have to see it."

She thumped the screen. "I keep thinking I'll probably never see white curtains billowing into warm sunlit rooms on a lazy summer afternoon. We haven't left yet, and already I'm nostalgic."

"For me, it'll be surfing."

"Glory has oceans. A moon, pretty small. Maybe they have waves, too."

"I didn't bring my board."

He saw the Arctic Ocean ice was at least visible, a heartening symptom of a planet slowly backing down from the Hot Age. The big chunk of Antarctica that fell off a century back and caused all the flooding was slowly regrowing, too. The Pacific islands were still gone, though, and might never appear again, worn down by wave action. No surfing there, ever again.

He noticed a phalanx of officers in blue uniforms and gold braid, standing smartly in ranks. Most were from the Oort crew and would not go out on *SunSeeker*, so were here for formality. The leaner Glory-bound crew stood behind the tall, craggy figure blinking into the spotlight but still quite sure he belonged there.

"Captain Redwing is about to speak," a deck lieutenant's voice boomed out over the speakers. They stood at sharp attention beneath the other banner proclaiming,

STAR-CRAVING MAD FAREWELL

Redwing was in full dress uniform with medals blazing, beaming at everyone, face ruddy. Cliff recalled he had divorced the wife who was to go with him, but he had not heard the inside story. Redwing kept his posture at full attention except for head dips to junior officers. He maintained a kindly smile, as if he were pleased the other officers were sharing their nice little thoughts. Still, he was an imposing man in uniform.

"A great exit line," Cliff whispered, trying to edge inconspicuously toward the door. He cast a long look at Earth on the screen.

"Last night for separate quarters, too," Beth said. "Would you like to stay over?"

"Wow, yes, ma'am."

"I believe it's customary."

"Customary where?"

"Wherever it's Saturday night."

They threaded their way through the crowd, but the feeling still plucked at him. The noise and strumming music, the drinks and snog-fogs and quick darting kisses, faces lined and hopeful and sad, all passing by—but still, somehow, as if he wanted to freeze them in amber.

In an eerie way, this was like a . . . ghost story. All these support people, likable and irritating and officious and sexy and, soon enough—all dead. Left behind. When he and the other crew awoke in orbit around Glory, more than half of these would be centuries gone. Even with the standard life span of 160 years now, gone to gray dry dust.

It had never struck him this way. Not knowing it, but *feeling* it. All this greatness, the human prospect—all that would be far behind them when they next awoke.

Cliff smiled a thin pale smile and thought, *This is the last time I'll see Earth.* He looked at the swimming majesty of it, sighed with a sense of foreboding, and followed Beth.

PART I

WAKE-UP CALL

The possession of knowledge does not kill the sense of wonder and mystery. There is always more mystery.

—ANAÏS NIN

ONE

Life persists.

He recalled those words, his nervous mantra recited as the soft sleep came closing its grip with chilly fingers—

—and so he knew he was alive. Awake again. Up from the chill-sleep of many decades.

He was *cold*. His memory was blurred, but it told him he was on an odyssey no biologist had ever ventured on before, a grand epic. He was going to the stars, yes, and they had given him the stinky sulfur gas, yes, the first creeping chill . . . and that was . . . it.

But beyond that flash of memory, all he could think of was the incredible, muscle-shaking chill that spread like a sharp ache through him. He was too numb to shiver. Somewhere a loud rumble rolled up through his body, not heard but felt. *The cold* . . . He thought hard and with effort opened his sticky eyes.

Trouble. His gummy eyelids slammed closed against a crisp actinic glare. He must be in the revival clinic. Slowly he pried them open, still numb with cold. He focused with effort, looking for the joyous faces of his fellow colonists.

Not there. Nor was Beth.

Instead, the worried frowns of Mayra and Abduss Wickramsingh made him groggily anxious as they worked over him. Their faces swam away, came back, drifting above like clouds as the cold began to recede. He was *tired*. His bones ached with it. After decades of sleep . . .

Hands massaged his rubbery legs. Lungs wheezed. His heart labored, thumping in his ears. His throat rasped with a sour wind. He was finally starting to shiver. Sluggish sleep fell away like a mummy's moldy shroud.

Think. The Wickramsinghs were paired by ability, he recalled in a gray fog, self-sufficient and solely responsible for the three years of their watch. Mayra piloted, and Abduss was the engineer. They were fairly far down the queue, maybe twenty-seven watches. . . . How far along were they? It hurt to figure.

They turned him on his side to work on his stiff muscles. The massaging sent lancing pain, and he let out a muffled scream. They ignored that. At least he could see better. Against the hard ceramic glare, he could see that no others of *SunSeeker*'s 436 passengers in cold sleep were being revived. A capsule was running its program, though, so someone was coming out behind him. The bay was empty. Carboceramic tiles were clean, looking like new.

As a scientist, he was not slated to come out until the infrastructure staff was up and running at Scorpii 3, the balmy world that everybody called Glory, that no eye had ever seen.

So they were maybe eighty years into the voyage. Not enough to be near Glory. Something was wrong.

Mayra's lips moved, glistening in the hard light, but he heard nothing. They worked on his neural connections and— *pop!*—he could hear. The dull rumble hammered at him. Interstellar surf.

"Okay? Okay?" Mayra said anxiously, mouth tight, her eyes intent. "What's your name?"

He coughed, hacked. Once his throat was clear of milky fluid, his first words were, "Cliff . . . Kammash. But . . . Why me? I'm bio. Is Beth still cold?"

They didn't answer at once, but each looked at the other.

"Don't talk," Mayra said softly, a smile flickering.

Definitely trouble. He had known the Wickramsinghs

slightly in training, remembered them as reserved and disciplined, just what a cryo passenger would wish in a caretaker
watch team.

And they were good. They got his creaky body up off the
slab, kind hands helping, his muscles screaming. Then into a
gown, detaching the IVs. Up, creaking onto his feet. He
swayed, the room reeled, he sat down. Try again. Better . . .
a step. First in eighty years, feet like bricks. They helped him
shuffle to a table. He sat. Minutes crawled by as he felt air
swoosh in and out of his lungs. He studied this phenomenon
carefully, as though it were a miracle. As perhaps it was.

Food appeared. Coffee: caffeine, yes, lovely caffeine. Nobody spoke. Next course, soup. It tasted like nectar, the essence of life. Then they told him, as he eagerly slurped down
a big bowl of fragrant veggie mix grown aboard. Halfway
through his third bowl, he became vaguely aware that they
were talking about an astrophysical observation that required
his interpretation.

"What? Mayra, Astro is *you*," he shot back. "Every pilot
has to be."

"We need a different viewpoint," Mayra said, her dark
eyes wary. "We do not want to bias your views by explaining
more now."

"We are reviving the captain, too," Abduss said.

He blinked, startled. "Redwing?"

"It's that important." Abduss was unreadable. "He will
awaken in another day, his capsule says."

Cliff felt a chill that was not thermal. Stores of food,
water, oxygen couldn't be recycled forever. That was the point
in riding semi-frozen: They would reach Glory with enough
stores to survive until they could replace what was lost.

"Four of us. Waking too many people would run us short,"
he said. "What's up?"

Again, the Wickramsinghs looked at each other and did
not answer.

• • •

As soon as he could walk steadily, they showed him the viewing screens, and for a long moment he could not speak.

The spectacle was striking, both for what was familiar and what was not. *SunSeeker* was forty light-years from Earth, and yet he could identify many of the constellations he had known as a child in Brazil. Their familiar faces swam among a bright swarm of lesser lights, twisted here and there. On the scale of the galaxy, light-years did not count for much.

He immediately looked for their destination. A star not much different from Sol, Glory's primary should be a white point dead ahead. It was there, reassuringly bright, though still five light-years away. Perhaps its brilliance was enhanced by *SunSeeker*'s velocity? No, that was a small effect. More probably, brightened by his own longing to see, to breathe, to touch an Earthlike world, named Glory out of pure hope before any human eye had seen it. Pixels and spectra didn't do the job.

Other stars brimmed in the rosy night lit by *SunSeeker*'s bow shock. The ramscoop's plowing through the interstellar gas and ionized hydrogen was an unending rainbow light show, filmy incandescent streamers curving around them as they plunged into the infinite night. Beyond that prow wash lay the spectrally shifted universe. Some of the glimmering stars were intriguing, constellations rearranged—but nothing compared to the nearby red sun.

"That's the problem?" Cliff asked.

Abduss nodded. "It is a problem, but there is another, larger. We have been wrestling with this more difficult issue, but that can wait for the captain."

Can't these people ever say anything straight? He made himself say deliberately, "Okay, tell me what's the big deal about this star?"

"We are overtaking it. When we came on watch, the star

was not visible. There was a mild recombination source nearby, rather odd." Switching to another channel, Abduss pointed out a diffuse ivory plume behind the dark patch.

Cliff frowned. "How long is it?"

Abduss said, "About three astronomical units. This is a signature of hydrogen recombining, after it has been ionized. This linear feature seems to be a jet, cooling off and then turning back into atoms. That's the emission I made this map from, you see?"

"Um." Cliff wrinkled his nose, trying to think like an Astro type. "A jet from a star. It didn't jump out at you?"

Abduss tightened his mouth but otherwise did not move. "At first we did not even *see* the star."

Uh-oh . . . , Cliff thought. Best to shut up, yes.

"We had much to measure. The jet did not attract much attention, as it seemed unimportant. Yet now we can see it to be related to the star—which suddenly appeared."

Cliff nodded, smiled, tried to defuse the man's irritation. "Perfectly understandable. Our problems are inside the ship, not outside. So . . . the star popped into view because it came around the rim of this . . . thing."

Mayra murmured, "We became alarmed."

"Nobody noticed the star before? Earlier watches?"

Abduss blinked slowly. "We could not see it."

Cliff shrugged. In moderate close-up, the dwarf showed as a disk: it must be close. It was perched at the lip of a much larger arc of light. An ordinary star, little and reddish. He raised an eyebrow at Mayra.

"The spectral class is F9," Mayra added helpfully. "Most likely the plasma plume means that this star must have been recently active. Early stars often display this." Under magnification, the expelled matter looked to Cliff like a thin nebula, dim and old.

"But we don't know it's a young star," he said.

"No, stars of this class have very long lifetimes."

Cliff had never been much concerned with the fate of failed stars as they erupted and faltered. Spectacular, sure, easy to sell to contract monitors—but biology demands a stable abode. Still, he immediately guessed that this veil was a remnant of an earlier era in the star's life, when it was blowing off shells of hot gas. A good guess, anyway—but of course, not his field. These details of stellar evolution had never interested him very much, since they had little to do with his specialty, the evolution of higher life-forms on worlds similar to Earth. A largely abstract pursuit until the Alpha Centauri discoveries of a simple but strange ecology there. That was what drew him to Glory; Beth was an accidental benefit.

So he shrugged. "Gas from a small star. Why wake me up?"

"You are the highest-ranked Scientific," Abduss said.

Marya added, "And your specialty may be quite relevant."

That remark just perplexed him. He felt hungry and tired and disappointed. And miffed, yes, with a raspy sore throat. He sucked in a deep breath. "I'm supposed to assess Glory's biology, not be awakened to answer questions from the watch crew!"

They blinked, startled. He wondered if he was betraying more than the typical awakened-sleeper irritation they all had been warned about. Chill-sleep was reasonably safe, but coming out of it was not. Every crew member under its enforced hibernation cycle ran a 2 percent risk of subtle neurological damage from a revival, an irreducible price of seeking the stars. By waking him, they had forced him to double that risk. He'd be going back into the chill when he'd done what they wanted. He had rather blithely accepted the risk of several revivals when he became a senior science officer, he recalled, when it was entirely theoretical.

As well, no sleeper could be immediately returned to the vaults after revival. The medical risks were too great. So he was stuck for at least a month in the narrow rumbling quar-

ters of the starship, eating the pallid food generated from pon-
ics tanks. There was no way to avoid the perpetual growl of
the fusion ramscoop. Filters could not erase the ever-shifting
tones of turbulence as the ship surged through clumps of
denser gas, riding waves of ionization—a moving electrical
discharge, lighting up its neighborhood.

He had not been slated for revival on the passage at all, so
his sensitivity to noise had not been an issue. And indeed, the
shifting, grating clangor already irked him a bit. There was
no way to damp it, so he would have to use noise-suppressing
headphones. Certainly he would not have made the cut for
active, awake crew.

The Wickramsinghs glanced at each other yet again, as if
to say, *Humor him—he's a senior officer.* Both inhaled deeply.
Abduss said, "Please tolerate our unveiling this anomaly so
that you may experience it as we did."

"Um, yes." He still felt irked, but ordered himself to behave as an officer should.

Mayra said, "Notice that the luminous gas, as you put it,
is very straight."

Cliff zoomed the image—and blinked. He had expected
a ragged cloud of expelled debris, the star's outer layers blown
off. The plume seemed to point at the star ahead. "Pretty, at
least. Why so sharp?"

Abduss said carefully, "We wondered, too. None of the
astronomical analysis systems had an explanation. But it did
alert us to the infrared spectrum."

"Of this plume? Why—?"

Mayra switched to the middle infrared bands, and his
mouth fell open. An orange circle stretched across the sky.
The plume was an arrow stuck in the exact center of some
target.

"The plasma apparently comes from the center of that
massive infrared region. It is mostly of hydrogen, and its ions
eventually find electrons and they unite," Abduss said, as if

he were talking to a student. "That is the hydrogen line we see, the plume cooling off."

Mayra added, "But it did lead our attention to the huge region of soft infrared emission."

"Hey, I'm a biologist—"

"We awoke you because the infrared signature is clear. The circle we see is solid, not a gas."

His irritation vanished. Even a biologist knew enough to be startled by the implication. All he could manage to say was, "That's impossible."

Mayra said mildly, "When I first saw it, I, too, assumed it to be gas. The spectral lines prove otherwise."

He studied it, trying to allow for perspective. "A disk? . . . It's *huge*."

"Indeed," Mayra said.

"But it can't be a planet. It would be bigger than any star."

Abduss nodded. "We are approaching from behind it, and at present speed will come directly alongside within weeks. The . . . thing . . . is about three hundred AU away from us." He smiled quickly, as if embarrassed. "Allowing for that, look closer."

"This is why we awakened you," Mayra said.

He blinked. "It's . . . artificial?"

"Apparently," Mayra said.

"What? How—?"

"We have just come into view of this object, by coming alongside. It drew our attention because its star suddenly appeared—presto! We could not see it before because the . . . the cap, whatever it is . . . blocked the starlight as we overtook it."

Abduss added helpfully, "Infrared study shows that it is not a disk. It's rounded. We witness it from behind, with the plasma plume coming through a hole at the exact rear center. The cap radiates at the temperature of lukewarm water."

"A . . . sphere?" He saw it then, the image snapping into

perspective. He was looking at a ball with a hole in its bottom. Through that hole, the star glowed. His imagination scrambled after an old idea. "Maybe it's a, what was the name—?"

"A Dyson sphere," Mayra provided. "We thought so at first, too."

"So this is a shell?"

She nodded. "A hemisphere, perhaps—a sphere halfway under construction. Perhaps. Only—the old texts reveal quite clearly that Dyson did not dream of a rigid sphere at all. Rather, he imagined a spherical zone filled with orbiting habitats, enough of them to capture all of the radiant energy of a star."

Abduss thumbed up a reference to these ideas on a side screen. Good—they had done the homework before awakening him. But if not a Dyson sphere, what—?

Mayra said, "We have watched and run the Doppler programs carefully. The hemispherical cap is spinning about the same axis formed by the plume."

Abduss said helpfully, "Only by rotating such a shell could one support it against the star's gravity."

"Like this ship." He nodded, trying to guess Abduss's point. "Centrifugal gravity. But a complete, rigid sphere . . . spinning . . . that would be impossible, right? Gravity would pull it in at the poles."

They both nodded. Abduss said, "Still, the configuration is not stable."

They both looked at him, so he went on, thinking aloud. "The shell should fall into the star—it's not orbiting. There's some sort of force balance at play here. Odd construction, indeed. Just spinning isn't enough, either—the stresses would vary with curvature. You'd need internal supports."

Mayra said, "Quite right, I believe. My first degree was in astrophysics and I have some ideas about this object, but—" She bowed her head and shrugged.

As matters developed, there was a great deal behind

Mayra's modesty. In the next day, eating five meals to build himself up, he learned as much about the Wickramsinghs' subtleties as he did of the strange object they had discovered. They were deferential toward him, unveiling their ideas slowly, allowing him to come to his own conclusions. This helped greatly as the magnitude of implication grew.

He didn't even ask about Scorpii 3 until hours later, when Abduss and Mayra were using the control room facilities to lecture him. The planet, their destined home, was a long way off still, and deserved the nickname Glory. Scorpii 3 was the second nearest habitable-seeming world ever found, after the Alpha Centauri base. A fast-burn probe had verified the bio-signatures found by deep space telescopes two generations before *SunSeeker*'s launch. A wonder, with strong ozone lines, a lot of water, and tantalizing hints of green chlorophyll in the spectrum. A dream world. No sign of any artificial electromagnetic emissions, after big dishes had cupped their ears toward it for decades. Plus the mysterious grav waves that made no sense, considering that there were no big masses in the system to send out such quadrupole emissions.

He looked at it in the high amplification forward scope, but it was just a flickering blur through their bow shock. Scorpii 3 was barely visible because it hung near the edge of the structure ahead, though it was many light-years away. He looked at the screens, trying to get his head around what that vast bulk could mean. But emotion overwhelmed him. Pure wonder.

Unimaginable, yes. Bigger than the orbit of Mercury, huge beyond comprehension, the hemisphere was an *artifact*, a *built* thing, the first evidence of another intelligence in the galaxy. Not a trickle of radio waves, but a giant . . . riddle.

He took a long breath, relaxed into the observer's chair and headpiece, and let the slow, long wavelength rumble of the starship run through his bones. And thought.

The Wickramsinghs felt it was a matter of biology. Wake the biologist!

Cliff wrinkled his nose. He had been irked, sure, but the Wickramsinghs were right: You see trouble, you call for help. But he wasn't prepared for this. But as well he saw that none of that now mattered.

Science had speculated about intelligence for centuries, as probes spread out through a desert of dead worlds. The Big Eye telescopes in the twenty-first century had found warm, rocky worlds resembling Earth, and some had the ozone spectral lines that promised oxygen atmospheres. There the promise had ended. Here and there flourished slime molds in deep caverns, or simple ocean life, maybe—cellular colonies still unable to shape themselves into complex forms, as Earth's life had more than a billion years ago. Sure, there was life, the consensus said . . . boring life.

To find an artifact of such immensity . . . it made his mind reel.

Then Abduss said, almost casually, "There is something more. Why we realized the protocols demanded that you be awakened. We have detected narrow-band microwave traffic from near the star."

Cliff realized that he should have seen this coming. "Coded?"

"Yes. It may be broadcasting from near the hole in the center—the angle is right—and we're getting some scattered, reflected signals."

"Are they hailing us?"

"There's nothing obvious that we can figure out, no," Mayra said. "There are many transmissions, not a long string. It looks like a conversation, perhaps."

"So they don't know we're here, maybe."

"We could hear the traffic once we were within view of the hole, I believe. Perhaps it comes from within the hemisphere, and leaks through. It is not broadcast for others to pick up—or so we think. And unintelligible, at least to us."

Cliff eyed them both and said carefully, "I agree that the protocols call for my revival. But this is more than anybody ever visualized, when those protocols were invented. . . ." He was still dazed after a day awake. And cold; he rubbed his arms to get blood moving. "I wonder if you didn't wake me too early, though. We're not looking at plants and animals yet. If we wake too many of us . . ."

"Yes," Abduss said.

"We'd run short."

"We're short now," Mayra said. "That is the other problem. It is high time someone woke the captain, we felt."

"So you did, right after me? Me, because my secondary specialty is in rations and ship biology. Mostly, though, I'm a field biologist. But sure, call me up. Then the cap'n, to take over all the other implications. Right."

"And now we are happy to turn both problems over to you." Abduss gave him a broad smile without any trace of irony. Mayra beamed, too. They had faced all this together, and the weight of it showed in their evident relief.

· · ·

It didn't take long to see why they were handing off to him and the captain.

The opportunity: an artifact bigger than planets.

The problem: *SunSeeker* was not performing to specs. The ramscoop drive was running at 0.081 of light speed, instead of the 0.095 engineering had promised.

Not a big difference, but in starflight it was crucial. At 0.081, their trip would take 550 years. They had stocks for a bit over 500 years.

Early space travel had been like this, with tiny margins of safety. Reaching the Moon six out of seven tries had been a miracle. They'd run aging X-planes for a quarter of a century, losing two shuttles before they built something better. Interplanetary travel still cut close to the bone, and interstellar was a crapshoot. And still there were always those who would take the gamble.

Of course, *SunSeeker* recycled everything—and, of course, the accounting never quite came out even. The flight plan had them arriving at Glory with time to find what they needed. Glory had a world with oceans and free oxygen, all carefully checked in the ozone spectral line seen from Earth orbit. And in the infrared, they had seen a broad disk of asteroids, too, comfortably farther out and with traces of iceteroids among them. The world or the rocks would give them the elements they needed: water, oxygen, dust to be turned to soil.

But this slower speed was eating their safety window.

He checked the log. Five watch cycles had worked on the problem in their ramscoop drive without really spotting a cause. None of them had wakened the captain. It was an engineering problem, not a command structure one. And they were on a centuries-long voyage.

The big magnetic fields at *SunSeeker*'s bow drove shock waves into the hydrogen ahead, ionizing it to prickly energies, then scooping it up and mixing it with fusion catalysis, burning as hot as suns—but somehow, the nuclear brew didn't give quite the thrust it had during field trials out in the Oort cloud. Considering how new relativistic engineering was, maybe this was not truly surprising.

Still, it had huge consequences. "We won't get to Glory in time," Cliff said.

The Wickramsinghs nodded together. Mayra said, "So . . ." She did not want to draw the conclusion.

"We have cut our rations to a minimum, all five watches, yes," Abduss rushed in, eyes large. "It was a major decision we made, you see—to revive you and the captain."

Cliff slurped down more coffee. It tasted incredibly

good—another symptom of revival. "You've done the calculation. Can we make it?"

"Marginal at best," Mayra said precisely. "The last five watches have run at the minimum crew number: two. Plus we are pushing the hydroponics to the maximum. We fear it is not enough."

"Damn!" Cliff grimaced. Starve to death between the stars. "That's also why nobody woke the captain. One more gut, one more pair of lungs. Until . . . yeah." Until they saw the strange thing up ahead.

· · ·

He knew the deeper reason, too. What could the captain do, after all? If the engineers could not find a solution, mere managerial ability would not help. So the engineers had followed the protocols that had been drilled into them: Follow mandates and hope for the best. Especially since an error could kill them all with relativistic speed.

They gazed at him, calm and orderly and patient, the perfect types for a watch crew. Which he was not. Too restless and a touch excitable, the psych guys had said. That was fine with Cliff; he wanted to see Glory, not black interstellar space. All crew were calm, steady types, or they wouldn't have made the first cut in the long selection filters.

The Wickramsinghs were waiting. He was in charge until the captain woke up. That he did not understand the situation did not matter; he was a superior officer, so he had to make the decisions.

First, he had to rest. About that, the revival procedures were as hard-nosed as the mission protocols. At least that would give him a little time to think.

· · ·

They found him twelve hours later, in the kitchen.

The first thing he ordered was a thorough study of the star

they were approaching. The Wickramsinghs called up screens of data and vibrant images. This gave him a jumpy image of a star massing about nine-tenths of Sol's mass. There were plenty of those in the galaxy, but this one was not behaving like a serene, longer-lived orange dwarf. Fiery tendrils forked and seethed at the center of the apparent disk. "There is blurring in the image," Abduss remarked, "by the plasma plume."

Squinting, at first he did not understand the implication of the roiling spikes that leaped from a single hot spot, a blue white furnace. "Ah—that spot is directly under the center of the artificial bowl, the cap."

Abduss nodded. "Something is disturbing the star, making it throw out great flaming tongues. Very dangerous, I would think."

They were coming up on this system pretty fast. Cliff thumbed in the whole data field. The obviously artificial disk—okay, call it the cap, because he could sense from the image that it was curved away from their point of view—the cap was not at all far away, maybe a few hundred astronomical units, where an A.U. was the distance from Earth to Sol. You got used to such enormous distance measures, in the relentless training all crew had to undergo.

He tried to remember when that was . . . centuries ago. Yet it seemed like just a few weeks.

He looked at the image and let his eyes see it as a curved hemisphere cupped around this side of the star.

They zoomed the optics in on the disk's flares, having to go through several settings that blanked out the blue white hot spot on the star's surface. The glare of the hot spot was fierce, actinic, bristling with angry storms, a tiny white sun attached to the bigger pink star like an angry leech.

Above the white spot raged the filigree spikes of streaming plasma. They whirled around one another like fighting snakes, burning as they rushed up from the hot spot. It looked like they should bathe the hemispheric bowl in licking flames. But before they reached the curve of the bowl, they dovetailed into a slender jet. Among the streamers, Cliff could see little blobs and bright flecks moving out from the star, swarming up along the jet, toward the neatly circular hole in the bowl and out into the sky.

Cliff wrestled with the images. "Let's see the earlier pictures, from the last watch."

Automatically, the ship kept records of the local sky. Its software was spectrally sophisticated and framed its own, limited hypotheses about the class and type of every luminous object it saw. They checked the records. The muted minds that murmured among themselves, struggling to understand the bowl, had spun endlessly in parameter-space confusions.

In the infrared, there was a glow where the "bottom" of the bowl would be. None of the instruments showed any image of the bowl during the years while the ship was approaching from behind. He thumbed through uninteresting pictures. The bowl blotted out a small dot on the sky, but nobody had noticed such a minor thing from light-years away.

The bowl's infrared radiation showed a temperature around 20 degrees centigrade. Room temperature.

"Ah, balmy," Abduss said. Across that vast curve, tropical conditions prevailed. The back face was cool and appeared stony. But the warmed side was at 20 degrees C. The star was less luminous than Sol—but, of course, the bowl was in continuous sunlight, so it would get pretty warm. No night.

Cliff had a mind's eye picture of the bowl as a colossal construction, even though his common sense was screaming. When something appeared impossible, it seemed best to simply study it until understanding emerged. And wait for the captain to wake up, yes.

The first shock came from simple geometry. Mayra gave him distances and angles and he quickly found that the area of the inward-facing cap was two hundred million times that of Earth. Hovering over its star, the rim of the bowl would provide a vast, livable surface. (The biologist would wait for the captain's take, but . . . *Air. Water. Stores to replenish a failing ship.* The Wickramsinghs nodded and smiled when he spoke of this. . . .)

On that area, peering through the small hole they could see, Abduss picked up reflecting optical emission . . . and found the spectral signatures of water. Then, with a bit more effort to see through the rippling plasma that shrouded *Sun-Seeker*, he found oxygen.

So it was an immense area designed for living . . . by what?

Cliff checked their distance from the bowl: 320 AU— about a hundredth of a light-year. *So close!* And coming up fast.

But they were still looking at the back of the cap, in the dark. He looked at the waiting faces of the Wickramsinghs and thought. They were left with some brute astronomical facts—velocities, times, food supplies. . . .

At their review meeting, the Wickramsinghs eyed him expectantly.

"It's beyond me," he said—and watched their faces, despite their best efforts, show disappointment.

"Surely we can learn more?" Mayra suggested hesitantly.

"Not at this distance," Abduss said. "And I doubt the captain will authorize a trajectory change to get closer."

Cliff looked at them and thought unkind thoughts. Five crews didn't wake the captain, because there wasn't an answer. They had been trained to keep the ship running. Schooled to stay steady. But here was something the Earthside planners had never imagined.

"I think we have two problems," Cliff said with what he hoped was a diplomatic tone. "Supplies, yes. And this strange . . . object. Too much here for us to deal with."

Abduss said carefully, "We had thought somewhat the same."

"Look," Mayra said directly, "it's nearly time to take the captain up to his conscious stage—"

"I want Beth Marble brought up, too."

Both of them blinked. "But she is—"

"Capable, right." He could see a lot of trouble coming, and he didn't want to be alone. Who did?

"But there is no protocol requiring—"

Cliff held up his hand and looked across the table steadily, letting them think about it. "Let's just do it."

"She is . . . not your wife."

"No, but she has ship skills and can pilot."

"Not until we can ask the captain," Abduss said. His face was firm.

TWO

They told the captain when he came out of cold sleep, bleary-
eyed, stiff, still lying on a slab—and then his eyes began
blinking with startling speed, alert.

Abduss said, "You aren't going to believe this."

Captain Redwing's skeptical grin crinkled the leathery
skin around his eyes as he said, "Try me."

So they told him, while they gingerly massaged his stiff,
cold muscles and applied the necessary chemistries. Cliff
hung back and bided his time while the Wickramsinghs took
Redwing through the whole story.

Redwing sat up and shook his black mane, his bronzed
skin blue-veined at the wrists, and said, "You're *sure?*"

So they told him some more. Showed the screens, the
time log, and finally the close-ups of the back of the bowl.
The captain stared at the bowl image, and Cliff could see him
mentally put it aside to concentrate on the supplies issue.

"The drive not running to specs. Five crew changes! You
couldn't do *any*thing?" He jabbed a finger at the Wickramsinghs.

"We did not know what to do," Mayra said reasonably.
"There were—"

"We've run this way for—what?—decades!"

Abduss bristled in her defense, face stiff. "This was not
in the protocols."

"Protocols be damned. I—"

"The leptonic drive is one issue, Captain," Cliff said, "and this thing ahead is quite another—"

"You're Science." Redwing cut him off with a chopping hand signal. "This is crew."

Cliff sat back and nursed his coffee and remembered all the rumors before launch. How Redwing was from one of the families that had made a bundle out of the Indian casinos. How he'd breezed through MIT with great grades and a wake of surly enemies. Made his rep in the Mars exploration and exploitation. Been a real sonofabitch, sure, but he had gotten things goddamn well *done*. Maybe not the worst recommendation, considering. Cliff was going to have to follow orders.

"We cannot go on like this," Mayra said, ever the diplomat. "Our external diagnostics are working well, so we are sure there is not some property of the interstellar gas that is the root of our drive problem. We rely on the microwave view to diagnose the ramscoop fields—"

"We'll review it all," Redwing said crisply. He bit his lip. "And the earlier crews—Jacobs, Chen, Ambertson, Abar, Kalaish—all top people . . ."

• • •

Redwing went through an extensive engineering review with them. Systems, flows, balances, malfunction indices. After hours of work, he was just as stumped as the ship diagnostic systems, which were better engineers than any of them. Nothing seemed wrong, but the ship could do no better. *Seeker* had performed perfectly in the first few decades, achieving their terminal velocity when the pressure of incoming matter on its ram fields equaled the thrust it got out of hydrogen fusion. They had been losing velocity through tens of light-years— slightly at first, then more.

Crews had tested the obvious explanations. Maybe the interstellar gas was getting too thin, so they weren't taking in enough hydrogen to drive the fusion zone at max. That idea didn't pencil out in the detailed numbers. The fusion drive was a souped-up version of magnetic cylinders, each a rotating torus that contained fusing plasma. Boron–proton reactions were the burning meat and potatoes, the protons shoveled in fresh from the ramscoop. The rotating magnetic equilibria held fusing plasma in their bottles, releasing the alpha particles into the nozzle that drove them forward. It had worked steadily now for centuries. It looked fine.

The next crew thought there was too much dust ahead, so perhaps the fusion burn was tamped down. They found an ingenious way to pluck dust samples from their bow shock and measure it carefully. Nothing wrong there, either.

There were more ideas and trials, and now it was getting serious. They had started with plenty of spare supplies, but now it wasn't going to be enough.

"Our big fat margin of error got . . . eaten," Redwing told them.

Seeker would arrive nearly a century late. They might barely squeeze through, if the expected level of leaks and losses did not happen . . . but nobody wanted to calculate the odds of that. Because they all knew the odds were bad.

· · ·

They all slept on their problems, and the next ship-day Cliff was first up. Another revival symptom—insomnia sometimes lasted weeks. Along with that, and no surprise: irritability. The damn noise wasn't helping. The best solution was to say as little as possible. Meanwhile, his mind churned away at the deeper puzzle of the bowl that hung like a riddle on their optical viewing screens. The image rippled from plasma refraction, but Cliff could make out tantalizing, momentary patches of detail in it.

The world as a bowl, he thought, trying to think of a better term. Flamboyantly artificial. What would choose to live in such a place?

They held a meeting, and then another, without anything new turning up. At the end of another frustrating conversation, Cliff said quietly, "I want Beth revived. We need more minds on this problem, and we're stalled."

Redwing pursed his lips briefly and shook his head. "We'd better keep lean."

"Only if we're going to just forge on and hope things improve without our doing anything." Cliff said it in a rush, finally getting out what he and Abduss had agreed upon.

Before Redwing could respond, Abduss chimed in, "I found another slight decrease in our velocity this morning. Nearly a full kilometer per second."

A long silence, Redwing carefully letting nothing show in his face. The signs of strain in the man had been mounting. Little gestures of frustration, a broken cup, time off by himself, little social talk. The psychers back Earthside had a high opinion of Redwing's leadership style, but to Cliff the man had seemed to be best at bureaucratic infighting. *No managers to game around out here, though.*

"So whatever's wrong, it's getting worse," Redwing said.

Nobody answered.

Cliff said carefully, "Beth has piloting and engineering skills, pretty broad."

Only when the words were out did he recognize the pun. Mayra smiled but said nothing. *A pretty broad.* And of course, Cliff's longtime "associate," as the polite social term had it.

Redwing let a wry smile play on his face for a few seconds. "Okay, let's warm her up."

They started Beth's revival. The protocols were straightforward, but every case had variations. While the slow processes worked in her, they spent another two days looking at the slowdown problem, getting nowhere. The ship was flying hard, hitting molecular cloudlets and, increasingly, vagrant wisps of plasma. "That's the plume from the jet we see," Abduss said. "We're starting to hit the wake."

Then the ramscoop would need to navigate, and there would be no data to let it know how to work. The artificial intelligences that tirelessly regulated the scoop fields were smarter than mere humans, adjusting the magnetic scoops and reaction rates—but they were also obsessively narrow. The AIs worked as well as they could, making estimates based on many decades of in-flight experience, guessing at causes—but they could not think outside their conceptual box. "Savants of the engine," Mayra called them. Cliff wondered if she was being ironic.

"Look, we need to make a decision," Abduss insisted. "Yes?"

"I do, you mean," Redwing said. He made a cage of his fingers and peered into it. He was pale and drawn, and not all of that came from his recovery from the long sleep. Nobody had slept much.

Cliff said, "Maybe this is a godsend."

Redwing shot him a questioning glance. "You always had an odd sense of humor."

They had not gotten along particularly well in staff and crew meetings. Redwing had held out for making all Scientific Personnel de facto crew members, rigidly set in the chain of command. Cliff and others had blocked him. Scientific Personnel had their own, looser command structure that dealt with Redwing only near the top of the pyramid. Cliff was the highest-ranking Scientific Personnel officer awake. Of course, all that procedural detail was decades ago—no, centuries, he reminded himself—but in personal memory, it still loomed as recent.

He tried a warm, reasonable tone. "If we hadn't been slowed down, we'd be blazing right by this weird thing. No way we could even swing around that star—say, let's call it Wickramsingh's Star, eh? With joint discovery rights for all."

Thin smiles all around. They needed a little levity. Nobody aboard would ever make a buck from interstellar enterprises. . . . "But now, going slower, maybe we can make a small correction with a pretty fair delta-V, get a closer look at the thing."

Redwing looked blank. So did the Wickramsinghs.

Cliff said carefully, "It's artificial. Maybe we can—"

"Get help?" Redwing's mouth twisted skeptically. "I admit, that's a bizarre object, but it's not our goal to explore passing phenomena along the way. We're headed for Glory, and that's *it*."

Cliff had thought about this moment for two days. He spread his hands as if making a deal, splitting the difference. "Maybe we can do both."

Redwing's face had already settled into the firm-but-confident expression that served him so well back Earthside. Then he paused, puzzled, and almost against his will asked, "How's that?"

"Say we use the plasma plume from the star. We're running up into the fringes already. It's rich in hydrogen, right?" A nod to Abduss and Mayra. "And a lot more ionized than the ordinary interstellar gas we've been riding through, scooping up with the magnetic funnels and blowing out the back, all these decades. For a ramscoop motor, this is high-quality input. Let's use it to pick up some speed."

A heartbeat went by, two. Cliff thought, *Keep it simple*, and said, "That jet's spurting straight out the back of the thing. Let's fly up it."

Redwing asked, "Abduss, isn't that plume moving at relativistic speeds? In the wrong direction? It'd slow us down."

Was Redwing right? Mayra was nodding. Recklessly, Cliff said, "That could work, too."

"You make my head hurt," Redwing said. "What are you on about now?"

"With what we've got for consumables, we're going to arrive dead at Glory. If we can't speed up, we'll have to stop for supplies. Here, now. Make orbit around Wickramsingh's Star. Deal with the natives."

They stared at him.

Cliff played his next card. "We're overtaking the star. Every hour makes a velocity change tougher."

Mayra's eyes widened, startled—but surely she had thought of this?—and then she nodded.

Redwing wasn't a man to leap at a suggestion. But he screwed his mouth around, eyes seeking the low, mottled carbon-fiber ceiling, and said, "Let's do the calculation."

. . .

That took another day.

While the others checked their screens and fretted, Cliff watched Beth come up out of the long dark cold and into his arms. He claimed the right to massage her sore self, rub her skin with the lotions and soothe away the panic that raced across her face, coming up out of decades'-long sleep. He watched her pretty face fill with color, rosy with freckles, her red hair still a vibrant halo. She had been uneasy about the whole prospect, kept it from him and failed, and now here was her fear again, in fluttering eyelids, vagrant jitters that flickered in her face—until her cloudy eyes focused, squinted, and she saw him hovering against the ceramic sky and a flush brightened in her, surprise racing, and she smiled.

"I . . . what . . . *cold* . . ."

"Don't talk. Just breathe. Everything's fine," he lied.

"If you're here, it's gotta be." She reached for him anyway, grimacing at the effort. It was like a new sun coming up.

THREE

Beth Marble felt life coming back into her like a muddy, warm flow. Seeing Cliff first made her last thoughts—those fears of decades ago, as the sedative swarmed up in her—trickle away. *He's here! Looking the same. It worked! We're at Glory, then.*

A few minutes ago in relative time, she had felt the old clammy panic. *This could be the last sight I see.* . . . And the adrenaline surge of dread still pounded through her. *And I thought I was so ready, so sure.* . . .

She smiled at this memory of her former self and carefully put that past aside. What was that mantra in high school? *Be here now.*

Cliff spoke, his words warm and steady. "Everything's fine."

She answered with a croaking, "If you're here, it's gotta be."

His hands on her felt wonderful and she followed his whispered orders. Lie back, just take it, enjoy. Smell the cool metallic air. The spreading glow of tissues swelling, blood flowing at speeds her cells had not known for years, tingling, surges of pleasure as her senses revived . . . *Hey, I could get to like this.*

Then she heard the growl of the ship.

The vast majority of the crew had gone into sleep before *SunSeeker* even started, but as pilot she had stayed up for over a year as *Seeker* gathered speed. It felt *good*, to be at the helm of a starship, she recalled—even if the yoke helm was nearly superfluous, since electronics really steered the magnetics and lepton-catalytic fusion burn.

So she knew the thrumming long bass notes that told her the ship was running full bore. She didn't need to hear that; she could feel it.

And the subtle tenor in the background, when *Seeker* was in reversed configuration, and so decelerating—it wasn't there.

She listened hard as Cliff's hands welcomed her back into the world, and no, they weren't at Glory. Something was wrong.

· · ·

Redwing's well-managed face was a study in guarded reluctance.

He did not like any of the alternatives on the table. Nobody did. But Cliff could see in the doubting downturn of his mouth that he did not want to forge ahead into long, lean years, hoping the drive would improve.

Abduss scribbled on a work slate. By this time, Cliff could read his expression pretty well. The man was steady and reliable, risk averse, with an automatic distrust of radical new ideas—just right for crewing the long years out here. Yet despite himself, Abduss was trying out the idea, and liking it. Now he had a share in a great discovery, and it was dawning that he wanted more. So did Cliff, for that matter.

But mostly, Cliff wanted to live. With Beth. They could marry, after the longest courtship in history.

Cliff knew enough to let the silence in their wardroom lengthen. Beth sensed the score now, and her careful look took in the tension: Redwing's folded hands, Abduss and Mayra keeping their eyes on their slates. The background rumble of the ramscoop fusion engines was like a persistent reminder; Newton's laws don't wait. Redwing stared into space. In the end, Abduss looked up. "We could make such a maneuver, yes. But very vigilantly."

"What do you make of it, Beth?" Redwing asked softly.

"I'm pretty sure the ship can be helmed in that accurately," she said. "It's within specs, the delta-V and aiming. I can tune the comm deck AIs to smooth it a bit. It'll be a ten-day maneuver. But I do wish I knew why the engines aren't working to design."

"Don't we all," Redwing said ruefully, unfolding his hands. "But we play the hand we're dealt."

It was as though fresh air had come into the room. Four faces awaited the captain's word.

They had awakened him to make this decision, and so far he had shied away from it. Now Cliff had a slender moment to wonder at his own ideas, if he'd followed them far enough. *Life's a gamble.* He had a gathering, foreboding sense—and a heart-pounding curiosity that would not give him rest. *Life persists.*

Redwing's mouth firmed up. "Let's do it."

· · ·

Beth had the flight plan Alfvén numbers tuned just about right. She found it gratifying to see the ship respond to her helm, even though it was a bit spongy. It took eleven days to make the swerve. There were dark days when it was not clear whether *Seeker* was responding correctly to the maneuver. The magnetic scoops rippled with stresses but performed to code. With Abduss checking her every move, she brought them through, though not without some polite arguments.

Cliff and Beth spent a lot of time in their room together. The warm comforts of bed helped.

She preferred taking ginger snaps from her recovery allotment of "indulgences." These she had selected for just this, a crisp bite floating on sugar, to the richness of chocolate chip, which she also had because Cliff liked them. Though with either she always had a cup of cocoa, the warm brown mama she needed, Cliff had carried none but stern Kona coffee in his wakeup stash. No cookies at all.

"What do you remember about going into the chill-sleep?" she asked while they licked crumbs off each other.

He smiled dreamily. "They said I would feel a small prick in my left hand and I thought that was funny but couldn't laugh. Could barely crack a smile. Then—waking up."

Beth grinned and finished her cocoa. "I thought of the same dumb joke. Not that, in your case, I know what a small one feels like."

The remark got more laughter than it deserved, but that was just fine, too.

Beth said with a thin voice, "Y'know, looking at that round thing from this angle, first thing I thought was, it seems like a giant wok with a hole at its base."

"You're thinking about food again. Time to eat."

Her old fear subsided while she worked, and to keep it at bay she indulged herself with Cliff. He was the sun of her solar system, had been since the first week they met during the crew selections trials. Her parents had both died the year before in a car crash, and that cast a shadow over her application, in the eyes of the review board. They wanted crew with a long history of steady performance, no emotional unsettled issues that might boil over years later.

Losing the two central figures of her life had eclipsed her joy, made her withdraw. She had not thought of the affair with Cliff as an antidote to her grief, but its magic had played out that way. He brought out the sun again, eclipse over, and it showed up in everything she did. Especially in her psych exams and, more tellingly, in the return of her social skills. Later, in training, she had learned that about the time she met Cliff, she was slated to be cut in the next winnowing. As she put it later, "Then Cliffy happened to me." The visible changes in her had saved her slot. Then her performance at electromagnetic piloting, a still-evolving new discipline, had excelled.

She was here because of him. She let him know that, in long, passionate bouts of lovemaking. Sex was the flip side of death, she had always thought—the urge to leave something behind, ordained by evolution way back in the unconscious. Their sweaty hours "in the sack" (not a phrase she liked, but it sure fit here, because Cliff used a hammock) certainly seemed to confirm the idea, as never before in her admittedly rather scant love life. At meals, she was afraid that it showed in her face, which now reddened at the slightest recollection of how different she was now, wanton and happy and well out of the eclipse shadow.

One evening, after she had set them in a long, curving arc toward the bowl, the captain allowed spirits to be broken out. They held a sort of impromptu group brainstorming session, with Mayra presiding as de facto referee. Ideas flew back and forth. What would they find up ahead? What the hell could the bowl *be*? Squeezebulbs were lifted, and lifted again. Beth got them all laughing. There was singing, predictably awful, which made more laughter. The captain drank more than the rest of them put together and she began to understand the pressures the man was under.

. . .

The maneuver they were planning was astonishing. The jet was far denser than any plasma *Seeker* had been designed to fly into. But *Seeker*'s specs were broad enough to include collisions with molecular clouds. You never knew what you would run into in interstellar space, Beth thought. Never the bowl, not that, but *SunSeeker* had been made robust.

Stars buried in a cloud could ionize spherical shells around them. *SunSeeker* might have to brave a cloud, and so the plasma spheres. Its prow sprouted lasers that could identify solid obstacles up to the size of houses, and vaporize them with a single gigawatt pulse. The lasers were tough, hanging out in the plasma hurricane near *SunSeeker*'s bow shock. They were going to need that.

Wickramsingh's Star was moving counter to the galaxy's rotation. That was somewhat unusual, though not rare. They were headed the same way, because Glory's system lay behind Sol, in the sense of the rotation most stars share in the immense beehive pinwheel that is a spiral galaxy. That was why they had not noticed the star's oddity before—the bowl cupped around the star, so they could not see it from *SunSeeker* or from Earth. As *Seeker* overtook the system, moving directly behind, the star had suddenly seemed to pop into existence from behind its shawl. And it was quite nearby.

"Mmmmmm. It's moving how quickly?" Beth asked in the next meeting. Five of them just fit five monitor chairs in the control room.

"More than ten thousand kilometers per second," Mayra said.

"Look, that's damn fast."

Mayra beamed. "Yes. I was keeping this precise fact for the right moment."

"And that's nearly our ship velocity. Sure seems high for a star."

Abduss nodded. "A bit less than ours, so we overtook it. But yes, unusual for a star."

They glanced at each other and Beth wondered why the Wickramsinghs liked unveiling mysteries one step at a time. A cultural thing? Maybe they just hadn't wanted to shock her too much, so soon after revival? She had to admit, her head was still feeling a bit woozy—and not from the cold or the drugs. Conceptual overload. If she hadn't seen the thing on the screens with her own eyes . . .

Try to think straight. Beth asked, "Could . . . could the flares we see at the center of the star be responsible?"

Mayra shook her head. "How? Surely they are caught by the cap."

Beth drew herself a sketch with an unsteady hand. "The flares point toward the cap, and the star is accelerating away from the cap? And there's a hole in it."

Abduss said, "I wondered about that. The cap keeps away, even though the star's gravity attracts it."

She thought of such colossal masses in flight, the balance of forces necessary to keep them from colliding. How? "What's moving all this?"

"The jet escapes, driving the entire configuration forward," Abduss said. The Wickramsinghs shook their heads, apparently still amazed at the immense contraption. She could see why they had awakened Cliff first, rather than Redwing. Cliff's specialty lay in dealing with the oddities of life that Glory might hold, at being flexible. A biologist, true, not an astrophysics type. Yet he had devised the idea of flying up the jet, and they hadn't.

A long still silence . . . and an idea came, lifted an eyebrow at her. She recalled suddenly that old phrase for understanding: to see the light.

"The missing element, it's—the light," she said. "The whole setup has to be using the starlight from Wickramsingh's Star."

"How?" Redwing asked skeptically.

"Let's get as many spectral views of this thing as we can on the approach," Beth said.

She had her add-ins working so sent a question and got back

SPECTRAL SYNTHESIS-BASED ABUNDANCE

MEASUREMENTS OF Fe AND THE ALPHA ELEMENTS

Mg, Si, Ca, and Ti—

—so she realized she would just have to rely on ship's diagnostics visually presented. This was going to be the perfect collision of shipboard smart systems and the unknown—with her in the middle. At hallucinogenic speeds.

She had a big fat intuition and nothing more. Everyone had a right to their own intuitions, but no one had a right to their own facts. Best to let the facts speak.

· · ·

Now came Beth's moment. Piloting is not a committee event. Even Redwing could only watch and make decisions, while the artistry of magnetic steering lay in Beth's hands.

"Wish me luck," she said with strained bravado as the ship drifted into the pearly plume of the jet.

Cliff hugged her and kissed her cheek, but she was already riveted on the lively screens curving before her acceleration couch. He whispered, "Good luck, yes," and retreated to his own couch, within watching distance.

Wickramsingh's Star was a smoldering beacon seen through the knothole that let the jet escape. "What'll we call it?" Beth asked from the board.

"Knothole, then," Redwing said tensely.

Near the star's hot spot, at the foot of the blossoming jet, coronal magnetic arches twisted in endless fury. Storms jostled one another all over the star, brimming with X-ray violence. It almost seemed as if the red dwarf had a skin disease.

They swept in behind, lining up. The speed of overtaking was now visible from hour to hour as the bowl swelled. Beth went with little sleep, aided by mild performance drugs that she carefully monitored. Abduss and Mayra spelled her when she started to nod off. She stayed with the board, trying to remain steady through her jittery anxiety—*but aren't pilots supposed to be rock-steady, girl?*—and couldn't help but speculate. The bowl's outside, seen in infrared, was crusted and simmering in the eternal starlight. Colossal structural beams coiled around it in a dark longitude–latitude grid. It hung there, spinning, dutifully following behind its parent star. Its cool nightside scarcely reflected any of the bright stars.

"The spectra look to be some metal–carbon composite," Mayra observed. "Not like our alloys at all."

Cliff had no important role in all this. He made the meals and washed up while the crew worked their bridge stations with unrelenting devotion. Every plot change they checked and rechecked. Beth could tell that Cliff was impressed by their close teamwork, once the goal was clear. They could focus on technical details at last, and were obviously happier to do so.

Cliff made himself fade into the background. He had little role here, but he didn't sleep much either. Beth could read his unspoken thought: If he was going to die, at least he wanted to be awake.

In the unending din of the scoop engines, it was a struggle not to let feelings overly influence her thinking. Irritation mounted as she tried to do precise calculations and maneuvers. She projected all kinds of fantasies upon the growing mote as they screeched around, the ramscoop fields readjusting to a turning maneuver they had never been designed for. Artfully, Abduss and Beth used the star's gravity to swing *Seeker* into the exact vector that the dwarf sun was patiently following.

Beth got edgy with their eyes on her—or was that the fatigue talking? Redwing sensed this, so he and Cliff spent their time writing the report for Earthside, with full data and visuals. They were on the bridge, sending it out through the laser link at their stern, when it struck her. What were the odds that *SunSeeker* would come upon Wickramsingh's Star when their velocities were aligned?

Redwing looked startled when she pointed this out. "We're both headed toward Glory. Damn."

"They want to colonize Glory, too?" Mayra asked.

"Can't be," Abduss countered when he came onto the comm deck. "What would be the point? That bowl has tens of millions of times the area of a planet."

This seemed an obvious killer argument. Still . . . their velocities were aligned. Bound for Glory. With Sol dead aft.

"Maybe they just wander from star to star?" the captain asked. "Interstellar tourists?"

Nobody answered.

Redwing said cautiously, "You were briefed on the gravitational waves?" and looked around.

They all nodded. "Can't keep secrets from the tech types, boss," Beth said without moving her eyes from the shifting displays.

Abduss said, "You suggest perhaps this construction, this bowl, is seeking the source?"

"Makes sense, I'd think. A puzzle, isn't it?" Redwing looked around again.

Mayra said, "It is noise, or so scientists thought when we departed."

"Any chance this bowl thing could be the source of the grav waves?" Redwing gestured. "Maybe this jet?"

"There are no masses of size that could make such waves," Cliff said. "I read up on it while Beth was waking."

Abduss said, "The Glory system has no obvious enormous masses either."

Redwing thought. "Maybe they're going to Glory for its grav wave generator?"

Cliff shrugged. None of their ideas sounded right.

"Not that intuition is a reliable guide here," Beth said wryly, over her shoulder. She never took her eyes from the panels. Soon enough they got back to work, plotting and piloting. The intense work was a relief to them, a respite from the uncertainties of their lot. Beth saw Cliff come onto the bridge; he clearly envied them. At least their days were full.

They vectored in on the center of Wickramsingh's Star's bowl, keeping a respectful distance. Beth trimmed their velocity by cutting back the engines. "Maybe letting them rest a bit will make them run better later," she said, but she didn't believe it. The jet plasma running through the Knothole had plenty of fast ions in its plume, and these pushed steadily against their ramscoop fields. Shudders ran the length of the long ship. The deck hummed with long, slow tremors. For the first time in her life, Beth felt like an old sea captain, riding out a hurricane.

Now the jet was visible to the unaided eye as they neared it. They could see it as a pearly churn lit with darting flashes of blue and yellow—recombination of the plasma, Abduss said, atoms condensing out of the torrent and sputtering out their characteristic spectra. The control deck lights were ruby for visibility, stepped far down. A direct view through a window would have burned out their eyes and set the room aflame.

As it flowed away from the bowl, the long jet was oddly tight. Beth close-upped the views. "Looks like the jet narrows down at the Knothole, then flares out. Look, some regularly spaced bright spots in the outflow."

"An instability, I would gather," Abduss said. He was fidgeting but he kept his voice calm. "The jet must have been magnetically squeezed as it passed through the Knothole."

Corkscrew filaments crawled along it, Beth saw, like one of those old barber poles. They could now see longer along the luminous lance of the jet as it speared through the opening, an exact circle far bigger than the span between Earth and its moon. Mayra trained all their scopes on the rim of the circle. The microwave spectrum crackled with bursts of noise from the spaced bright spots: pinched-in electrons singing their protests.

· · ·

Abduss close-upped the bowl at a good angle and Cliff felt his heart leap as the resolution grew.

In the side-scatter of the star's somber rays, they saw what looked like enormous coils, bathed in lukewarm beauty. "Those are bigger than mountain ranges," Abduss said in a whisper.

Without thinking it through, Cliff had expected that whatever built the bowl had long since died out. Decay, collapse, extinction—these were the fates of whole species hammered on the anvil of time, not merely of civilizations. This thing had to be *old*. But it still worked. The star's solar wind got funneled stably into the jet, pushing the whole vast construct to high velocity. What could have thought of this, never mind actually build it?

Beth began getting stronger signals in the microwave spectra—a rising buzz of electromagnetic signals as *Seeker* neared the cap. Mayra began to detect a haze of watery nitrogen at the innermost edge of the circle, farther in than the coils.

"Air?" Beth asked aloud. No one answered. Cliff thought about the inner surface of the bowl, a land holding millions of times Earth's area.

And more: Close-upped through the churning refractions of *SunSeeker*'s plasma shroud, the shell clearly rotated as a single piece. "Of course," Mayra said. "Centrifugal gravity."

They merged their measurements and built up an image on the main screen. The bright plasma jet pierced the bowl's hemisphere through a ribbed hole. "Kind of like a weird teacup," Redwing said. "Cupworld."

For long moments no one spoke. Then Redwing said with elaborate casualness, "Abduss, check if there's any new tightbeam traffic from Earth."

"There has been none for—"

"Now," Redwing said firmly. Beth understood: Abduss needed something to do.

The deck took up a long, deep vibration none of them had ever heard before, an ominous bass note they felt rather than heard. "We're entering the edges of the jet," Beth said tersely. "Picking up—well, plasma surf, I guess you'd call it."

Redwing frowned. "Full brake. Cycle the magnetics."

"Roger." Beth worked the large board, eyes never still.

The bowl seemed to swell quickly. "We're locked in on the jet." The deep bass note swelled. "And—slowing. We're flying straight up the jet."

SunSeeker made its agonizing turn. To pivot the ship on its plasma plume demanded the skill of an ice skater, combined with an acrobat, spinning in three dimensions under thrust. In interstellar space, where most hydrogen is a gas and not broken into ions and electrons, *Seeker* ionized the gas ahead with a shock wave driven by its own oscillating magnetic snowplow. The pressure waves plunged ahead, grabbing the electrons available and smacking them into the hydrogen gas molecules. Properly adjusted—which took Beth only moments to tune—there was enough time for the hydrogen to break up into protons and electrons. The gas fried into a torch of fizzing ions. That left a plasma column just ahead of the ship, ready to be netted and swallowed by their magnetic dipole scoop, then fed down into the fusion reaction chambers. The trick was to torque the ship while riding atop this angry, spitting column.

Seeker curved sideways by a mere few degrees, letting the target star gain a little on them. Then they curled behind it. Lacy filaments played before them as the jet grew near. They swerved fully into the jet with a hard, wrenching turn that slammed them all against the left arms of their couches for . . . forever.

. . .

Starships do not easily change directions. Sweat popped out on Beth's brow; a swipe of her hand on a touchpoint started a cool breeze. Throughout *SunSeeker*, joints strummed, echoing in the long corridors. Auxiliary craft shifted and strained on their mountings. Beth wondered if the ship could take it, and then if *she* could.

Finally they straightened and felt the push of the sun's jet against their magnetic collector fields. Beth surged forward from the deceleration, straps cutting into her. In the wrap-around omniview screen, set to all parts of the spectrum, plumes of incandescent plasma skated and veered around their prow. Their total speed was higher than the star's, but as they came around under the great bowl and into the furious jet, another force came into play. She felt it, became alarmed, then understood. *SunSeeker* began to twist, cork-screwing steadily around in the rushing plasma torrent. They all felt the grinding force of it, a giant's slow twirl.

"Y'know, I was kinda wondering what held this jet so straight and tight," Beth said in a conversational tone, her hands moving quick and sure over the many induction controls. "Magnetic fields do the job, generated by a current in the jet itself."

"Uh, so?" Redwing said. He was not a technical type, she recalled.

"Somebody's designed this to use the star's own fields, sucking them into a jet. They form those helical filaments we saw on our approach."

"Currents?" Mayra was alarmed. "We are mostly metal, a conductor—"

"So the currents are running around us, but not into us. Conveys angular momentum. Same as airliners flying through lightning on Earth. But—what a ride! Feel the twist!"

Beth turned to grin at them all and saw startled dismay. *Okay, not everybody likes surfing.* An acquired taste.

"Hey, I've got us under control. No sweat. It's a big magnetic helix." *Put forward the best news, worry about the rest later.* "And that means we'll follow a longer path, take more time—so we'll get more deceleration out of the jet."

No change of expression. *Passengers!* No fun in them . . .

· · ·

They ran hard and hot for hours and then hours more. Beth felt the strain, but somehow didn't mind. Riding the plasma knots without battering the ship was . . . well, fun. Her heart was pounding away joyfully. Excitement did that for her as nothing else could. She had been a skydiver and surfer and skier, savoring the sensation of dealing with artful speed. *Zest!*

But whenever she grinned, Redwing frowned. After a while, claiming that she needed the stretch, she got out of her harness and couch and stood while she worked the board. The AIs were laboring hard, carrying out a lot of the minor adjustments. For a while there, the ship gained a lot of charge on seams and edges, and Beth was afraid something would start shorting out. Too many electrons jockeying on the skin. But then she blew the charge off with a proton-rich plasma pulse—pure inspiration, plus freshman physics—and they got right with Mister Coulomb again.

She stayed standing. This was like surfing the longest wave in the universe, buffeted and sprayed and *rough*—but it thrilled her to her soul, every zooming kilometer of the way.

And here came the Knothole. She got back into her couch. *Fun's over . . . maybe.*

Somebody was talking behind her and she let it go. Pilots don't listen to passengers, not if they're smart.

Beth lunged painfully forward into her shoulder straps. The bowl ahead yawned like a flat plane—with a bull's-eye target. She could see intricate ribbing around its polar opening, a ridge around the Knothole. *Engineered current-carrying circuits, bigger than continents?* Something had to make the magnetic fields that shaped plasma from the sun, fields that were also pushing against their ship now with a fierce, blinding gale. Something huge.

"No trouble decelerating now," she said matter-of-factly, to calm the others. She need not turn to look at them; she could *smell* their fear. They swam upstream against the jet. Now the magnetic braking was worse than anything *Seeker* had ever been designed for. The ship popped and groaned. The bowl came rushing at them. Deep bass notes rang through the ship, vibrating Beth's couch, rattling everything. . . .

Focus. She flew through the bowl's exhaust Knothole, hugging the edge to avoid cremation. A noose of magnetic fields at the Knothole boundary tightened the jet like water in a constriction. Flow velocity rose against the ship. Running creases crossed the shock waves they rode. She saw the bowl was thicker at the Knothole than elsewhere—to carry bigger stresses? And eerie lightning played along the Knothole rim.

She dispatched an AI to map the Knothole magnetic geometry and in seconds a color-coded 3-D map unfurled on a screen. "The noose we're going through is bounded by dipolar fields," she said abstractly. "And the dipoles are kept in line with another field, perpendicular to the dipoles—so the magnetic stresses can't reconnect and die. Neat."

Murmurs from behind her egged her on. Analysis, tension-relieving talk, cheers—all just a chorus she ignored.

"Plus, ladies and gentlemen, it's radioactive as hell around here," Beth said, adding brightly, "but an interstellar surfboard—that's us—is designed for that."

They slammed ahead, losing speed. She surged forward in her harness, adjusted, and surged again. *Surfing the big one. Ride of a lifetime. If you survive* . . .

The prow tried to fight sideways but she jockeyed it back. Again. And again. Each time she got the feel of it better. Offhand she noticed she was drenched in sweat. *No wonder I can't smell their fear anymore.* . . .

She caught a glimmer refracted through the streaming

plasma ahead, a small sphere wobbling toward them—Wickramsingh's Star. The bowl flattened, became the sidewise horizon. The ship howled with its labors.

For Beth, time ceased to mean anything. She countered every veer and vortex, kept them straight, swore, blinked back sweat—and they were through.

The sky opened. Abruptly they were rising above a silvery plain. The jet hammered at them still. "Wonderful!" Cliff choked out, still hanging forward in his harness. Hollow cheers, ragged. They were rising above a vast white plain, but slower, slower—and then they turned again.

"Getting out of the jet," Beth said, as if passing the butter. If they stayed in the jet, they'd be slowed further, back through the Knothole and out again.

"We're taking a lot of ohmic heating in the skin," Abduss said, voice tight with worry.

"I can barely hold the vector," Mayra said calmly. Cliff knew by now the subtle tones of tension in her voice.

The white-hot jet plume thinned, then seemed to veer aside. Rough turbulence struck, slamming them around in their couches, bringing fresh metal shrieks from the ship.

"Out!" Mayra shouted. "We're out."

"I'd say we're in," Redwing said.

They cheered and all eyes were on the screens. Now they could see the inside of the bowl . . . and it was a vast sheeted plain brimming with light. They rose swiftly, peeling off from the jet to the side, plasma falling behind, vistas clearing. Again there curved away over the misty distance great longitude and latitude grids in sleek, silvered sections the size of worlds. The sections had boundaries, thin dark lines, demarking different curvatures of a greater mirror—and from that their eyes told them that these were all focused far away.

Silence. In a whisper Abduss said, "Mirrors . . . reflecting the sunlight back, inward, onto the star. That's what causes the hot spot."

Beth nodded, awed. Yes—otherwise the huge curved mirrors would have blinded them instantly.

They slewed to the side, turning, the screens taking in, across the immense celestial curvature, hazy tinctures of . . . green. She zoomed the scopes pointing inward along the great spherical cap. The lower latitudes of the inner bowl teemed with intensely green territories and washes of blue water. Lakes—no, oceans. The eye could not quite grasp what it saw. They were cruising along near the jet axis, and before them unfurled a landscape of arcing grandeur.

Beth calculated angles and distances. Any of the grid sections had a larger surface than the entire Earth. Each boasted intricate detail, webs strung among green brown continents and spacious seas, framing immense areas.

And her vision was all getting foggy with fatigue. Aches seeped through her.

"I've had enough," Beth said. "Climbing up that jet burned away our velocity enough. The bowl and star system were moving pretty fast, and now we're in their rest frame. We're marginally trapped in the potential well of that star."

Captain Redwing said, "You what?"

"Captain—"

"No, it's okay, I get it," he said suddenly. "The scale of this thing, it's just mind-scrambling, Beth. The bowl is the size of a little solar system, right, and you can just leave the ship circling the sun, right? Are we too close? Will we heat up too much?"

"We'll be okay." She visibly straightened, her pale lips firming. One last effort. "I'll leave the ramscoop idling, keeping the fields high, so we won't be sprayed with radiation. It runs rough that way, but we have no choice. We've matched velocities with the system, so it'll be *months* before we could be in trouble. We'll be in an eccentric orbit, right, Abduss? I'll be back at the controls before anything can happen, but somebody stay on trajectory watch, please."

Redwing looked puzzled.

Beth gave him a weak smile. "I'm going to sleep."

She staggered out. Behind her she heard Redwing's, "How can anyone leave *this*?"

And then Cliff was with her, guiding her, but lurching a little himself.

FOUR

Beth thrashed and jerked awake. The hammock shuddered. Her legs and arms were cramping from armpit to fingertips, hip to toes.

The dream faded. The controls weren't under her hands; the ship wasn't roaring through a plume of star-hot plasma. She hugged herself and tried to sleep. Cliff wasn't there. How long had she been sleeping?

Presently she gave up and went to the bridge, her boots thumping, bringing her fully awake. Her hands were trembling, though. Not what you want in a pilot . . .

"Hi," Cliff said, grinning. "Redwing left me on watch. Abduss is computing an orbit for us, unless he flaked out, too."

Beth was famished. She got out bread and fruit and ate as she watched the displays. She was just a little jealous of the others, who must have been watching for hours. And it was glorious.

Structures fanned out from the Knothole. She was now watching from the other side, gazing down at a vast sprawl. Her eyes kept tricking her, making her think this was all nearby, like looking down on Earth . . . but she was gazing over interplanetary distances. The tubing around the Knothole must be tremendous, the size of continents.

Far below the ship stretched away the wok-shaped mirrored shell, faring into a ring of green-tinged ocher. Between

SunSeeker and those lands was a shimmering layer—atmosphere, she guessed. Held in . . . how? She squinted and thought she could catch a sheen, the star reflecting from some transparent barrier. A membrane? She squinted at what seemed like millions of square kilometers of clear plastic sandwich wrap. The diffuse layer stretched away toward the distance, where she saw the lands of the belt—the great cylindrical section that formed the thick rim of . . . Cupworld? She didn't like Redwing's term but couldn't think of a better one. No mirrors there. Continents, yes, cloud-shrouded and green. Deserts as well, sandy and bright under the unending glare of a star that never set. Indeed, never set on all this colossal construction. *And what lives here?*

Her hands were trembling even more.

This immensity was impossible, too much; Beth looked away.

"They've made a world . . . a habitat out of the bowl," Mayra said wonderingly. "A vast green thing."

Beth took a long breath. For safety—*pilots must be focused*—she took her hands off the command boards.

Cliff thumbed up a display board. "We worked up a sketch to get the essentials of this thing in one view. Have a look."

She studied the line drawing, feeling woozy. "Yes, right. You've labeled the regions out from the axis with the equivalent gravs . . ."

"Yup, and the clumps in the edge plain are supposed to be topological features. Only my splotches are bigger than whole planets, a lot bigger." He waved his hands helplessly, grinning. But he frowned, too, worried at her fatigue.

"Right, hard to grasp the scale—this is inconceivable, but a sketch helps. You caught how the jet bulges out near the star."

More hand waving. "Looks to me like the magnetic fields in it are getting control, slimming it down into a slowly expanding straw . . ."

.   "A wok with a neon jet shooting out the back . . . and living room on the inside, more territory than you could get on the planets of a thousand solar systems. Pinned to it with centrifugal grav . . ."

"They don't live on the whole bowl. Just the rim. Most of it is just mirrors. Even so, it's more than a habitat," said Cliff. "It's accelerating. That jet! This whole thing is *going* somewhere. A ship that is a star. A ship star. We humans only built a star ship."

•   •   •

There wasn't much redundancy among *SunSeeker*'s auxiliary boats. Designs were modular: tanks or skeletal cargo carriers could substitute for passenger shells.

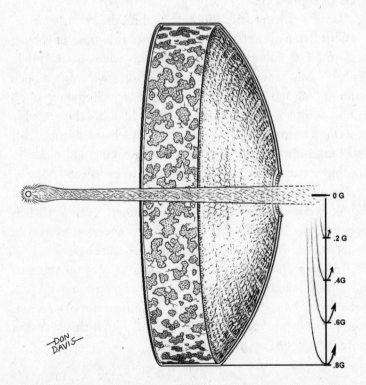

There were two fliers, Hawking and Dyson, twin lifting body designs. "We can't use reentry vehicles," Redwing decided. "We'd tear holes in whatever's holding the air in."

Abduss said, "Captain, these *are* the tankers."

"*Ceres* and *Eros* are tankers, too, for mining asteroids. We just add the tank," Redwing said.

Mayra said, "There aren't any asteroids or comets. The locals must have cleaned out everything that might have threatened their habitats, or even used it all to *build* the bowl."

"Really?"

"We haven't found anything at all," Mayra said.

"What, in four days? Four days to do a thousand years' worth of astronomy in a brand-new solar system?"

The Wickramsinghs were silent before Redwing's sarcasm. Indeed, the autoinventory had found no asteroids. "It's been vacuumed clean."

"Um," Redwing said. "So nothing hits the bowl."

Cliff listened with half his attention; this wasn't his business yet. The automatic search cameras were smart, quick. Probably Mayra was right: The whole solar system had been scoured long ago. But he didn't want to cross Redwing over a minor point; best to husband his credit with the irascible captain. The man had gone without much sleep, too. Cliff had found him pacing the corridors, checking and rechecking ship status, when he was supposed to be asleep.

He wished he had someone else to talk to about this, but the Wickramsinghs kept their own counsel. And Beth was sleeping. She'd done a lot of that, still recovering from cold sleep and the grueling flight through the Knothole.

Redwing chopped air with his hand. "Okay, for the moment we'll take that as given. No asteroids, no comets. We'll put a tank on *Eros*. It can carry water, mine it out of a comet, even—and it can *land*. Landing legs and a high-thrust fusion motor. We thought there'd be moons."

Mayra asked blandly, "Where are you planning to land, Captain?"

"Down there." Redwing waved toward Cupworld's green-tinged rim.

"Yes, I thought so. If you land near the Knothole, you'll be millions of klicks from any water source, and right on top of the systems that shape the electromagnetic fields. We could be perceived as a threat."

Redwing blinked. "You think so?"

Mayra kept her face blank, apparently her way of being diplomatic. "We have no idea how the builders of this thing feel about visitors."

Cliff couldn't resist saying, "At least they didn't shoot at us."

Redwing grimaced; he had not been chosen for fighting skills. "They haven't tried to talk to us. I don't like that."

Cliff put in, "But, Captain, the rim is where all the water and farmland is. They must live there."

Mayra added, "It's spinning around at thirty-four klicks per second, too."

Redwing nodded. "Higher than our orbital speed, right? Do we have onboard fuel to catch up with that spin?"

Abduss said, "It will take a significant fraction of our onboard reserves, principally water for the nuclear rocket."

Redwing snorted. "*All* our onboard ships are fusion powered. We can fly wherever we like if we can get water from Cupworld. We'll need the same trick to use any of them. Okay, say we see a lake. We'll put *SunSeeker* in a nearer orbit and drop the lander from there. Beth will know how to do that. Cliff!"

Cliff jumped.

"Where shall we land?"

They were asking him as the biologist. "It all looks like farmland and meadows and forests," he said. "Different habitats, probably—see those ice fields? I don't know how they create those, but our telescopes can't make out individual trees. All I've got is a light spectrum, but clearly from spectral reflections, the plants are using chlorophyll, Captain. Land anywhere near water on the rim, I'd say, and refuel the tanks first thing."

Mayra asked, "Do we land on the inside of the bowl? Or the outside?"

Redwing frowned. "Inside, of course. That's where they live."

Mayra pursed her lips and said evenly, "They surely launch their own spacecraft from the outer surface. They could simply put their ships in elevators, lower them through an outer air lock, and let them go. Immediately the ships would have a thirty-four-kilometer-per-second velocity. All with no need to fly through an atmosphere, or out through the film that covers their atmosphere."

Cliff grinned. Mayra had been thinking as he did, asking how the hell this enormous contraption worked. "You think we could go in through their outer air locks? From underneath? Maybe to reenter, they have magnetic clamps or something to catch incoming craft. Maybe we could use those."

Mayra shrugged. "Suppose we do. How do we knock on the door?"

Redwing mused, "They must have safeguards. . . ."

"Even if we get in the door, they control the locks," Cliff added. "We'd be caught."

Redwing liked that. He sat back and gave them all a glassy grin. "Makes it easy to choose, doesn't it? We must retain our freedom of maneuver until we know what—whom—we're dealing with. We go down through the atmosphere, then."

"We'll have to bust through that film they have," Cliff observed.

Abduss added, "They might see that as aggressive. *I* would."

Redwing nodded. "But it's the only way not to be cornered from the start."

"Makes you wonder, doesn't it?" Cliff said casually. "They must have seen us. How come they haven't come out to pay a call?"

Abduss said, "Good, yes. I have received no electromagnetic transmissions, either."

"Funny," Redwing said. "You'd expect at least broadcast radio."

"Perhaps they use point-to-point comm, laser links," Mayra said. "Just as we do."

Redwing sat up straight, switching to his command voice. "Abduss, would we have time to hover? Pick a landing spot?"

"Not much."

"We'll take *Eros*," Captain Redwing decided. "Get it ready as quick as we can. Now, do we need to thaw anyone else?"

Maybe this was Redwing's way of "building consensus," as the leadership classes taught. Cliff said the obvious: "We'll need twenty minimum to do anything on the ground."

"Let's get started, then."

FIVE

They kept wary eyes and instruments on Cupworld while they tended to the auxiliary ships. Beth brought *SunSeeker* into a useful orbit for making the *Eros* drop. They maneuvered carefully, but though they could see landscapes far below, the distances were vast. Even orbital rendezvous took weeks. This was not a planet.

That gave them time to revive a selection they would need—engineers, maintenance people, "groundpounder" types who expected to wake up on a planetary surface. Redwing kept the numbers revived as low as plausible for the exploring party. They needed replacements for the current crew, who were all going down to the bowl, since the revived wouldn't be physically able in time.

Unsurprisingly, those woken up were quite surprised.

Just looking at the external feeds could cause these newbies to freak out. Redwing quickly learned that it was best to have the recently revived brief the next batch. Cliff got tired of explaining their incredible situation.

He spent his days surveying the lakes, rivers, and oceans of Cupworld—or as some called it, the Bowl; Cliff had tried to think of something descriptive yet high-minded, and failed. The dotted blue expanses had been well planned, apparently—no huge deserts or wastelands, good circulation of air currents and moisture.

They awoke Fred Ojama first, so Cliff could work with a

geologist while making the survey. "This isn't geology," Fred pointed out immediately. "It's a, well, a building."

"A building the size of the inner solar system, yep," Cliff answered. "But somebody thought it through. Look at how the lakes, rivers, and seas follow a fractal distribution."

Fred thought that through. "Best way to distribute water. Avoids deserts, maybe . . . but that patch looks like desert. And that patch of forest might be . . . No, never mind."

"Like symbols," Cliff agreed. "Looks like writing. A super landscaper leaving messages. Like in *Hitchhiker's Guide*, the guy who designed the fjords."

Fred looked blank.

Redwing had hesitated to wake Fred Ojama. Fred's bio listed him as borderline autistic. He'd barely made the height requirement. Nobody actually knew him very well. Not all the crew were social mavens, for psycher reasons. Redwing remarked that a cocktail party with no listeners was a noise fest, and there was an analogy there about teamwork. The list claimed Fred was a near genius, too, with a history of original ideas, and Cliff had wanted that.

Cliff pointed to the boundary where the cylindrical part curved smoothly into the vast mirror dome. "I'm trying to figure out how it would be to live on the surface, when it starts to slant. The whole thing is rotating together, so as soon as the slope changes, centrifugal grav will be at an angle to the ground."

Fred zoomed on that area. "The rivers go away there. Just vanish into the sands." He snapped his fingers. "I got it. The centrifugal grav works against the inward-sloping curve of the high Bowl. So water can't flow up into the mirror area. That means the gravity alone can keep that big zone clear of life, I guess. Maybe even air."

Fred was smart. There weren't dumb people on *Seeker*, just people with other tales or people you disagreed with.

An important point to remember in arguments. "Sounds right. The mirrors are important. The builders don't want them growing lichen or anything."

"So the whole structure has a clean division. The cylinder's for living, the mirror for propulsion." Fred shook his head. "What an idea."

"What kind of mind would even think of it?"

"Something with a long time horizon. This whole construct accelerates *very* slowly." Fred looked at the jet in the distance, a brilliant ivory pillar of ever-shifting tendrils. "That plasma's pushing a *star*."

"Odd minds, gotta be. But engineering's a universal. Things work or you change them."

"You want to reverse engineer this place?" Fred grinned, nodding his bald head so it caught the gleam of the lights. "Good. Good."

Cliff had close-upped the region where sunlight reflected off the atmosphere membrane. He and Fred kept up their banter while he tried to see deeper. The shiny surface was probably some tough but thin layer to keep their air in—19 percent oxygen, 72 percent nitrogen, and traces of carbon dioxide and noble gases. Then he saw it. A patch that didn't reflect.

They used the maximum magnification of the scopes and then called Redwing. "I think we've found an area sealed off from the membrane," Cliff said, showing him the barren circle. "It's about a hundred kilometers across."

"How can they tolerate it? Won't their air leak out?"

Fred said, "Maybe they opened it for us, just recently. A thing this big can take a little loss."

Redwing looked at every view, across the spectrum, before finally saying, "Open areas, yeah. Makes sense. Apparently for landings from space?"

"That's what we figured," Fred said.

"Solves our landing problem, then," Redwing said with a thin smile of satisfaction. "Let's go in."

SIX

If your heart is large, Memor thought, and contains volume enough to envelop your adversaries, then wisdom can come into play. One can then see their transparency, and so then diffuse or avoid their attacks. And once you envelop them, you will be able to guide them along the path indicated to you by your own hard-won wisdoms.

He shook himself. This insight came from some new part of him . . . the restless part of his mind that would soon be *her* mind. For Memor was now amid the fevered straits of the Change.

Not the optimum time to confront a crisis unlike any within the last eight-squared of generations. Lifeshaping should be done in peace, but that was not to be Memor's destiny. He would be female within a few short cycles, but he had not yet lost the male's sense of reach and joy, the Dancing. He could even smell the seethe of fructifying change within him. Hormones raged; molecules fought for dominance in his bloodstream. Fevers came in like chemical reports from a raging battlefield. These changes had been designed by the Founders and their following generations, now well sanctified by endless eras. Memor knew his shifting moods and jitters paid the cost of acquiring greater wisdom. But the cost was high and hard to endure amid a crisis.

"Order descends," the Prefect called in ancient tones for the assembly of Astronomers.

"Order prevails," came the answering chorus as they took their places of rest beneath the great dome.

Memor let the details of unfurling discussion play over him. He kept his body still while his inner mind fretted at the vagrant impulses within his changing self. Even his Undermind, normally serene, showed a surface wrinkled by fretful winds. Waves of knotted concern broke across its steady currents.

The technical summary was as he had heard. A starship of boldly simple design approached from aft. Diagnostics astern had seen it turn and approach, as though their flight had not been directly for the Bowl. Perhaps they were bound for the star ahead, where the gravitational waves emerged?

The audience of Astronomers murmured. Speculation fueled their excited chatter. Monitoring the approaching ship's transmissions picked up several bursts directed back along the ship's path. Trailing satellites had picked up these, yet intensive study by the linguist minds gave little more than a simple sense of their grammar and contextual constructions. Their habits of mind as revealed in language did not seem remarkable. Linear logics, few layers of meaning. Indeed, they seemed like their ship—primitive, yes, but ambitious to undertake full starflight in such a flimsy craft. The consultant engineers—small creatures, timid in the presence of full-sized Astronomers—pointed out odd features in the magnetic configuration, and announced that they would like to inspect the long, slim craft. Much sharp discussion followed.

Memor felt distracted by the marinating changes within him. He sat out the usual time-honored dispute, Watchers—pejoratively called Sitters—versus Dancers. The Prefect called up ancient records and even voices from the far past.

Past lore supported the Dancers, Memor thought. Unsurprising—stories of change are always more interesting than stories of stasis. Change is the essence of story, built into the mind by evolution's strict dictates.

Astronomers of ancient times had fired upon many ships, usually with the Gamma Lance. They had passed by many planets, explored and then ignored. These cases did not have many stories. The Watchers kept referring back to them.

Memor stretched and tried to look alert. Watchers were boring, ponderous. But then, Memor was still male, and like Dancers favored variety, engagement. Wisdom came later. The Watchers were nearly all female.

So Memor was in the middle here. He could sense the change to come, but he hadn't lost the male's sense of reach yet.

The assembly took a long, deliberate time to glide through the vast library of the past. Memor coasted through the old records as if they were his own adventures. Zesty, colorful, shot through with ancient exploits. They enthralled him.

The Bowl of Heaven never came too near a sun. It was too ponderous for that, and with its mass could perturb the orbits of life-bearing worlds. They did send ships, of course. But the Astronomers' telescopes had always been superb; they knew the nature of a world or moon before an exploring ship ever set forth, fired into a solar system from the rim of the Bowl. Voyages to interesting planets always took hundreds of long cycles, aboard one or more great cruisers usually equipped with landers, sometimes with orbital tethers.

Memor sat up, snorted, and focused on what had been mere droning history. Here, in one thrilling tale, the Bowl had come near a heavy world, too massive to support any adventurer. The mother ship hovered in the quasi-stable point beneath the largest moon. Ships angular and strange rose like sparks from the heavy world's surface, rocket propelled. There was no orbital tether. Simple technologies. This was how the finger snakes had reached them—an artful species indeed.

There followed hundreds of long cycles of negotiation, of studying one another. The little finger snakes had gained from this dialogue some trivial enhancement in their technology, nothing that could threaten the Bowl. The Bowl had learned little from them, of course.

Then 256 finger snakes had returned to the Bowl aboard the mother ship. The small colony had needed little in the way of integration. They were more dexterous than most Bird Folk, good tool-users, and crafty repair artisans. You rarely saw them now; they lived underground. Memor was impressed that such small beings had ever attained spacefaring skills, considering how they loved their buried warrens.

Lessons of ages unwound. The past scrolled on within Memor's mind. Around him, other Astronomers huffed and grunted as they, too, experienced the deep realms. An elder snored. Out of respect, all let her sleep.

Here, a bandit species had attacked approaching Astronomers' exploring ships. The Astronomers had retreated. The Bowl's defenses proved adequate, and so they had continued on, out of their range. A few scores of invaders had landed, been captured, been bred for docility. Four-limbed bipeds, they were, and they made good farmers.

These named Sil had come as plunderers; they'd seen the Bowl as a high-tech civilization and wanted its secrets. Their early days after capture proved turbulent. Training worked its slow magic. The Sil were limber, dexterous creatures, invaluable today. Space suits allowed them to work on the Bowl's understructure. Their docility was not quite dependable, even now, after twelve million long cycles.

Memor moved on through the stories. Images filled the air around him, long dead voices spoke in somber tones of musty triumphs.

Here, a gas giant planet was home to living dirigibles. Probes managed to scoop up enough infant balloons to make a stable population. They bred in air, seldom touching down. The Bowl's deep atmosphere gave them free, safe range. The bioengineers deftly tuned their genes for docility and strength. A million long cycles later, they were an indispensable part of the Bowl's civilization. To take to air without expending fuel was a great pleasure, available to all the master Folk.

Memor moved on through the annals of history, all the while fighting his trembles, fits, fevers. *Is it worth all this to become female?* Judgment is never wise while in restless agonies. He focused, lifting mind above body. His unmasked Undermind dealt with the aches and fevers, beneath his burrowing consciousness.

Here, alien visitors had failed to accommodate to their new station in life. Genetic trickery had failed them, too . . . but a life-form derived from that world had become the skreekors, a valuable and tasty prey animal that could be eaten raw for the relishing. Memor hungered for one now, stomach squeezing, just from viewing the savory pursuit-and-devour sense concerts.

Tales of successful change rolled by, all leading to today's ideal ecological and political balance. The Bowl was a living thing, not a static tool. This incoming visitor was the first in many a million long cycles. Flaming them with the flare would be easy, though not trivial: it demanded managing huge energies with a deft touch. They'd done it before.

"The Gamma Lance is primed," a senior female said. She gestured at the star bowl. The starship plainly intended to fly into their jet. *Foolish!* The senior female said.

Memor rose on unsteady legs to dispute. *But what would we all lose?* An interstellar ramjet of unusual design and audacity, at the very least. New modes of thought. Strangeness. *Adventure!* Memor sat, and others sang their vying songs. Discussion rolled on.

Memor tried to follow the discourse, while giving no sign that he wrestled with his inner self. Strange emotions flitted through his mind, mingling with the ancient records in strange symphonies of thought. The best stories were never of maintaining stasis. Change meant action meant zest. Watchers held the balance of the Bowl, but Dancers had all the best songs. Of course, there had been times when a visiting alien was simply destroyed, but where was the entertainment in that?

It might be that Memor, and Memor's peers, would give too much weight to tales of change and advancement.

Time would tell. But for now, Memor was a Dancer. He had to be.

His inner struggles and outer sweats so preoccupied him that he very nearly failed to note that the Dancers carried the argument. Only when a friend pounded him with hearty congratulation did Memor discover that he had been made Master of the Task—and would have to deal with the approaching aliens, if they should dare land.

"Why?" he asked a friend Watcher.

"Because you are inventive. Also, you have enemies."

"My enemies would—?"

"Hope you fail, yes."

Memor paused, but decided to go with the tide. He strutted a bit and bellowed hearty masculine thanks to all. *Let them come!*

PART II

THE TOUGH GET GOING

Man is a small thing, and the night is large and full of wonder.

—Lord Dunsany

They left a skeleton crew of five aboard SunSeeker, *with Red-*wing plainly sorry that proper ship command protocols demanded that he stay aboard. The crew left were enough to handle the hundreds in hibernation and maintain ship systems.

The descent team took ten down with them—Beth, Cliff, Fred, the Wickramsinghs, and five recently revived, who were still taking it all in. Cliff was nominally first officer, mostly because Redwing wanted to avoid the delay in reviving a ship crew officer. Cliff could barely keep the various ranks straight in his head and suspected they would quite soon matter very little.

Terry Gould and Tananareve started as per regulations by checking everyone's gear and organizing it for rapid use if necessary. They had field packs, rations, water, lasers, and tech gear, all compact and rugged. The lower Bowl grav made it possible to carry more, so they had packed to do so. Cliff, Beth, and Fred spent most of the long flight checking and rechecking their gear, then reviewing the many multi-spectra maps they had made. On the flat regions there stood pillars, barely resolved—not pylons, but raised land formations.

"Buttes," Beth said, sipping coffee. "Black-topped. Kinda like the American West but lots bigger. Looks like they rise all the way up to the sky roof. So the sealing barrier, that light blue stuff, ends at the rim of the butte."

"Pretty high, too," Fred added with a grin, plainly enjoying himself. "Nearly seven kilometers. Not as high as Everest, and certainly nothing compares to Olympus Mons, but worth climbing for fun. Always wanted to do Everest . . ."

Cliff kept his voice even and warm, and even managed a smile of sorts. "We'll have to arrange it for you." At times, Fred was touchy. As the ship rumbled, Cliff eyed Fred, who was lean and muscular and sported a permanent suntan. How had he gotten that in all their training time? Cliff had hardly been able to sleep. At least Fred didn't talk much now as he concentrated on work.

• • •

The last long swoop of their descending orbit was tense. The cabins filled with a sour smell and everyone was on edge. It felt odd to be coasting down toward a huge landscape that stretched away to all sides, filling the sky—and yet still be in space. The Bowl wrapped around them.

No tug of deceleration or singing of thin air. Cliff looked at the wall screens. One showed *SunSeeker* above them, a pale blue thread of flame trailing. Another showed the top of the butte, nearly edge on and still a featureless black. Another, the "overhead" view toward the jet.

Cliff watched the ivory and orange streamers fight and roil along it. An idea struck him. "Abduss!"

The man was in the next acceleration couch, face pale, looking none too well.

"You studied the jet, right?"

"Uh, yes, Cliff . . ."

"What does it emit?"

"X-rays, microwaves, plenty of IR."

"And?"

"Not much visible light. A lot of broadband radio and microwave noise," the wiry man said, obviously glad to have something else to think about than their landing. "Very loud. Very beautiful."

"I'll bet that's why we don't pick up their transmissions—they avoid the visible region of the spectrum. Probably use direct laser feeds, instead—so no side lobes for us to pick up."

"Ah, yes, they are clever," Abduss said, and went back to looking fixedly at the land sliding below them. His mouth worked.

Lightning forked around the oval. Some kind of electrical process, like the big sheets of luminosity that came cascading down from Earth's ionosphere? Cliff watched the quick, orange streamers. They slid around the butte, with glowing fingers probing at the lip.

The atmosphere's membrane was a light blue shining sheet under them now. It was visible only at an angle. Sunlight glinted off long wave fronts that rippled in the sheet's surface, making it look like a transparent ocean. Cliff marveled at the illusion, seeing beneath it craggy mountains and long, sloping green valleys as though they lay on an ocean floor. Somehow this made the whole construction both eerie and yet like a planet.

Now they tilted and their thrusters roared, rattling Cliff's teeth. They skated along just above the membrane, and he saw that the waves were moving slowly, great undulating troughs driven by—what?

Like an ocean on Earth. Perhaps the rotation of this colossal artifact unleashed such waves, and they in turn affected the weather below. So did Earth's atmosphere, after all; hurricanes came from the planet's rotation about its poles. What oddities could they expect on this unimaginable scale?

He watched a long line of rain clouds caught in the crest of a wave. Angry blue gray clouds were corralled in the high peak, as if in rising they cooled and let go their moisture. His eye followed the cloud-racked crest to the far horizon. A marching regimental rainstorm. He felt a cold sensation of strangeness at this sight. The idea of a rainstorm that stretched long and slender over distances far greater than continents made him suck in his breath.

Now they were above the black pillar, descending. Cliff's stomach fluttered up into his throat. He clenched his teeth as *Eros* rolled and dived, wrenching around as Beth slammed them hard into their couches.

"The butte!" she shouted. "Damn!"

Abduss shouted, "What? What is it?"

Pause. "It'll be fine," she said flatly with forced calm. "I can figure this. Keep your crash webs tight. Someone should have noticed." Beth was talking through clenched teeth.

Abduss frowned. "What is—?"

"That's no butte. We're inside a hollow tube! The surface is—I don't see a surface, it's in shadow, seven kilometers down." Thrust went away. "I don't want to run out of fuel. I'm going to assume there's a floor and it's flush with the forest. Abduss, can you get me anything with radar?"

Cliff's throat was dry and his voice cracked. "Floor as opposed to . . . what?"

"As opposed to a hole that goes right through the Cup-world and out into space!"

Abduss said, "What?" His eyes showed a lot of white.

"Suppose it's a through-out tube, to save the trouble of going around the whole Bowl. That's what it looks like in a full-spectrum picture." Beth gestured at a stack set of views. In some, stars hung in the opening.

"Uh, so?"

"We could go right through. What's radar say? You can get an angle on the floor now, right?"

Abduss nodded and worked his board. He was sweating.

Cliff ventured, "We'd be picked up with *SunSeeker*, no problem."

"Maybe," Beth said tensely. "Unless somebody slams the door."

"There's a bottom down there," Abduss said. "Watch yourself, radar says it's not flat."

The motor thrummed again. High thrust. Pings and pops in the ship.

Cliff didn't try to speak. Beth was talking her way through it, and that was nerve racking. "It's flat, Abduss. There's a hole in it, a pit with stars at the bottom. We want to land, right? *Not* go through to the outside. Hey, there's light at the bottom! And here we go—"

Eros surged, then danced sideways under Coriolis force.

EIGHT

She set them down less than two kilometers from the butte wall, on a cluttered ledge that was perhaps four kilometers across. There was a wall along the inner rim. Beyond that, the universe peeked through a hole ten kilometers across. She made the ship linger on its jets, finding a bare spot. They thunked down and felt the tug of centrifugal gravity.

She looked toward the butte face. Pale ivory light spilled out along the bottom of the wall, from a row of windows running from tiny to huge.

They all felt the significance of the moment, but there was no time for reflection. They didn't know what waited outside, but talking wasn't going to tell them anything.

They emerged from the scout ship in full space gear. Cliff listened with half his attention to Fred reporting to Redwing. The lightspeed time gap was seventeen seconds and rising. They stood at the foot of *Eros*, looking into the light. Into a row of glass boxes of increasing size, with forest on the far side.

"Air locks," Fred said, and laughed happily. "With transparent walls." He stopped laughing when nobody joined him. "That one at the far end is fifty or sixty times as big as *Eros*. I guess they have to pass big machinery, given the scale of this, well—" He groped for a word, then laughed again. "Describing all this isn't easy. Captain Redwing, are the helmet cameras working?"

"We want one of the little locks," Cliff said.

These gigantic structures weren't funny; they were daunting. The one ahead would easily pass *Eros*, and it wasn't the largest.

Redwing, lightspeed delayed, barked on comm, "Cameras are working. Definition isn't good. Keep talking, Fred. We're lonely up here."

Beth added, "And nobody's coming out to greet us, either."

. . .

The smallest hatch that seemed to be an air lock wasn't a good choice. It was no bigger than a child. Cliff had picked one big enough to pass a couple of elephants, Beth judged. They brought the cart rovers down the ramp from *Eros* and lined up their cargo in front of the air lock. Their suits weighed lighter on them in the lesser grav.

Beth felt odd indeed, looking through two walls of faintly blue cliff to see . . . trees. Spindly black trunks, soft pink fronds, carrot-topped—but trees. They set to work opening the air lock.

Only they couldn't.

. . .

For three days, they tried to find a way into the air lock. The task took all the gear they had in the lander. Beth got tired from lugging apparatus out to the working area, setting it up, trial testing, integrating, then listening to the arguments about the results.

People under stress, she observed, need to argue. It lets off steam.

The team looked for obvious controls in the window/ walls, but the surfaces were translucent, smooth, unmarked. They were synthetic diamond, at a guess. Carbon, anyway. Mounted on a blue interior wall were odd protrusions that might be controls—"For something with big fingers, or clumsy," Fred reported to *SunSeeker*, now half a lightspeed minute away. But on the outside there were no manual assists, nothing like a computer interface they could recognize, not a lever or a valve. In a way it made sense: defensive architecture.

They tested the cliff wall—a hard shell, rising straight up with a vacuum on one side and on the other an atmosphere. They could see the weather was heavy with sleeting rain the second day, and cloudy the next. Looking up the height of the transparent inner wall was like taking a cross section of the sky, with clouds sometimes stacked against it. Slowly winds blew the clouds around the enormous boundary of the butte. While the others labored, Beth and Cliff took time to watch the trees and soil and small darting things that flitted among the swaying trees. Something foxlike almost escaped a pouncing bird. . . .

An alien world. It was like standing on one side of a museum diorama, only they were in skin suits and packs. And the other side was a living world just doing its business.

Quick flitting birds like swallows, but much bigger. They were fast and sometimes flew in formations. Bright splashes of color amid snarled undergrowth looked like flowers with petals, but threw tendrils through the underbrush. Why? Trees of curious zigzag trunks and branches. Scampering slick-skinned blue gray things—*like squirrels? same niche?*—leaping on the ground and into trees. Odd angles in the tree limbs, gnarled things like nests or goiters, a broad-winged thing flapping through . . .

Howard kept making analogies to Earth life. Sometimes they worked, but other features made no immediate sense. Strange and wondrous. Gradually Howard stopped talking to Cliff and just made notes.

Redwing got irritated that they could not find a way in. He started giving orders in a stern tone. *Eros*'s crew stopped answering. People got prickly, Beth noticed without surprise.

Beth figured there was some signal they were supposed to

give, but the blank, smooth, slick face of the air lock wall gave no clue about what to try. Here was the abstract problem of communicating with aliens, brought down to a concrete level.

Beams of particles, laser pulses, microwave antennas brought to within a meter—none made any difference, or provoked so much as a change of color in the eggshell blue wall.

The third day they were standing around the big microwave beamer they had hauled out, Beth with her gloved hands on her hips, gazing down in frustration at the rig, which had done nothing to the barrier. Fred said very calmly, "Something moving in there."

They all turned and saw a big colorful creature walking out of the trees. Swaths of blue, yellow, and magenta seemed splashed over it in elaborate designs. A big narrow head, with a long nose between two large eyes, swiveled and watched with stately elegance. The native looked to be at least three meters tall and strode forward on legs that articulated gracefully, taking great long strides. Mouth like a stubby beak. Spindly long arms ending in complicated hands. It came forward quickly, carrying something tubular, and then three more like it appeared from the trees. They seemed to stroll, taking their time but covering ground quickly.

Beth stood absolutely still, but part of her realized that this would be the first remark at the sighting of intelligent aliens. She said quickly, "They're . . . beautiful."

"Birds," Cliff said. "Those colors—they're feathers."

"Smart *birds*?" Fred asked.

"Hey, crows are smart," Irma said. Then shrugged. "Somewhat."

Howard Blaire just gaped at the Bird Folk, his gloved hands flat against the glassy surface. He'd run a semi-private zoo in Maryland on Earth. He'd collected animals too. He'd been something of a star, bringing weird animals onto television shows. Cliff had asked Redwing to revive him because he was familiar with varied environments and animal behavior.

They stood there for long minutes and the Bird Folk did just about the same, staring through the wall. They made quick, jerky movements with their two slender arms, moving their long necks sideways and jerking their beak-mouths. It was easy to see them as birds who had replaced wings with arms, but as well, they had a lightness and grace to their gait, an elegance of motion that recalled no creature of Earthly origin. Beth found this enchanting, a sort of dance she had never seen before.

The newcomers did not make any move to open the lock. After a while, Cliff poked a finger at Fred and Irma Michaelson. Irma was one of the recently revived crew, a plant biologist. "Go forward. Make hand gestures about opening the lock."

The Bird Folk seemed excited when Fred and Irma approached, beaks flapping—but they did not answer the hand signals and gestures. They gawked. They talked to one another. They fingered the various burdens they carried on belts and vests.

Beth watched them closely—the humans were all recording visual and audio, of course—and decided the Bird Folk didn't wear clothes at all beyond appliance wear like packs and belts. They had long swaths forming colorful patterns all over their bodies, particularly at the neck. Some wore what looked like headsets, or else ornamental hats. The backs of their heads had multicolored coxcombs of astounding profusion. Every one was different, with intricate bursts of color interwoven in rubbery pink combs, some nearly a meter long. They were tall, the biggest maybe 2.5 meters high.

Redwing's voice said on comm, "Company. About time! Fred, keep me posted." Fred didn't answer.

More Bird Folk appeared, came forward, and seemed to

talk to the others. Body language: strutting, bowing, fluffing of feathers. Plenty of beak flutter, speaking. Cliff reported, "We've got two species—at least two species—call them big and medium. Medium is still bigger than we are. Big defers to medium. Big carries sacks under the neck or on the ramp of its back."

First contact was turning out to be entirely a spectator event.

They stopped using their beamers on the wall for fear that the Bird Folk would take it as an attack. So everybody stood there and looked.

Beth chuckled. They had come light-years, met an obviously intelligent species—and neither could do much but gawk.

The tension of it finally got to Cliff. "Let's all go back inside. Maybe that'll provoke them to do something."

Beth thought this was a good idea; their suits were running low on reserves of air and power, anyway.

Nothing happened the next day, either. Some Bird Folk came and went, but came no closer to the lock.

The humans made a more elaborate camp: pressure tents, stores of water, microwave stoves. Maybe that would give the aliens some idea of how they lived, Beth thought. With guard duties assigned, someone was always watching the Bird Folk, capturing every move on video.

They all invented theories about why the Bird Folk did nothing—Captain Redwing had half a dozen—but without any way to check them, it seemed futile. So they had meetings and talked to *Seeker* and tried ideas.

More Bird Folk appeared. They formed loose ranks and stretched beyond view. Over a thousand of them, by Abduss's camera-count. Irma wondered, "Maybe they don't have much technology anymore? Or are they just the local animals?"

"They're carrying things," Abduss pointed out. "Not just

the neck sacks. Those three Bigs are towing . . . what? Something big, five meters long. Made of metal, looks like."

More waiting. More Bird Folk.

Cliff, mostly just to break the impasse, suggested they cut through the wall. Even diamond wouldn't stand up to what they had for tools. Go straight through the outer door of the air lock. Maybe they could find and work interior controls.

There were objections, of course. This was a crucial moment; don't make any moves that might be taken as aggressive. This view held sway for a full day, until Irma asked just how long they would wait, doing nothing. Until *SunSeeker* ran out of air? That would be centuries.

Biggest of all, there was the problem of cutting their way in. Nothing had worked before. So a team tried high-intensity gas lasers, tuned to an ultraviolet frequency that the air lock wall totally absorbed. It worked in trial runs, cutting in quickly, blowing off a carbon vapor.

They set up the laser outside the air lock. By now they had an extensive audience of Bird Folk. Beth felt uneasy working under their gaze. They just watched. Were they waiting for something? Certainly their steady stares implied a remarkable calm. Or, she reminded herself, a remarkably alien consciousness.

Redwing wondered on comm if this was some sort of test. Maybe the Bird Folk weren't interested in strangers who couldn't figure out how to get in?

They started in the middle of the outer lock door. As they worked, their acoustic detectors on the lock picked up a hissing sound. The Bird Folk were filling it with air! Celebration!

. . . but the lock did not open. What did this mean? The Bird Folk just looked at them, eyes glittering. Beak-mouths working. Even some odd moves, like dancing.

Pressure in the lock, with vacuum outside, made the job more difficult. Nobody wanted the atmosphere jetting out suddenly. For safety, they built a chamber around where they wanted to cut, to hold the pressure. Then the laser punched all the way through.

Through their first cut they slid a small pipe, just to sample air. Breathable, barely—high in CO_2, warm, a bit lower in oxygen, humid and with minor differences from Earth's. Had the aliens figured out human tolerances? That seemed unlikely. But the molecular ratios fit the measurements *Sun-Seeker* had made in its first studies.

"Earth's oxygen level is as high as it can be without igniting spontaneous fires in summers," Howard said. "Maybe biospheres generally run up to that limit, then stop—or else they burn themselves back to our levels."

"Never thought of it that way," Beth said, her voice hushed. "This place stays warm all the time. Maybe that draws down the optimum oxy level a little."

They were all in awe of this place, moving quietly, trying to take it all in.

Howard said, "The more I see, the less I know. Some of these plants and animals are clearly evolved from Earth. Some clearly aren't. Cliff, I think this thing—Bowl—went to Earth and picked up some life-forms. The birds are a maybe. I'd need to see a skeleton. Cliff? Anyone? What do we do next?"

This was clearly the captain's call, despite a lightspeed gap of four minutes. Redwing dithered; this was far outside his leadership skill set. They all finally got him to realize that they needed an exploratory plan. Some wanted to explore the Cupworld, at least enough to restore *Seeker*'s depleted stores. But they needed crew with the lander, too. The Bird Folk wouldn't wait forever . . . would they?

Cliff won the draw to lead an exploring party through the door they would cut. As pilot, Beth stayed with the shuttle party. The two of them didn't like this, but they were short of crew, and nobody else had the right mix of skills.

Beth grimaced at Cliff, and they made it up to each other that night.

Or at least that was their excuse. Nobody wanted to admit being afraid.

NINE

They started the next morning—not that there were any sun-rises here.

Cliff's team were four men and Irma, all muscular and tall and athletic. Beth and Cliff did not like being more than a few meters from each other, but they overcame that.

They followed Greenwich Meridian morn, of course, because the sun never set on the British Empire and certainly not here; the reddish star always hung in the sky at mid-afternoon. The star's jet was a furious neon line scratched across the sky, adding diffuse shadows. The eerie landscape confused their eyes and unsettled the mind.

They could not be sure if the Bird Folk slept, though Irma had compared camera runs and found that each did take a few hours of closed-eye time, still standing up. They never seemed to sit; maybe their knees locked. Nor did they fly.

Cliff had come to think of them as like ostriches. Far prettier and more graceful, but there was a similarity. Could such birds have built the Bowl?

The gas laser took three hours to eat through the outer lock door. On broad-beam, it then cut an arc big enough for humans to squeeze through. Cliff went first. He felt very vulnerable, hurried and impeded by his pressure suit, crawl-ing through a hole not much bigger than his torso.

By then the laser was short on charge and overheating. The operators—two engineers, Lau Pin and Aybe—shut it down and worked over the gas chamber fittings, which were looking the worse for wear.

Irma passed him some gear, then wriggled through. Cliff watched the Bird Folk for reactions. The big ones nearby fluttered a little, stamping their big feet, then went back to their steady stares. Much rippling of feathers, glorious runs of color.

Irma was through, and Terry Gould was having some trouble. "Let's move!"

Cliff felt alien eyes on his back as he got his five through the hole. Aybe came through, and Howard Blaire. Hustle, hustle, hustle. They had planned to put a plate over the round bore hole and let one of the party partake of the lock air. Getting set up for this, Cliff happened to look behind them.

The hole had changed. It was lopsided . . . and smaller.

He blinked some sweat from his eyes, smelled the sour flavor of the helmet. He had spent too much time inside. The hole still looked lopsided. As he watched, the rim of it wrinkled, changed color, crinkled at the edges and . . . grew. Inward.

Not diamond after all.

"Block it!" he cried, lunging at the hole.

They wedged some fittings into the gap. Abduss had a hand laser on his tool belt and he cut some more metal bars to jam the hole from the butte side. These stuck . . . then bent . . . and snapped in two and flew away with lethal force, bouncing like shrapnel around the air lock as the hole tightened further.

Howard cried, "*Ow!*"

"It's self-repairing," Beth called over the comm. "Get out—now!"

"Can't—it's already too small." Cliff eyed the rate of closing. "It regrows just about as fast as we can cut it."

They stood helplessly watching the wall ooze into place, like a liquid. The laser team struggled to get it back in operation, but—

"Too late." Cliff stepped away from the narrowing hole. He scowled at the Bird Folk. "Why do I think they saw this coming? No wonder they didn't look bothered."

"They knew something else, too," Beth said. He followed her pointing finger.

He hadn't noticed the dust motes rising behind *Eros*. Cascades of white light came from everywhere.

"That dust. It's been there, ticking at the corners of my eye," Beth said. "More every minute."

Until suddenly they were all glowing, as if bright sunlight were falling into the butte. Cliff heard shocked voices in his earphone, and Beth shouting, "Into the ship! Tananareve, you at least, get into *Eros*!"

Four of Beth's team were still in the pressure box they'd built around the air lock's wall. The fifth must be Tananareve, and she was running for *Eros*. She stopped when a hexagonal thing covered with lumpy protrusions rose through the Star Pit behind *Eros*.

Jets of ice white lowered the hexagon toward the floor of the butte.

Everybody was talking over comm—panic and anger and shouted orders that made no sense. Cliff watched the thing descend in the vacuum outside, tremendous compared to *Eros*. All happening only hundreds of meters away.

It might as well have been a light-year. The hole in the air lock kept narrowing, and the ship that looked like an assembly of boxes and rhomboids and coiled tubes settled down nearby. Out of it came a lumbering machine on wheels.

Soundless, the horror unfolded. The machine had a transparent cowling that looked like the atmospheric membrane, a shimmering pale blue balloon. Inside that sat three Bird Folk, working controls, staring at consoles that flitted across the walls in splashes of vibrant color. They moved with jittery intensity. Cliff made himself study the three and saw that they had different feather markings, and looked larger than the bigger variety on his side of the air lock. They moved with a lumbering, muscular purpose.

Three more of Beth's team were free of the pressure box. Coiled tubes unwound on the wheeled tank. These reached Tananareve, caught her. They plucked her up none too gently and dropped her into a cargo hold behind the cabin. Arms reached for the other crew, yanked them up one by one, added them to the hold.

Then the tank rolled back toward its ship, up a ramp, and was gone. Just like that, Beth disappeared. Just like that.

Horror paralyzed him while his own crew still fought the hole's steady closing. Nothing worked. Cliff watched but could think of nothing to do. Their shouts came through on comm. But he heard it all through a cottony buffer, the words hollow and refracting. Meaningless. He dimly realized that he was in a state of shock, numb, unable to process the events. Part of him had shut down.

The hole sealed itself up—a neat engineering trick, Cliff admitted distantly. He did not see the flicker of motion outside. Three tall Bird Folk were standing beside the air lock. They were of the third variety. They had the same markings as the ones in the crawler outside, and with a level, steely concentration they gazed impassively in at the humans.

Something thrummed up through his feet. He turned and on one of the lock walls a set of symbols flashed, rippled, changed in a cadence. He sensed a change in the pressure. Behind the three taller Bird Folk the crowd backed away, their leathery mouths working. The three were somebody important. Maybe a funeral guard . . .

"They're going to open the inner lock door," Irma said with an odd, flat calm.

Cliff said, "Aybe!" The man's head jerked around, wide-eyed. "We're going out the instant there's room. Here, give me that hand laser."

Someone called, "We shouldn't make any fast moves. Just be—"

"We'll make a run for it," Cliff said loudly. "Everybody, get all the gear you can into your packs."

He had to try the laser himself. It worked, a brief flash. He watched the aliens. This was dangerous and he was in charge. But he was damned if he'd let his crew get scooped up like Beth.

What to do? He looked up into the bowers of the forest. Some looked dry. Last night's rain was long gone.

"Burn the trees," Cliff called. "No shots toward the birds." The lock door somehow slid aside, though Cliff could see no housing it fed into. The door just shortened along one side. A puff of ivory fog swirled around it, humidity freezing out as it expanded. Cliff shouted "Stay together!" and was first through the opening.

The big Bird Folk, third variety, were twenty meters away. The Mediums and Bigs were edging back, giving them plenty of room. Cliff aimed the laser at the trees nearby and blew hot spots in them. They burst into licking, hungry flame.

The Bird Folk backed away, all of them, arms up in defensive gestures, legs stuttering in fast, short paces. Aybe helped the fire along with dried brush he snatched up. The rest of the crew copied him, moving to their left, behind Cliff. Irma was pulling Howard along.

The trees crackled and gave off plumes of oily smoke. Cliff heard high-pitched calls that he guessed came from the Bird Folk, but there was no time to think, only to run and shoot at the trees, keeping as many burning trunks between them and the Bird Folk as he could. Bowers in the trees exploded with muffled bangs, showering the air with sparks.

The aliens did not move fast. A breeze whipped down from the muggy sky and slid down the butte wall. It gushed out at the base, pushing the flames toward the Bird Folk. Cliff and Aybe formed a team, Cliff watching to be sure they did not get flanked, Aybe shooting at more trees, the others staying close. Inside their suits, they did not have to fight the smoke. Cliff could see legions of the Bird Folk staggering away from them, into the safety of the forest.

They kept on the move long after the Bird Folk had vanished in the growing firestorm. The land began to rise and they pushed on up it, getting enough height to see. The forest ran to the fuzzy distance. Nowhere were there any signs of a town or even a tall building. The fire had gathered momentum and now surged away from the butte wall. They had created a disaster.

Cliff was elated. Panting, the others grinned . . . except Howard, who sat like a sack of potatoes as soon as the rest stopped moving. Cliff finally had a chance to look at him. A three-inch sliver of metal protruded from Howard Blaire's arm, through a slashed sleeve. Nasty and bloody—shrapnel from the attempt to block the closing hole.

Given his ripped suit, Howard was breathing local air already. Tananareve got his suit peeled down, extracted the metal shard—Howard refused even to wince—and stopped the bleeding. She had him patched within minutes with a "walking anesthetic" that would not impair his ability to move. Howard stayed silent through it all, looking at the many odd details of the flora and fauna, still doing his job. He even caught something like an insect with his free hand and held its buzzing body for inspection. "Big wings, eyes I don't understand. It seems—ouch!" The creature shot away.

Cliff gave a hand signal and they gingerly opened their suits to the outside air. Fragrant with odd odors, thick, a bit sour—but the first natural air any of them had breathed in years.

Victory, of a sort. Cliff savored the moment.

He took time to pull the metal spar out of Howard's arm. It stuck in the bone, then jerked loose. Irma had her medkit open; she handed him antibiotic gel, then superskin spray. They all pooled their medkits and made a selection. Howard asked, "Painkiller?"

Irma asked, "Could you still run? Wait, here's a local anaesthetic." She rubbed white cream generously over the bleeding wound.

Beth and the others were back there, probably captured by now. He tried not to think about that.

They pushed on. Howard was able to run with them, but he didn't speak. He sweated a lot and seemed in shock. He'd been one of the last to be warmed up from the sleep. Cliff suspected he'd been hit with too much strangeness. Just like them all.

TEN

Beth's team took positions to cover all directions. Tensely they waited and watched. Things were moving. They crouched at the edge of the great bare plain, their backs to the closed air locks.

The space above the Star Pit had become dusty, vague. Dust motes don't behave that way in vacuum, floating, sparkling, drifting up in currents. Beth never noticed. She and the others were watching Cliff and his team in the air lock, still trapped, still trying to find controls they could work. Then—outside the pressure box, above the tremendous pit in the floor of the butte—space came alight.

All the motes were aglare, lighting *Eros* and the bottom of the butte and the line of air locks. Through the Star Pit rose a building, a skyscraper, a tremendous hexagonal prism festooned with coiled gray snakes. Metallic snakes. They began uncoiling. Some of them glared white at the head end. Others ended in grabbers, mechanical hands, clusters of nostrils that might be little rockets or sensors.

Beth and three others were inside the pressure box, up against the air lock wall. Tananareve was outside. A huge boxy thing was descending on them. "Look out!" Beth had time to call. "Get away from the Big Box!"

A look and a gasp, and Tananareve ran. Behind her the Big Box settled carefully. A wall in it split. A smaller wedge-shaped thing rolled out on tractor treads.

Consternation blared in her earphones. Beth turned

around to see that the hole they'd burned through the aliens' air lock was closing. The Wickramsinghs and Lau Pin were trying to jam stuff into it, blocking Cliff from climbing through. *Shit!* Howard Blaire started to try anyway, then pulled his arm and head out and hurled himself backwards as some of the blocking struts bent, then exploded.

A snaky arm from the tractor plucked Tananareve from the shadow of *Eros* and set her inside the Big Box. Another, much larger grab reached out of the bigger vehicle and closed around the human-built pressure box. Air puffed in momentary frost, and Beth felt the pressure change. She looked for the chance to escape, to run.

The crumpled pressure box had already risen too high. If she let go, she'd be killed. Like Beth herself, Mayra and Abduss and Lau Pin were clinging hard to whatever they could reach. The pressure box descended into a much larger cargo bin in the larger vessel.

Many of the walls in the alien ship were transparent, like thick, murky glass. Beth and the rest rolled or crawled out of the wrecked pressure vessel in time to see grapplers close on *Eros* and lift it against the Big Box's hull. The thing was immensely strong.

The Big Box rose fast. In sudden hard and tilting thrust, Beth eased herself against the floor of the cargo bin, a smooth transparent surface covered with wedge protrusions so big that she had to wrap both arms around one.

Lau Pin's voice rose above the general sounds of dismay. "Tananareve? Tana—Oh, shit."

"Lau Pin? Where are you?"

"She rolled. We're over . . . up against a wall. She's out cold. Her arm's broken, I'm pretty sure."

Thrust eased. Vanished. They were falling. They clung to the tie-downs and waited.

ELEVEN

Beth shook herself, trying to keep track of time, at least.

She didn't believe her in-suit displays. Days had passed.

Beth wrenched around, feeling sluggish. Bile slid up into her throat. She clenched, swallowed, forced it back down. Not the time to get sick.

She blinked at the passing scenery. Beneath her feet lay deep space, yawning vacuum. To the sides, slabs and beams and walls stretched away.

The back of the cup was sliding past. Occasional grapplers and other machinery came into view, some of it working. No living things, just robotic arms and, in the distance, locks. A weird, stressing vision.

She moved slowly. Her body felt numb, as though senses came through a filter. It took hours to get her crew together and make them work.

Fred recovered early. He watched passing scenery, mumbling notes to himself.

They spent the time taking care of Tananareve, and tying harnesses onto the lockdowns available on the walls. Nobody else had suffered anything but bruises and banged joints. Tananareve's ulna was broken. She clenched her teeth and said little. They tried to set it and splint it, with dubious results. She had broken ribs, too, but there was little to be done about that. Mayra could inject painkillers through the suit. Tananareve fought it for a while, groaned, then went slack.

Meanwhile the Big Box rose behind the wok-shaped section of the Cupworld. Very little noise came through the walls of their chamber. Thrust came and went, with no sound of rocket motors. They must be moving by magnetic interaction, hovering so close to the cup that its curve was almost lost. They were close enough to make out hexagonal plates that made up the mirror, and tiny-looking motors on their backs, all mounted to a grid that seemed no thicker than spiderweb.

That trip was their first good chance to see anything of their tremendous prison. Stars shone in the hard black. Brute slabs of metal passed by. Clangs and grinding noises, usually with small jerks and electromagnetic noise.

A long series of plates passed by as they rose. These were a city block or larger on a side, with enormous arms to move the plate's position. Beth felt that she was seeing the rear view of a giant array, devised to tilt the laminated wedges. Yet the huge areas were not thick. What could this be?

The mirror lands. They had seen those areas on their flight along the jet. Abduss had figured they reflected sunlight back onto the star's hot spot, to boil the surface and drive the jet out. These plates, then, were able to tilt and yaw, adjusting the reflection of the mirrors on the other side from their Big Box elevator line. The whole array was like the smart telescopes Beth had seen, only not used to look at stars across interstellar distances. These drove their own sun through interstellar space.

The Big Box rumbled as it rose up the back of Cupworld, taking its time. Sometimes there was rattling thrust, sometimes not. The big alien Variety Three Bird Folk didn't like heavy gravity, it seemed. No wonder, given their size.

They ate the food paste in their helmets, and thereafter went hungry. Not thirsty; the suits were made to recycle. They talked about food. They talked about whether they would starve. They wondered how much those huge aliens ate, and what they ate, and if humans could eat it, too.

Occasional thumps, surges, rattles, hums. Mayra collected pictures of everything on her all-purpose phone, which had no reception, of course. She watched her team bear up.

Fred—was he watching everything? Or just wrapped within his own mind?

Nothing to do but look at one another and worry.

Their chronometers clocked four more days.

TWELVE

They slowed down as their adrenaline high faded. Cliff could feel the energy leak out of them. It left a sour taste in his mouth. They trotted, then walked. His own breath turned ragged, wheezing.

Cirrus clouds overhead fuzzed Wickramasingh's Star into a gauzy reddish blur. Strange, layered forest lay in all directions. There were several decks to the high trees, separated by open air. Cliff wondered if these had evolved to allow the constant sunlight to reach separate layers as the tall trunks swayed in breezes. The oddly spray-topped trees were getting bigger as they moved over a ridge and down its slope. The trees were strange, often thick at the top and with rough bark.

He glimpsed plenty of birds flitting among the branches, and some very large, broad-winged ones hanging in the sky. Odd songs and squawks resounded in the high, thick canopy. At 0.8 g, it must be easier to stay aloft. Smaller birds flitted across the sky, too, in great chirruping flocks.

He suppressed the biologist in him and concentrated on seeing if they had pursuers. No sign of it, and the first two hours went without incident. All eyes surveyed the forest. Heads jerked at the sound of small things scrambling in the bushes. They were tense at first but slowly relaxed.

"We've got to live on the land," Terry said at a break. "Conserve our supplies. Cliff, you're the biologist. What can you see that we can eat?"

"Can't tell at a glance, Terry. We need to do checks to see

what here we can even digest. I've been looking for what's chasing us."

"Stay away from those aliens, right," Aybe said. "We need to figure out what's going on."

Cliff had doubts as to what was possible, but kept quiet. This was a small group, and they had to learn to work together first, and stick to essentials. "How much food do we have?"

A quick inventory showed that he was carrying more than the others. They did carry gear that worked in concert, compact food, and not much else beyond personal gear, comm, and tool sets.

"Say, let's hunt," Irma said brightly. "I used to do that. Liked it."

"Using what?" Terry's expression told them he would not have expected her to be an outdoors type, though she was tall and strong. "Lasers take a while to recharge."

Irma turned to show her hand-sized solar panel riding at her upper spine. "Mine's already done recharging. Hunting is a good way to scope out the wildlife."

"And vice versa," Aybe the engineer said crisply.

"We should find water first," Howard said, looking dry already, his clothes sweat-stained. His arm was healing fast and he showed few signs of any slowness. Vibrant health and response to treatment had been an essential in crew selection.

"We're too easy to spot up here," Cliff said, eyeing the horizon. "Water's down below. Safer, anyway."

They set off toward a denser stand of trees, using cover as they could, working down from the ridgeline. Irma insisted on taking the point position, hefting her laser intently, eyes jittery. After her came Aybe, and Cliff decided to give the man his own laser. He didn't want to be the marksman and also have to scan the terrain, figuring things out as a biologist. As soon as he let go of the laser he felt downright naked, which was the point. Not having a weapon reminded him that he was not a hunter, but rather the wary, hunted stranger. They all were, but some didn't know it yet.

Everyone seemed to accept Cliff as at least their temporary leader. It was best to appear pretty sure of yourself, he knew, so he did not share his own doubts.

So . . . What to do? Deal with the immediate. Learn, let time educate them all.

His first major decision came when he stumbled over a gnarled tree root and fell flat on his face. Getting up, tasting the sour taste of the soil here, he realized that he was tired. They all were.

His eyes felt grainy. "Let's take a nap," he said.

They groused a bit. Aybe was still pumped up with what Cliff judged to be adrenaline energy, but the others looked gray and drawn in the full daylight.

"How can we sleep in this glare?" Irma asked, fidgeting, ready to push on.

"In the shade." Cliff said it flat and sure . . . and after a long moment, they accepted it.

Aybe said, "Let's build a fire."

"We could make some hot soup, tea," Irma said, brightening.

Cliff shook his head. "The smoke will draw attention."

Irma blinked. "From who? The aliens?"

Cliff nodded. "And maybe something else that we don't know."

"What's our strategy here, then?" Aybe stood, hands on both hips. "Hide?"

"Yes. If we can."

"For how long?"

That was the nub of it. "For now, yes. Get our bearings first. Then we'll see."

Aybe sniffed. "Not much of a strategy, I'd say."

Cliff was tired, his back ached, and he didn't want to deal with this now. "Luckily, you aren't saying."

Aybe shrugged and glowered. "What's that mean?"

Cliff kept his voice mild. "We have to get oriented first."

Aybe held the glower. "You're giving plenty of orders here."

Cliff sighed. He really *was* tired. "So I am. We're in strange lands. I'm a biologist and the senior science officer in this team. Learn the life-forms first, find out what we're dealing with—yeah, seems like a good strategy."

"I don't recall us electing you."

Now Cliff shrugged. "This isn't a constitutional convention."

"I'll say." Aybe grimaced and opened his mouth to say more, and Irma broke in. "Running around here on our own, strange goddamn place, aliens, hell—where I come from, sounds like we're cruising for a bruising."

They all gave dry laughs and glanced at one another.

"Let's get some rest, guys." Irma looked at each of them in turn, beseeching.

Cliff nodded again. This issue wasn't over, but it would keep. He might even remind them that he was first officer. Scientists didn't pay much attention to chains of command usually, but this was not a lab.

Once they sat and ate, the momentum seeped out of them. They talked little and stared off into the distance—the forest that just *felt* strange and low valleys fuzzed by blue gray water and dust haze. The view was idyllic, still. A breeze blew through, aromatic and soft. Comforting. They were each still processing the dramatic events just past, trying to get some perspective. Too much had come at them too fast.

Then in the distance, Cliff saw a round blob high in the air. Dark, small, impossible to tell how far off even with zoom lenses. No discernible movement. He watched it for a while and wondered if it was some suspended artifact. Another mystery.

Cliff drank some water and curled up under some low hanging limbs. He conspicuously pulled his hat over his face.

This was an important test, he sensed, peeking at them. They looked at one another once more. Irma shrugged. They settled in.

Cliff took the hat off and said, "Aybe, you up for taking the watch?"

"Uh, sure." The lean, muscular man climbed up on a thick limb to improve his field of view.

The others laid out soon enough. Hats went on faces. Within minutes, somebody was snoring. The hard bright daylight remained.

He woke—two hours later, by his left eye watch—and sat up, disoriented. He had been dreaming of Beth, a jangled bunch of lurching images and a vague sense of threat offstage. Aybe was lying on the branch, head turned the other way. Cliff walked around and looked up at his face. Aybe's eyelids fluttered and he jerked up. "I, I was—"

"It's okay. Sleeping rhythm's going to be a problem for a while."

They roused slowly. Howard still was gray, worn. Irma looked at his wound, and his eyelids fluttered with pain. In the enduring sunlight, they ate and drank and didn't talk much. The air was dry and dusty and a breeze had kicked up dust clouds in the distance. Cliff wondered how anybody could figure out the weather here. There might be something like the Hadley circulation in the atmosphere, since the Cupworld wasn't a perfect spherical surface—but the scales were immense. Surface gravity varied over the entire hemisphere, but not solar heating. He found it hard to think through the atmospheric dynamics. It seemed unlikely that Cupworld had seasons; no axial tilt. What carried moisture around, in what patterns? What happened to evolution, without the seasonal cycle?

He made them go downwind, slanting off the ridgeline. That way they could see whatever was interested in them, coming up ahead. Their rear guard could be pretty sure of no surprises—from animals, at least. The sapient aliens were after them with smart technology, so they could come from anywhere.

Out of the sky? Cliff gazed up into the gossamer blue bowl. Birds of many sizes flapped across the immensity. Their body designs were familiar, excellent examples of convergent evolution shaped by the laws of physics—but some were huge, oddly angular, and rode thermals until they vanished in puffy high clouds. He could not see the rest of Cupworld through the high white water haze, or the jet. No sign of industrial pollution, at least. The aliens were somewhere out there, looking for them. Their only advantage was the size of this place, its refuges.

They made their way down a valley, seeing nothing much. Yet the air of strangeness kept them uneasy, on guard. Cliff led by example—always looking around, keeping them from talking. That way they could let their ears do the advance warning.

Irma got it. "Think like we're in Africa," she said. "Lions around every corner."

The two new guys, Howard Blaire and Terry Gould, seemed capable tech types, but with little field experience. They didn't hike well, kept talking. Irma shushed them a lot. The trees got shorter, and on all sides were brown bushes and tall gray grass. Birds trilled and sang in the tree bowers and stopped whenever anybody spoke.

They crept carefully into the high grass. In the dry perpetual afternoon, the stalks rattled as they brushed by. Thirty meters in, Cliff sensed something moving up ahead.

He felt a cold adrenaline shock trickle down his spine, his chest tightening. They went to ground in tall grass and watched a bobbing, tawny spike move across their path at about twenty meters ahead. Cliff saw the spike—a tail?—turn and then stop, directly downwind of them. They all tensed.

Then it moved off again, faster, at an angle. Maybe they smelled funny to it. Or maybe, he thought, it was going to get some buddies.

Crossing the grass had been a mistake. Their lasers gave them control of a ten-meter perimeter, but that shrank to how far they could see in grass or dense forest. They all got edgy. They got out of there fast and headed partway up the side of the narrow valley, to get viewing range. They were still seeking water. Cliff had them do an inventory on the way.

He had chosen to fill out his backpack carry weight, fifteen kilos, with other gear. Luckily, he had guessed right, and brought a light sleeping bag and cooking equipment. He had left behind all the techy gadgets and gimmicks available in *Seeker*'s supplies for planetary landing. Most of those presumed a power supply and backups. One item he had found and brought was a pair of sturdy boots and, most important, spikes for climbing trees—or anything fairly soft. Light, foldable carboaluminum, they weighed little and clamped snugly around the boots. They popped out on a sharp heel-clinking command—smart tech, quite cute.

They moved carefully and kept down talk to a minimum, but they were basically city types, able to keep the expedition's technology running. Not a bad group for this place, which was, after all, an enormous machine. Their attention wandered after the first hour.

Without warning, something like a wiry, fanged slick-skinned squirrel leaped down on Irma and tried to eat through her hat. Howard snatched off her hat by its brim and hurled it like discus. The squealing creature hung on until the hat landed in thorns, then dived into the briars and was gone.

Irma snatched at her hat as if it would fight back. She was flushed and trembling. "Why'd it do that?" she asked.

"It thought you looked like some tasty thing, I figure," Cliff said. He wondered what that thing might be, but kept the thought to himself. "Or maybe he liked your hat."

There were worried faces all around. He waved the matter away and changed the subject. "Try to listen for water. Or better, smell it."

"Smell it?" Aybe frowned. "Water doesn't smell."

"Sure it does." Aybe and Terry really were a bunch of office engineers and computer types, he thought, living out their lives indoors. And they had been inside for a long time. Good thing they didn't have to learn to build a fire or make bows and arrows. Or at least, not yet.

Except Howard Blaire, who was grinning at Aybe. Howard had run a private zoo, and collected for it, too. A field guy, he'd know the smell of water. "It smells fresh, kind of," he said.

They sniffed the air as they moved. Cliff wondered why they had seen no aircraft. It was the obvious way to search, and anyway, wasn't there routine air commerce? Anywhere on Earth, they'd have seen commercial flights by now. He recalled a glorious week rafting through the Grand Canyon, when the only sign of civilization was contrails scratched across the deep blue.

But this place was alien, and they should learn from it. What had his mother used to say? *Problems are just disguised opportunities. Sure, Mom.*

Maybe the natives were afraid of aircraft puncturing their atmospheric cap? He filed the puzzle for future study and went back to scanning the woodland they moved through.

They were halfway across a clearing when something charged them.

Irma got off a shot at something that looked like a giant red badger. The shot didn't slow it down much. Cliff and Irma both walked backwards fast. Without a word spoken, the other three ran for the trees.

Irma shot at it again, and Howard, but it didn't seem to notice. It turned away from them—for Cliff.

His fingers itched for a laser, but instead he ran for the nearest tree. He jumped, clicked his heels in midair, and had his spikes dug into the tree bark before he thought about it. Then he was up and over, just as the badger clawed up at him. He could hear teeth snap behind him. It was a pretty nasty beast, all big teeth and claws and temper. Smelled bad, too.

Cliff scrambled out onto a thick limb and looked around. His team was intact, making for higher altitude. The badger hadn't gone after Irma, not after she hit its muzzle with a laser bolt. Aybe had been light on his feet and was now far up a big tree.

They were spread out but safe. The badger jerked and snarled when Irma and Aybe gave it some encouragement to leave. Cliff could see the laser bolts spouting puffs of gray smoke from its fur. They could not get through the thick mat.

Impasse. It prowled around their base trees for hours, spitting mad. Their laser bolts made it angry, but it didn't go away. Maybe it was used to a waiting game, Cliff mused. And didn't like to climb trees.

The badger seemed mammal-like, but that was just appearances. Convergent evolution fitted life to niches. Like marsupials compared to placental mammals: similar forms but completely different physiology.

Finally, after much shouted talk, they started to quiet down. Fatigue, again. At least it was shady here. He took a deep, moist breath from the twilight air beneath the trees, and let himself relax. He could feel the tension ease from his back and legs. This was the first real rest he'd had since coming through the lock. A long time ago, yes. His stomach growled. He fetched out stiff blocks of protein/carb mix and munched them thoughtfully. Their taste burst with lemony richness in his mouth and he carefully let himself have a gulp of water. *Ah.*

Then, resting despite the badger, he heard this world. It

buzzed (insects?) and barked (predator pack signaling, territory assertion?) and twanged (what the hell?). The symphony of life, singing strange in a colossal zoo . . .

He fell asleep without meaning to. And dreamed of Beth—dark images, fraught with lurid worry.

PART III

Good judgment comes from experience.
Experience comes from bad judgment.

—MULLA NASRUDIN

THIRTEEN

A Serf-One brought Memor a delicious skreekor, fragrant with the scent of its own fear. She ate it with lip-smacking pleasure while she watched the invaders.

The skreekor was an ample beast, about the size of the new invaders, but certainly far more tasty. This one was lightly spiced and big enough for a midwake meal, six or seven bites. It had been preserved by radiation; its taste was savory but slightly stale. It did not wriggle, in a final gesture of its knowledge of the right order of things. Memor paid no attention to the smaller bones that snapped as she ate. She would disgorge them later.

She'd wondered if the invaders could do magical things, tricks beyond known science. This was most unlikely. They had not presented any real problems, though the Folk had responded slowly. The aliens now seemed safely confined. One was injured or dying. Their gear was unfamiliar, but it seemed crude. They fumbled with their toys and jabbered endlessly. Primates always seemed to do that, as ancient Bowl records showed from similar adaptations of the four-limbed. In their simple forms, it made them easier to hunt, though they never seemed to learn that.

The group that escaped had shown not cleverness, but panic. Mere luck had aided them. But luck was occasional. No matter what their strange origins might be, their frenetic movements showed intelligences not able to deal with new elements. Or incapable of planning, an even worse sin. Perhaps, indeed, the only true sin.

They were dull creatures, as well. They had no coloration feathers—indeed, no feathers at all. Camouflage was therefore beyond them. How simple! From what odd world had they descended?

They seemed incapable of conveying meaning with even their elementary skin signals—and so incapable of nuanced speech. Talk from their wiggly mouths, and antic hand gestures, had to somehow suffice. The females displayed mammal signatures, bumps and curves, and lesser mass. Curious. How did sexual selection occur? Through such constricted pathways? What sour, diminished channels they used! And so tiny! Memor wondered how to teach them to speak the Tongue.

Of six Astronomers and twice that many Serf-Ones, only Memor had been trained in TransLanguage. She had long thought there would never be a chance to use her training. Vast time would pass before the world came near Target, where they expected to find their first intelligent species in many million-folds of time. Now Memor's TransLanguage and neurological sensing arts would advance her prospects. Her pulse quickened agreeably.

The Target Folk were powerful; that much was obvious to any telescope array. But they had never shown interstellar ambitions, judging by the lack of visible fusion torch signatures near their star, or large constructions.

Still less likely was this startling appearance of visitors. Such were discussed in the Long Records, but none had come for a countless time. Until now, suddenly, from behind. A crafty approach. The Astronomers were plainly disconcerted by their drawing near. A vast failing, really. Yet now that Memor was female, all seemed somehow clearer. This was an opportunity!

But at first it was not Memor's, for it had not been Memor's watch for many, many Turns. Plus, she had been *he* in those times, and thus had less judgment. Yet she, in the racked torture of the Change, had seized the moment, banding with others of the Dancers, and so now could show her newfound abilities in judgment. This would surely help her career. The prospect warmed her, beyond the pleasure of anticipation. She was on the cusp of a great era; of that, she was sure.

Memor had been trained long and diligently in TransLanguage, because one of every generation must be educated, to pass on the skills. She'd never hoped to use those elaborate methods of transcending ordinary language, designed in antiquity for speaking with these Target species, these candidate Target Folk. The Bowl's beamed transmissions at the approaching ship and at the Target had never been answered, but that did not reflect a failing of TransLanguage. There could be many reasons why the Target Folk did not reply.

Or . . . Were these aliens Target Folk at all? The thought struck her, apparently from her Undermind. She would have to trace its origin.

No doubt they might be from the Target sun, still scores of light-years ahead. Memor's great heart thumped agreeably at the very idea—but their big ramship had come from *behind* the World. Unless, of course, they thought to conceal their origins. But Memor was sure routine Astronomer observations would have picked up their fusion plume, had they approached from the Target direction.

Call these chattering things something else for the moment, then. Call them Late Invaders.

There were feeds from cameras in Sector 1126. Memor watched in hope of learning more. A second group of Late Invaders was running loose there . . . but for five wakes they never came near a camera. Perhaps they were more clever than they seemed at first?

There must be living invaders in the big ramship, too. Memor watched it on her input screen as it now arced around the sun, shedding momentum, grasping its way forward with magnetic claws. She had wondered if it would come back, if it would attempt rescue of its small invaders. But in over five wakes, it did nothing but maintain its almost-orbit, thrusting a little against the pressure of stellar gas. Perhaps they were benign. For now.

Memor bristled her feathers, air humming richly through them in a darting pride-song, to match her thumping heart. *Joy of life, that brings such opportunities.*

She opened her Undermind, a narrow window for now. This could refresh her thinking. It was like a sudden shaft of crimson light, startling to her Overmind. She could feel thoughts and emotions wrestling endlessly there, combining and mating. A rich bed of vibrant murk. She thought of these roiling notions as a sort of food for her Overmind, endlessly wriggling. *So different, so oceanic, as female . . .*

Deftly she dipped in. Notions purred. Slick sounds keened at moist harmonies. *Richness!* She might need some new combination of previous ideas, properly cast in a pale glow of fresh scrutiny, to deal with this emerging situation. Perhaps she would even have to let the Undermind churn until it produced something fresh. That had happened seldom, but the possibility was exciting. Memor would come into her own then, her talents in demand. She could ride her Undermind to become perhaps even Overlord. Thus did Astronomers rise in the pyramid of status.

Moving the invaders was going to be tricky. She needed ideas there, yes. Memor wondered how long they could go without food. They couldn't eat anything through those pressure shells, could they? Better to get them out of the vacuum.

And now the Serf-Ones were docking the Maintenance Craft. Carefully they worked, with much worried chatter, afraid of giving the slightest offense to their superiors. As was proper.

The invaders offered no resistance. There would have

been no point, and this behavior showed some modicum of intelligence, plus that rarer quality, judgment. Compared to those who escaped, these might be a superior type of primate. If there were such among such a ragged, hairy species lacking any of the lushness that came from alluring feather discourse.

Three huge Astronomers surrounded them and urged them forward with stamping feet. That signal transcended language. The invaders moved, half carrying, half towing the injured one of their kind. They huddled close together, puny things overawed by the size of the Astronomers. Their anxious primate gestures gave them away.

Seven much smaller Serf-Ones went ahead of them through the air lock, carrying gear.

The invaders stopped moving on the other side, eyes agog—an expression of wonder common among many species. Perhaps they were startled by the contrast: grass and huge trees and vast flocks of wide-winged birds, all in microgravity. Memor saw that teams of Serf-Ones had set up a force-fence. Excellent. The invaders were properly imprisoned.

Now Memor sent an Astronomer off with a flock of Serf-Ones to fetch food. She instructed the crewperson carefully: They must find something of every kind. Skreekors, hairies, bugs, fruit, bark, grasses. No telling what these things might eat, though their amino acid composition was common in Bowl experience. Memor was aware that most life-forms were restricted in their diet, their environment, cycles of sleep and mating and feeding, heat and cold . . . a thousand things, but particularly diet. These creatures might starve to death no matter what she could do.

So Memor was eager to feed them, but also to teach them. She let her Undermind purr forward on ideas of how to do so. These poor creatures must learn something of her, and she of them, before they died in microgravity.

• • •

"Mayra," Fred said, "did you get pictures of that chain of bubbles?"

Mayra looked at him. She said, "Buildings. Domes, but not just half spheres. We build that way too in lunar gravity. I snapped some pictures on my phone, but I thought you might have seen something. . . ."

Fred said, "I was too sick, and hungry. Didn't notice."

"Well, we followed a ridge after we passed the bubbles. You saw the ridge? It ran right here."

Beth said, "It's not going to matter. We're fenced in. Do you suppose they'll let us starve?"

"We're in a garden. There must be something to eat. Rabbits?"

FOURTEEN

When Cliff awoke, Irma was sitting next to him, hat tilted, standing watch with concentration. She winked and said nothing.

It still felt funny waking up in this perpetual daylight. Humans had evolved in a daily rhythm, and the strangest thing about this place was its constancy. No sway of day and night, no dance of the hours. The sun stood still, a permanent glare in the sky. He could read nothing from the slant of sunshine, since it never varied, and he missed the sunsets of the California coast. Living in perpetual day was the ultimate jet lag; it never went away. He knew from Earthside experiments, done in preparation for starship building, that people in constant illumination tended to develop longer sleep cycles.

Above, the scratch across the sky that was the jet bristled with festering luminosities. He could see tiny hairlike threads slowly flex and turn amid the tossing motes that burned with furious energy. Was this what a galactic jet looked like up close? It was brightest near the star, cooling as it coasted outward toward the Knothole. The nearer jet reddened so it sent diffuse, pink shadows rippling among the leaves. Nothing as spectacular as a sunset, but intriguing and unsettling.

The badger had wandered off, Irma told him. They gave it an hour, though, in case it was lying in wait.

They set off again, more cranky than before, from the odd sleep they had managed to get. Like a clotted rain forest, the dense copse of slender trees enveloped them in moments, fronds and puffball clumps blotting out the sky. The soil was a soft loam, with little bushy understory. This reminded him of dry eucalyptus groves in California, still and aromatic and whispery. The smells were tangy, odd, not at all like the medicinal eucalypt aroma. Game paths laced through it, hard packed dirt with some brown droppings. He sniffed some; turds appeared to have a universal pungency. The same basic chemistry, he surmised.

And more than game could use these bare throughways. Or stalk parallel to them. He waved to the others and they angled away from the easy game paths, not without some grousing.

"Carnivores lie in wait along these," he explained in a whisper. "We might look like tempting game."

"We're primates," Howard shot back.

"And nothing ate monkeys in Africa?" he retorted.

When he started his fieldwork in grad school, he could barely tell raccoon tracks from bobcat. Now he knew earthly tracks and scat and had been automatically cataloging what he saw underfoot here. Alien tracks fell into the same general categories, hooved and padded and birdlike, but some had spindly hexagonals, which he could not fathom. Scat looked pretty much the same.

They saw some game, too. These were flickers of tawny flanks among the trees, glimpses of hides with natural camouflage that faded away into the hushed silence. Howard whispered that maybe they should shoot one.

"And carry it along?" Cliff answered. "We can hunt when we set up camp."

"Near water," Irma said. Cliff nodded.

They passed under a chattering locus in the high branches and stopped to gaze upward through binocs. "Monkeys," Howard said. "Swinging around, with big tails."

"Really?" Cliff recalled the barking bands at the San Diego Zoo and used his binocs to bring one of the quick shapes into focus. A rude purple throat display, huge yellowed teeth, darting small red eyes, but—"Yeah, kinda like monkeys, anyway. But not mammals, I'd say. No obvious genitalia. Can't see teats, either."

"So primates evolved here, too?" Howard let it trail off into a question.

"Maybe they're just getting started," Cliff said softly. He wondered if, given a few millions of years, these protomonkeys could overcome the aliens they had seen. Not likely. As soon as the primates became noticeable as competition, the smart aliens would prevail. Established forms usually had the advantage, and there was nothing automatically better about primates.

"Look down there," Aybe whispered, pointing. A creek glinted green among the shade trees below.

They approached too fast, in Cliff's opinion—he called out to them to hold back. Predators liked watering sites. This wasn't Earth, where dawn and dusk were the natural hunting times, as herbivores came for a drink. Carnivores could be hunting any time at all.

But there was nothing waiting near the creek, so they all had a good long drink. It tasted cool and fine, and on impulse Cliff plunged his whole head in, glad to be free of the grit and sweat of the last few—days? There were no days here, he reminded himself. He would have to think of a new word.

He recalled a calculation Wickramsingh had done back on *Seeker*. Take the Earth and spread it into a bowl the size of this Cupworld and it would be maybe a centimeter thick. Here in the stream-cut hills, he could see cross sections of the land. The soil was a conglomerate, like coffee grounds peppered with chunky gray rock. No strata, of course. There had been no real geology here.

To get hills hundreds of meters tall, the Builders (he thought of them as deserving the capital) must have chewed up Jovian-size masses. They had transformed a whole solar system. That explained the absence of asteroids and other debris around the star. They'd had to be removed; otherwise they could've smacked into Cupworld later, punching an unfixable hole, draining the atmosphere. He had to stop thinking of their surroundings as being just a planet. It was . . . well, a vast contrivance. With all kinds of weirdness living in it. On it.

After resting above the creek, they followed it downhill. The creek bank revealed more conglomerate rocks, round yellowish balls fixed in grainy sand. Cliff wondered how the designers of this place had laid soil and water down on a huge, spinning carousel.

Plainly they had to put down some mass, a meter or two of rock or water, to keep out cosmic rays. But the scale . . . again and again he came back to the vastness of this place. The whole idea seemed both gargantuan and surrealistic—mute testimony to the deeply alien nature of its builders. Who—what—would do such a thing? Those birds? Somehow, he couldn't see it. They didn't seem that smart.

In a while they came to a dense spread of trees and within it found a lake. Flies buzzed around a thick margin of reeds, and they found no easy way to get to the water. Cliff wondered if he could take a swim in it. His skin itched. Maybe later.

A thing buzzed by his head. It had six wings, about the size of a sparrow. Maybe it played the role of dragonflies in freshwater wetlands, he guessed. Convergent adaptation. Willowlike trees hugged the shore, but taller and with twisted, helical trunks. Convergent evolution seemed to have led to pollinator plants, too—bigger stamens and longer, twisted pistils, but the same strategy. Shrubs somewhat like laurel sumac mingled with tall trees vaguely like closed cone pines. Still, some of the plants were bizarre, with canopies permanently pitched toward the star, and bunched leaves like parabolas. There were mosses, too, bryophytes, ferns.

Howard was whispering into his phone. He was loving this.

. . .

They camped, but still Cliff thought it a bad idea to light a fire. They slept again, badly, with Howard and Irma taking watch. Voices called in the woods—chirps, snorts, ominous grunts, buzzes and bellows, oddly pleasant trilling songs. Alien melodies.

They circled around the lake, keeping to bristly brush and trees. They were getting better at keeping a clear field of fire; the badger had taught them well. Three people covered while two moved, then the reverse. This meant eyes caught any reaction among the nearby foliage. They startled game but did not fire.

Sharp odors welled up from everywhere and peculiar fowl flitted noisily. They honked and sang and sometimes sounded like fire alarms. Cliff noted that there seemed to be plenty of small birds darting in and out of the bush branches, slipping their pointed snouts into the many long-tubed, sweet flowering plants. Never was there a species he could recognize, yet the patterns were recognizable. *Sunbirds, hummingbirds, same strategy.* When threatened, some fluffed up their feathers to make themselves look larger and barked odd calls—territorial defense as in most nectar-eaters, like orioles. Others had the sharp beaks of those who preyed on insects, like wrens or the short, triangular beaks of seed eaters like finches and sparrows. Evolution here had produced skills similar to those on Earth; he found this reassuring. In the lesser gravity, birds had apparently beaten out many land animals. They were bigger, too—fat and confident. Apparently a 10 percent or so difference in local g made a big change in the balance of living types.

He'd have to talk this through with Howard when they had the chance.

He had seen flying frogs leap from stream levels to high branches, flapping short distances on webbed legs. The predators of the high sky hovered long before they dived, able to sustain their altitude with big, slow-flapping wings. The insects here were bigger, too, for some reason, though with the same many-legged gaits as on Earth. This was indeed a different place—and how different, how truly alien, they could not fully know yet.

Plus, the smart bird aliens. Was he being narrow-minded at first, thinking smart birds unlikely? But of course, these were huge birdlike ones . . . and he had not seen any fly. Maybe they resembled ostriches who gave up flying and gained technology.

Howard held up a hand, pointed, hunkered down—they were getting better at hand signals.

Along a narrow stony beach lay some long reddish brown things like bulging crocodiles, lounging in the perpetual noon. They grunted as they moved. Their bodies were long and scaly, with a short, blunt snout. A lazy yawn showed many serrated yellow teeth.

"Those are for tearing chunks out of big prey," Cliff whispered. "Our crocs dine on small fish, chickens, small pigs. These eat bigger things."

"Let's give them plenty room," Irma said.

Aybe pointed. "But what's—?"

It rose out of the deeper dark water. A long neck uncurled upward with strands of weeds dripping from its flat, rubbery mouth. The brown eyes gleamed with wet curiosity as it looked at them, mildly interested but taking its slow time.

"An herbivore," Cliff said, awed. "Like a . . ."

"Dinosaur," Howard supplied. "What the hell kind of place *is* this?"

"Convergent evolution?" But that seemed unlikely, and he stepped back as the thing rose like a slippery mountain—dark with a white belly, legs like pillars, long slick neck and tiny head. "It *is*. It's a . . . dinosaur," Cliff said, a chill running through him. "From Earth. Has to be."

Irma said, "The aliens, they stopped at Earth?"

"Must've sent ships, anyway. They must've picked up some of our—Earth's—ecology," Howard said as if entranced, eyes rapt, prophesying. "Like we were doing, bringing species alone in sleepstate—only more so."

"It's interested in us," Aybe said, taking a step backwards.

"How do we know it's not a meat eater?" Irma said.

"We don't." Terry turned to leave.

"Their native ecology here must been overrun with alien species. So . . . Cliff? It's too good, this place, too like Earth. That's why. They imported Earth life."

"Maybe. Maybe," Cliff said, grimacing. "Reassuring, isn't it? If that's the explanation."

Irma backed away, too. "Let's go."

Cliff smiled. "Don't miss the lesson. We can eat some things here, and it can eat us."

"Y'know," Irma said, "they could've just hauled some dinosaur eggs and other life here on ships, passing by our solar system, a long time ago."

Cliff nodded, eyeing the massive, slow shape with fascination. It grunted. "So the Earth forms could've taken over parts of the Cupworld, and lasted this long."

The huge thing sluggishly waded toward them, pausing to rip reeds and lily pads from the water and gulp them down. A muddy reek came from it on the soft wind. It was slow but steady, and Cliff motioned them to back away. "It's a herbivore, I'd say, but interested in us."

"Not for eating, though," Howard said, "so why—?"

"If it steps on you, what's the difference?" Aybe was moving faster, towing a grunting Howard by his belt.

They got away from there. Irma led the way, in case some predator moved to block their exit. None did. They faded back into the forest.

Cliff now felt apprehensive. He realized that they had been taking this place as a pseudo-Earth, and indeed in many ways it was—but that also meant it held forms that summoned up in them ancient fears. None of them had seen dinosaurs except in movies, but the sight of one tapped also into a deep reservoir of primate vigilance.

Aybe said, "Now we know the trajectory of the Cupworld better. We extrapolated a naïve straight-line trajectory and folded in star motion, too. It may have been near Earth over sixty million years ago."

"What's 'near' mean?" Irma asked.

Aybe rolled his eyes as he calculated, adjusted his hat, shrugged. "Say, five light-years. How old was that dino back there, Cliff?"

"Maybe a hundred million years ago. I don't recall the classification or the dates real well. I'm a field biologist." Abruptly he laughed. "Didn't think at the time I'd have any use for those paleontology classes."

In a clearing, Irma automatically moved to their right flank and said, "Y'know, Earth wasn't in the same place in the galaxy hundred million years ago. So Cupworld might've been following some different trajectory, not just some straight line from Earth to here."

Howard said, "Right. Stars move a lot in that time."

Irma kept a wary eye out, whispering, "Face it, we don't have a clue what these aliens—the smart ones, I mean—are doing. Touring the galaxy on a slow boat? What kind of mind does that?"

"A slow mind," Terry said. Cliff had noted that the man didn't say much. When he did, it was well thought out. "Maybe an immortal one?"

"As a biologist," Cliff said, "I kinda doubt that anything lives forever. Once you stop reproducing, the force of natural selection stops working. Traits that gave you short-term benefits come back to haunt you."

Irma said, "But if you have biotech galore—?"

"All bets are off," Cliff admitted. "Maybe the Builders—that's what I call them, the ones who made all this—lived pretty damn near forever. But Cupworld has been on its way for at least millions of years. Maybe even sixty million—that's when the dinosaurs died."

This sobered them all as they made their way upslope, keeping their eyes on the surrounding forest. Cliff recalled a training hike into the Ecuadorian rain forests he had taken while he worked on his doctorate. The instructor had told them that the three weeks they spent upriver of the Amazon would be "meet-yourself experiences," and that seemed to capture a deep truth. Exploring made you know yourself better, like it or not. *Self-knowledge is usually bad news.* . . .

Without warning, a leathery thing the size of a greyhound came at the point man, Aybe. It ran quick and sure, as if it had preyed on something that looked like them before. Aybe shot it at a one-meter range, blowing a laser hole in its forehead. The big yellow eyes of the thing fluttered and it fell, kicking, rasping out a last breath. It looked like a reptilian dog, scaly and tough, with thick haunches and a powerful set of clamping jaws.

They stared at it. "Good shot," Terry said.

Irma said brightly, "Let's make a fire, roast up big chunks of meat."

Cliff worried about detection, but didn't stop them from gathering wood. Their amino acid scans had shown the basic same as Earth, and DNA had the same structure too. Maybe they were universal? An old folk song about moonshine cooking rang in his mind. *Don't use green or rotten wood, they'll get you by the smoke.* . . . "Don't use fresh fallen branches," he called out. "Look for dried-out ones." Terry looked scornful at this, but others nodded. They had uneven woodland skills. Cliff still had to remind them often not to talk so much, a rule every field biologist knows.

Around the campfire—carefully set under dense leafy boughs, to capture and spread the billowing gray stink, which was nearly transparent—they set into the fresh roasted haunch meat with gusto. Terry wished for a good red wine to go with it, got some laughs.

They ate but were not sleepy. So they pushed on, looking for a safe water source, a spot with clear fields of fire. Nobody wanted to spend a sleep time in trees. But what was the alternative? Cliff was still wrestling with the problem of what to do, but he had to shush them after the meal, and that made him worry more. Leadership was a bitch, he decided. More like being a schoolmarm . . .

"Look, we've got to remember one big fact: These creatures don't have any natural caution about us," Cliff said as they made their way up a steep slope under spreading canopy trees of fat emerald fronds.

Aybe said, "Doesn't that mean they'll be easy to hunt?"

Cliff gave him a wry look. "Sure. But it also means the predators have no reason to fear us. Remember that."

FIFTEEN

Memor decided to isolate her prisoners from the vast species richness of the World. Her Undermind provided the idea, and she instantly knew it was correct. She had watched the logics working in their moist, blue green connections, and understood the entire thought-chain.

The World's wealth would stun them, surely. The blue green abundance would prove shameful to such primitives. They might even commit group suicide, humiliated beyond tolerance. Their cages she ordered made hospitable, but nothing more.

Further, her underlings saw that these small creatures found every avenue of escape blocked. Isolation was best, both for them and for scientific study. It was simple to devise transport to put them tens of millions of miles from natural air, water, vegetation, the ripe bounty of the World. Ancient records said something of the sort had worked well against the last invaders, rendering them compliant. Then again, she had to feed them.

She had found a good solution. The greenhouse was a series of verdant ledges set near the World's axis of rotation and thrust. The Jet burned a searing injunction in its sky, pointing back at the Star. Sunny and mild, this was a unique preserve, a rightful richness that fed the Astronomers and gave them restful grounds for strolling and contemplation.

Surely, as the species that tended the course and the health of the World, and so provided for their servant species,

Astronomers deserved such cloistered wealth. Since time immemorial, the plants that grew there, the animals and birds that lived on the plants and each other, had all been deftly altered to match microgravity. Such was the wisdom of the Ancients.

In this lush paradise, Memor allowed the Invaders some small latitude. She had not stripped the Invaders of their equipment, because she didn't know what would kill them. No doubt some of their implements, so odd and crude, were sacred to them, or used for amusement. Very well; Memor was generous.

She and the other, lesser species watched to see if the Invaders would divest themselves of their pressure suits. They did strip the wounded one, but failed to learn from the experience. For some no doubt primitive reason, the rest remained dressed for vacuum when they went to sleep.

They slept twice as long as an Astronomer would have, and all woke more or less at once. Perhaps this was a species defense mechanism?

They stripped down then to a lower layer of cloth. So scrawny! Memor doubted they were hiding anything from her. More likely they kept themselves covered as a birth control measure, taming their primordial impulses. Or perhaps they used outer coverings to control temperature in an altogether wilder environment than the World's. Lesser species of the World had similar mechanisms, and could even use simple tools.

Memor watched carefully as they designated a toilet area, and used it in turn. No sharing. Perhaps a status ritual? They tried various bits of what Memor had set for them as food, an elaborate crescent array that would serve as a biology lecture, too. They did not eat grass or bark or water weeds, but they did eat an amazing variety of higher protein content foods. Omnivores! Memor had once wondered if they could feed themselves at all. In the World there were species that could not; they needed servants who could process and serve food. Biology had many strange flowstreams.

Some of what they had were tiny cameras. Memor watched them making records of what they saw. They spent much of their effort recording the arrays of possible food sources. When she knew they used meat, and knives, she supplied whole carcasses; they photographed these and the dressed and cooked meat, too. Plants raw and peeled. Servitors and Memor herself.

Her lessers had returned with reports on the cell cultures harvested from the Late Invaders. The Late Invaders had similar methods of genomic patterning methods. Was DNA a universal, then? Memor knew that it was not. But they could come from one of the Seed Worlds the Ancients reportedly tried to fertilize.

Memor wondered if these Late Invaders could genetically engineer tools and machines not to degrade in a biosphere. The Ancients had bequeathed enzymes to synthesize devices, so the World grew apparatus needed by the Folk.

Turning sunlight and water into machines was the Higher Way, and these Late Invaders did not seem to have mastered that pathway to greatness. They might be able to edit genes, or transplant them to another crop; such was simple. But their devices did not have the elegant cast of grown apparatuses. So they quite probably ate simple foods, too, and lived lives of primitive needs. Yet built ramscoops.

Memor pondered this and decided to try fish. She ordered admitted to their ample cage some varieties with appropriate chemistries. No need to not be generous, after all. They should be made comfortable in their final days.

SIXTEEN

Coarse, smelly, wet soil stretched away, embedded in a gray metal mesh. You couldn't call it the ground, Beth thought, not in almost zero gravity, not with a straight face. More like a sheet of stucco with plants growing in it. The stuff ran away from them in muddy sheets for what looked like thousands of kilometers.

She had climbed into one of the spindly, triangular trees and surveyed the landscape. The soaring fence was far off, tens of kilometers. Beth judged that it ran up as far as the plastic sky. "It's as if they've imprisoned us in a dull, wet, brown Australia," Mayra said. "Lots of room. Lots of space to hide."

Abduss grumbled, "We're about to starve to death, too."

"Working on it," his wife said, grinning.

Lau Pin said, "Let's at least get out of these damn suits. We can do a better splint job on Tananareve."

In the early, fractured talk the big one in charge identified itself as Astronomer—a rank, apparently. She—definitely a She, a slit wreathed by crimson feathers—used star charts and pictures to make the point, assisted by slowly pronounced words in their language of grunts, call, piping songs. The Fourth Variety of locals Beth called Porters. Like other varieties, they were feathered like flightless birds, but built more like lizards. Their limbs and toes were long and limber. In the near free fall here, they were still flightless, but they could leap long distances. The Astronomer, whose "close-name" was Memor, had shown them this right away. Beth thought this might have been some kind of display to instill submission; certainly the long, hooting calls Memor gave sounded joyous and dominant. Most of the other Astronomers wore harnesses, and used them for carrying.

The big Third Variety who led them was a hunter. Was the alien a he—or she? Where were the genitalia? Anus under the tail, just like Earth's birds. Call it he, then—he carried a long-tubed gun and gleaming, curved knives. He looked like an efficient killer.

They never went past the fence. The Porters did the carrying. In short order they came straggling back with small corpses and bigger slabs of meat—and roots and fruit and grain and twigs, all gathered at the Astronaut's direction.

The Astronomer had big, nimble four-fingered hands, though she wasn't doing much with them. Porters did most of the work, and their long hands were dextrous too. They laid their loot in a pattern, a long arc, plants to the left, meat to the right. Swallowing saliva, stomach rumbling, Beth waited for them to finish.

The Porters backed away. The Astronomer came ambling forward, and she was huge. It amazed Beth that she could pick up such little things with her long, jerky arms: bunches of grain, a ravaged muskratlike corpse, a small globe that looked like a striped melon. The moving mountain picked up something and grunted or trilled, raised it toward her huge, thick-lipped mouth and made a warbling, keening sound— the same sound each time for that gesture.

"Eat?" Beth wondered aloud. The Astronomer made a deep bass sound. Gestured with an arm.

They were being taught.

Until Lau Pin snarled a curse, stalked forward under the Astronomer, and reached up.

People froze. Beth waited for him to die.

The Astronomer dropped the little melon.

Lau Pin caught the melon. He held it up and brandished a knife big enough for killing. "Melon. Knife." He cut the melon, "Cut," and bit into the slice. "Good," he called back. Buried his face in the orange flesh. "Eat." Lau Pin jogged back, turning his back on the Astronomer, and cut a slice for Tananareve. "Give. Eat," he said, and she did.

They all did. Eagerly.

Each time Lau Pin spoke, the huge feathered Astronomer replied with a bellow and a gesture, his long fingers tracing curves in the air. Those might be easier to repeat than the sounds, Beth thought. She noticed that Tananareve was awake and paying rigid attention. Her hands moved in response to the Astronomer's Sign language.

• • •

The Astronomers also included some called Astronauts, who seemed to be those who could patrol the vicinity of this place. They were big, lumbering sorts who barely noticed the humans. They hooted at one another in long, rolling calls.

But more important, the principal Astronomer had buckled her knees in what seemed to be good-bye, and gestured: She had left them their tools.

That seemed amazing to Beth. Lau Pin had used a knife and he still had it. That was reassuring. Beth tried something else.

She chose a slab of red meat—"Steak," she pronounced it, optimistically—and set it on a rock. "Beamer," she said, and held up a microwave projector. They'd tried to use it to cut through the wall of the aliens' air lock. She plugged it into her backpack power. Turned low, it cooked the meat in a few seconds. They set the beamer aside, cut up the meat, and ate. Beth carefully plugged the beamer into its solar panel charger. The meat tasted wonderful and in her hunger she forgot about the alien.

Mayra and Fred, of course, were photographing everything with their cell phones, and now so was Lau Pin. Good. The power wouldn't run out for months.

When they were finished, they still had the beamer. And several knives, Abduss's gun, and the pressure suit helmets. *We must look pretty harmless*, Beth thought wonderingly. A matter of size?

Abduss stretched, yawned, and said, "I'm wiped."

With her belly full, Beth suddenly felt the wave of exhaustion. She thought, *Don't be silly, it's only . . . well, duh.* The sun was at sunset, vertical to the glassy wall and horizontal to wet soil embedded in a coarse mesh, and it wasn't going to set. Ever.

She called to the Astronaut, "Sleep," and to her companions, "Sleep."

Memor spoke a word. She watched, and when she saw her captives turn unresponsive, she turned toward the air lock. Beth tried to watch her, but her legs dragged. She felt soooo very tired. . . .

So did the others, she could see. It was logical. They were trapped, depressed, so took refuge in sleep. It made sense. Let their unconscious selves sort out all the new, strange, and alarming. No reason to fight it.

SEVENTEEN

They had a long slog through the rumpled hills. That took days.
Without more understanding, they had no plan, no destination. They needed to learn. But without a goal, Cliff knew,
morale would evaporate. Even fear, which was driving them
now, would ebb.

When they got tired, Cliff called a rest. Nobody argued.
They soaked their hats with water and put them over their
faces, falling asleep instantly. Gratefully.

• • •

They stirred themselves nine hours later, but without breakfast. Food was short.

Cliff led by example, roving through the nearby copse of
trees and bushes in search of edibles. There were plenty of
berries and some fat leaves, but testing by taste was dangerous even on Earth.

But what choice did he have? He smelled them for sourness, tried a tongue touch, and if all seemed unthreatening,
would bite in. Sometimes this worked with berries and the
fat-leaved plants and he got a sweet burst of juice. Other candidates stung like mad and he quickly washed them away
with water. He did this several times, returning with a hatful
of berries or flavorful leaves. He made them memorize the
plant features before eating. The others welcomed fresh food
and some caught on, following him in his prowling. Irma was
best at this.

The guys seemed to think that they were cut out for hunting. Howard and Terry said they had some experience. Cliff half listened to their bragging amid a discussion of guns. He had glimpsed something large in the bushes—a quick flash of brown hide, then a soft flurry that sounded like hooves, fading. If this had been Earth, he would have guessed it was a deer.

Howard and Terry went out together, making a show of it. Surprisingly, within an hour, they brought back something that looked like a large rabbity grazer, furry and with ears that pitched upward from the flat, level skull. Cliff looked at the odd ears that cupped skyward, and realized that they must be for hearing birds—diving predators, probably. He had never seen such an adaptation on Earth. It was testimony to how important flying was here.

Skinned, the critters had interesting skeletal structure and internal organs. Cliff sectioned them out and tried to understand how they worked. Odd fans of bones, lumpy organs with no apparent function. Some made sense, most not. He needed a real lab. . . .

They cooked the pseudo-rabbits over a small fire, taking care to keep it hot and show no smoke. Under some spreading canopy trees, the little smoke that did rise got trapped and spread, so they hoped nobody could see it at a distance. Cliff thought they needed their spirits lifted a bit, and warm food again did the job. The meat was tasty, dark and gamy, and very welcome. "See anything that looked like a deer?" he asked them.

Terry nodded. "How'd you know? Four-footed, at least, and meaty—but it had teeth."

Howard added, "And antlers. Looked pretty weird. Kept sniffing the wind, like a predator. Looked like more trouble than it was worth."

Aybe said, "We should save our lasers for defense, anyway. I thought we should have tracked and cooked that badger thing we shot before."

"It looked hard to kill," Cliff said. "And we were in a hurry."

Aybe shot back, "And now we're not."

Cliff took a long breath of musky air. Might as well bring up the tough issues while they were all relaxed, bellies full. "Look, we're wandering. We need an agenda."

That brought on plenty of discussion but few ideas. He had expected that—they needed to vent. Anxiety came out as talk, rambling and vexed. Danger and hardship made for bad reasoning, but if he could defuse their frustrations, they could all then work better together. So they talked for a while, mostly hashing over we-shouldas and we-couldas, and finally Cliff said, "The past is prologue. What do we do next?"

"Find the others," Howard shot back.

"How?" Cliff asked.

"Maybe make a link to *SunSeeker*." Howard paused, obviously not having thought very far ahead. "They can maybe link to Beth."

Cliff did not want to step all over anyone's ideas; give and take was how you worked forward. He said carefully, "We don't have anything that can reach *SunSeeker*."

"How about our lasers?" Irma said. "If we could send a simple Morse message . . ." Her voice trailed off, seeing the difficulty of even locating the ship in a sky that never darkened.

Aybe saw how this was going, his eyes moving swiftly around their little circle, and said briskly, "First, figure out how this crazy place works. That will tell us how to get on top of our situation."

Cliff agreed, but it was best to let the ideas come from others. As they tossed thoughts around, he wondered at his own developing social skills. His career had focused on technical abilities—mostly useless here—not management ones. Here he would have to get this little band through unknowable threats—much harder than just keeping employees happy, a task that had always bored him. But this was lots more interesting, and nobody else seemed to want to lead. None of the expedition's actual, official leaders were here. Though as someone had remarked in Leadership Training, the important skills can't be taught.

They kicked this around for a while and finally agreed to what Cliff thought was obvious, without his having to say a word. Good—but talk took time, and he doubted they had a lot of time to spare.

The next two Earth days, they spent moving warily across the strange yet oddly familiar landscape. Trees with limb decks, zigzag trunks, spirals—on low hills with running streams and shallow arroyos. Cliff kept track of how long they all slept and found it was steadily increasing.

Irma commented on this. "Y'know, they did Earthside experiments while preparing for starship life. People under constant illumination had sleep–wake cycles that got longer and longer. Without the sun, they lost track of time."

Terry said, "So that's why shipboard lighting follows the sun cycle."

Aybe asked Cliff, "How does anything get regulated here, then?"

"I don't know. Biology without outside timing, no day or night—we have no experience with that."

They hunted small game, using spears they made—and got nothing bigger than the pseudo-rabbits. Still, it was fun and they celebrated their rare victories with ragged cheers. They were urban types, and the skills of stalking came hard. Maybe it helped that the rabbity grazers were used to attacks from the sky, so were less adapted to ground predators.

But there had to be intelligent life somewhere here. They could see fields in the distance—great plains of crops stretching between the forks of two converging river valleys. Grass crops, Cliff guessed. They worked their way closer, staying in the hills and staying within the trees. Still, Cliff was startled when they came up behind a few silent, trudging figures. Not human.

"Careful," Cliff whispered. They crouched down.

The shapes were crossing a foggy slope ripe with thick aromas. Out of the mist came shambling shadows, slow and silent. Cliff switched his distance specs to infrared to isolate movements against the pale background and found the figures too cool to be visible. In the mist they were ghostly, slim shapes. Legs, but no arms.

"The farmers?" Howard whispered.

"No." Aybe peered closely at the ponderous, spindly forms. "Plants."

"What?" Now Cliff heard the *squish squish* as limbs labored.

In the murky light, they watched as crusty pods popped from the trunks of great trees. Stubby limbs peeled away from their parents and found unsteady purchase on the ground. They were about two hands high and a mottled green. The slow, deliberate birth came moist and eerie in the quiet.

Cliff watched in awe. Working their stubby legs forward with grave slowness, the roots freshly pulled from soil and then moved onto wetter ground that enjoyed better sunlight. The air brought the scent of their sharp thorns to him, a tinge of acrid poison. The young needed defenses here.

They watched the animated seeds find new spots and with great, slow care settle down to take root again. To Cliff, this method extended animal mobility to plants, perhaps made easier in lower gravity. The others looked incredulous and uneasy, though Irma nodded when he advanced his idea. Certainly these plants were not dangerous, but their strangeness unsettled. Cliff realized that they had all been thinking of this place as mildly different, just the sort of world you would see in a movie, complete with dinosaurs. Reassuringly ordinary in just the right way. He had to guard against such comfy illusions.

They moved on warily. Soon they saw spreading below their hill a vast plain of green grain. A heady aroma blew up from the crops on winds that wrote sweeping patterns across the valley.

Irma pointed. "Look—those farmer folk we saw back at the lock."

With time to observe, they could see the farmers were leathery at some joints but otherwise sported plumage that rippled with colors in intricate designs. Clad in loose-fitting coveralls, they formed teams that worked on snaking tubular watering systems, focusing the misty, arcing plumes over great distances. They worked hard in their fields, using four-footed animals to draw and plow.

"It's like farming centuries ago," Terry observed. "Hard work, very little powered machinery."

"It's not as though they can drill for oil, is it?" Aybe said.

"Plenty of solar power available," Terry said. "And this has gotta be the most high-tech place in the universe."

"Maybe they *like* manual work," Howard said. He looked at their skeptical faces and shrugged. "Just because we've been living the rugged life for a while and find the idea un-appealing doesn't mean *these* things do."

Irma raised skeptical eyebrows. "Could be, I suppose. But—" She zoomed her vision and stared at the field below. "—they're coming."

Cliff looked closer. "Not the farmers. Something else."

Irma added, "Yeah. Fast."

These were even bigger, with long necks—something like elongated, feathery racehorses that strode on two legs, with long wiry arms held forward for balance as they cantered. Plenty of rich plumage but a muscular look to them, espe-cially in the legs. Clothed only at the middle, they had thick belts with things like tools dangling from them. As Cliff watched, one of them looked around and eerily looked right at him. It was running hard but held its head fixed, the eyes large and glittering. Not farmers, no.

"Looks like they're about a klick away," Terry said. "We must've hit some trip wire or detector."

Cliff had wondered how this place could have developed different intelligent species. Specialization for labor or life niches? They probably had genetic technology, so maybe had developed new species from some early root genetics. Humanity had yet to do that.

Enough thinking; it was hard to avoid it, his head full of questions. The runners, he saw, were perceptibly closer.

"Let's get going," Cliff said, and did so.

The menacing pursuers were fast and far more than anybody wanted to fight. Terry led the way, running as if devils pursued him—and just maybe, Cliff realized, they did. Humans had invaded this biosphere unannounced. They had not surrendered meekly, but instead fled from the air lock. No negotiation. Now they were ranging around in somebody's territory, killing local wildlife to eat. The farmers seemed peaceful and simple, but that couldn't be the whole story here.

But could they outrun those things?

On the run they decided, amid hoarse, barked consultation, not to return along their earlier route. There seemed little shelter there. Instead they headed downhill from the next ridgeline. They had learned a long, loping stride that took advantage of the lower gravity. No sign of pursuit yet in the forest behind them. They stopped to listen—panting pretty loudly, then holding their breaths to hear.

A distant chippering cry. Beneath that, low growling. Coming closer. "And they know the territory," Cliff whispered.

They ran. Nobody suggested negotiations.

They hurried into a broad, low valley of gnarled trees. Some bore fruit, and Cliff felt a pang of hunger as they ran through these. It was moist here and soon they heard the snarl of water over rapids. The river was broad and Cliff wondered whether they could ford it. He glanced left and right and saw a long arched bridge. "That way!" They all veered toward the bridge, puffing heavily now.

Terry, who had started off fast, now brought up the rear. *Not a distance guy*, Cliff thought, and knew that he wasn't going to last much longer, either. He tried to think of something to do. Anything.

He studied the bridge as they slogged toward it. He could hear the high, skating cry clearly now. Closer.

The bridge was made of stone cemented together, very old style construction. On the underside, though, were thick metal beams, ribbed and with flanges at each side. Rugged.

They reached the foot of the bridge. Maybe the lighter gravity gave them some edge here, but it was all gone. He slowed, thinking frantically. Stopped. An idea flashed.

"Hey. Let—let's hide."

Aybe gave him a sharp *you're crazy* look. Irma was so winded, she just bent over and gasped.

"We'll get run down," Cliff said. "I wouldn't count on our lasers taking these things out, either—they're big and look pretty damn tough to me. And . . . they're clothed. Belts, tools. Maybe they're armed, too."

He let this sink in while he puffed, and now they could hear the cries behind them quite well. They all looked at one another, gasping, coughing, and finally Irma said, "I can't go much more. Let's try it."

The men nodded, looking relieved. Good psychology, Cliff thought—they still felt that they had to protect the woman. He trotted around to the underside of the bridge and grabbed one of the ribs. He hadn't really thought this through, but when he put his boots on the side flanges, he found they fit, barely. The others watched as he climbed up the ribs. He then turned carefully to face down toward the water that swirled and chattered over rocks. With some effort, he could strain back and support himself against the beam.

The others looked up at him doubtfully. Aybe said, "Hanging with both hands? We can't use the lasers from there."

Cliff called down, "What else can we do?"

That decided them. They inserted themselves into the nooks between the beam flanges and with some grunting got pinned into place. It was an effort and he could feel his arm muscles working hard.

"Hold on as long as we can," Cliff said. The chippering was close. *"Quiet."*

Pounding of heavy feet. Growls from deep guts, wild shrieks, quick barks like commands. Thumps. Feet hammered at his back, or that's how it felt, and most of them passed on. But then he heard a huffing from above, heavy long breaths. Feet padded around, slapping on stone. A rumbling bass grunt that seemed to go on forever. His stinging arm muscles had locked solid, his fingers trembling. The thing above wouldn't leave. Maybe the pursuers had left one here to block their retreat?

He didn't like this conclusion, but as moments crawled on he saw that it wouldn't matter. Irma's face was white with strain and Cliff wasn't going to last much longer, either. At least they had caught their breath.

He didn't dare whisper. Catching the eyes of the others, arrayed in the beam slots, he nodded down at the riverbank. They frowned, then got it. Cliff listened intently and caught footfalls above, a scraping that moved to the left of the bridge.

The stream splash might mask any noise they made. He nodded vigorously to them all and jumped down, landing as softly as he could. They followed as he moved to the right. Irma landed off balance, but Aybe caught her before she fell into the stream. Lasers at the ready, they ventured out from the bridge's shadow.

The shape above came back toward the high stone railing. It towered above, a long snaky head looking across the river—and Irma hit it clean and sure with a long bolt. The head jerked, looked down at them with those big, glittering eyes—and toppled backwards. They raced around, got on the bridge—and stopped to gaze at the big thing.

A deep burn at the top of its skull trickled pale blood onto the stones. The eyes blinked, but the eyeballs did not move. Cliff unbuckled the belt from the thick waist and put it around his own. The tools were odd and heavy. He was tempted to take a look at them, but—

"What'll we do with it?" Irma asked, beaming.

"Leave it," Aybe said.

"This body will float away pretty quick if we toss it in," Howard said.

They looked at one another and without a word lifted the body at several points. Getting it over the stony parapet was not as difficult as Cliff had expected. It was a bird, after all, something like a monster ostrich. They flung it over.

Irma said, "Its blood—I don't think we can mop it up easily. There's a lot."

"Let's get moving," Aybe insisted.

"Which way?" Cliff asked mildly, scanning the far riverbank for movement.

Terry said, "Across—oh, I see."

Cliff said, "They left this guy here to block our return. They're probably trying to cut us off from those hills beyond and drive us back to the bridge. Pin us against the water."

"So we stay on this side?" Irma asked. "Move downriver, say? At least it's downhill."

They looked at one another edgily and then all nodded. Collective decisions, Cliff realized, made it much easier to take if things went wrong later. Otherwise, they'd blame it all on him. They ran.

EIGHTEEN

Lau Pin hefted an eighteen-pound fish, turning it this way and that, inspecting it. A row of fins ran down each side, eleven on a side, diminishing toward the tail. Yet the fish looked odd, with ventral fins, long and wispy, narrow eyes, mottled green skin. "I'll have to be careful," he said. "Parasites."

The Astronomer had left Lau Pin a ten-inch knife. He gutted and filleted the creature and cut it in slices. The flesh was pale, like a red snapper, Beth thought. There were angry red spots Lau Pin cut out. "I think I got them all," he said. "Sushi? Or shall we start a fire?"

"Fire. Cook it," Mayra said. "I do not feel lucky. It's ugly."

They broiled the meat on twigs. It was delicious, rich in oils and savory with a strange, tangy flavor. Spirits lifted and there were jokes about finding the right white wine to go with the fish. Or maybe margaritas all round? Beth was glad to get them in a good mood. The meetings with Memor had fascinated them all, but the brute fact was that they were prisoners listening to lectures. The thrill of contact with a real alien, telling them strange new views—even that had to fade. They were not idle scientists or philosophers. They had signed on to explore a new world, make a fresh home for humanity, to sail the stars. Their patience was limited.

Lau Pin rummaged through his tool belt and then gave a startled cry. "My beamer is live. It's got signal."

They gaped. He showed them that the signal light gleamed

on his handheld communicator. "It's tuned to the *Eros* systems. I'm picking up data from its onboards."

"Any internals?" Tananareve asked wanly.

"Just status reports. Everything looks normal. It's on auto-standby."

"We must be somehow in line of sight," Tananareve said.

Lau Pin scowled skeptically. "We're an astronomical unit away from it, easily. This Bowl is huge. How could we hear from it?"

Beth felt a surge of hope. "It's a smart system. If *Eros* doesn't get pinged for a while, it must amp its transmission power to get a response. Maybe Cliff's group can get it, too."

"If we can negotiate our way out of here, we can use homing to find Eros," Tananareve said.

"Yes, great." Beth made herself sound more optimistic than she felt. They had last seen *Eros* crushed into a bin in a Bird Folk spacecraft. "Lau Pin, can we use your beamer to send signals from *Eros* to *SunSeeker*?"

Lau Pin worked on it for moments, staring intently at the small solar-powered beamer that was barely larger than his thumb. "I'm trying the 14.4 gigahertz band, then the subs. . . . No, I can't do over-commands from outside. Some kind of safety precaution."

Abduss growled with frustration. They all looked crestfallen.

Beth couldn't let that continue. Best to distract them. "Let's review what we've learned, class," she said with a smile. "Mayra?"

The normally quiet woman blinked and nodded. "When Memor brought those visuals—big constructs, dazzling perspectives—I got a feeling that she did that partly to impress us. You know, show the visitors some flashy capabilities."

Lau Pin said, "I like that it—okay, *she*—uses voice and gestures. Easier to remember that way."

Mayra said, "I liked those visuals it gave us on that screen.

One was some kind of macroengineering in a planetary belt. I'll bet that was their history. How they built this place."

"She's using those as attention getters," Beth said. "Then she showed us those 3-D keyboards. I think she wants us to manipulate display machines. Only—she just spoke to them."

Mayra asked, "So you think she wants us to learn their language, by picking up how to instruct those 3Ds?"

Lau Pin waved this away. "Maybe. Those images it showed us could be fauxtography, too. A phony story. Distractions, anyway. We've got to escape, not just sit and learn language."

Beth nodded. She liked the wildlife around them, wanted to learn about it—and Cliff would love it, might be loving it now—but—"Right. Our bones are getting worse as we speak. We've got to get back to gravity."

· · ·

Cliff's troop were doing badly on the basics: sleep and food. After crossing broad grasslands with clumps of trees for shade, they had seen no game worth pursuing for the better part of an Earth day. Some berries helped, and they found fresh water, a tinkling clear stream without signs of fish.

Following protocols, Irma went upstream and provided cover guard. The four men slipped into the cool waters gratefully. For several days they had all had intermittent dysentery and all needed to soak, a morale booster. In the first days, they had added a chloride pill to the drinking water but now used a solar-powered UV source in the caps of their water bottles to sterilize it.

Something broad, ribbed, and horned scuttled into a burrow at the shore. It looked to Cliff like an oval-shaped turtle with a razor-sharp crest. The burrow reeked, repulsive and rank, so they let it go.

Howard floated in a small muddy pool. He lay slack, grinning widely. "Y'know, I've been thinking. I figure our getting the runs is from chirality."

Aybe asked, "Chirality? Spin?"

Aybe was an engineer, right. "Direction of rotation of molecules. Handedness. When a molecule isn't identical to its mirror image." Howard didn't talk much and kept getting hurt, which made him even more closemouthed, so Cliff listened carefully. "Most biochemists think it was a historical accident that all our sugars are right-handed and our amino acids are left-handed. I think some of the life here has molecules opposite-handed, versus what we know."

"How?" Terry asked.

"Remember how, two sleeps back, you were all raving about how great that purple fruit tasted?"

Aybe grunted at the memory. "And got ravenously hungry again in an hour. Pretty much like Chinese food, as the cliché goes—then we all got diarrhea."

"That's why I'm always hungry?" Cliff asked. He wished they had the chirality gear in the *SunSeeker* landing supplies. They couldn't bring everything on the first lander.

"We all are," Howard said. "We're moving cross-country, burning calories, but some of our food is going straight through us—and burning our guts some, too."

"We cook the meat," Terry said.

"Sure, but all the prior biochem work we had, back Earthside, can't offset microbes no human ever met. Montezuma's revenge, y'know."

Cliff said, "That comes from microbial pathogens, different problem. I ran the DNA checks. This ecology uses the same basic double helix structure in everything I checked."

"Sure, but on other planets, the accidents of evolution could make the proteins and sugars different. If this Bowl has been cruising along, sampling ecologies, then there may be whole ecologies here based on L-glucose rather than our D-glucose, and D-amino acids rather than our L-amino acids."

Aybe shrugged. "Sick is sick."

Howard glared. "So L-glucose is interesting because it tastes just about as sweet as D-glucose, but passes through the gastrointestinal system completely unmetabolized. Throw left- and right-handed ecologies together here, and every life-form in the food chain has to choose one isomeric biochemistry or the other. Fruit sugars, fructose, will behave the same way."

Cliff recalled that Howard had been a media figure of sorts. He ran a semi-private preservation zoo in Siberia, after the climate warming ran wild there, exhaling methane. He'd never have left Earth if a disaster hadn't wiped out his patch of land, animals and all. The mission planners put him in because *SunSeeker* carried the makings of a zoo, intended as an ecology for the colony. Some critters wouldn't survive and most wouldn't be revived right away, but Howard could handle them. He and Aybe were butting heads for a bit until Cliff held up a hand.

"That explains why we get the runs? How sure is that?" Cliff said. "I thought I'd seen all the problems when I did that air sampling as we came through the air lock."

"Biology never rests." As if to illustrate, Howard slapped at gnats that swarmed around his eyes. "Better if we learned what's got our handedness and what doesn't." Howard held up his phone. "I've got notes in here, beginnings of a menu."

Cliff clapped him on the back. "Good stuff. You're the food guide now."

It made him glad to get some clarity on an issue they'd shied away from. Just talking about it and making rude jokes helped. Irma came ambling back and laughed, too.

Howard finally said, "Meat's the best for us. Kills a lot of nasty stuff. Let's find some."

"Where?" Aybe asked.

"Look to all points of the compass."

"Compass doesn't work here," Terry pointed out, and they moved on, following the stream.

At a rest stop hours later under some zigzag trees, Cliff wanted to get some game into their bellies and sleep, so when Howard pointed silently into the distance, they all crouched down and peered through their binocs.

"Looks like a squashed ape," Irma said. "Meaty."

It had a gray pelt and walked with a swaying motion, hips throwing the legs forward. A narrow head kept wary watch, and it was coming toward them.

"At least two meters high," Aybe judged.

"Plenty of meat on it," Howard said. His stomach growled.

"With that thick coat, lasers won't be much good," Terry said.

Irma said, "A head shot is tough, too. Look at those eye ridges—bony and not a large skull."

"It's not carrying anything in those hands. They look nearly like claws," Howard said.

Cliff thought about killing a primate but . . . they were really hungry. He decided to say nothing.

"Let's go to Howard's points of the compass," Aybe said, "and close in on it. Maybe get some spears?"

This zigzag tree had limbs that slanted backwards as the trunk angled left, then right. They cut off four limbs that were fairly straight and trimmed them down, sharpening their points with knives, searing the points hard with their lasers. They had all gotten quick and sure, handling their field gear, and the gray "ape" was only a hundred meters away when they circled through the tree line, working around it as it moved steadily on. The quarry looked around a lot but didn't notice them.

On Cliff's signal, they all closed in. The target was bigger than they were, he judged, by fifty kilos at least. It was watching the ground as they quietly edged closer. It climbed a short knoll and crouched down among the grassy tops. This helped shield them as they moved to within twenty meters of it. The quarry's attention was focused on the ground and Terry, who edged up the slope, gave the hand signal to attack.

They ran up the slope with makeshift spears and the thing suddenly sprang up, eyes wide. Terry charged at it with a high-pitched yell and then suddenly stopped. "It's got a tool kit!"

"Hold!" Cliff shouted. They stopped, spears still at the ready.

The creature drew out a slender instrument and pointed it at them.

"That a gun?" Aybe asked.

"Doesn't look like one."

Silence. Edgy foot shuffling. Cliff now saw their potential prey was not covered in gray fur but rather a formfitting garment of close woven cloth. From a distance it had looked like a pelt. It backed up, saw that it was surrounded, and crouched low. At its feet was a square opening, revealed by a hatch tilted back by a large handle. It had used the slender tool to unlock the thing, and the lid of turf swung wide open on a big, rugged hinge.

"It's intelligent," Terry said.

The creature stepped carefully over and took hold of the lid. It murmured something and gestured with its long, angular hands. They ended not in simple fingers but with an array of flexible, multi-jointed appendages.

Cliff dropped his spear and stepped closer. About a meter below in the hole was a complex mechanical array. As they watched each other warily, a slight rumble came from the ground, vibrating his boots. The creature bent down and tripped two flanges to a new setting, ignoring them.

It's got to be pretty confident of itself, Cliff thought.

It swung the lid back into place with a thump that broke the strained silence. It put away the tool and held out its hands, appendages up. They were twice as long as human hands and fingers.

"Is that a peace gesture?" Irma asked.

Intelligence gleamed in the quickly shifting eyes. It focused on Irma and Howard, who were standing together. Slowly it walked toward them. They glanced at each other uncertainly, and Cliff said, "Stand aside."

With what Cliff thought was supreme self-confidence, the thing walked past the humans and continued on its way. It did not even look back or seem concerned that they might follow it. They stood awhile and watched it walk into the distance with a dignified, measured pace.

When Cliff turned from watching it, Aybe had the lid up and was examining the space below. The rumble was louder with the lid off but soon faded away.

"This is interesting mechanical engineering," Aybe said. "I could squeeze down in there and—"

"I'm hungry," Terry said. "I was already figuring out how to roast that thing."

"Can't eat a smart alien," Irma said tersely.

"I suppose not," Terry allowed with a nod.

Cliff thought, *People do on Earth . . . even primates.* But said nothing.

They went back to the stream and managed to catch one of the oval turtles with the razor-sharp crest. They were all in a bad mood. They hit it with a rock and roasted it over a spit. Cracking the shell, they found leathery meat sizzling from the fire and giving off heavenly aromas. Tough, but no one hesitated.

NINETEEN

A small set of rocky ruins lay downstream. Big stones cemented in place, no obviously advanced technology. They seemed abandoned. Cliff wondered at their age.

They skirted these, and the river broadened into a lake that smelled of sulfur. A swamp dominated one side and unfortunately it was theirs. They tried moving through it but the sour muck sucked at their every footstep. A hundred meters of this made them stop.

"Leaving prints in this muck makes it easier for them to track us," Irma said.

Terry looked exhausted again. "Look, we can only run so long. We're not trained for this."

Cliff nodded. "There's gotta be a better way."

There was, but not easy. They found logs and lashed them together with vines and strips of bark from the rotting fallen trees. No high chippering cries from behind, but they worked quickly together. Their discipline was getting better; nobody spoke more than the minimum. Cliff thought to himself, *The forest always has ears.*

At 0.8 g, the raft didn't have to be as strong as on Earth. Cliff and the men took off their belts to bind together the gray logs. The mud reeked and they were glad to cast off into the shallow lake. Paddling with some broad branches was slow, but they caught a breeze and the smell got better. Cliff set them facing all four directions in case anything came after them. He could tell from their faces that they were worrying.

Only partway across did he recall the dinosaur-like thing that rose from the last lake they had seen. That thing could capsize them easily here. But nothing did. Fish splashed, making them all jumpy, but nothing more came. This lake wasn't deep enough to support something like that.

They landed in a thin forest on the other shore, a kilometer away from the swamp. Wind was increasing, sighing through the trees. At Cliff's orders—he was getting used to just making them clear and direct, when speed was crucial—they hauled the raft beyond view, into the wispy trees. Then he had them take a break. He needed a pause and they must, too.

They ate the pitifully small provisions they carried, maybe thirty grams each. Irma made a joke about losing the weight she didn't need, and they all laughed ruefully. Soon enough, it wouldn't be funny. Cliff could feel his overalls clinging to him because he was burning up his stored fat, always hungry. He wished they had time to stop and take a swim just to clean their clothes. But who knew what was in those murky waters?

So they pushed on—and found a wreck within minutes. They had seen rusting debris before, but this was different, fresher. It was a crashed light plane, made of light composites, its rear section crumpled. The passenger seats were two meters apart. A two-seater for giants, no bodies, one wing smashed to fragments. The engine had plunged out of the body and jammed into the sandy soil. Most of the fuselage was smooth, though, undamaged. Some sort of carbon composite, he judged.

Cliff again wondered why they had seen no aircraft. This wreck looked recent. Then it struck him—if a big aircraft fell, it might punch a hole through the entire structure, venting the life zone to vacuum. So only small aircraft were allowed. And not many of those.

Only a few hundred meters farther on, they stepped from the wispy forest onto a flat plain of sand. There were no hills

visible in the distance through a shimmer of heat haze warp-
ing the perspectives. Warm tan sand simmering beneath the
eternal sun. A steady breeze at their backs seemed to urge
them into this desert.

"We sure can't go slogging across that," Terry said, his face
sagging.

"But those nasties behind us . . ." Irma's voice trailed away.

"We need to get some distance between them and us,"
Howard said.

Cliff let them toss it around and then said, "I don't like
the idea of standing out nice and clear against a desert." Not
an idea, but true.

"We're trapped!" Irma said angrily. She looked wan, worn.

Aybe kicked at the sand and knelt down and used his
magnifying scoper on grains in his palm. "I *thought* this stuff
felt odd. Look."

They took turns peering at the grains. Cliff was surprised.
"They're all round," he said.

"Manufactured," Terry said. "Maybe condensed out of a
hot silicon and oxygen mix in zero grav?"

"Could be," Aybe said. "If you're building this place in
high vacuum, starting from scratch, you don't have rivers and
beaches to make sand."

Cliff looked at the stretching expanses, as flat as the lake
had been. What moved well on—? And it came to him.

"Sand without edges has got to have less friction," he said.

Irma looked at him. "Uh, so?"

"Less resistance to a sliding surface. Let's make a . . . sail
craft. Let the wind blow us across this desert."

"What?" Aybe was aghast.

Irma snapped her fingers. "Remember that downed plane?
We could use the airfoils, cobble something together."

At first they were puzzled, then disbelieving, then—
remembering their pursuers—grudgingly, they tried it.

They had to drag the cut-down body of it for hundreds of

meters. Terry pried the damaged wing away, and they used the wheels to keep the thing rolling. Cliff had time to look through the tool belt he had taken off the alien body. That seemed now like many days ago. He knew this meant he was getting near his limits. That was now a bigger problem for them all—telling when an Earth day had gone by.

In his stupefied fumbling, he finally saw that most of the tools were alien wrenches, hammers, screwdrivers for pentagonal heads—and huge. Hard to use, but not impossible. One he couldn't understand turned out to be a laser. He spotted it because it had leads to attach to a solar panel that unfolded. The gear was quite well designed.

It flared on with a virulent pop. Everybody cheered. They cut through the unneeded metal with its actinic beam, slicing elegantly thin lines. It took care and contortions to shape the body into something clean and usable.

They reconfigured it into a sand-sailboat, making the usable wing of the plane into a sail. They screwed that in place with their new tools.

Luck was with them: the wind was picking up, still howling at their backs.

They set off by pushing the fat-tire wheels into the sand and then letting the wing turn into the full wind. Cliff held his breath. If it failed, they were stuck, backs against the desert.

It failed. The wheels got stuck in grit and they had to lever them out of the sand, digging with their hands. Then, with them all crowded into the long passenger compartment, they got stuck again. Sighs, drawn faces.

Terry had another idea. Cut off the wheels. Let it be a true sailboat, running on its skin. Cliff was so tired by now, he really had no faith in anything but sleep. But he let Terry shear off the wheels and struts with the alien laser.

They got out of the boat's body and pushed. Sand ground beneath it, the wind blew—and it started to gain speed. Cliff ran alongside, pushing with raw hands until it had some momentum. Only then did he call, "Pile in!"

They yelled and shouted and got inside with weary last energy. In a few minutes, Cliff looked back and could no longer see the tree line. The wind purred around their sail as it picked up. They were skating across a great sand lake with no idea of what lay ahead. Into the unknown.

So what else is new? Cliff asked himself, and fell fast asleep.

PART IV

The real voyage of discovery consists not in seeking new landscapes, but in having new eyes.

—MARCEL PROUST

TWENTY

Tananareve stared at the shambling beast looming over her and made herself not cringe.

Keep your head held high, her mother's spirit reminded her. She had to, anyway, because the alien towered over her like a mobile mountain.

This thing smelled, too. Its thick musk made her eyes water and she sneezed.

Memor had brought yet again an odd thing made of plasticlike, squeezable stuff. The vast beast set the thing before her and stepped on it. It squawked, hissed, then got up and walked around on stubby legs. A life-form? Now it ran off in a panicked, lurching gait, as if afraid.

Just the way I feel, she thought. Each time, Memor brought a little thing that surprised her a bit. But what did they mean? A calling card?

Memor made a resounding speech of woofs, yips, and growls. Plus the seemingly mandatory feather-fluffs, fan displays with suites of multicolored synchronization, and ruffles that sounded like whispery drumrolls. Tananareve got the drift—was she awake?

"Of course I am," she said back, in words that sounded more like growls. This seemed to please it. Every meeting began this way, and Tananareve still hadn't figured out why. Or the calling cards.

Haltingly, Tananareve asked Memor for help in finding food they could eat. She felt somewhat comic, mimicking the alien's huffing, bass word-structures in her high, lilting notes. But her meaning got through somehow.

Memor bowed, a gravid gesture of understanding. The huge thing lumbered around, trumpeting orders to its lessers, trying to find leafy boughs that the human could try. She caught a combination of rough consonants that seemed to mean, "fodder for eaters of meat and grasses." At least it apparently knew some organic chemistry.

She kept to the ropy vines Beth had settled her into for comfort. Tananareve felt safer here, too, lounging back among this aromatic wealth. Her dark skin blended into the shadows.

Anything was better than the awful rattling box they'd had to endure coming here. She had felt better from the moment they were shooed out of that by Godzilla-like birds.

The forest was oddly comforting. Plants here, adapted to near free fall, looked odd. The usual supporting structures were gone, so huge leaves and blooms hung in the 0.1 g from slender branches. Many had no obvious parallel to Earthly vegetation. They looked like slender spiderwebs with splashes of puffball decoration.

Serf-Ones, as the Astronomers called them, had been busy building an enclosure when the humans were harried into the Greenhouse, as they called it. The Serf-Ones inside the enclosure worked steadily but avoided people. Maybe they were scared of crushing the much smaller humans.

The atmosphere seemed to cling in her lungs, muggy and sweetly fragrant. After the ship's carefully modulated air, it was pleasant, moist and not chilly. They were still in low gravity, though. The Bowl here had just enough spin that stuff tossed up would eventually settle.

The aliens thought *big*. Their enclosure was far larger than it needed to be. Of course, the entire Bowl exceeded any imaginable idea of limits. Should that tell them anything about the psychology of those who built it?

Tananareve noticed that Lau Pin was getting restless. He paced, climbed some of the thin, layered trees, got into arguments seemingly out of boredom. After several days of this, he announced that he was going to explore. He didn't want company, either. Beth didn't like that, but she had no real authority here. She wasn't going to go herself, not with Tananareve injured and needing looking after.

She was trying to convince Abduss to go with Lau Pin when abruptly he just hiked away, not waiting. Beth shrugged and said with lifted eyebrows to the others, "Guess he just doesn't like us." Still, Tananareve knew that Beth worried. That was her nature.

Lau Pin was gone for well over a day. He returned (he admitted) when he started wondering if he could find the way back, even though he used slash marks on the large, barked trees to guide him. He reported finding nothing different, just endless vegetation. No hills taller than fifty meters, just enough to get streams to glide downhill. It was eerie, he said, watching a broad creek easing along over rocks, but not chuckling with the splashes it would have made on Earth. Low g did that, taking the zip out of life in odd little ways. He had never reached the turning back of their enclosure. Even in 0.1 g, the wall was too high to jump and its smooth lattice made climbing impossible. He guessed that the Serfs had dropped the tall, chicken-wire walls from some craft flying above. "It's enormous, this cage they've stuck us in, at least tens of klicks across," he said.

"Maybe they want us not to get claustrophobic?" Abduss suggested. "Living in the Bowl, maybe they've evolved to like room."

"So we should, too?" Lau Pin rolled his eyes.

"Come on, Astronomers are *huge*. They *need* room," Mayra said. "Fred, what do you—?" Fred was glowering at one of the skyeyes hovering nearby. "Never mind."

Fred Ojama wasn't taking imprisonment well. He was withdrawn, sullen. In some ways, he was worse off than Tananareve.

Beth asked Lau Pin, "Were there more of those head-sized sensors floating around?"

Lau Pin grimaced. "Two followed me the whole way."

Nobody liked the ever-watching spheres the size of a human head. They seemed to navigate by whispering jets. Lau Pin had studied them and found there was a strong magnetic field near them. Mag lift? Indeed, it was nearly a hundred times Earth's surface magnetic field, running parallel to the ground here. Abduss guessed it might have to do with running the Bowl, perhaps helping stabilize it with magnetic pressure.

Tananareve listened to all this behind the soft insulation her meds gave her. She was content to lie back and observe through cottony air. There were plenty of vines that in small gravs didn't bow in graceful catenary curves, but shot straight out. These connected to plants that were crowded layers of great broad leaves. The leaves were as big as Tananareve and firmly attached to barnacled branches. Those long limbs were so large, she could not see where the gradually thickening, dark brown wood ended. Among the green and brown leaves scampered and leaped many small creatures. They capered among odd long, pearly white strands as thick as her arm. These connected like spokes across the open spaces—lanes that cut through the thick green stands of web-trees. She could not figure out what the pale fibers were part of, unless it was some plant of enormous size, its details lost among the distant growths that lay along the big tunnels that brought light and air.

She suddenly saw that her whole mind-set was wrong here. This was not an Earthlike forest. *The landscape is designed. Sculpted. But it looks like Earth's nature preserves.*

Memor sent a small underling into that tangle. It was a

ferretlike thing with a big head and darting eyes. It fell from one leaf to another, slid down to a third, and landed on a cat-like creature—which squashed like a pillow. With a shudder the prey died, provoking in Tananareve a pang of guilt. The cat-thing had wings and sleek orange fur. Her heart ached at the beauty of it.

Memor gruffed approval. With a few movements of its razor-claws, the ferret hunter skinned the cat and plucked off gobbets of meat and scampered to Tananareve with them. She bit her lip at the reek of the red gobbets, and pointed to the people tending their fire.

Tananareve watched as Memor's minions snatched at tu-bular insects and crunched them with relish into a hash. They especially enjoyed ripping big fronds to shreds, picking out packets of ripe red seeds. Tananareve videotaped them at it, watched and learned.

One of the ferret-things brought her crimson bulbs that grew profusely in grapelike bunches. Memor reassured her with feather-fans of certainty that these were humanly di-gestible. She reached for some, and the bulbs hissed angrily as she plucked one loose. All bluster—the plant did nothing more as she bit in. She liked the rich, grainy taste. Far better than ship food, for sure.

The taste rode atop the bland dryness of the sedative she had taken. Here she was, in the most fascinating and terrify-ing moment of her life—and she was injured, dulled. Tanan-areve stopped herself from rubbing at her cracked ribs and her upper right arm, which throbbed from a nasty break. Nothing to be done about broken ribs except not move around, as Beth said, and risk jabbing a rib through a lung. Beth had splinted her arm quite deftly. Their emergency med kit gave her some pain relief, but that didn't stop her restless mind.

She knew she wouldn't be much use for a while, even with the quick heal salve Abduss applied to her aching arm. She hung relaxed in a secured bower of vines and plants and wondered how all this profuse life had evolved in near-zero gravity. Time to sit back, watch, and learn—which turned out to be, fathom what the alien called TransLanguage.

At university she had been good at the language game, learning French and Russian. Her secondary expedition job was to be alien translation. So now she had the job of dealing with the giant who identified itself as Memor—the name itself an approximation she had worked out to a sound like a bass humming, deep in its throat. She had imagined that, if they met aliens, there would be some orderly exchange of texts and recordings and, well, a method. Something like SETI messages, maybe, across a proper desk. Not here.

The other people were distracted, finding and choosing edibles, building a shelter, classifying Bird Folk varieties—which kept appearing to do work nearby, openly gawk, and flare their brilliant feather displays, rainbows of vibrant color. Squawking, too, in a language Memor dismissed with a gravelly grunt: unimportant.

Beth came to watch with her and change the dressings on her broken arm. "That bush over there smells like cooked meat," Beth said. "Strange . . ."

They watched it uneasily. A ratlike thing as big as a dog but sporting an enlarged head came foraging by. Humans bothered it not at all. Beth pointed out that the animals here had no fear of humans because they had no experience. The rat-thing caught the meaty smell and slowed, tantalized. It lingered—and the bush popped. Spear seeds embedded in the rat. It yelped and scampered away.

"A victory for the plants," Beth said. "That rat will carry the seed, I'll bet, until it dies."

Tananareve said, "So then a fresh bush grows from the rat's body. Smart."

Memor approached, huffing and rumbling, and they both tried not to shrink from its size. It spoke and Tananareve translated to, "I, like you, have a meat tooth."

Beth said, "Uh, charmed, I'm sure."

"We try for you to find the eatables," Tananareve translated again. She thanked Memor, and the mountain of flesh and rippling feathers seemed to bow at a sideways angle, lowering its arms and head.

Memor took them for a stroll in the awkward low g, explaining, gesturing with head and hands. It felt good to walk. All this helped improve Tananareve's translating abilities. They passed by colonies of plants that clearly had a social life, communicating through pollen-sprays their needs and distresses.

Tananareve bit her lip and summoned up the courage to ask, "How do you . . . manage all this? Your . . . world-ship?"

Memor stopped and regarded them with big, solemn eyes. She spoke in long, rolling cadences and Tananareve struggled to translate. Her voice came in bursts as she got the meaning. "Fast learns, slow remembers. The quick and small instruct the slow and big by bringing change. The big and slow urges—dammit—call it constraint and constancy. Fast gets attention; slow has power. A robust system needs twice—I mean both. There is one great commandment: Stability is all."

The sound of her voice was like stones rattling in a jug. Very large stones, boulders, in an immense jug.

Beth asked, "How old is this . . . world?"

After translations, Tananareve shrugged. "We don't have the same time measures, but it's *old*. I get the feeling Memor doesn't want to say."

"What's it—okay, she—doing now?"

Tananareve looked up as Memor tilted her head back and went into the long trancelike state she had seen before. "I don't know. She says it's like talking to another part of her mind—that is, if I'm really getting the gist of her meaning."

Memor wandered away, still in a daze.

Beth smiled and sat back into a conical bower of fleshy

plants. "I'm amazed, just like all of us, at how fast you've learned."

She gave Beth a quick, flinty look. Tananareve knew that her honey-toned Mississippi vowels made most crew members discount her. *Talk that way, and people will knock twenty points off your apparent IQ,* her mother had said. But she liked the soft, supple play of her accent, the stretched vowels and rounded consonants. "I'm even more so. Who would've thought that an alien language would have sentences at all? Much less, relating in a linear configuration with structures, a system?"

"And they're not even mammals," Beth mused. "I think."

"I suppose, but we don't really know. Kinda a hard subject to just bring up." Tananareve frowned. "It was so easy to learn from Memor, just from pointing and acting out. Maybe the underlying chemistry and stuff doesn't matter so much. I guess there are essentials in language after all. Not just in vocabulary and grammatical rules, but in their semantic swamps. Gad!"

"But you did it," Beth said simply.

Tananareve shrugged. "Memor says she's using 'artful intelligences' to help her. I suppose that means she's computer linked."

"Well, we don't have that," Beth said. "Maybe that's necessary, to run a thing like this huge thing."

"Could even our most inspired programmers, just by symbol manipulation and number-crunching, have cracked ancient Egyptian with no Rosetta stone? I doubt it."

"Maybe they've met other aliens, learned something of how the whole galaxy talks."

Sobering indeed, Tananareve thought.

"Still, it means we're dealing with beings who have unseen resources," Beth said.

"Hey, just the visible resources are incredible! Yeah, that may explain why Memor can teach me so well. She's flexible.

Nearly all human languages use either subject-object-verb order, or else subject-verb-object. Memor says she uses both, plus object-verb-subject, so she can adapt to us easily."

Beth sat up quickly. "Something's happening."

Animals came fast, yelping, flitting through the nearby foliage. An insectlike thing fluttered by them. It was like a dragonfly whose wing sets moved at right angles to each other. A long-limbed jumping rat streaked by, using Beth's head as a touchpoint, then gone. She flinched but managed not to cry out.

Then they both heard a long bass note sound through the bowers. Nearby, some of the long, thick white strands trembled. Something was tugging on them, sending low frequency waves ahead.

"Get down, cover up," Tananareve whispered.

The deep note was louder. Or maybe it just sounded that way since everything else got suddenly quiet.

She looked down the long strands. They laced through the foliage with a clear path around them, almost like a tunnel in the air. Every hundred meters or so, they had an anchor on one of the thick, rough trunks.

A big hairy thing came into view from the distance. Fast. Spherical and ruddy, with six long legs or arms that moved with liquid grace. It flowed as if it were swimming, flicking long, thin legs out to pluck momentum from the white cables. Soundless. Tananareve judged it was ten meters across at least. A flying house.

She and Beth wrapped themselves away, but Tananareve left a slit open to watch the enormous creature pull and fly, pull and fly—zooming on by them with quick, nimble movements of the legs. It swept by, leaving a slight breeze with a prickly, acid aroma.

Then another. It looked the same, maybe slightly smaller, but even faster. Its legs sang with humming as they plucked, all a blur.

It followed the first around a far curve maybe a kilometer away. The sharp odor lingered.

The area around them was dead silent. Nothing moved. Slowly, slowly small rustlings started. The forest went back to business throughout the three-dimensional volume.

Beth whispered, "What was that?"

"A spider designed by an art deco mind."

"I thought Memor was the top predator of this biosphere."

"Me, too. But even we have bears and sharks."

"What'll we do?"

Tananareve thought to herself, *Send not therefore asking for whom the bells toll. And if it starts ringing, start moving.* "We'd better be getting on."

Beth nodded, eyes big, face pale, and lips drawn. Tananareve was startled to see that Beth, who had always seemed to have rock-hard confidence, was scared.

TWENTY-ONE

The moist heat here felt like it could be cut into cubes and used to build a wall. Beth was glad to feel it. It wouldn't be long before their clothes would get worn. At least there was a nearby stream running through so they could bathe and drink. Plus, the Astronomers let them make fire. She had wondered if Memor would intervene when they used the tools they wore around their waists, too, but apparently the immense aliens thought puny humans could do no real damage.

Damage, no. But maybe they could escape.

It had been several days since the huge spiderlike things came zooming through. Beth hadn't been able to sleep well after that. Others remarked that the huge beasts—Abduss called them spidows—had ignored the humans. Maybe they weren't predators at all, just large herbivores. But Beth had seen their bristly palps moving in a blur as they clutched the thick strands. It called up a fearful image of spiders that still made her shake.

Tananareve was healing quickly from the speed-heal salve Abduss had in his med store pack. But they were all getting restless, now that they had food and the basics. Mayra deftly climbed to the top of a particularly tall frond tree, lashing herself in with ply ropes when she got above a hundred meters' height. She found feathered lizards that sported gorgeous fan plumage and could fly among trees, apparently evolved toward a monkey lifestyle. One variety she called mammoth monkeys. Like many things here, they were huge but not gorilla-like. They were shy, with attenuated, long arms and long torso, just built big and limber as a snake. They liked to swing on vines, apparently for amusement.

She could see farther from there, she reported, above most of the tree canopy.

Lau Pin and Mayra spent their time with heads together, inventing one scheme after another to escape. They even got Fred involved. His notions were crazier than theirs, but nothing stood up under examination.

Find if there's some key to their enclosure, steal it. Only there didn't seem to be anything obvious the serf breeds used to seal and unseal the boundary.

Find a way to fly away; in low gravity that should be pretty easy. But that wouldn't get them out of their warm prison. It just meant they would be on their own, without the serf breeds to help them find food.

Surrender. Somehow. Already they were talking, sort of.

Lau Pin hotly objected to this view. "Should we sit here, as prisoners? We can explore a whole huge world out there!"

Tananareve said mildly, "How about those spidows?"

That sobered them all. Beth let their discussion run; it kept them busy and they might find a good idea. She got up to get some water from the daisy-cup cistern Lau Pin had made. Far up among the bowers, orange flashes arced and snapped from treetops into the gray, clouded sky. Only moments before, those clouds had been cheery, popcorn-white puffballs. Now they slid aside to reveal angry purple towers that tapered to infinity. Her hair stood up on her neck, and a warm wind tickled her hair, sure sign of air freighted with electricity. She turned to say something—

—and got knocked off her feet by percussive force. It felt like getting hit with a baseball bat and blinded by a virulent yellow flash. The others were sitting in the giant leaves and nearly got walloped by a felled tree that crashed through nearby. The air reeked of ozone. Small creatures lay around, some twisting and the others clearly dead.

None of Beth's people was hurt, but they were certainly shaken. There had been no warning except the instant when she felt her neck hairs rising. She had always thought lightning struck golfers out on fairways swinging 4 irons to the sky, or farmers sitting on tractors in flat fields. Earthly lightning descended on anything taller than the rest of the landscape, like a sailboat on open water. But here she had been among trees and massive foliage.

Abduss said, "You were the only one of us standing."

Beth frowned. "So?"

"Lau Pin measured a strong magnetic field here. We are on a spinning conductor that carries a strong field."

Lau Pin snapped his fingers. "The same as a generator—a rotating magnetic field drives current. Charges move around on Earth because of that, so it's the same for the Bowl."

Abduss grinned. He always seemed happiest, Beth knew, when he was solving a puzzle. "Lightning is the celestial housekeeper, balancing out the overcharged land with the ionized top layer of the atmosphere."

Beth said. "This came up through the ground, though."

"Upside-down lightning, yes," Abduss said thoughtfully. "Somehow opposite from our experience on Earth."

"Upside down can still kill you," Tananareve said. *Goes with the territory.*

They returned to the discussion. Tananareve repeated her remark about the spidows, and Beth said, "They get into this enclosure anyway. If we escape, we can just stay away from tunnels in the foliage. Back off if we see the spidow strands."

They all nodded, but she could see they were grudging nods. Abduss made the point that they had now set up "housekeeping" here, had food and water and help from Memor's servants. "Meanwhile, we know nothing whatever of Cliff's group and of *SunSeeker*. They could be negotiating with the locals right now. Let's wait. Give them a chance to make some progress."

More talk as they ate some of a spongy, spherical fruit, and Abduss's view emerged as the consensus. Beth had to admit there was some logic to it. "But we can negotiate, too."

Tananareve said, "I'm getting better at translating. I'll approach Memor about a deal. But what's on our want list?"

In the way group decisions often occur, this was the signal to abandon escape plans. More talking to Memor got everyone off the hook. Their faces said they were glad to play for time. Escaping would be scary, and they had been scared plenty already.

TWENTY-TWO

The tiny primate learned quickly. Memor had the Serfs bring in a mindscan. This was an oddly compact version of the ancient devices. At her order, the techserfs had been working on it diligently since Memor summoned forth the customary device used by scholars, but scaled down to these small bipeds.

Here in the Greenhouse Terraces—a privileged verdant garden of vast natural wealth the size of the Old Continents— dwelled many vibrant, quite different creatures. The Astronomers had studied them since ancient long-gone eras of the Voyage. Their mental processes, as viewed in mindscans, told of the slow press of evolution even under the constant condition of the World. But now such crafts could aid in dealing with the Late Invaders—an idea that had come to Memor while letting her Undermind gush up into full view.

Memor persuaded the translator primate to enter the machine. Indeed, it—yes, *she*—seemed to like the prospect of leaving the corral. Serfs had erected the scan tunnel near the corral entrance, and the primate gazed about with quick interest at the technologies assembled.

Memor spoke warmly, using soothing tones and featherfans of quiet resolve. Serfs attended the cautious Invader, chattering in their simple tongues, and soon all was ready.

The device worked surprisingly well. The Serfs had tested it against the arboreal simians, simple forms that were the nearest approximation to these Late Invader aliens. The primate female submitted to the device after being told that it would help the translations. False, of course. But useful, as so many passing illusions are when dealing with those less adroit. Memor sighed, a long, slow, and satisfying vibration it used to let its mind process data.

The scan revealed a brain startlingly different. Strange, yes—but Memor's Undermind could see structural connections, similarities (primitive, to be sure) to the Astronomer-class minds honed by more Cycles than time could count.

The female disliked the incisive, magnetic lacing of the scan. Clearly so. She became uneasy, and with the Serfs attending to the process, Memor could see her anxieties forking like dendritic lightning fingers through a mind cloudy, veiled, mysterious. And . . . divided.

Memor experienced the exquisite tremor of an insight. An idea emerged fresh and flowering from her Undermind.

These awkward, tenuous aliens lived in a sort of middle scale. Their senses had evolved to perceive things on their own puny scale. Of course, they could not see bacteria, but they could sense minor dimensions. The larger scales of a world were beyond them, though—no doubt because they evolved on some gravitational mass, as Memor's own ancestors had. They had a perceptual horizon limited by the curve of primitive worlds, seen at heights no more than their own stature. They must feel trapped here.

Still more shrunken was their sense of time. Typically they sensed the grind of orbital cycles, seasons, incessant day-night, the brute revolutions of planets. They lived in the mire of cyclic mechanics, sleeping and mating to the tick of some planetary clock. Slaves to time.

Memor had the Serfs interrogate the primate's innate mind-time scales. They scampered about, using their instruments. The result was desperately plain.

The creature had a summing time of a few of its own eye-blinks, a trifling interval. It used that scale to integrate information. That meant that it could not delegate to its lesser parts the usual boring business of keeping itself alive. It had to keep incessant watch.

This was difficult to believe. The Folk had abandoned the drumming rhythm of short cycles long ago. That was the informing idea behind their pursuit of constancy—of freedom from the ticktock of early origins. Instead, the Folk dwelled on the eternal Quest through the Voyage.

This small, intense being was forced to worry about its housekeeping, such as digestion, excretion, even the intake and outblow of oxygen. Could it be so pointlessly busy? Difficult to know, but depressing to contemplate.

Such a short processing time meant that it could seldom spare computational power on issues beyond its own heart rate. It lived a poor, distracted life. Yet it had built a starship!

Did it even sense the gyre of evolution? Or of the World?

Memor pondered. Her Undermind worked, fretful and persistent as always, yet came forth with nothing. She inspected her Undermind workings, peeled back layers—yes, nothing. The Undermind was justly perplexed. So many questions remained!

Could these hairy bipeds fathom why their slavery to oscillations in dark and day made them primitive? Once even the Folk had submitted to such endless toils. But they had learned otherwise, had in the Deep Times built the World to escape such bondage to primitive cycles. In its way, this small thing represented the ancient past, brought forward by circumstance for Memor's instruction.

When the alien came out of the scanning, Memor tried to get the female to speak. It was staggering a little, waving its small arms for balance. "I see you find our insightful machines a trial," Memor said.

"You trying to pick my brains?" it—no, *she*; hard to remember; how could one tell?—shot back.

"I have analyzed your capabilities," Memor said, which in a way was true.

"You goddamn smelly elephant-bird! You have no right—!"

Its noise carried little information. Hot-eyed fervor marked it, and even more its limbs whirled entertainingly, as if they were beset by breezes. The effect was comic. She had noticed this one was darker in hue than the others, which might mean it had spent more time in starglow, and so was older, and thus wiser. That was why Memor had selected her—hoping for a faint trace of wisdom in it. Futile, perhaps. But Memor did not know enough yet.

So Memor had the Serfs return it—her—to the scan. It squalled, of course.

Ah. Revelation dawned up from the Undermind. New data flowed into Memor, and she could see it working amid the low minions of her own mind. She could flick back and forth between her own mental understory and that of this Late Invader primate. A unique experience, laced with shadowy strangeness.

So . . . could she question the female while she was in the scan? She had never known this to be done, in all Astronomer history. Yet her Undermind pushed this concept up from its ripe swamps, and Memor saw the value of the idea. Onward, then.

The Serfs stood in awe as she called up the image-data, learning from it in quick bursts. She let the Undermind hold sway. Serfs could not of course understand, as they—indeed, nearly all of Creation—were all linear minds. Unified minds, yes—but with little Undermind. Serfs used a variant of linear thinking, just as did these Late Invaders, but apparently the Late Invaders had strengths Serfs did not. Certainly no Serf could have escaped from the traps laid for generic Invaders.

She scrutinized the alien brainscan with care. Hereditary neural equipment governed them. Primitive, indeed. Their minds were divided! Straight down the middle, a clear cleft. Most of Creation was so configured. Evolution had apparently used this often as an early, rudimentary precaution. The Folk shared this property as well, and it was common in this explored region of the galaxy, at least.

But there were new features here, as well. Simple forms of animals divided functions so that they could not interfere with basics, and so interrupt the fundamentals. Later, further up the evolutionary pyramid, various utilities like digestion, heartbeat, the underlying housekeeping—all became walled off in the mind, their work uninterrupted except in emergencies.

But some fundamental features of advanced minds were beyond these Late Invaders. Higher intelligence needed not mere utilitarian modes, but rather the creative ones. The source of cross-association, and thus ideas, had to be accessible. The Undermind was common to all sentient creatures— yet these primates could not see theirs! Only a mind unified at the upper levels, above the shop floor of bodily business, could have deep ideas, surely? Then a mind could manipulate them, force them on the twin forges of reason and intuition, into great leaps.

These aliens had no such ability. Their greatest drives, intuitions, associations—all lay concealed from their foreminds, the running agents and authorities of the immediate, thinking persona. They were primitives.

Yet they had built a starship.

Memor was shocked. In a while, she got control of herself and pondered. Interrogated her Undermind. Found no lurking answers. Perhaps the Undermind needed a rest. Often, sleep brought ideas.

TWENTY-THREE

Beth listened to Tananareve's summary intently, brows fur-
rowed. Better to hear it first and hash matters over, well before calling a group meeting.

"Incredible! They put you into some kind of device and
then asked you to *think about* things?"

Tananareve shrugged. "A sort of CT device, I suppose. So
I thought on command about astronomy, about *SunSeeker*,
about what my left hand was doing while they put my right
hand in cold water. Memor found it interesting, I guess."

"Um. We have to use this. . . ."

Beth realized that she was acting instinctively like a leader
now. *Think, judge, act.* That was what irked Lau Pin, she knew.
But she intuited that the others didn't want the sometimes
impulsive, emotional, very young Lau Pin to take over. Too
bad Lau Pin didn't know that.

"It didn't bother with the rest of your body?" Abduss
asked intently. "No medical exam?"

"No, just that suffocating box with its foul scent. We had
some of that in our physicals, remember?" Tananareve shuddered. "But this time—creepy, like snakes swarming over my
skull."

Mayra put an arm around Tananareve. "Maybe it was trying to improve translation?"

Tananareve snorted derisively. "I doubt it."

"What did it feel like?"

Tananareve gazed off into the distance. "Like fingers in

my head. I'd think something, then feel it slip away, as if something was . . . feeling it."

"Um. Creepy."

"You bet. Next time, if Memor does it again, I'll deliberately think of something lurid. Just to poke at her."

Beth started diplomatically, "I know how you feel, but that might provoke—"

"Hey!" Lau Pin shouted, and came trotting over to the bower where the women sat, using the leafy enclosure to muffle their voices. His eyes danced. "I got a beamer signal—a message!"

"From *Eros*?" Tananareve asked.

"No, that's what's amazing. It carries *SunSeeker*'s bitcode. Message is loading now."

Beth felt her pulse quicken. Lau Pin's little beamer beeped and he put it to his ear. And scowled. Lips pressed into white lines, he handed it to Beth. "Captain Redwing. For. You."

Redwing spoke rapidly in his usual growl, as if afraid the connection would drop out. She restarted the recorded message. "We saw the big electrical discharges up near the top of the Bowl. Filtered out the noise and found this beamer flag frequency. So if this works, here's our situation: We can't get much out of signaling the aliens. They acknowledged us, but they take their own sweet time about getting back to us when we transmit. We demanded your return. They say they're learning our language 'in person,' so it's more efficient to keep you. It's just you, too, Beth. They won't tell us anything about Cliff. So for now, try to transmit back. Beamers don't have any real focus, but we're now to the right of their star, as you see it, maybe thirty degrees. I'm focusing all our high-gigahertz-range antennas on that spot where the big electricals went off. We're seeing flares, lightning the size of continents. Hope that didn't fry you! Over and out."

Beth smiled. The old-fashioned *over and out* was typical

Redwing. To her surprise, she felt affection for the old hard-nose. He butted his head at problems until they got solved.

She glanced at Lau Pin and saw it was time to mend fences. "Here, try to send. Tell him we're okay but captive. Trying to talk to the aliens. Ask if there's any chance they can send us supplies in one of the auto-landers?"

Lau Pin nodded and his mouth lost its irritation. "I'll send some visuals, too," he said. "Mayra? Mayra! Can I have your file of photographs? I'll send mine also."

"Sure," Mayra said, and handed over her phone. "I don't see what use he'll get out of them."

"Not him." Lau Pin looked at Beth and said, "He'll get Cliff sooner or later. We've been photographing what we can and can't eat. Cliff's party needs to know that." His smile said, *Why didn't you think of that?*

Cliff might have starved by now, she thought. Beth walked out into the middle of the little clearing they used as a gathering spot and called with more joy than she felt, "Hey, everybody! We caught a break."

TWENTY-FOUR

Memor was puzzled. Only lowly beasts used divided minds. That was a known method of letting parts of the mind work separately, so that some efficiencies emerged from specialization. But it also meant that the mind could not function with all its many parts in the mix. That stunted split minds. This was conventional evolutionary theory, well verified by contact with many planets.

These Late Invaders had brains split into hemispheres that did not always interact. Yet they had built high technologies! Quite shocking. Some of them had even evaded the Folk, as well—a shock in itself. These affronts to both experience and even reason demanded explanation.

So Memor summoned the female she had tested before. Had she overlooked some essential clue? Perhaps another viewing of her divided mind in action, plus active simultaneous use of her Undermind, would reveal an insight.

To do this she had to do the necessary mental work first. Carefully, she isolated herself from the Serf breed chatter. First she withdrew, letting sight and sound drop away from her. Inner peace came, sliding slowly. The world fell away. Gingerly, to avoid startling the working elements of her mind, she opened the vistas within.

Into her higher levels swept ruminations galore. Some of these thoughts mixed senses, as the unruly Undermind often did. Liquid amber lightning shot through her Inmind with a sharp, bristly scent—and Memor knew she was amid the chemical swamp of associations. Buzzing red flaps peeled back to reveal punctured pathways.

She was ready. So prepared, she began inspecting the biped's mental landscape. Alarm rang down its corridors.

She delved into this and felt something else, a sort of . . . memory. Only it came freighted with feelings of desire, moist expectation, flaring scents. She saw the female as if in a mirror, looking at her and yet—yes, it was locked in embrace with a large male. They were lunging at each other.

She shot a glance at the female, lying flat on the preceptor bed. She was agitated, moving her legs and hands, clasping herself—

Memor realized that she was showing Memor how her kind reproduced.

Then, unmistakably, she heard her cackling rise. Laughter, it must be. The biped was making fun of Memor.

She rocked back, red anger flaring. This tiny thing was jeering at her, using her mind to send the insult.

She let her Undermind deal with this fresh event. Soon soothing cadences passed through her, damping the prickly irritation into milder currents. As this happened, she saw that the biped was now back to a normal state. Perhaps it—she—felt that she had made her point, and was now calming down.

Very well. She would do the same. This had taught her something profound—the bipeds were quick-witted beyond their limitations. She must remember that her brain was as large as Memor's own.

The biped spoke directly to her. "I want to go back to my friends now."

Of course. These were social creatures, and she felt—she could see directly—fretful emotions down in her Undermind. The Late Invader female could not feel this clearly, though, because she could not directly see her own mind.

Instead, she sensed a vague unease. In such moments, apparently, she wanted the company of her kind. Now that Memor saw this, she understood with her Overmind the sense of it. Evolution had to converge on such social chemistries, on any world. Because more often than not, the most adaptable thing one could do to survive and reproduce was to be cooperative and altruistic. This knowledge was an Absolute, time honored and proved often in the enduring history of the Bowl. Evolution never slept, even in the great constancy of the World.

Memor answered her warmly, trying to defray her inner, vexing storms. These aliens showed much mental evolutionary selection. Whether this arose naturally or from their own genetic tailoring, she could not perceive. Their hidden Underminds were an adaptive unconscious that let them size up their world quickly, set goals, decide. Of course: these bipeds had evolved in a place where speed was vital. In contrast, the Folk prized long-term judgment, because they planned for a larger scale of time. These primates were a fresh, young species, untried.

Somehow the bipeds' methods worked, even at the chemical maintenance level. Their minds worked largely out of view of their "running-selves," the surface mind that thought it was in charge, simply because it could not see its own minions below. Indeed, she now recalled that this female had used an expression, once: "I just had an idea."

That must mean that notions simply appeared in their Overminds. They had no concept of where the ideas came from. Worse, they could not go and find where their ideas were manufactured. Much of their minds were barred to them.

Astounding! Yet it worked.

Still, the danger of this strategy was their lack of true awareness. These creatures were strangers to themselves. So they decided issues without knowing the true elements behind the decision. Perhaps they did not even know why they chose mates!

This implied a further thought.

Did they have *more* mental freedom than the Folk . . . or less? To mask the Undermind from view—could that convey some benefit? Even though it was clearly a fearsomely destabilizing element, as the ancient history of her species had shown? The Undermind could unleash vast passions that swept whole societies. Unless, of course, their deep natures could be seen and regulated.

She had never thought this of another intelligence—that there could be any advantage to concealing the Undermind. The question struck at the boundaries of the Folk, their superiority—even their freedom.

She knew that one must believe in free will, despite the ability to analyze the mind to great detail. This rule applied even to these aliens. Its logic was simple: If free will was then a reality, one had made the right choice. But if free will did not exist, one had still made no incorrect choice. One had made no choice at all, not having free will to do so.

In this, the Folk and the Invaders were equals.

These tiny creatures had a rich mental life, but it was actually deeper than they knew. They had no overlook, from which they could view the vast continents of the adaptive unconscious below. They did not see the sobering landscape of the mind in all its fervent glory.

In their curious vessel, they voyaged amid a ship environment surely unlike their natural world. Perhaps they had not considered building a Ship Star for proper exploration of the galaxy. Or more likely, they could not attempt it, and so set forth in simple machines. They were young and raw, willing to suffer.

Their situation was then tragic. They had launched forth into the stars with brains evolved to deal with a world that bore only slight resemblance to the vast, messy crowds of information in their present, awkward mind-machinery.

Perhaps, then, their deaths would be a proper release from such unnatural tortures.

TWENTY-FIVE

The message from Redwing had given them a lift. But the mood faded before a clear, quick question: *So what?*

Lau Pin's beamer couldn't rouse *SunSeeker*. It was a long shot, of course—Redwing could focus a megawatt of 14.4-gigahertz power on them, but Lau Pin's beamer, even fully charged, delivered only a watt or two of unfocused signal.

So they were stuck. Beth watched them react to this. Then Abduss produced his own miracle, after a desultory day of chores.

"I have a bit of joy here!" he called to them all. In his hand was one of the useful flasks the Serfs had given them for their own housekeeping. Now that they had established their chore routines of getting and preparing food, the usual details of a stationary life, they had time to amuse themselves as they wanted. So they assembled, not expecting much. Abduss passed around the little cups the Serfs had made for them, ladling into them a murky fluid. "Toast!" he said loudly.

They drank. "Moonshine!" Fred called.

Abduss looked hurt. "Wine. It is a wine I made from the esters of the fruit they give us."

Lau Pin and Mayra both said, "Rotgut!" Mayra even hugged her belly in comic relief.

But they liked it anyway. Beth waved away her second cup and watched the others. They grimaced when they drank but that didn't stop them, or their increasingly high-pitched laughter, the rude stories, obvious lies, raucous laughter, bright eyes. They needed release, after all that had happened. Alcohol was the easy road to all of that. *Let this pass,* she thought. She watched Fred Ojama, but he only grew more torpid. Presently he said, "I shouldn't," and set the cup aside.

The next morning most of them were hungover, griping and shaking their heads. They got their housekeeping jobs done and sat around and then the lumbering, smooth-feathered Serfs brought in cylindrical canisters, laying them at the feet of Mayra. She opened them carefully. Sniffed. "It's—it smells like alcohol."

Beth grimaced. The aliens had caught on that fast. To keep the prisoners quiet, give them the ancient chemical that consoles without illuminating. Smart, in a worrisome way.

Lau Pin, to his credit in Beth's view, said, "I don't like that they watch us. This proves they're trying to . . ." He didn't complete the thought.

Beth said, "What? Keep us sedated?"

Mayra objected, waving her arms. "They're just catering to us!"

Lau Pin twisted his mouth into a sardonic curve. "Worse. They've got organic chemists, sure. But we're lab animals here, not guests. The alcohol is an experiment to see how we react."

Beth agreed. They broke up, since it was time nearly for lunch—according to their suit clocks, not of course to the unending sunlight here. Lau Pin drew the job of expanding and deepening the latrine, while the others cooked the fish and vegetables they had learned to harvest from the ample surroundings. Even simple jobs here demanded some learning, since working in 0.1 g changed everything ingrained in them. They managed, though without spirit.

Beth worried. No new word from Redwing, and they were settling into a routine now. Jobs assigned, a routine set up.

Lau Pin shouted. He came running from where they'd dug the latrine. "Come see! This topsoil is only a meter deep."

So it was—which made complete sense. The Bowl was a thin layer built to face the central star, capturing sunlight. But it couldn't be very thick without imposing huge stresses on the tension that held the Bowl together, just from mass loading. Here they saw that the entire ecology was rooted in soil only as deep as needed. Lau Pin had uncovered metal sheets and pipes, the underpinning of this odd building bigger than any world.

At lunch they mused aloud at the possibilities. "How about tunneling through?" Mayra asked. "How could we use that?"

Fred smiled derisively. "And let the vacuum suck us away? These aliens have some way to patch really fast, I'd guess—but not before we die."

They all nodded. Beth looked around at their faces going slack and thought, *We need to have a goal. Otherwise, we'll turn into passive prisoners.* She had learned what to do from her training. Get them focused. *Do the next right thing. Now.*

She knew it was true. In a tough situation, don't avoid acting just because it's easier or comfortable. Don't lapse into a passive state. People who give up, die.

Abduss mentioned something in passing that cut off Beth's reflections. "I found these strands of spidow web, must've been tossed aside when a Spidow repaired the network. They spin this stuff out, just as Beth said they must. I saw one doing it. Creepy! Anyway, I got the strands to fuse—"

"Fuse how?" Beth pressed him.

"With a laser. Just warm the ends, stick them together." Abduss smiled, obviously happy to have something to do. He produced from a sack he carried two meter-long pieces of the filmy white stuff that made the spidow web. "See?

They can be retied, with heat. I suppose these pieces got cut off in some way—"

"Then they can be made into long ropes," Lau Pin said, eyes on Beth. "So we can use them."

Beth smiled. "To get out of here."

TWENTY-SIX

Never before had Tananareve wished so fervently for blessed night.

They had all slowly adjusted to sleeping in the incessant daylight, wrapped away in the long, moist, flexible leaves of the giant bowers. With pieces of the stuff, Mayra made them masks that helped them all get some shut-eye. Still, sleep was always troubled, her alarm senses waking her often to the occasional scamper, rattle, or caw. So when they agreed to arise and move, she was thick-eyed and muzzy.

Now they had to sneak away without the Serfs catching on. That was hard. Lau Pin led them stealthily away along routes he had explored. Tananareve had insisted she go, too, even though she had trouble getting through the root-rich terrain. Thin soil meant that trees spread their roots along the surface, making for tricky footing.

Abduss had risked his life for the long, ropy strands they carried in teams. He had walked kilometers away along the flat, forested terrace that confined them, to separate his acts from the others. A simple precaution, in case the spidows discovered him at work. Then he cut long segments of the spidow fibers and carried them away from the thread-corridor before a spidow came to repair it. This meant only minutes. Slicing through a thread sent a signal along the webs, and the huge things raced to make repairs. They looked and moved like a nightmare on a caffeine high.

"Time to light out for the territories!" Tananareve said

gladly, when they had it all assembled. She saw Fred's grin; nobody else got the reference to *Huck Finn*. They were tense, ready.

Time to go, then. But the pace wore her down.

Tananareve struggled to keep up with Fred and Lau Pin as they hauled the coils along on their shoulders, with leaves to separate the fat threads so they did not stick together. Her arm was mostly healed, but it hurt now and sweat popped out on her brow, trickling into her eyes in big fat drops, and stinging. Sweaty work, silently done, as they crept away from their campground. Serfs did not all sleep at once, apparently, and Tananareve had monitored them to find the time when a minimum of them were awake. The Serf sleep cycle took about three Earth days, by her reckoning.

They quietly stole away, leaving behind dummies of wood wrapped in the leaves, looking somewhat like sleeping humans. No Serfs raised an alarm.

Moving silently took concentration. The air seemed to coil up into her nose, filling her lungs with thick musk. They reached the barrier just as Tananareve was starting to feel woozy. Her arm ached. Lau Pin thought the tall, slick wall was slightly lower here, due to some sagging. A huge tree had fallen into it from the other side, pulling it down somewhat. It was uncomfortably close to a spidow corridor, too.

Quickly they deployed their loops of spidow string. Lau Pin and Abduss began linking the coils, fusing them together with quick bursts of laser light, raising a stench like burnt milk. They had practiced this craft and now could seal the ends within seconds, playing the beams along the ends until they bubbled.

Tananareve took her position along the barrier, as they had drilled. The wall was transparent and slick, probably to keep animals from climbing it. Easily a hundred meters high, too. She looked through the wall at the jungle beyond. The wall was like ancient glass, with whorls and ripples that toyed with the view. She realized that that must be exactly what it was—glass so old, it had warped through its slow slide downward, for glass was a fluid. These must be some sort of standard wall, used for keeping animals within their range. But not, apparently, smart animals.

Working quickly, Lau Pin and Abduss fused the end of the coiled filaments to a chunk of wood. Lau Pin had cut and sized these days before. He had proved handy at woodcraft and more. The ropy, rubbery vines nearby he had built into a curious kind of slingshot—taut vines, a cantilevered flinging pouch, artfully angled struts. He and the others cocked his array back, grunting. The men had practiced this and seemed confident it would work. A tanned and stretched leaf held the wood block payload, the ropes straining at it. They all took their positions as Lau Pin counted down.

Tananareve had to admire how Lau Pin had made this with Abduss. The entire taut machine was like something from the Middle Ages—and they had built it from scratch.

"Fire!" Lau Pin couldn't resist whispering.

The energy stored in the stretched vines sent Abduss's payload shooting upward, arcing high. It cleared the barrier lip and started down on the other side. In 0.1 g, a slingshot had ten times the range it would have on Earth. That simple physics had led to many comic miscalculations as they learned to walk and work here on the terrace, but now the difference paid off. The soaring block pulled the spidow thread smoothly out of the coils. The block struck the ground with a thump she could barely hear.

"Over!" Lau Pin called.

Beth scrambled up the threads, hand over hand. The pale fibrous stuff was strong and slightly sticky, just enough to get a hold. She went up fast in the low g.

But something moved behind them.

Tananareve turned and saw two spidows moving off the

threads about a hundred meters away, in the channel of their threads. *How did they know?* she had enough time to think. *Vibrations? The stench?*

Then the spidows came at them.

Abduss turned and fired his laser at both the approaching shapes. The spidows kept coming. He hit one in the four eyestalks and it bucked back, showing a mouth of converging black teeth like pincers. They made not a sound, but the wounded one reared up, as if to frighten them with its size. At that moment, Tananareve fired her laser into its belly. The thing came down with a crash. It didn't move.

But its partner did not slow. It brushed aside big trees as if they were saplings, ripping some out by their roots. Abduss held his ground and Tananareve saw the others were going up the thread, hand over hand. She fired again but the second spidow seemed invulnerable. It took the bolts without a pause. She heard from it a high, thin shrill.

"Go!" Abduss called to her. "Up!"

She fired one last time at the spidow. It was moving slower but was only twenty meters away. Tananareve tucked her laser into her belt and leaped for the thread. Her arm gave a sharp spike of pain. She favored that arm and went up, hand over hand, kicking off against the wall to try to get more momentum.

The spidows could climb the thread, of course. She had not thought of that before. They had worried about the Serfs and Memor, but the spidows were the present threat.

She was halfway up when she heard a scream. She could not help looking down.

Abduss was under the spidow, and with a gurgle the screaming stopped. But the spidow did not linger. It tilted up and with its arms it grabbed at the thread. The arms were long and sinewy and moving so fast, they were a blur.

It launched itself upward. Behind it, Abduss looked like a tissue someone had crumpled up after a nosebleed.

It was coming for her. The thin, cutting shrill was loud now.

She pulled furiously at the thread, kicked with her toes. She could hear the huge thing sucking air in and out now with long, windy breaths.

The thread jerked with the weight behind her. She looked up and there was Lau Pin, aiming down from the top of the wall. A crisp sizzle raked the air near her head. Dazzles flashed in her eyes, evaporated away. Another sizzle. Her breath rasped and she ignored the snap in her shoulder.

Lau Pin held out a hand and when she took it he lifted her bodily free of the thread. With one hand he brought her to the lip and she angled herself over, rolling to stay out of his way.

He said, "No way I—" Another sharp sizzle near her hand. The thread went limp in her hand.

She canted over the lip, gasping. Her hands grabbed it and she tumbled over, facing the wall. The brown and gray spidow mass was just below her. She thumped against the wall, mashing her nose. Blood drooled down her face.

She looked around. Lau Pin was falling away below her. He had laser-cut the thread and—the spidow was falling. It went straight down, getting smaller in slow motion. No sound now.

She hung there, holding on, watching it thud below. And flatten down, graceful and quick as a cat. Scrabbling legs, a long low mournful sound. It got larger then. It had absorbed the fall in its legs and now—it leaped for her.

Missed. Fell back. Would try again.

She let go with one hand, the weak arm, and turned her back to the wall, clunking into it.

Below were faces. The thread had fallen into coils below her and the others looked up at her. A long fall, over a hundred meters. They waved their arms and their mouths moved, but with the pulse pounding in her ears she could not make out what they said.

The spidow was coming. Maybe it had a way of clinging to the wall. She did not wait to find out.

A treetop beckoned about fifty meters below. It looked leafy and thick, with few branches showing. In this low g— no, not the time to do a calculation.

She gathered her feet and pushed off—toward the treetop.

She tumbled and tried to come down on her boots. When she hit, the leaves lashed at her. Branches snapped against her boots, arms; one caught her smack in the face. She hit a large limb, pain lancing into her ribs. It hurt badly as she tumbled headfirst through—into clear air—and managed to get her boots under her.

She hit hard. Collapsed. Rolled away, trying to get a look up at the spidow.

It came through the tree after her. Slamming through, snapping even the big branches, showering leaves and limbs down. It had punched its way through and crashed to the ground right beside her.

Beth shot it through the enormous, many-eyed head. It jerked, gave a high, thin wail—and went still.

When Tananareve looked through the wall, she could see Abduss, as still as the spidow.

PART V

*Nothing in biology makes sense
except in the light of evolution.*

—THEODOSIUS DOBZHANSKY

TWENTY-SEVEN

The Citadel of Remembrance loomed larger than Memor recalled from her young days, so long ago. The high ramparts loomed like mountain cliffs over the gathering assembly. Fog trailed strands of pale luminance that frayed into brilliant amber fingers, like a twisting dome over them all. She admired the new additions to the Citadel, feeling the immense powers lodged here. That august force seemed more like a state of nature than a power, but such was the point.

That the Citadel could well be her place of execution did not fully overcome her awe. Instead, it gave her a delicious blend of fear and strangeness that her Undermind relished. She could feel the strumming presence of it and knew she would have to keep it carefully controlled. Her Undermind could slip words and even phrases into her speech, in its eagerness. And eager it was; she could feel the hopeful spikes of feeling. Drama was rare in an Astronomer's life.

She shuffled her feet in the required way, said the right things, and needed scarcely any promptings from her inboards. They knew the steps but not the sway, and it was safe to ignore them here.

Memor hung back from the slowly ambling crowd of Astronomers, relishing the trumpeting salutes of greeting they gave. She always used the tone of these as a diagnostic of the collective mood, and today seemed more testy than usual. Some glowered at one another, while others passed in stiff silence, feathers turned to muted tones. Riffs and small songs danced among the bass notes of the many, a leitmotif. These came from the few young males, who walked quickly and greeted loudly, joyfully.

Memor had been male when young, of course—the great, vibrant stage of life. Then that Memor of vivid passions and great conquests had gone through the Revealing. It had been a passage of legendary ardor and travail. Mercifully, most such memories had been blotted away by the experience itself. Yet the lessons of being masculine lingered and blended with the feminine insights she was now acquiring. This merging led to the path of wisdom.

As with all mature Astronomers, Memor became a She of the Folk, after learning by direct experience the male view of the world. While a He, there came to the higher Folk the legendary great desires, an easy willingness to risk, to change and innovate. This phase of zest and emotion lasted nearly twelve-squared Annuals. Memor still recalled the He sadness when those vivid feelings fled, and the bodily shifts began. Memories remained, leaving their residue of longing for a He who could never be again.

In the Revealing's changes, Memor had felt His/Her body shift with wrenching desires. The pains and startling fresh urges were also the focus of much Folk literature and dance, but few were nostalgic for that jittery chaos.

From the Revealing, Memor had acquired the long views of a She, while retaining the experience and fathoming of the He era. This conferred judgment and sympathy-from-experience on the Astronomers, a vital stabilizing element evolved by the Folk over many twelve-millennia in the truly ancient past.

This essential balance—more a dance, truly—between the He and She Memor now struggled to apply to the most unsettling event of her long life: the radical alien primates. Luckily, she had the Revealing when these aliens first appeared. That dual view of them should help her now.

"Memor! We have not greeted in longtimes," came a solemn, deep voice.

Memor turned and saw the slim head of Asenath, the Chief of Wisdom. To be welcomed by such an august figure was surely a good sign—or was it? "I have longed to see you again," Memor said. "I need your counsel."

"And you shall have it," Asenath said mildly. "I like your problems—they are more intriguing than our usual fare."

Asenath turned to use her bulk as a sound screen, anticipating the arrival of someone out of Memor's field of view. Memor did not have time to turn to see. Asenath said deftly, "Boredom need not come with every task, Memor, but it may seem so as you go forward."

"I am honored," Memor said with a suitable sub-murmur of respect. She filed the words pointedly with her inboards for later review. She was about to say more, but another voice intruded to her left, "I shall have much interest as well," in tones more threatening.

Memor turned with a sense of dread to confront Kanamatha, the Council's Biology Packmistress. "I hope to please you," Memor said.

Kanamatha said, "I shall have many questions," and in her quick-tongued way turned to Asenath and said, "Following yours, my dear."

Memor knew she should say more, but the chimes sounded final call. Amid heady perfumes and sweet music, the cohort assembled beneath rippling lights. In their twelves they began entering the high chamber in all its splendor and beauty. In reverent silence they passed gleaming alabaster edifices, oversized onyx statues of the Builders lining the inward paths to the Citadel of the Council, small temples dotted with animal gods in ancient dress, grottoes for quiet negotiations—and perhaps for amorous assignations, when the time was ripe.

The following retinue included scribes, small musicians burdened with their instruments, waykeepers, lampists and mathists, stewards of the Savants, oil masseurs—and all trailing sycophants galore.

Formalities consumed some time, and then routine reports. Each bloc applied their own torque to the proceedings, peppering the reporters with questions.

The Council had three major factions—the Farmers who ruled the vital living self of the Bowl, the Governors and Bowlcrafters who integrated the Farmers' intricate networks with the Bowl's physical structure. Overseeing all this in the larger perspectives were, of course, the Astronomers.

All three sought more power, though of course none wished to be overtly seen as desiring it. Humble achievement was the goal. But having a particular goal could not be too obvious, or one would never attain it. Memor remained silent throughout this. The occasional reports came next, and Asenath declared a mealtime to separate the two. The twelve-squared all retreated to the banquet hall, nominally to feast but actually to make deals and sniff out new alliances.

Memor ate little, wanting to keep her wits sharp. When they returned to their seats, Asenath nodded to Memor.

"Please lead me," Memor said to place the conversation in the right ranking order. She reported at length on the primates, their odd actions and even odder bodies. Full pictures of them floated in the chamber air, rotated to point out features. The genitalia were unexceptional but their carriage caused remarks. Memor skipped over the escape of some, stressing instead her studies of those captured. She showed the neural and brain interrogations and estimated their capacities—below the Folk, of course, but perhaps somewhat above others of the Adopted, those aliens already encountered and integrated into the Bowl.

She bowed with regret to report the escape of the second party, as well, from the high latitudes. Her ending was of course humble. "Apologies to you all for my failure to retain or recapture these strange primates."

A rustle of reaction, hard for her to judge. The Council had many questions. Obviously, some had not read or even prior-memoried Memor's reports.

Why did they wear clothing here in the Bowl's mild climate? Was their world colder or more hostile? These coverings over all but head and outer extremities—were these rank symbols? Could the clothing hide subtle weapons? Or could their bodies be perhaps recently reengineered, and still fragile, needing to be wrapped?

When Memor described how the primates remained clothed except when sleeping, others asked if they were competing with one another, making declarations of self with clothing?

The primate hindfeet had thick coverings. Had they evolved on a world where their every step was threatened? How to explain that curious gait—their continual, controlled toppling must be a transitory style, surely? Bowl creatures used more certain gaits, to avoid falling injuries. Two-legged forms were few.

A Crafter had a detailed set of questions, embedded in her description of inspecting the primates. The teeth appeared to be all-purpose, but did that mouth truly need an ugly protruding flap of muscle? A proper design would have sheltered the protruding eyes better, yes? Did the tiny knob nose mean they could not smell well through the tiny nostril bump-with-holes? How useful could those modified forefeet be, versus the obvious better choice to remain on four legs and have arms as well?

They seemed to use base ten, rather than the more efficient base twelve. Why?

"Their hands have ten digits."

"Surely the obvious advantages of twelve—first three fractions are integers, many other easeful facets—would outweigh that, in an intelligent species."

Memor could not contest this, and so moved on. "They display an odd adaptation—"

She showed short clips of several humans talking, their odd mouths flapping rapidly. Across their narrow faces quick muscular changes flew, a darting sequence of eyebrow lifts, shaped lips, eye moves, nostril flarings, tilts and juts of chin and jaw.

"They have this much expression, yet never evolved feather flaunting?" Biology Savant Ramanuji asked.

"Apparently they use their heads alone. Plus hands."

Sniffs and rumbles of disbelief chorused through the high vaulted room.

Omanah the Ecosystem Packmistress said slowly, "A collective good, I would predict." This came in feather tones designed to convey her well-earned wisdom, and augmented by self-deprecating, somber themes in a three-layered suite of browns and grays.

"How so?" Memor said. "Lead us."

"These facial moves are apparently signals from their Underminds. Thus the speakers do not know all that they convey."

"Surely they must!" a young Astronomer spoke suddenly. All turned to gaze, and the young one realized she—or was this one in the neutral Revealing phase?—had overstepped.

Omanah twisted her crested head and rippled her ambers and grays subtly. "Memor's points elude you. They do not know how to access their Underminds. So, in a kind of evolutionary retaliation, the Unders speak in ways the Overs cannot know."

Another stir of respectful understanding worked through the gallery—huffs, sighs, soft flares of ruby tribute to Omanah.

"I kneel to your insight," the young one said, eyes closed.

Omanah said, "Here is an example of group selection. The party speaking does not know fully what it says—*but the listeners do.* For they can see the Undermind voicing in swift flurries of expression, the signals flitting by, using little muscular movements in eyes, mouths, jaws. So the group learns the true thoughts and emotions, yet the speaker does not fully comprehend."

Memor added, "Thus the species gains a collective good."

Omanah bowed in agreement. "And so it was with our self-modifications. The Uncovering made the Bowl possible by revealing to us our Underminds."

A large, thick-plumed Overseer Astronomer asked in slow-sliding words blended with singing, sharp chirp signatures and plume-shaking, "Do you imply, Flock Head and Packmistress, that these primates have deliberately engineered this face-flutter method?"

The Packmistress pondered this, and in the respectful silence Memor saw the assemblage's feather tones shift from bright attentive colors of magenta and olive into hues tending toward grays and subdued deep blues—signs that they, too, contemplated, trying to anticipate what the Packmistress would say. Time crawled as each of the members consulted their Underminds, trawling deep, long, and slow for insight. This was how the joint Undermind of them all, in concert, learned—accumulating in linear additions, all cross-correlated to achieve greater force—the steeped wisdom of collective thought.

Asenath as Wisdom Chief called them back to Uppermind. "Of course, these creatures have features from which we can learn. At least we recovered the body of one dead primate—not killed by Memor's efforts, I remark—and have learned much from it. Their DNA is like ours, as it is with several of the Adopted. This fits the accepted view that earlier life dispersed through our galaxy on wings of sunlight."

Then she turned with dramatic effect and called, "Attendant Astute Astronomer Memor! How to deal with these escaped aliens—*that* is our issue. And you let them escape."

So here it was. Memor dodged with, "Knowledge speaks, wisdom listens, Ecosystem Packmistress Asenath."

"I expected more of you."

"I can explain some features, Packmistress, and then describe—"

"On with it."

"These primates have to live with a spectrum of desires driven by natural selection, as do we all. Their starship is a simple design, as if from a society that has developed quickly. That surely means they now operate in a world much different from their primitive lives. Yet still driving them are their deep desires. These, as our own species long ago learned, are hard to govern with learned experience or even medication. Their morality, as did ours, often fights with their desires. So to understand themselves is impossible for them, unless they can *see* their inner, unconscious minds."

"They are retarded, then," put in an Ecosystem Savant. This provoked feather-ripples of amusement, but no one made noises of glee; the occasion did not invite such.

"Indeed," Memor said. "We could help them with this—"

"Help them?" Asenath showed vibrant oranges and reds in a dancing pattern, half in jesting colors, half in rebuke. "They got away from you!"

Memor stepped back, bowed, hooted in the notes of sorrow and beseeching. "They proved more clever than their ship implied."

"Certainly more clever than their approach suggested," Judge Savant Thaji injected. "They simply landed and came through our air lock. No caution! So young!"

"I can see that as misleading," Asenath remarked without a single feather display. "Or subtle. They gained entrance, we thought we had them—then they got away."

"And now they roam at will!" the Judge Savant said. "Doing damage! We have reports of several dead in 12-34-77 district—their doing, no doubt. They captured a car, as well."

"Very grave," a Biology Savant said. "Grounds for removal."

"Or a more exacting measure," the Judge Savant said with

display of scorn and censure, gray and violet fans dancing in rebuke.

Memor stood and let the discussion run, for it would harm her cause to speak now. Instead she let her Undermind rule the moment. It conjured up for her a memory of a visit to the funeral pit, in all its elegant yet somber majesty. At its center was the Citadel of the Honored Dead, who would be churned into a matrix they shared with plants, animals, insects, and the depleted topsoil the honored would enhance. Subtly hidden machinery adjusted the slowly roiling mud-fluid for bacterial content, acidity, temperature, trace elements. First the Pit, then the Garden: the fate of all.

When the Undermind let go of the memory and was satisfied, Memor turned attention to the argument rustling all about her. Harsh things had passed her by in a flurry of hot words. She deliberately let these go, as was best in such heated moments. Insults are best not remembered. She let it all go, following the long-ranging talk but not engaging with it. Here, the Undermind helped.

The Judge Savant pressed her case for execution, calling it "a just recycling." Others differed, calling for Memor's replacement. Much talk. If Memor had followed it, laid it deep and solid in memory, she would then go through doubt and regret—which would in future impede her work. Better to let the moments glide by.

Yet questions about the primates called her out of her needful reverie. Refreshed, Memor pointed out that she had used classical methods of psychological control, since these primates were strongly social animals. She began by keeping them in comparatively small areas, and gave them just enough food to be sure they did not starve. "Still, hunger began to play a role in their behavior. Within ten of their sleep intervals—they seem to come from a planet with a fairly long day—they showed classic symptoms. Some began to communicate with us more often. This was obvious food-seeking.

Slowly, I believe, they began to identify less with their fellows, and more with us—specifically, me."

"Yes, very good," a helpful underling allowed himself to say. All else ignored him, of course.

"Within five more sleep intervals, their mood shifted. Disputes began, often in their talk during meals. This, too, fits classical theory—eating brings food to the front of their minds, their hunger drives competition, then disagreement."

"You broke down their social code? Their solidarity?"

"In part," Memor said, hoping this would come over as modesty. In fact, though, she was unsure that she had. Hurrying on, she said, "They were obviously crew on a distant voyage, so we cannot expect to break them down quickly. Time is our friend here."

"Any signs of the early stages of Adoption?"

"I believe so. They often brightened when one of my team gave them a bit of food, or allowed a small favor."

"Your analysis of their minds suggests they can be Adopted?"

"In time, yes."

This gained her shuffling fan-gestures of approval, and the air eased.

In the end it came down to a vote. Memor suffered through the moments as each voter consulted her Undermind and finally cast an electronic signal. Asenath displayed the results, and—a shocked hush.

"You have survived in your office," Asenath said, letting a pitch of reluctance skate among her words. "But I shall monitor you, and report you to this assembly when needed."

Memor allowed herself a relieved bow. There came hoots of derision, and a background soft melody of approval, expressed in sighs and foot-claps of applause.

In the great vault the gathered began a rhythmic chanting. The Protocols called for some group expression, and the momentum of the moment gave it forth. The chant called out an ancient rhythm. It spoke of what the Essence is not, instead of what it is. This set the Citadel into a great rolling call, amid hooting songs and vibrant bass notes. *Joyful joined we are, eternal. . . .*

This was clearly a rebuke of Memor, a reminder of what the Universe of Essences demanded of all the Folk.

She felt grateful to escape with a mere reproach. She even roared and stomped and joined in with the chorus. The humming calls grew and she began to enjoy it all. Release.

But the memory of the Pit, then the Garden—these remained long after.

TWENTY-EIGHT

Cliff awoke to feel the ground trembling. Blinking, eyes gritty, he looked around at the small copse of ellipsoidal ferns they had sheltered under. Nothing visible in the shadows. No odd scuttlings.

But he could make out a faint, ominous rumble from below. There was no actual geology here, so it had to be machinery moving on the outer face of the Bowl. He got up and walked barefoot, feeling the vibration. It seemed louder in one direction and as he moved, the ground trembled a bit more. Birds rustled and chirruped in response to it.

Then it began to fade, though he kept walking, and by the time he reached a slab of fused rock, he could feel nothing. The source must have passed, so maybe it was a moving platform on the other side, an elevator or similar.

Then he noticed he was out of the trees. Feeling vulnerable alone, he glanced at the mercifully empty sky and quickly sought the canopy cover. *Like a terrified rodent*, he thought ruefully.

But he couldn't get back to sleep. He had been deep in a softly erotic dream of Beth. Their biggest problem was the unending day. They all had trouble sleeping because there was always something up and active, rustling through foliage, setting off their apprehensions. Now, though, the others were snuffling and snoring and he envied them. At least he could use the time to think, to plan.

He lay back and looked through the canopy at the dim

presence of the star. The jet was a scratch across the sky, flexing with whorls and tendrils. Near the star little flashes of brilliance lit the base. He was getting used to this sky, to this place—and that was dangerous.

So much here had a familiar feel—the sudden sizzle of lightning splintering a sky, a patter of rain, moaning breezes— but the tremor just now gave him an important warning. Here they all lived with a strangeness made all the more discomforting by its deceptive likeness to a world they all knew, and would never see again.

So they had to use everything, especially deception. They were torn between the need to stay out of sight and the drive to explore. They had disguised their craft, making it sand colored. From a distance, the sand ship made no impression, but close up it did move and attract the eye. The fixed wing aerial surveys they occasionally saw in the distance had missed them. Cliff hoped their pursuers were losing interest, because the fliers were getting spotty. Luckily, no intelligent aliens seemed to live in this vast desert.

But his gang of five was getting surly and hungry. They had learned to spot and shoot the large, savage lizards that lived in the rock outcroppings. The meat was nearly as leathery as the brown hide, but over a roaring fire of hardwood that did not give off smoke, it supplied protein they badly needed. No talk; they ate eagerly. Carbohydrates were harder to find, and water always an issue.

He had tried to forage for edibles, but the problem was tough. Not only was this an alien ecology, but it was also one that worked without night. What did that do to plant evolution? What kind of defenses did plants have here? On Earth, poisons were defenses against predators—tobacco was a particularly effective one in the tropics, where there was no winter to kill off the insects.

But in this Bowl, no winter saved plants or animals from constant predation. So Cliff expected to find plenty of poisons, deceptions, disguises. He had already seen plants that looked like rocks or even skeletons. The leathery lizards could bound sideways, because they had two forelegs and one hindleg designed to give them startling leaps. What hunted the lizards? He expected that the evolutionary arms race meant that a big predator was around, but he saw none. Maybe the lizards ruled this region, the top predators.

Humans were new here, so creatures mostly took no notice of them. But big birds smacked them in the head, or dived for their eyes, apparently mistaking them for some easier game—but what creature was that?

They had all lost weight. Howard, who was always recovering from some accident or injury, was now downright pallid and scrawny. They all leaned on Cliff to find more edible foods, and he had some successes—but was running out of ideas.

He heard some movement nearby and turned, automatically reaching for his laser. "You woke me up," Irma said, sitting down beside him.

"Spotty sleep is better than none," Cliff said, holding out a piece of the odd fruit they'd found. It looked like a puffer fish with spokes of purple hair, but tasted sweet and dark.

"Good call on this one. Better than mangoes, even."

"Sliced it, smelled it, tip of the tongue—that's all we've got to go by. I wish I had some testing gear to use on candidate food."

Irma nodded. "Those woodlands we first went into, the soil was more acidic and moist. The soil here, though, seems alkaline and dry."

"Like most Earthside deserts."

"Right, so we can use our intuition from what works there. Look there—"

Within a few meters were fernlike plants, thorny bushes, prickly globes dangling temptingly from enormous trees. "Okay."

They climbed partway up the crusty bark of the tree and brought down two of the large oval fruit. "Funny," Irma said. "They trail these coarse leafy strands, look more like tendrils."

He cut into one. "There's this fuzzy red tinge to the skin, like blister rust on Earth. But what's that mean here?"

He sniffed the rosy skin and found no stink of decay, but again, what would rot smell like here? So he sliced off a chunk, bit in—and found a gusher of warm soft sweet succulence burst in his mouth. "Maybe poison, sure, but soooo good . . ."

She grinned. "I'll wait, see if you topple over."

He waited to see if his stomach rejected it, but nothing happened. Irma said, "I think we should sleep in shifts. Keep two guards up, spell each other every four hours."

"Let's try it. But it's hard to sleep on the sand ship."

"We have to keep moving if we're going to learn much."

"Yeah, sure—but I'm wondering what we're doing, running around. We sure as hell aren't getting closer to understanding this place."

She patted him on his shoulder. "Don't get down about it. The guys take their cues from you."

"Huh? I'm not in charge."

She grinned. "Like it or not, you are."

"Who said?"

"Primate politics. Ever notice? They say their piece, argue, then look at you."

He sniffed. "No, I hadn't noticed. Aybe and Terry give me plenty of grief."

"They're scared. We're all scared. Sometimes that comes out as anger."

"Uh, glad you brought that up." The scent of her, after yesterday's swim in a pond, was messing with his concentration. He felt uncomfortable somehow, so resorted to safer generalities. "I see some old patterns emerging under the stress. The guys are summoning up their inner macho, like putting on armor. Not that I'm immune, either."

"You don't flex it like they do."

He chuckled ruefully. "Look, as a teenager I practiced cool smoking in the mirror—" She laughed and he blushed. "No, I really did. Cancer sticks! I also impressed dates by revving the engine at stoplights."

She laughed. "No! You had a combustion car?"

"An heirloom, the license cost a fortune. Once I tried on thirty sunglasses to get the right ominous look. With guys like Aybe and Terry, I talked tech and .45 automatics, usually while holding a beer bulb. And—" He glanced at her. "—I wore jeans so tight, I got sore balls and a red rash."

She cackled, slapped her knee. "That's so bad, it must be true."

"Sure, it was ridiculous then, it's ridiculous now—but Aybe and Terry are faking a calm they don't have."

She nodded. "Sometimes it's so thick, you could cut it with a knife. I see them eyeing us, hiding their fears. Good deduction, Cliff-o."

He turned to her. "We've gotten used to being scared, maybe. But I don't—"

Without warning, she reached over, hands on his shoulders, and kissed him. Held it, long and hard. Let go, sat back, looked at him levelly. "Had to say that."

Say what? he thought. "I, look, I'm—"

"Married, I know. So am I."

"I hope I didn't—"

"Give some sign? No, damn it." She took a deep breath and rapped out words in a rush. "We're on the run across a goddamn artifact we don't understand and could get caught any minute, or killed, maybe worse than killed—so, way I see it, the usual rules, they don't matter."

"I—"

"No real argument, Cliff. But you and I have got to keep

this little bridge party going and, and, I'm feeling *so* lonely, so like I'm on the edge, have got to—hell, I don't know what I'm saying."

He smiled. "I don't either, but I . . . liked it."

They just sat and stared at each other for a while, letting the moment brew.

She raised an eyebrow, gave him a twisted grin. "Y'know, what anybody thinks of us means, to me, less than zero."

"You make a good case." Cliff wondered what he was doing, mind boiling. But something strong in him knew he needed this.

"I never liked sex in daylight, though."

"I never was so picky."

. . .

Terry said, "We're getting nowhere."

Irma sniffed and poked at their small, popping fire. It burned old wood, which did not give off smoke. "We're alive, right? And I wouldn't have given us good odds on that last week."

Aybe sniffed, his wide mouth twisted skeptically. "Week? This damn place makes time meaningless."

Irma lifted her phone. "Standard time."

Techtypes all, they then ruminated on keeping a time standard here with their digital devices, which got updated aboard because *SunSeeker* had significant relativistic time effects versus Earth-normal time. Aybe cut this off as he leaned forward over the fire, where stick skewers turned and dark lizard meat sizzled. "This place was made to *erase* time, that's my point. What kind of thing makes a big thing that hasn't got seasons, change, variety?"

Cliff said mildly, "Something that likes life predictable."

Terry pounced on that. "Yes! Something really strange. Those big, feathered things we saw—they run this place. We ran away from them!"

"They were taking us prisoners," Howard said. His injuries made him wince as he adjusted his seating around the popping fire.

Terry said, "Maybe they just wanted to talk."

Irma said, "It didn't seem like an invitation."

"Hey," Terry said, "the thing about aliens is, they're *alien*. We may have misunderstood them."

Aybe shook his head. "That doesn't matter. We can't live out here forever. What's our agenda?"

Cliff sighed, but put his hand over his mouth so they didn't hear it. They all looked at him; Irma was right. He wished he were more certain, but said anyway, "Lie low. Work the sand sailer toward the mirror region. We're making good time. We could get there in maybe a month."

"Month means nothing here," Aybe said.

Irma said, "Hey, we need to keep time straight. Call it a million seconds, okay?"

They managed a low chuckle, the most they could muster as a group identity. Cliff watched their faces and seized the moment. "I'm hoping to find some access at the mirror zone. We saw that there were big constructions up there, close to the Knothole. Whoever runs this place probably hangs out there."

Terry furiously shook his head. "We need to talk to these aliens. Look at what they've built!"

Irma said, "So?"

Terry sat back, blinking. "Let's get close to one of their living zones. Stop hanging out here in the desert."

Howard said, "I agree."

Irma said, "I don't like going in under their terms. Maybe they think aliens like us should be eliminated—who knows?"

Aybe scowled and jutted out his chin. "We escaped, remember? They may not take that kindly."

Terry shook his head once more. "All I know is, we'll learn

more observing them near here, instead of trying to move millions of kilometers up to the Knothole."

Irma pressed, "How?"

Aybe pointed. "I climbed that big skeleton tree yesterday, got a look at a dark patch off that way. Green, must be a forest."

Terry said, "Better game, better concealment. Let's go there, see if we can find some natives. Watch them, learn."

Cliff watched them as this got tossed around. He had realized that Terry was the sort of guy he had known in university. He liked to sit around and drink and philosophize, and if he got drunk, he would tell you what you could expect in life for the sort of person you were. That met the legal standard for an asshole, Cliff figured. When the crew was getting shaped up—centuries ago in real time, yes—he had barely met Terry. But now he knew what type Terry was and was thankful that there was no alcohol here. With a few drinks in him, the man could do real damage in a small group like this. Maybe without the drinks, too.

So now Terry was far from what his skill set could deal with. Fleeing across a huge contraption nobody had ever imagined, Terry kept himself oriented, Cliff could see, by staying sharp of chin, assured, with eyebrows clenched behind aviator glasses. Sure of himself. Dangerous.

Assurance in the face of uncertainty was a good pose for a leader, sure. But not without plenty of thought to back it up.

"I say let's vote," Aybe said.

"Sure," Howard said, his only remark in a while. He kept picking at a nasty scratch he had scabbing over on his calf.

Cliff said, "All in favor of following Terry's idea."

Three hands: Aybe, Howard, and Terry. Cliff shrugged. "Okay, after breakfast we set sail."

Irma said wistfully, "I wish I was back on *SunSeeker*, not hiding and running."

They all nodded.

Irma had a point, Cliff realized a bit later, but there were compensations. Here they got to deal with the crux of the problem, understanding this place, not just watching it from the orbiting ship. Plus, no boredom. *An adventure is someone else risking their life far away.* . . .

And he had just dried off from a great swim in a warm desert pond. He felt great. He drank a cup of water, and snapped open one of the pods that held tangy little silky strands, like eating sweet cobwebs. The water was far better than *SunSeeker*'s recycled, bland water, and the air here had a fresh zest. Also, their chem tests showed it had no gutbuster microbes they could not nullify. Redwing certainly wasn't breathing anything so good.

It took two days to sail to the distant forest, over crusted sand that sang beneath them. The surface was glazed, and when they stopped he took small samples to study under his field microscope. The stuff was hard yet living—bacteria, lichens, and mosses mixed into sand. Maybe all these were waiting for the next rain to flourish. They learned the hard way that their sail ship had to skirt the darker patches, which were rough and once poked a hole in the bow. Sticking to the tan-colored zones gave them better speed. Somehow the place seemed ancient, even the occasional sand dune firm and polished. There were parabolic dunes, star dunes, straight dunes with radial crests. The emptier the land, Cliff realized, the more luminous and precise the names for its features.

They passed by a raised bluff, tan and barren, and suddenly saw a canyon open in the steep stone walls. "There's green in there," Irma pointed out.

Their sails flapped in the lee of the cliff when they lost the wind. Howard said, "Let's have a look, take a break."

All heads nodded; they were getting stiff, sitting in the craft and managing the ropes to steer.

They left Howard with the sailer, since he still had a

gimpy leg from a fall. Marching two kilometers up the dry canyon was hard, working against the drifts of dun-colored sand in a broad streambed. A soft breeze swept their sweat away.

The side channels looked ancient, and Cliff kept a wary eye on their shadows. Ruins of stone and twisted metal stuck out of the erosion plain. Terry tried to make sense of them, prying fragments from the soil, but most of it was rusted away. Breezes sighed around them as they came upon a larger wreck, a tumbled-down building of curiously long rock slivers, pale along their lengths and burnt at their edges. "Fire?" Aybe asked.

"Looks abandoned," Irma said, pulling a slab free of the rest. The whole stack of stone gave way, sliding down and tumbling so they had to lurch out of the way.

"What's that?" Aybe asked about a buried structure, and they spent fifteen minutes uncovering a hard metal carapace. The building's collapse had dented but not breached the boxy thing.

Aybe used up a lot of his laser charge cutting in. He used razor mode and the highest frequency, but the stuff was much tougher than any steel alloy. They levered the metal open to the music of wrenching screeches. Inside, wrapped in polycarbon, were fine metal grids and some mysterious black boxes with ports and plies in their sides.

"Hard to figure this out," Terry said, fingering the stuff, "but must be electrical."

"To do what?" Cliff asked. Not his area of techspeak.

Aybe spread the metal grids across a slab of the pale, hard stone. "Doesn't matter what it was for. Point is, what can it do for us?"

"Like what?"

Aybe grinned. He had been moody the last few days, but now a tech challenge animated him. "Amp up our antenna function. For our beamers."

"That'll be tough, getting an impedance match to a beamer."

"I like problems."

They found little else but buildings that had collapsed a long time ago. No obvious resources, no primitives among the ruins as in a bad movie; nothing.

The electrical stuff was too heavy to carry, except Aybe wanted the grids. Howard said, "Fine, so long as you carry them from here on out." On the move, everything was about mass.

As Cliff marched back to the sailer, he wondered how this huge desert zone had formed and whether the climate here needed vast, largely inert areas to function. There must be large-scale atmospheric movement of water, like the Hadley cells of Earth, but even with the occasional patterns of passing clouds, he could not figure out how things worked here. Earthly air moved in several circulating patterns, and the poles were the final place where matters got resolved. But on this Bowl, the only pole was the Knothole region. What did that do?

The Bowl and Earth both rotated, so both felt the Coriolis force—which brought all its complications, like hurricanes. But the sheer scale of the Bowl made him wonder if the same rules of thumb about weather could possibly apply. Matters of heating and atmosphere, not just the planet's rotation, set the scale lengths of Earth's circulations. Here, those scales were immensely larger, about a thousand times!

Then there were the oddities and intuitions that were wrong even on Earth, but might not be here. People thought whirlpools in baths circled differently in Earth's north and south hemispheres, but that was an illusion. It might be fun to see if that was true here, though.

All that seemed a long way off, slogging beneath the constant sun. They traded occasional comments, but it was a good idea to shut up and watch their surroundings. Except for the birds, who were conspicuously larger than Earthside ones, Cliff noticed that few animals advertised themselves. Caution seemed the universal policy.

So he mused as he helped with the steering, pulling ropes to adjust their sail, listening to the buzz as their bow rasped over the stiff sand. He watched his sweaty team and wondered how long they would hold up. Nobody in *SunSeeker*'s crew was given to big shows of emotion, shouting, brags, insults, tears and drama, big proclamations of love or hate, stomping out of meetings. No bipolars, no geniuses. Rather, they were members of the sober, hardheaded, but soft-spoken race. Educated to a fault, practical as a paper clip. Considered, deliberate, oatmeal steady, skeptical and sharp-eyed when they met new ideas, unflappable, but—and this was what cut down through the applicant list like a hot knife through ripe butter—with an appetite for adventure. An odd assortment of those realists nonetheless willing to dive down the funnel of time and come out centuries later in a strange new place, ready for the dangerous and eager for the grand. This made them short on hugs and compliments, quick with the narrowed eye, short on the soft warm armloads of comfort.

Their spirits rose as the forest grew from a distant line on the horizon to a dense stand of trees, even though their food and water were running out. They hid the sailship, ventured in with lasers drawn, and soon found a stream. Yellow big-finned fish lurked in the darker pools and Howard managed to catch five with a simple line and hook, no bait needed. A feast! And the water was as sweet as champagne.

A kilometer farther on, there were dense stands of fragrant bushes that, when they crawled into it, gave them something like a day/night ecology. They fell asleep immediately.

Over breakfast of more fish, Terry said, "Time to set up a base, drop some of our body gear. I'm tired of backpacking everything we've got."

Aybe nodded. "And reconn."

Cliff didn't like leaving anything behind, but they had a point. Even in the lower gravity, the straps cut into their shoulders by the end of a day's march.

They hid their heavier gear in a stand of angular, skeletal trees, marked it with subtle signs, and moved out, using their practiced methods. Aybe and Terry took point to left and right. Cliff and Howard brought up the rear to the sides, with Irma in the middle. No talking, hand signals only, stay out of clearings.

The foliage here was strange. Vines made convoluted turns, as if trying to find a way out of their thick mats. Small, unseen animals clattered and called in the canopy. Birds gave fluttery songs, not like Earthly chirps. Then they heard ahead a low, ominous hum and circled it. A dense clump of webbed brown plants teemed with brightly turning leaves that sounded like bees. Cliff could see no role for this in plant dynamics, unless—"Maybe they're windmills generating power," he whispered to Irma.

"For what?"

"Dunno."

They skirted the humming network, which was a hundred meters wide. He wondered if this artificial ecology used directly generated electrical power somehow, reactors and plants, and not just solar energy. The whole structure could be a giant electrical grid. Only a few meters away lay the high vacuum of space, and the understructure of metal could conduct electricity to distant points. For the usual question—*why?*—he had no answer.

"There's some odd noise that way," Terry said, pointing left. A clatter, some yips and snorts. They followed his lead.

After a few minutes Irma said, "Over there, a hill. Let's get up in those trees to survey."

They found a slight rise of a few meters and shimmied up

the zigzag trees at the top. Howard stopped halfway up and whispered, "The birds."

Cliff worked his way out on a limb that kept jabbing him with tiny spikes, the big tree's defense against some sort of predator. He got a view of a distant meadow where odd things hovered. Four aircars, holding a meter or two above the emerald green. Inside their open tops were two or three of the Bird Folk. The aircars moved in a circling path, and Cliff saw their prey—a large thing that dodged across the meadow, hemmed in by the aircars. It had three legs and danced away from the encircling hunters, its big hairy head jerking around, seeking an escape.

A lance arced out from one of the aircars and hit the big animal in the haunch. It yipped, a high insulted cry, and dashed away. A big Bird stood up in its aircar and threw another lance at it, missed. The aircars rushed around in some kind of pattern, weaving in and out as if this was a game, or some ritual. The animal yipped again and screamed when a lance caught it in the middle.

It collapsed, gasping so loud, Cliff could hear the plaintive cries. Another lance ended that. The thing slumped.

The Bird Folk landed and Cliff wondered at the vehicles' soundless grace. Were they magnetically suspended? That made sense if they carried powerful electromagnets in their thick undercarriage. The Bowl's conducting frame a few meters below the meadow would provide the surface that opposed the magnetic fields, allowing the aircars to ride on the magnetic pressure.

"That thing's a carnivore," Irma whispered. "Mostly bone and muscle. The birdies are hunting for *sport*."

She was right, Cliff saw. Nine of the Birds had formed a circle around the dead creature and did an odd dance, strutting in, whirling, dancing out with spindly arms raised, making quick leg movements. Then came a honking shout. They circled the beast, raised the lances they had pulled out of the carcass, and hooted again.

It looked primitive and yet understandable. Terry said, "They're like primordial hunters!"

Howard said, "They're not using impact weapons, like high-caliber guns. I saw some with long spears, arrows, a flung garrote."

Irma said, "Maybe low impact because they don't want to damage the underpinning of the Bowl? It's only a few meters down in spots."

They nodded and climbed down, moving away from the Bird Folk. Cliff realized that this immense world was a park, in a way. For the Bird Folk.

They spent hours working through the dense vegetation, returning to pick up their gear, then moving on to explore further. It was too risky to leave anything behind—except for the sailcraft, their escape route into the desert lands.

Cliff and Irma took note of the many life-forms they saw, including a long thing like an armadillo. It crawled without legs, using its sliding plates of armor to inch forward. "An armored snake," Irma said. Terry wanted to kill it for meat, but Cliff was unsure it would be edible. And he hated to kill creatures on spec, even when they were hungry.

They found enough of the nasty lizards lurking near streams and shot them. They were aggressive but stupid; it was simple to kill them. Aybe gathered dry wood to keep their smoke down. As they ate the greasy lizard meat over a low fire, they tossed around ideas about the Bird Folk, and what they had seen. Not reassuring, no.

They napped, got up with the usual aches from sleeping in the open, and after a breakfast of more lizard, moved on into denser woods. This was a search-and-understand mission, and Cliff moved carefully, not letting the uncertainties get to him.

A distant high noise came rolling through the tall trees as

they moved forward. A *skreee* came from their left and they cautiously moved that way, faces puzzled. Some bass rumblings, then more *skreee*. They saw a broad clear area and circled it, Terry gesturing to keep low.

A chattering alarm burst out in the branches high above them. Cliff felt his pulse rate rise as he duck-walked forward through low brush. The whole forest was alive with excitement and arcing above the din came the shattering calls he recognized as those of primates they had seen before. Monkeys, though larger and stranger. But the *skreee* sounds had structure, chopped notes floating on the underlying base line, like sung words. These were different primates, riffing up in the high canopy.

He peered through the ropy strands of a vine plant. Much movement. He brought up his binoculars and studied the moving figures.

The Bird Folk. On foot this time.

About two hundred meters away, moving right to left across a broad, rocky plain. They ran in long loping strides, eight of them, carrying instruments in their long arms. Their feathers rippled with flowing patterns of yellow and magenta. Their heads were tilted back, which pointed their long, broad noses forward, their two large eyes glittering. Knobbed legs articulated gracefully, eating up the ground between them and their prey.

Bunches of running figures were nearer to Cliff. Primates, running with their own loping grace. The primates were tall with long arms and even longer legs, running it seemed from a stand of zigzag trees several hundred meters to his right. Their angular heads jerked around, looking back at the birds, who were angling toward them from farther away. Cries spilled from the primates—harsh, barked shrieks. They ran faster and broke into groups of threes.

At first Cliff had thought the ragged, fleeing band were, somehow, humans. But these were primates nearly as tall as the Bird Folk, and had four arms. They ran in clumps of three, the one behind turning to fire something that looked like a crossbow at the Bird Folk. The shots were inaccurate and the Bird Folk dodged them anyway. The primate that fired then ran ahead while a companion in the group of three stopped, aimed, fired. The one in the middle was reloading.

Arrows flew everywhere. Primates and Birds shrieked and howled and chattered—a din.

An arrow hit one of the birds, but it simply lodged in the thick feathers. The Bird plucked it out and tossed it away. Then the primate ran on and the next one stopped to fire, a classic delaying tactic. This shot hit home. A Bird went down in a tangle of legs.

A long, hooting cry came from the Bird Folk. Angry rumbles came from the surging Birds. They sped up, long legs taking great bounds. They closed in on the primates and swept to both sides, a flanking pincer movement.

Something bright flashed from the huge running Birds, and a loud boom rolled across the open plain. Several fired at the same time, and primates burst into flame. Shrieks, bodies falling, limbs jerking.

Cliff smelled an acrid tinge and watched the remaining primates panic. They scattered, bunches breaking up. Some fired arrows but most fled.

The Birds ran them down. Some they did not shoot with the quick, darting beams, but instead ran up behind them and leaped high in the air, coming down on a primate in a crushing fall. Cliff could hear bones snap.

The last primate turned and howled at the Birds and they simply ran it down, trampling the body again and again.

The Birds danced on the bodies. Their mouths opened wide and they emitted sharp, harsh calls, like trilling fire alarms. With their stubby beaks they stabbed the primate bodies. Some danced on the dead. Spindly long arms shot toward the sky, jerking with joyous energy, and they circled, making a quick-footed dance, shrieking in a melodious chant.

Cliff backed away from the spectacle, shaken. He straightened up a bit and retreated, duck-walking backwards. Terry came alongside him and whispered, "My God."

"Yah. Yah." Cliff could barely absorb what they had seen.

The party came together, united in a single purpose— move fast, get away.

Cliff remembered thinking that this place was a park, in a way.

Certainly not for mere primates.

TWENTY-NINE

Redwing dipped into Meal 47, a pomegranate-rich sauce and artificial meat mix with long grain brown rice, green vegetables on the side. It tasted the same as always, of course—pungent, hearty. And since he'd had it more times than he could count, boring. Still, its savory tang was somewhat enjoyable because it appealed to the dimmed senses he had developed in the austere, rumbling caves of *SunSeeker.* And every meal reminded him of their dwindling supplies.

Any semblance of a sensory life was heartening in the ceramic claustrophobia here. At least when the ship was driving through interstellar plasma, noise-canceling headphones could subtract most of the sound. Not here, now, when *Sun-Seeker* was laboring hard, its Reynolds bosonic drive coughing in electromagnetic stutters. Some crew said they just forgot about the engines' steady din, but Redwing could not—though he hid this, of course. He had to seem calm, steady, oblivious of their desperate uncertainties.

Getting contact with the Beth group had been their sole breakthrough. Before that, Redwing found himself commanding a ship that had constant navigation problems and no contact with the ground. He had nearly written off the whole landing party.

Redwing raised an eyebrow at Ayaan Ali, who came and sat at the mess table, waiting respectfully. Ayaan was an Arab woman who dressed in deck uniform like everyone else, but occasionally at dinner wore a stylish veil and glinting emerald earrings. "Ah, good," Redwing said formally. "Report?"

"We've got the high-gain antennas ganged together."

"How's Beth's signal?"

"Strong and—"

"Can you get me visual?"

"Hell, Cap'n, we're working with a damn field phone signal here!"

"Answering my question comes first, then the complaining."

Ayaan's face stiffened and there was a three-beat silence. Then Ayaan said slowly, "No, sir, don't really know yet about visuals. Doubt we have the bandwidth."

"It's a bandwidth problem, or a signal to noise and coherence mapping?"

"At this stage, that's rather a moot point."

"Ah." He looked at the slabs of illos she showed him in a long silence. "Good, then. No complaint?"

Ayaan blinked and her mouth firmed up. "No, sir, and no excuses."

"Excellent." Redwing permitted himself a slight smile.

Ayaan laid out a diagram on his slate, pointing to the array she had mounted outside, jury-rigged from interior structural beams. "As soon as we work the kinks out of ganging the dishes, and optimize Beth's incoming, we'll have a coherent, linked system."

"Which means you can go after Cliff?"

"Yes, but remember, we don't even know what gear they have."

"Field phones, too, as I recall."

"But have they hung on to them? I'm getting no pings back at all."

Redwing understood the tech enough to know that grouping all their microwave range antennas together outside was a hell of a tough problem. Software and hardware together had to gang the antennas so they were coherent in phase, like making them into one big eardrum. Doing that on a constantly moving platform swooping above the Bowl, and focusing them on spots in the moving landscape—he couldn't even begin to imagine the problems. "You're doing a great job, Ayaan. I know the problems. Just keep trying for a ping."

Ayaan blinked rapidly at the notoriously rare Redwing praise. "Yes, sir."

Redwing nodded and strode with visible energy—more performance for the crew—the five meters to the bridge viewscreen. The whole hemisphere had been converted into a complex display that could flit from real images to overlay dynamics charts. Look too long at them, flip back and forth, and you had to sit down and let it seep in. He had ordered that their interior centrifugal grav be Bowl normal, 0.8 g. They would all be ready to go down and help, if that was necessary. But he wasn't going to put another boot on the ground until he knew more.

He felt a sudden surge, twist, and correction strum through the deck and walked over to the operations chair.

"How's the induction coil?" Redwing asked the pilot, a short man named Jampudvipa, always shortened to Jam.

"Sputtering. I got it back right, using the three-zone thrusters. We're getting barely enough plasma to keep the system from going into parasitic oscillations."

"Damn. Can we make the delta?"

Jam wrenched his face around and shrugged. "Perhaps."

The Bowl image spread across most of the glowing hemisphere. It always made him stop and stare.

The landscape unfolded at speeds hallucinatingly fast, because they were moving at about ten kilometers a second over it, orbital speed. So much wealth: forests brimming with green promise, clouds towering a hundred kilometers high over shallow seas, spare bare deserts of golden sand, crawling muddy rivers snaking through valleys rimmed by low hills. Hurricanes roaring and churning across continents larger than Earth itself. An immense, impossible geography. A contraption devoutly to be wished, yes. But, by whom? By . . . what?

He watched the comm bands. Beth's signal was down to zero, but her party had gotten through earlier for a few minutes. To keep Beth within range, Redwing and Jam had to maneuver the ship constantly, spelling the watch with Clare Conway, the willowy blond copilot. But the solar wind here was a puny wisp, barely enough to keep the induction chambers from shutting down. Space was everywhere a very good vacuum, but the red star's wind was even thinner than Sol's. Plasma blew off stars, but this smaller sun's somehow got swept up into the jet. Magnetic focusing, apparently, though how it was done seemed a mystery to the engineers. Indeed, Redwing thought, this whole weird place was an implied slap in the face to human endeavors. Even *SunSeeker* was a mere bauble compared with it. A huge bowl whirling around so fast, it covered a perimeter about the size of Earth's orbit, every nine days.

Jam's job in all this was to keep them close enough to the Bowl's atmosphere to let Beth's weak phone signal get through to them. He steered them so close, the land seemed like a flat plane below them, an infinite wall of blue green dotted with clouds hundreds of kilometers high, of seas bigger than any planet. All of it hung under the constant glare of star and jet, which cast different glows across the deep atmosphere, in long blades of shadow and radiance.

Redwing could see the strain in Jam's face, but the man would never mention it, of course. "How long can we keep doing this waltz?"

"A day, perhaps two."

"Then what?"

"We must use the reaction motors."

"We can't afford to burn real fuel."

"I know." Jam's watery eyes studied Redwing's face. "But I cannot alter the laws of mechanics."

"To me, Jam, that means something between diddly and squat. Time to do some hard thinking, or we're going to lose touch with our people."

Redwing had almost said *my people*, but thought better of it. Too possessive, even for a captain. He had to seem sober, focused, yet somehow above the fray, thinking about the larger prospects.

To give Jam some time, he walked the length of the full deck, eyeing the display boards for signs of trouble. They had few crew up, to conserve on supplies, but heads looked up as he passed, his face observing yet detached.

He passed by the Bio Preserve and on impulse cycled through the lock. A strong stink of dank animal sweat wrinkled his nose. One of the pigs had gotten out of its enclosure. It ran up to him, squealing, sniffing, and farted. This turned out to be an overture. It crapped on the deck, turned, and dashed away.

Damned if he would clean it up. He called out to Condit, the field biologist, and pointed to the mess when the woman appeared. She shrugged. "Sorry, Cap'n. It got around me while I was recharging their food."

"What do they eat?"

"Anything. Table scraps, human dander from the air filters. Even their own dung if you let them."

"Maybe you should. Serve 'em right."

She nodded, taking him seriously. "It might help in the nutrient recycling, yes. We trap eighty percent of nitrogen value in our urine, but getting much out of solid waste is hard. Maybe we should feed our wastes to the pigs."

Something in Redwing liked that idea. *Let them eat shit! Marie Antoinette had it right.* But he kept his face blank and said, "Look into it."

Back in the central corridor, he sucked in the dry, stale

ship air with relief. He had to carefully avoid letting his sense of humor off its leash.

He hoped nobody here had access to records of his older self. Decades before *SunSeeker* was building, he had scorned the whole idea of interstellar arc-ships, and written a tongue-in-cheek send-up of the program. He proposed that they simply send out robot ships with a single message that read, *Make ten exact copies of this plaque with your name at the bottom of the list and send them to ten intelligent races of your acquaintance. At the end of four billion years, your name will reach the top of the list and you will rule the galaxy.*

A joke, quickly forgotten. The Review Board that passed on starship command hadn't seemed to turn it up, anyway. Or they overlooked it. But now he couldn't be that jokester.

As Redwing returned, Jam looked up. "Cap'n, I think we could—" He paused, as if this might be too much of a leap. "We could, ah, perhaps gather some reserve plasma by, by approaching the jet again."

"Too dangerous. We nearly lost it all, flying up that thing."

"We can come close to it, without entering the turbulent heart."

Redwing smiled. *Turbulent heart* wasn't a bad description of how he felt. "Scoop up plasma, store it?"

"I believe we can, using the capture cross section of the magscoop, when we extend it again."

"That'll take us away from the Bowl, though. A big delta-V."

"We can make it up, I calculate, with the reserve plasma gathered by an approach."

Jam's steady eyes said, *Your call.*

"We'll lose touch with Beth, right? No hope of reaching Cliff's party with Ayaan's jury-rigged antenna, either."

Jam nodded. "Surely true, yes. But we can make a strong boost when we arc down along the Bowl, and return within perhaps ten days."

"Plan it out," Redwing said slowly. "I want to give Ayaan a crack at reaching Cliff, then we'll see."

"Yes, sir."

Redwing paced again, wishing he had more options. Regret that he had not gone down in the landing party surfaced again—a gnawing black dog, but he submerged it. His judgment had been right, even if it did mean he spent his time bottled up here.

In some of the preflight training, to help them deal with the media, he had attended a showing of older ideas about interstellar travel. It was both funny and appalling. One of the earliest, from the Age of Appetite, had featured a dashing starship captain who always went down to planetary surfaces to investigate. Nobody questioned the practice! Of course, they had lots of other wish fulfillment trash ideas—faster-than-light travel (and this was after Einstein!), aliens who spoke English of course, teleportation for quick jaunts wherever they wanted. Nobody explained why that didn't yield an economy with infinite resources. After all, the transporter could just as easily make extra food or devices or money; anything at all, even people.

Yet those Age of Appetite people had the dream, too. They just didn't think much about how it would take hardship and death in the teeth of the unknown.

He made himself smile and say encouraging things as he paced the deck, and kept his musings to himself, as always.

THIRTY

They were rattled. Cliff could see it in their faces.

"I wonder," Irma said as they ate cold meat beside their sailcraft, "if the Birds planned to hunt us, back when we came through the lock?"

Aybe snorted. "Of course not! They were treating us as equals—"

"—and they tried to capture us," Terry finished for him.

"We didn't give them much chance to negotiate," Aybe insisted.

"They grabbed Beth's party," Irma said. "And look at what they did to those odd primates. They were tool users, too!"

Howard said mildly, "We can't gamble that they'll treat us differently."

"I agree," Cliff said. "Focus on what we do next."

Terry said, "I still think we should see what their society looks like, but at a distance maybe, see—"

"Too dangerous," Cliff said.

Howard nodded. "But sailing along in the desert zone, that's dangerous, too—and doesn't teach us much."

They all agreed. Terry said, "I'm getting tired of sitting in that rig, boosting it over outcroppings when we hit a snag, searching for water. And the dust storms! We've got to get some better transport, or we'll be hunted down."

More agreement. Cliff began to see an upside to the horrifying kills they had witnessed. Fear concentrated attention.

"Let's hunt up meat, grab some sleep, move away in the morning."

Howard and Terry brightened. They actually enjoyed hunting the nasty lizards, so they set out toward the nearest dry area. The black and brown things usually lived under cairns of rock they had shouldered into place. The trick was to catch them outside, and Terry had shown a talent for luring the quick-footed, hissing beasts with the old game meat left over from previous kills. They didn't seem to mind eating their own kind. "Maybe they're alien lawyers," Irma had said, and got a laugh.

Aybe fished out the mesh he had found before, unfolded it, and began tinkering with it, using his tool kit. Irma went looking for likely edible plants, but as their discipline demanded, always stayed within earshot. Cliff tried to relax. He had not been sleeping well. This ever-warm, sunlit prospect was as good as he was going to get, the new norm in his life—so he dozed.

Only to be awakened by a shout from Aybe.

"Uh, whazzit?" Cliff said, coming out of his sleep. He had been dreaming of Beth and didn't want to leave the warm comfort of the illusion.

"I got it!" Aybe had arrayed the mesh in a tree for support. His beamer was patched into it and he excitedly waved the phone at Cliff. "I got *SunSeeker*'s carrier indices."

Cliff snapped awake. "What? You can talk to them?"

"Damn low power, audio might not work—but I'll send them a text message."

Cliff watched and Aybe's face danced. "They answer! It's Redwing."

Aybe stared at the phone and called, "Sending a file!"

Long minutes dragged by while Cliff and Aybe stared at the phone display screen. Finally it chimed and a picture appeared—a big purple globe. A green upright finger symbol stood at the bottom right of the screen. "I've seen that thing,"

Aybe said. "The finger, green—maybe that means it's okay to eat?"

"Hit the next page," Cliff said.

A dozen pages confirmed several plants they had eaten. Cliff said, "How'd Redwing get this?"

"Must be from Beth's group," Aybe said, "relayed through *SunSeeker.*"

"Just what we need," Cliff said. "I saw one of those. That other one, too. Wait—I got it. This is a menu!" The next pages gave plant and animal pictures with two red fingers crossed, clearly warnings. "And an anti-menu. The red ones are dangerous to eat. The blue, okay." He looked up, grinning madly. "Boy, that Lau Pin is sharp."

Looking through the menu, Cliff thought about the colors of edible food here. Evolution geared animals and people alike to like the colors of things that were good or benign—blue for skies and clear water, white for snow. People disliked browns and dark colors linked to feces and rotten food, and reds that might mean spices or poisons. Plants had evolved those as warding-off signals. He hoped Beth hadn't taken risks to discover all the menu's contents. Then—

"Wait," he said to Aybe. "I'll bet they got that data straight from the aliens."

"So they're still in captivity. Um."

"Maybe. The important thing is, we're back in contact."

"Sort of." He sighed. "I lost *SunSeeker*'s signal again."

"They're moving, in orbit. Not easy to stay within range, even with these narrowband phones."

"Good thing they were designed to work at long range." Aybe chuckled ruefully. "Nobody thought they'd have to work over interplanetary distance, though."

Hearing from Beth brought up a subject he hadn't wanted to confront: that one quick moment of passion with Irma.

Sadly he remembered an old joke: *A conscience is what hurts when all your other parts feel so good.*

• • •

By the time Irma returned, Aybe could tell her which of the plants she had gathered she could toss and which to keep. Howard and Terry brought in an odd-looking two-legged thing like a badger, which was edible. They skinned and roasted it and felt joyous.

Then they sailed away into the desert, to get space between them and the magcar Birds. Half an hour of skimming slowly over the fine-grained sand got them into a region of rocky ridges. None they couldn't avoid, but it slowed them considerably. Howard was scanning the horizon for a better route when he called, "Something big coming."

It was a dot in the distance that steadily swelled. "We're more exposed out here," Aybe said. "If that's—"

"A magcar," Irma said. She had binocs and counted out, "Two, no, three Birds in it."

"No point in trying to run," Terry said. "Those are fast."

"But do we fight?" Howard asked.

Irma said slowly, "We don't know for sure they're hostile."

Aybe said slowly, "Angling for a mangling, we are."

Cliff silently cursed himself for not thinking how exposed they would be. "We can't run or hide, so let's do a reverse. Wave, hail them if they get close."

They all looked at him as if he were crazy. "Keep your weapons concealed. If things turn sour, we shoot. But first I'd like to get up into that magcar."

Howard said, "It'll all be in the timing. If we have to shoot, I'll take the one on the right. Terry, you get the left one. Irma, the third, wherever it'll be."

Irma followed the growing dot with her binocs and called, "Still coming, going left—ah!—they just turned toward us. We're spotted."

"Okay, now we look as though we want to be found," Cliff said.

"And keep our lasers out of sight," Howard added.

They spread out around the sailer as the dot grew rapidly. They started whooping and waving arms, dancing around. The magcar slowed, lowered until it was two meters off the ground. Three heads bobbed in the passenger area, and they still reminded Cliff of ostriches. As the magcar neared with a thin whining sound, he could see they wore harnesses that held odd-shaped tools. One was piloting, and all wore helmets.

The car stopped above the sailcraft, and he could hear a steady thrumming from it. He wondered how magnetic pressure could support such a mass so far from the conducting surface, which had to be meters below the soil. The Birds spoke to one another in high, chittering voices. Their heads jerked around, feathers danced in complex patterns. *Is that part of their speech?* The magcar rose to three meters.

This seemed ominous to Cliff. He backed away from the car and said to Irma, "If they produce weapons, we'd better shoot first."

"Yes," she said, "you call it."

He called to the others, "If I say 'start,' then shoot them."

Terry said, "I don't think that's necessary—"

"Let's *show* them we're peaceful," Howard said, spreading his arms with hands held open.

Seconds crawled by. Cliff's hand poised, tense, ready to go for his laser.

Two of the Birds stood up, and the magcar shifted a bit. It tracked a bit to the left, so the humans were bunched on one side now.

"Let's try harder," Aybe said, and called up to them, "We *are* peaceful." He spread his hands.

Terry echoed him, showing bare hands. "Speak mildly," he said. "Let them know—"

A net flew out of the magcar so fast, Cliff could not tell how it was flung. Quickly it wrapped across both Terry and

Aybe—*sssssssp.* Somehow the net's perimeter slithered around them and jerked hard—*ssssip-klick*—closing them in.

There was a snaky, thick ropy line at its peak, leading back into the magcar. It snapped taut. The net swept them off their feet. The line began hoisting them up.

Cliff was so shocked, it took him several seconds to realize that he was supposed to be in charge. "I— *Start!*"

He looked up. Three laser shots hit the Birds. One was hit in the head and toppled back. The other two shrieked and reached for something in their harnesses. Four shots threw them back and down, out of sight.

Cliff had fired one shot—and missed. He stuffed his laser away and sprang at the net. He snagged hands in the webbing and went up it fast. His boots hit Terry, who cried "Ow!" Cliff surged using Terry's back. He grabbed the line and hauled himself up. The Birds were milling around on the magcar floor, shrieking.

Over the lip of the magcar, tumbling, he fell on a Bird body. Feathers made it soft; then he struck the hard body beneath. He struggled up, breathing in the thick, sultry smell of the aliens.

The bodies were bleeding red. Two didn't move. One was twitching, but its eyes were closed. As he stood, he slipped on the blood, recovered, shook his head in the adrenaline haze— and looked down at a surprisingly simple control board.

Terry and Aybe were shouting, but he ignored them as he studied the board. To the right was what seemed to be a simple lever and release. Everything else looked like press plates and displays. The lever, then.

He tried it, and the line started to draw up into a receiver with a rasping noise. Cliff reversed the lever, and the line played out. He tried the release, thumbed it hard looking over the side, and the net dumped the men.

"Ow!" Terry hit the ground with Aybe on top of him.

"Wow," Aybe said, standing up. They all gaped at one another, amazed at what they had done.

Irma said, "That was so fast. . . ."

"Good shooting!" Terry said.

Cliff called down, "Let's grab this. Shinny up here, bring all our gear."

Terry said, "Think it's safe?"

Cliff considered for several seconds. "I can't tell if they sent any alarm. Seems unlikely, though."

Aybe said, "I never thought we could—it was so fast!"

Irma said, "That magcar is better than this damn sailer. Let's go."

Terry started, "I wonder—"

"Think later," Cliff said. "Act now."

They all looked up at him from below, faces scared and joyous at the same time. Seconds passed. Then, as if some unspoken agreement had been reached, they scattered to their tasks.

Howard came climbing up, and the two of them inspected the bodies. Their lasers had punched holes in vital organs, bringing shock, and then the aliens had bled out. Together they tried to detect signs of life. No pulse, and certainly there would have to be a heart. No reactions, no breathing, eyes blank and staring.

"Turd-ugly, aren't they?" Terry said, and kicked a body. "Solid, too."

There were many facets of these aliens Cliff wanted to explore, but there wasn't time. They got the harnesses off the bulky bodies before he and Howard pitched two Birds overboard. Cliff kept the one less damaged. Aybe started to argue with him and then shrugged.

By this time the rest were passing up gear. Howard said, "If they did set off some alarm, we'd better get away."

Everybody agreed, and voted Aybe into the pilot's chair,

since he had flying experience. The chair was too big for humans, but the seat wrapped anyone who sat in it with a gauzy strap restrainer, and Aybe managed to settle into it. He set to work systematically learning the control panel.

Cliff climbed down to check the bodies he had tossed out. Autopsies are best done fresh, and he learned a good deal in half an hour of cutting. Aybe shouted, "Hey, look!" and made the magcar perform some maneuvers. To their applause he announced in a stentorian voice, "Flight is leaving, folks."

They all laughed hard, letting the tensions out.

He helped Irma carry some gear from the sailer. She whispered, "Great attack! I knew you could do it."

"Well, that makes one of us."

THIRTY-ONE

The hell of it was, Redwing thought, that SunSeeker's *magscoop* seemed to act better as a brake than as an accelerator.

The deck veered and flexed under his feet, seams groaned, a low rumble echoed. The magscoop expanded, breathing like a lung, and *SunSeeker* slowed. Contract, and the ship accelerated.

Redwing hated the rumbles and surges, maybe because they echoed his own anxieties. To maintain flight control and keep their magnetic fields up and running, *SunSeeker* had to feed its engines with plasma. But the plasma density here was low and the ship had to keep flexing its magnetic screens to stay in burn equilibrium. So the whole ship followed a troubled orbit, skimming along above the Bowl and trying to pick up weak signals from their teams.

"Jam, can't we smooth this out?" he asked.

The slender man stared intently at the control boards and just shook his head. "I am trying, sir. Ayaan's array is slewing as we change velocity."

Ayaan herself called from a nearby control pod, "I can't get coherence! My antennas cannot focus."

Redwing felt frustrated, out of his depth technically. A ramscoop of *SunSeeker* class was an intricate self-regulating system, and no one could master even a fraction of its labyrinthian technology. It was not so much a ship as a self-tech entity, with artificial intelligences embedded in every subsystem. It behaved less as a ship than as an electromagnetically structured metallic can run by a dispersed mind, itself electromagnetic.

Beside it, an ancient automobile was an idiot savant, working because analog feedbacks and what the techs called "self-regulating networks" operated well enough, arrived at by incessant trials and some considerable deaths. Autos arose through a form of driven evolution. *SunSeeker* came from a two-century-long evolution of directed intelligences, none individually of great capability. Indeed, the subminds embedded in *SunSeeker* were no better than ordinary human intelligence, and some much lesser. But the sum of these subminds, as with whole human cultures, was greater than linear. Modern human civilization was surely of lesser station than its greatest intelligences, such as Gödel and Heinschlicht. So was *SunSeeker* an anthology of self-critical and disciplined minds. Each mind lived its life with a reward system and constraints, dwelling in a community of diverse talents. All that properly propelled *SunSeeker* into a social intelligence, one that ran beyond what the ship could entirely comprehend. In this it was much like human societies. While it nominally served Earthly society, the ship also had evolved over the centuries of its flight into its own, original society. Smart networks had to.

It could innovate, too.

"Cap'n! Our subsystems found a way to amp the coherence," Ayaan called out. "I've never seen it do that before."

Redwing walked behind her acceleration couch and watched the screens display a dazzling graphic. It showed linked armories of smart systems, adjusting in milliseconds to the fits and snarls of *SunSeeker*'s trajectory. The hundreds of elements in Ayaan's array glided to compensate, like a retina that caressed the light falling on it.

The signal grid shifted, its colors cohering. Suddenly, a strong pulse came through. "It's from Aybe's phone," Ayaan said, excited.

"Send Beth's bio data as soon as you can."

"Got it inserted already, right behind the carrier signature," Ayaan said crisply.

"What's their situation?"

"Here's their text."

GOT FREE OF ALIENS.

MAKING OUR WAY ACROSS THICKLY WOODED

TERRAIN. HEADED OUT OF DESERT ZONE.

"That's it?"

"I had to synthesize their signal three times to get even that."

"Can't they send up some detail?"

"I'll ask them to use store and transmit. That lets them set the phone so when it acquires us, it sends a squirt at optimal rates."

"No audio?"

"Too noisy for that. I squeezed this out of repeated text messages. Lucky it got through, considering."

"Considering what?"

"How weak their signal is, how fast we're moving, the whole problem of using a dispersed antenna—"

"I get it," Redwing said. "Outstanding work, Lieutenant."

She smiled and added, "I'll send what text I get to your address."

"I wish we had more people to analyze this," Redwing said suddenly, feeling his isolation.

Again, Ayaan smiled kindly. "Our experts are on the ground, gathering information."

He nodded, then lifted his head a bit. He shouldn't let the crew see his uncertainty. An old rule: If people can see up your nostrils, you're keeping your chin at the appropriate alpha angle.

"Has Aybe got the food stuff?"

"Just did. Sent back an acknowledgment—whoops, there goes the connection. Damn."

Redwing paced and turned back to her. "Y'know, just before they went down, Cliff was afraid they wouldn't be able to digest any of the food down there. Kind of funny. Now we're sending him menus."

Ayaan chuckled. "It's a major discovery, I should think."

"Really? Still seems like common sense to me. Food is food."

"Most biochemists think it was a historical accident that all our sugars are right-handed, while our amino acids are left-handed. It could easily have been the other way round."

Redwing blinked. He kept forgetting that crew were multiskilled, so the loss of one specialist couldn't crimp them a lot.

"Well, turns out otherwise," he said. "Beth's team said they had some dysentery at first, but some of their med supplies put them right. Prob'ly Cliff's did, too."

"Beth's text messages said she got most of her lore from the aliens."

Redwing nodded once more. "They knew the poisons, and maybe those are pretty near universal? Interesting idea."

Ayaan was observing him closely, he noted. "Sir, I understood Cliff's point, and indeed, I agreed with it. Particularly his suggestion that they do thorough sampling of the alien air, to see if it would be dangerous to us."

"Which they did. And it wasn't."

"Beth reported some flulike symptoms, dysentery, too— but, yes, nothing fatal."

"They caught a break, maybe."

She shook her head. "What interests me is that these ideas of Cliff's, and mine, they were quite plausible. Yet you ignored them."

"Not exactly. I said be careful but keep going. We had to go down there, had to take our chances."

"Yes, and that is what I find admirable. You made the decision, despite our worries."

He wondered briefly if she was just sucking up to him. But no—she wasn't that kind of woman, a brownnose climber. "That's my job."

She beamed. "And I am glad it is not mine."

"You're going to have to make decisions, too, as this whole thing plays out. Here's a tip: The biggest mistake is being too afraid of making one."

They both laughed together and it felt good.

· · ·

That evening he lay in his bunk thinking about the day and what Ayaan had said.

All the media back Earthside had played the whole ocean/space analogy to the hilt, making Redwing's job sound like that of Captain Cook or Magellan. But those sailors had plenty of experience, had worked their way up the naval ladder by sailing to nearby ports, learning command, getting navigation right, and gradually making longer voyages. The first generation starship commanders had to make a huge leap, from piloting craft around the solar system, then the Kuiper belt and fringes of the Oort cloud, then to interstellar distances. That was a giant jump of 100,000—like sailing around the world after a trial jaunt of about three football fields.

He had piloted a ramscoop on one of the first runs into the Oort cloud, and done well. But in all the trials, *SunSeeker* hadn't topped a tenth of light speed more than once, and they had run at that for only a week. Five ships had gone out before *SunSeeker*. In the first decade, none reported ramscoop troubles like theirs. That didn't mean much now, though. Communications from Earth had stopped more than a century back, for reasons unexplained. Silence says nothing.

They were sailing uncharted waters here, Redwing thought, to use a nautical phrase. Magellan, he now recalled, had gone ashore and gotten tangled up in conflicts in the Philippine Islands, and died in a battle he chose to start. He had been convinced that the angel of Virgin Mary was on his side, so he couldn't lose, even though he was outnumbered by a thousand to thirty. Later generations named a small galaxy after him, but he had made plenty of dumb decisions, especially that fatal one, out of emotion.

So maybe analogies could be useful, after all.

PART VI

Action speaks louder than words
but not nearly as often.

—MARK TWAIN

THIRTY-TWO

Even Tananareve was keeping up, moving steadily with grim, sweaty determination, but Mayra wasn't. She hadn't been making good time since their last sleep. Her forehead wrinkled with grave, deep lines and her lips moved in an interior dialogue. Beth could feel what it was doing to her, the loss of her husband eating into her morale.

That was how she had to think of it, Beth realized. Morale. Keep the unit together and deal with what happened. Leadership, they had called it in crew training. Every crew member had to be able to assume leadership if the circumstances demanded it. Which meant if the actual leader got killed or disabled or broke down in the face of things nobody had imagined before. Leadership.

She slowed her own pace, then watched as Lau Pin burrowed into the thick, leafy undergrowth and was gone in seconds.

Beth bit her lip. She would not yell after him. They were fugitives, best to stay quiet. She followed the torn foliage, thinking how easily a Serf-One tracker could do the same, or just follow his nose. The smell of smashed vegetation was rank.

But Mayra wailed and threw herself down among the springy leaves.

Beth glanced after Lau Pin, then touched her shoulder. "Mayra—"

"He's *dead*, and what's it for? We're just *running*. We're all dying of bone loss anyway in this low g!" She spat the words out, pressure released.

"Oh, Mayra, I'm so sorry." Best to just let this run for the moment, get the words out and be done with it. The emotion was the point here, not the health issue. There was plenty of experience in low gravs, and this region seemed to be about 0.3 g. Maybe not too bad—if they didn't spend months in it.

"And, and—where are we *going* that it was worth so much?"

Beth said softly, "We had to get out. We all agreed. He was a fine man, and he dealt with that spidow brilliantly. Bravely." Beth patted her arm, feeling useless in the face of such sorrow.

Mayra nodded, tears running down her face unnoticed. "He was just so, so—"

"I know." That was all there was to say, really. Sympathy seemed useless, but it was essential all the same. If the bereaved felt isolated, they got even worse. "I'm so sorry."

In a flash, she recalled her own feelings, looking at Abduss. A thick smell rose up from the body like fumes, stinging the nose. The spidow had flattened Abduss, and the bladder and bowels had let go. Already blood had crusted into reddish brown rivers and the face was squashed beyond even parody of the man who had once enjoyed sharp, symmetric features.

She had worked up spit and swallowed, taking deep breaths, and managed not to vomit. Then she walked away, expelling her lungs and getting rid of the dregs of the smell. Every encounter with death stayed with her, but this one would go to the head of the line.

Even the memory made Beth wonder if Cliff had survived in this strange place. She made herself stop thinking about it and sat beside Mayra, putting an arm around the woman who was sobbing softly.

Fred spoke, slow and even. "So am I, Mayra." A pause.

His head jerked toward the horizon. "Either way we decide to go, we should stick to the ridge."

This startled Beth; Fred could go for a day without talking. The other women blinked, glanced at one another, and decided to let the moment move on. They tended to look around when Fred spoke. He did it so seldom, so gravely.

Lau Pin was back in time to catch it. "Fred? We can't. It'll make us conspicuous."

"Not *on* the ridge," Fred said witheringly. "Keep it in reach. It orients us. Look—" His hands sketched a tented line. "When they brought us here, do you remember passing that line of bubble buildings? Then the ridge just went on, dead straight for thirty or forty klicks, under the wall and into the Garden. Under the dirt and rock, it's a, a structural member, don't you see it? How shallow the dirt is? If you're building here, you anchor the important stuff to the load-bearing . . ." He trailed off, hands waving.

Beth was nodding, hoping this would move them away from Mayra's grief. There was no solution for that but time. "Along the ridge, right. Stay off to one side and don't go near the spidows. Keep close watch, and we can see the spidow corridors."

Fred nodded, too, so she went on. "We already know some of what we can eat. Cook it with the guns so they can't follow the smoke. There's no dry wood here, so it'll smoke for sure. Folks, we need to think about not getting caught. No more ripping through undergrowth. We move along the tops of the trees. Tricky, but we can do it."

Lau Pin frowned. "Dangerous, and that'll slow us down."

"Safer, though," Mayra said, coming out of her mood. "How much spidow rope have we got? Lau Pin—?"

"I took Abduss's share of the rope," Lau Pin said, pointing to the loops of it around his waist. Beth realized that the way to keep Mayra involved was to present decisions to be made. Draw her into the group.

Tananareve said adamantly, "I think Beth's right. And it's only for a short distance. So, which way, Fred?"

Lau Pin said, "That was a spaceport, that line of bubbles. I never saw them clearly, I was too dizzy. But, but it has to be a spaceport, doesn't it? And warehouses and so forth."

"Could be," Mayra said, blinking some more and visibly bracing herself, getting back into emotional stability. "But that's just where they'll look for us."

"Yeah. Yeah," said Fred. "But if we follow the ridge the other way, we'll find something important."

Tananareve asked, "Like what?"

"Say, something that wants a solid anchor."

"Okay. Which way is the ridge?"

They looked at one another. Beth took a big breath, thinking, and said, "We need to climb."

• • •

From the top of a braid tree the ridge was obvious, a couple of kilometers away. They were on its long, gentle flank. Moving along in the treetops was more like swimming than climbing. The low grav helped a lot, giving their movements a slow-motion grace as they swung among the long, rubbery limbs of the tall trees.

Beth could see immense distances: the landscape was concave, unlike Earth's. Distant things rose up and got noticed. The ridge was conspicuous, a bony scrabble of boulders at the crest, four or five kilometers away. Beyond was a frenetic sky, the bright pink sun, and the glaring, restless white flare. The Jet cooled into rolling reds and strands of amber as it neared the Bowl. She watched a filament weave around another, each making a helical dance, like snakes dancing to slow music.

They stopped short of the ridge to talk it through.

"Spaceport," Beth said. "We need to find a way back to gravity. How's our dead reckoning working today? Fred, which way is that row of bubbles?"

Fred's eyes danced anxiously and he nodded toward his left.

"Should be that way. Left," Lau Pin gestured.

Tananareve used her binocs and said, "Folks, can't you see it? Like a black froth, that way. Left, like you said, Lau Pin."

"You've got good eyes. Anything to the right?"

They looked. The ridge dwindled, dwindled . . . nothing, nothing . . .

"Spaceport," Beth commanded, keeping her voice firm. "I wish I knew how to be less conspicuous. We're not hidden." She ducked suddenly. A big black bird with bright yellow canard fins just back of its head cruised above them, inspecting, unafraid. It swooped and dived away, honking.

"Ah, lunch," Fred said.

Lau Pin laughed. "Those will help. The Astronomers won't find us by our heat signature, not while the sky is full of big birds. If we can catch a few for dinner, we might use their feathers for camouflage."

. . .

Marching away from the spaceport, they would have left behind them vehicles that could take them back to gravity. Lau Pin was right: the spaceport was their obvious target.

Too obvious.

Canard bird flesh tasted like meat-eater, dark and rangy, a little like lion, Beth thought. She'd eaten lion at a theme restaurant, centuries ago now. She pushed away the thought that of all those she had ever known—parents, friends, lovers— only the *SunSeeker* crew were still alive.

She smacked her lips and focused on the meat. They conscientiously ate all of any game they got—fat, gristle, crack the bones and suck out the marrow. You never knew where your next meal was coming from here. They'd caught only four of the turkey-sized black canard birds before the rest caught on. Now they had to dip down into the forest to get

272   GREGORY BENFORD AND LARRY NIVEN

anything to eat. Water they found pooled in leaves. Shooting from the trees was easy, though; the midsized animals didn't seem to regard the sky as a threat, and just ambled along.

They'd used the black feathers to decorate themselves, smiling as if at a masquerade. Now they crossed the forest tops in low leaps, like flying squirrels. They'd tied spidow line in loops, to catch themselves in case of a fall. All their Earthside training in fieldwork paid off.

Snaps, pops. Branches thrashed without a wind, off to the left. Lau Pin halted, motioned them back. Fred reached, not for a weapon but for his camera phone. They watched for long seconds. Then Tananareve aimed a low-level laser into the rustling branches.

Branches fell, thrashing loudly on the long way down. Branches? "Tree octopus," Lau Pin said. "I swear, that's what it looks like."

"Couple of snakes, mating," said Mayra.

Beth said, "Seems more like a bunch."

Fred was replaying video in slow motion. "Snakes with two or three tails," he said. "Very strange." He showed them the phone. "See? Tails with . . . might be fingernails, or rattlesnake rattles. Look, they caught some lower branches."

They all paused to listen and heard rustlings below. Lau Pin suggested, "Go down for a better look?"

Fred began working his way down, without waiting. Beth called, "Fred! We need to keep moving."

"I see something."

"They could be venomous!"

Fred didn't answer. Mayra videotaped him until he was out of sight.

And here he came back moments later, waving something the size of a pillow, the shape of a sausage. "They dropped it," he said as he reached them. "Look, it's about as wide as they were, thirty centimeters around, snake-shaped. It's got straps. And—"

"Don't tear it!" Lau Pin said.

Rip. "Velcro."

Beth reached in, stirred the contents. A haunch of red meat wrapped in cloth. A knife with a peculiar handle. Tool with a button: Flashlight? Communicator? Both? Dared they try it?

"Folks, we have to keep moving," Tananareve said presently. Beth agreed. They resumed their flight, with the sausage pack tied at Fred's hip.

THIRTY-THREE

"What if we have to leave the forest?" Lau Pin wondered. They rested on the broad leaves that were the size of the main deck on *SunSeeker.*

Beth didn't have an answer. Outside the forest, they would find a vertical landscape. There might be nothing to grab on to. But the greenery seemed to run as far as that row of dots, which was beginning to look like hemispheres of varied size and color. They had decided to move toward large buildings in the distance.

Braid trees became scarce. Vegetation hugged low to the ground. The big canard birds were avoiding them now. *That last meal might have cost us*, Beth thought. Her stomach rumbled.

They prowled through the low scrub bushes and used their binocs. At any movement they froze. Astronomer-sized Bird Folk were wandering among the buildings. And canard birds wheeled over the trees near the bubbles, cawing and diving.

Their approach was slow, methodical. No shadows for cover, and the sky seemed hotter here. The first dome was a sphere as big as a ten-story building, standing up from the jungle on a single leg. Reeds and ferns surrounded it, of types the Bird Folk had used for food.

Beth carefully watched the distant figures as they moved at their bobbing pace, their long necks weaving back and forth to keep their heads stationary as their long legs stroked forward with lazy grace. Walking out from the spaceport, Astronomers would reach this structure last, she saw. It would be the culmination of their path, a final lesson, with a vast garden of delights beyond.

They crept forward warily. The air was fragrant and lush, and Beth listened for suspicious sounds, but there were none.

So what was this bubble? She studied the designs on its outside. Brown abstracts, some with white traces, and each shape surrounded by a dark blue. Almost like—

"It's a globe," Tananareve said in her ear. "A globe map."

"Damn, you're right! This garden, it's some sort of . . . gallery of planets?" She peered at the more distant globes—and, yes, they had the same color patterns, continents swimming in seas. But the spheres were comparatively tiny, not all the same size but no bigger than train cars or even the largest Bird Folk.

Tananareve asked, "So this one—their home planet maybe?"

"Or one they passed by, explored."

"They're headed the same way we are, so maybe it's Glory? At this range, their telescopes could pick out continent-sized features. And look, there's another big one at the far end of the chain."

Beth saw it: barely more than a dot. "One is their home world, and the other's maybe their ultimate target—yes, it could be. You'd think the home world would be treated specially." The Astronomers might actually know the shapes of Glory's continents, or this could be some planet they just mapped with big lenses as they passed by its system. If a world wasn't interesting, they might not land on it at all.

Lau Pin whispered, "What's up?" so they shared the idea. Beth stared at the nearer sphere, then began circling anti-clockwise. The rest came with her, moving in irregular jumps, staying hidden.

It mapped a planet, all right. There were no ice caps;

where were the poles? The thing wasn't rotating fast enough to tell. It might not be rotating at all, though it stood on a single axial pole. Oceans were a mottled blue; land was red and brown. The land masses were all clumped, and white streaks showed chains of snowcapped mountains. It was somewhat stylized, the continent and islands colored more like gems than landscapes, and the blue oceans—three-fourths of the globe's surface—were translucent, the deep sea floors showing through, subduction zones and midocean ridges clearly defined. Look hard enough, and you saw shadows moving in there. Life-forms the size of mountains? By now they knew that it was indeed rotating, but very slowly.

Tananareve whispered, "Somebody coming."

Fred sprang up on a strut and surveyed. "Yep." A handful of bird shapes were moving toward them. Lau Pin said, "We need to hide."

Fred jerked his head again—"Inside."

"The only way in is that post holding up the sphere," Lau Pin said. He loped away.

Beth said uneasily, "I saw motion in there. We don't want to have to fight anyone."

"I looked," Mayra said. "Holograms. Something's making pictures."

"Audience?"

"Nothing I could see."

Lau Pin waved an arm, and they followed silently, swiftly. The spindly metal pillar that held the ten-story globe would have collapsed in normal gravity. The interior was a spiral stair, steps narrow near the axis, several feet wide near the walls. Lots of room. Accommodation for various species, maybe not just Bird Folk.

They were hidden as soon as they entered the giant stairwell. Tananareve suggested staying in the stairwell, but even she wasn't pushing it. Wonders waited above.

They entered armed, as best they could.

The inside was even roomier, with a ceiling ten meters high above a single gigantic space. It looked like a museum: items standing free or floating on thin wires Beth couldn't quite see, all squashed into whatever space would fit. A vast ceramic green ramp ran round the spherical wall.

"Watch for anything moving," Lau Pin said. "Fred, Mayra, Tananareve, you in the middle. I'll take point. Beth?"

"Rear guard."

Here on the floor was a shifting mound, almost flat but with ridges and pools. Patches of ocher and pale green writhed and then spread out. After a minute, it repeated. It made no sense at all until Tananareve said, "Continental drift."

Beth said, "We still don't know—"

"Which planet. True."

They walked among what must be model spaceships, and with a flicker were suddenly in a three-dimensional movie. As they crossed some unseen threshold, it rose abruptly all around them, a starscape riddled with swarming dark dots.

Beth stepped back quickly. The dots vanished. That much furious motion, anything could be hidden . . . but there wasn't anything alive here except her own people, visible as long as she wasn't in the hologram. They had spread out a little, looking for enemies—barring Fred, who stood stock-still, caught by the dancing dots.

She stepped back in. Chaos danced in flickering light around her. Anything could sneak up on them under these conditions, but she couldn't look away. Fred sighed beside her, mesmerized.

THIRTY-FOUR

The sensaround opened in deep space.

A tiny knot of yellow white sat at the exact center of the display. The field of view was a hemisphere so big, she could not grasp it without turning her head. Stars sprinkled the sky, but she could recognize no constellations.

Slowly the point of view rotated. Maybe that was the nearest star? But, no—a ruddy yellow disk swam into view at her far left. The disk fumed with small storms, and she could see magnetic arches soaring above the brimming bright churn. Clearly this star was smaller and redder than Sol and pocked with dense black spots. The vision slid farther, the star moved right, and tiny ships came in view. They had blue bubbles midship, probably fuel blisters. They tugged huge hexagonal containers, hundreds of ships all heading toward . . .

A vast pale crescent swam into view. She watched the framework of long, spiky girders that curved around complex guts. Between these were long loops like wedding bands, glowing. The thing was so large, it cast deep shadows over a bee swarm of ships, all tending to the large structure like worker insects.

Farther away orbited tumbling rocks, mostly tinged with white. Flames shot along their faces, and fumes billowed out in spheres. Those must be immense smelting systems laboring in the high vacuum. Big clouds of white and amber gas rose from them, expanding until they dimmed to transparency and faded. The view crossed a smaller star, glare white, brighter than the rest of the sky.

Still smaller ships flitted among the mining operations. Some hauled massive girders through cylindrical arrays. Out the far end emerged long struts with a glaze on them, shimmering in the orange red starlight. Some kind of hardening process?

Dirty gray blobs hovered in the distance. Beth realized these were iceteroids, like those humanity exploited in the Oort cloud of Earth—condensed out when the sun was born, rich in volatiles. Beside them flitting ships shepherded enormous orange balloons. These filled with gas that was born in the tiny orange fires at their base. Mass and elements for the construction, she guessed.

Then the milling swarm of mote-sized ships became a blur. Time speeded up. The huge thing they were building took shape. Girders aligned and layered. Scaffolds unfolded and crossbars buttressed those. Joists and brackets the size of planets formed in the haze of buzzing motion. An enormous geometry emerged. It was the Bowl.

Flitting shapes, too small to see clearly, wove a tapestry of black lace around the budding hemisphere. This array glowed suddenly, a flash of white light. Gas blew away from the structure like a fading fog.

This is a history lesson, Beth thought. *The natives here must want to keep aware of how they came to be . . . and so leave places like this so the message is not lost, a tradition sent down through deep time.*

The camera eye view closed in. Beth could see intricate maneuvers of silvery ships as they worked their way across the surface of the Bowl in the making. They laid down layers and pillars that lapped around the hemisphere, and the camera eye followed them, sliding over the lip of the Bowl into . . . a thick flock of ships, all ferrying volatile bags, the orange balloons she had seen before. Flashes like lightning arced through the bags of gas. Above the bottom of the Bowl, these came free. They slipped through holes in a nearly invisible upper layer, gliding downward toward the floor of the Bowl.

The field of view closed in on the shimmering layer. It was the atmosphere's boundary shield. This billowed out as it held in the pressure of gases emptying forth. On the Bowl floor, gushing geysers spouted thick ivory clouds. Other ships skimmed along the ribbed understory of the floor, spewing masses of brown and black—the topsoil, falling into place.

This was an Origin Story. Somewhere, the small red sun had spawned the creatures who built the Bowl. Why didn't it open on a planet where the builders began? There were none in the black sky. If the red star had planets, they were small. So maybe the creatures' world was far away, orbiting the first bright spot she had seen. Maybe the builders came from near a distant companion of this small sun.

Now the measureless basin turned. The bee swarm of working ships was an earnestly working fog as they spun up this world in the making. The soil settled and blue haze spread throughout the skin of atmosphere. Darting flashes lit the troubled high clouds. Monsoons swept the ragged continents, and seas sloshed.

The system evolved. Storms lashed immense, windswept lands. A joist on the backside popped free and the bee swarm surrounded it as gouts of dirt and gas became a volcano into a vacuum. Patched, the system ground on, spinning up. The shimmering sheet holding in the atmosphere flexed and rippled as angular momentum warped it.

Time ran faster. She was not sure how she knew this, but surely it would have taken a very long time to form a working biosphere. Yet now she saw the air clear and gray clouds form in high stacks like pancakes. Green lands spread like a bacterium overwhelming a curved petri dish.

Beth could see the Knothole now through the clearing atmosphere. In an arc around it, mirrors blossomed in lines, like yarn wrapping around the floor of the Bowl. The dark patch of the Knothole bristled with large gray shapes that she supposed must be large magnet cores being built. Slowly the center resolved and she could see stars winking in it.

The winding up of the mirror fields slowed as the last strands of it popped into being. Now the mirror fields jittered and flashed as they came alive. Her view tilted and swam toward the edge of the Bowl, where knuckles of burnished metal grew. Quickly the mirror field gained a slick metallic sheen. Fitful sprays of blazing colors worked in it.

The mirror fields showed sparkling oranges and reds. They threw images of the small star into view, flickering and finding their patterns, settling in. Abruptly a thin line of boiling plasma arced in and played in the spaces above the Bowl. The plume steadied, stuttered—and lanced through the Knothole.

Thin at first, the luminous Jet thickened. Snarls worked along it. Dark spots. A filament broke free and lashed across the envelope that held in the atmosphere. The Jet snapped off. But the damage was done: the atmosphere's skin darkened and massive plumes of air shot out. A blur of worker ships stopped that.

The view turned toward the reddish star. Its corona boiled with hoops of magnetic force, making giant high bridges around a white-hot point. That was the mirror focus spot, and more ships tended to it with anxious energy.

With a jerk the Jet lanced out again. It speared exactly through the Knothole. The repaired skin of the atmosphere reflected a pale image of the Jet.

Now this Bowl of the past resembled the vibrantly alive presence of today. The point of view backed away from it, and the constantly flickering swarm of worker ships faded.

Imperceptibly, the system of star, Jet, and Bowl began to move. It swam across the blackness, the Jet's raging brilliance drowning out the icy stars. The vast contrivance glided with aching slowness away from the distant yellow white star.

Leaving the system, she guessed. It could not make a pass near that star without risking disruption of whatever planets might orbit there. The Bowl became a vessel bound for the distant pale lights, the firmament of beckoning stars.

Only the starscape remained.

Lau Pin, Fred, Tananareve, and Mayra looked around themselves. It was, Beth thought, a little like being on LSD. A trip into a distant, wondrous time.

In the dark she could see through the globe's smoky glass. Gigantic Bird Folk were walking underneath.

Fred said, "I think I see."

Mayra said, "We all saw, Fred."

Tananareve said, "I think I see why primitives died out when they ran across advanced civilizations."

Lau Pin said, "It strikes me that if there's only one way into here, there's only one way out."

Beth: "We can't leave now. We're surrounded."

"If any of them come in—"

"We're dead. Let's keep looking. All the secrets are here. By the way, Beth, this has to be the map of the origin world."

"Oh . . . almost."

. . .

Over the next hour, two dozen Bird Folk passed them by. The human folk spent their time examining hundreds of space-going tools. Most were too cryptic even to be described. Mayra took pictures.

They gathered at one point to share dried canard bird meat. It was all they had left, save for a bar of chocolate Tananareve shared out.

"I think the Bird Folk are gone," Beth said. "Do we feel lucky?"

"We feel hungry," Tananareve said. "Somewhere around us, there must be something to eat."

THIRTY-FIVE

Six little world-globes ran in a row, three or four meters in dia-
meter, half a kilometer apart. Worlds—big enough to show as
spheres—but not all Earthlike. One was featureless blue, bigger than the rest. One was stark ice white, cracked around the
equator. None of them had windows or openings.

The final bubble, an hour away, was another glassy sphere
marked with land masses in a great blue sea. They moved
carefully now, slipping from clumps of immense ferns to the
shelter of occasional tree stands. Bird Folk of a variety Beth
didn't recognize were streaming into a great arch. Beth's
troupe moved carefully, but the Bird Folk were paying no attention at all. They murmured and whooped with odd, high
singsongs.

Tananareve crept close against the glass, around the curve
from the entrance. "Dancing," she said. "It's a dance hall."

Lau Pin was beside her now. He stared awhile, then said,
"Mating ritual."

Beth said, "There's a difference?"

The chuckles that followed this weak joke told her how
tense they were.

Beth was up against the glass now. Slow, thumping music
with skittering undertones. A simple song, cascading chords
ornamented by lots of percussion. Lurching bodies, heads
turned upward to the ceiling.

With sun and flare behind her, she and Tananareve might
look like ferns, if they held still. There were platforms

throughout the interior, on narrow pedestals, some topped with . . . sofas . . . nests? Thousands of Bird Folk, including a few gigantic Astronomers, were paying no attention to anything but one another. Some were dancing, some fighting, some . . . head to tail . . . that must be mating. But the Astronomers weren't doing any of that. Were they there to supervise? Or as voyeurs?

"Nothing for us here," Mayra said primly.

"But, Mayra, it must be a map of Glory! It's the last globe in this park."

"Get some photos, then."

They did that, then went on.

The ridge continued toward the Bowl's inner well. Vegetation was sparse here, offering less cover. There was nothing to eat.

And the next dome was silver, as big as several football fields, with a tremendous square opening and tracks running into it. Floating railroad cars ran in and out. They were open cages, and inside—

"Live animals," Tananareve said.

"Plants, too. Warehouse," Lau Pin said. "Anyone hungry?"

They crept in, hidden by the shadows beneath a slow-moving car, and rolled away before the cars reached the unloading dock.

There were Bird Folk around, one of the big varieties. Some might be guards, but most were working, moving stuff on and off the cars. What went on the cars was recognizable: crates of melons and plants and creatures from the humans' garden-prison. What came off were ferns and reeds and grass, tons and tons of it. It must all be food for Bird Folk of various types, Beth thought.

She got the rest to hang back until they could see the patterns of movement. Once offloaded, the workers ignored the food. The humans waited, stomachs rumbling, and then approached a cage car. They kept to the shadows of squashes and melons as big as automobiles. They carved into the underside of one of these, juice gushing out, and began to feast.

Fred pointed to a grid on the wall, with a wind blowing into it. "We should be there," he said.

"Why?" Beth asked.

"We stink," Fred said.

They looked at one another . . . yeah. Nods. Bird Folk mostly had big nostrils. They would have a powerful sense of smell. Beth's team moved under the air conditioner, taking melons and fruit and a dead mammal with them. The wind there was refreshing.

. . .

They feasted, and slept, and feasted some more. "The easiest way to carry food is in us," Fred said, and was jeered for it, but they ate anyway.

"I think I see . . . ," Fred said.

Conversation had already stopped. Beth said, "What?"

"It's going to sound crazy."

Beth looked around her. "We're living like mice in a gigantic alien supermarket," she said, "inside a wok the size of the solar system. We're all lunatics here, Fred."

He said, "A lot of stars come in pairs. Maybe most of them."

Heads nodded.

"I think that sphere was a map of Earth. Earth before the continents split up."

Lau Pin asked, "Why would they build a globe of Earth?"

"They're dinosaurs."

Lau Pin laughed. "Yeah, right." The others were grinning.

"Some dinosaurs got smart. They developed space travel. They did some exploring. They visited Sol's companion star. Anyone ever wonder how the dinosaurs stayed warm enough? Sol used to be cooler, remember."

Lau Pin was still grinning. "Come *on*."

"Companion star," Tananareve said. "They stole it?"

"It was theirs. Earth was theirs, too. Left the solar system as it was, but maybe they took the planets around Wickramsingh's Star. Grist for the mill."

Beth noticed that Mayra had lost her smile, which meant she was thinking again of her lost husband. She put an arm around Mayra and listened as they talked Fred's crazy idea around.

She tried to think about it without a snicker. They'd watched the building of the Bowl. If you weren't here, on and in it, the Bowl itself would be . . . a laugh riot. Cupworld. The advanced version would have night and day, provided by orbiting tea bags. A spaceport in the handle. But Fred was so earnest.

Intelligent dinosaurs. Evolving into Bird Folk. Must have had feathers already. "It could fit," she said not quite seriously. "Dinosaurs think big."

Talk continued. It was good to distract them from their situation for at least a few moments. Beth began to think about how to get them moving. They weren't hungry and they weren't prisoners, but low gravity would still make them sick if they stayed here. Their bones would get brittle; neurological functions would steadily erode.

Lau Pin and Fred were watching the distant workers while they nibbled at a great wedge of green melon. Now Fred said, "Those are the same variety that were guarding us."

"Feeding us, too," Lau Pin said.

"No. A little different. That star pattern on their flanks, see? They're not moving stuff, they're just . . . meandering?"

"Hunting us."

"Yeah." Fred swept his arm across an arc. "They're moving in a wave. We stay here, they'll have us."

"They're not very good at searching or we'd be caught by now."

"Probably out of practice," Beth said, and peered at Fred.

"Have you got some idea? Because I don't see any way past them."

"Hide in a melon," Mayra suggested. "Or two or three. Wait while they go around us."

"I want a better look at that air outlet," Fred said.

They brought ferns with them, for cover. They lay beneath the grille in a howling wind, examining the grille and watching the searchers. The Bird Cops weren't all that big . . . bigger than humans, though. Earthy smells brushed past them: manure, crushed grass, big animals.

"There's plenty of room for big birdy engineers to work in there. We can get around the fans," Lau Pin said. "Carefully. We don't want to turn them off. The cops would notice."

They took as much food with them as they could carry. They didn't have any way to preserve it. Outside, maybe they could make a fire and smoke the animal they'd butchered. Then on to the spaceport ledge and try to find a ride. Or die trying.

PART VII

You can't depend on your eyes when
your imagination is out of focus.

—MARK TWAIN

THIRTY-SIX

"Slow down!" Cliff called out.

His stomach wobbled and lurched as the magnetics torqued them. The motors surged, growled, hummed. He held on as Aybe wrenched the magcar around, spinning it hard, testing its abilities. Up, down, around—surges faster than some damned amusement park twister, and not amusing.

Terry stood up to restrain Aybe, and a swerve sent him halfway over the side. Irma grabbed his arm and hauled him back in. "Damn it, stop!" she shouted.

Aybe brought the craft out of its spinning mode and the motors beneath their feet eased. "We gotta know what this baby can do!" Aybe laughed with glee. He took the magcar up and it slowed, stopped.

"Careful," Howard said. Terry and Irma did not look pleased.

Aybe's engineer eyes widened as he took the craft up. He pushed a simple control yoke forward to the max, and the magcar slowed against gravity, then stopped. "Looks like we can't go above six meters." He moved it forward, and the speed crept up.

"Let's get the hell out of here," Terry said. Cliff nodded.

Aybe took them down to near the ground and then away in a fast horizontal path. Cliff looked back at the bloody sprawl of bodies. Leaving these aliens was a dividing point, he felt. Once this incident became known, from here on the natives would probably give no quarter.

Aybe experimented with altitude and speed, getting the feel of the magcar. They got ten kilometers away before they found a narrow gulch that concealed them among billowy trees, swaying in a steady, strangely musky wind.

The others went through the dead aliens' gear while Cliff stood watch. He scanned the sky for pursuit. Nearby, undisturbed by the magcar passage, birds in flight broke from their immense, triple-decked formation. They curled in banks, forming a sphere, cawing and yawing in squawking concert. The sound was a rolling *skkkaaaaa!* and distracted him so he did not see coming from above the cause of it all. A huge slender shape shot down from a cloud and dived into the bird ball. Its jaws opened and scooped up several birds at once. He lost it in the thickness of the swarming birds. It poked out the far side an instant later, jaws closed now and turning away. Like a shark, he thought. A sky shark.

Irma sat beside Cliff and asked Aybe, "This wind is too much. Can't we shield it?"

"Yeah," Aybe said brightly, always happy to greet a new problem. "There must be . . ."

After a few minutes of his trying the oddly shaped controls, a narrow pole abruptly poked up from the magcar center, where the engine housing bulged, humming as Aybe drove them forward. It rose to three meters' height, and suddenly the wind pressure and sound eased away. They were all impressed. Aybe figured it was some field effect, and when Howard poked a finger over the car lip he got a shock. "Defensive, too," Howard said, nursing the finger.

Irma said, "We should decide where we're going."

"Shelter, I guess," Terry said.

"We have to think long term," Irma said. "What's our goal?"

Howard said, "Learn and stay free."

Aybe shrugged. "Learn what? How to find Beth's group? Or get back to *SunSeeker*? Or—what?"

Irma looked around at them. "Once I was supposed to meet a friend in Old New York. The whole comm grid was down, so I couldn't reach her—and she was a Primitivist anyway, so usually didn't carry tech or have any embedded. So how was I to find her?"

"Go to obvious places," Howard said.

Irma brightened. "Exactly!"

Howard nodded. "So you went to the Empire State Building museum, and there she was."

"No, Times Square, but—yes. Let's do the same."

"So what's obvious here?" Aybe barked as he steered, never taking his narrowed eyes from the landscape.

Everyone thought, looking at the alien landscape whipping by. They were going up a slight slope, and low hills framed the steel blue horizon. Green and brown vegetation clumped at the bases of hills and in the erosion gullies where Cliff knew predators would be waiting.

Terry said, "The Jet. It's the engine moving this system, and it passes closest to the Bowl at that opening, the Knothole."

"Ah!" Irma nodded. "So maybe whoever runs this place lives near there?"

Shrugs answered. "Seems dangerous," Howard said. "If that Jet breaks free—and why *is* it so straight?—I wouldn't want to be near it."

"Okay, but look." Irma called up on her phone a picture taken from *SunSeeker*. The big band of mirror territory gave way near the Knothole to a green zone. In a close-up view they could see complicated constructions nearer still to the Knothole. "Somewhere in there."

Aybe shook his head. "That's maybe a million klicks from us!"

"I'm not saying we fly there in this little car," Irma said.

"But look, we're living in a *building*. There must be some big, long-distance transport around this place."

"Where would it be?" Cliff said, face blank. He had no idea, but ideas came out in talk like this and Irma was right to kick it off.

"Something obvious," Howard said. "This place is so big, there's got to be some structure that contains transport. To be large range, it's got to be large. Irma's right, it's a *building*."

"Okay, let's look for structures." Irma held up more views from *SunSeeker*.

Looking at them, the angled views of the Bowl, Cliff recalled what was now a distant life. He had lived for only weeks after revival on *SunSeeker* and now—he checked his inboard timer—months here, on the run. Somewhere up there, *SunSeeker* soared serene and secure. *If we could get more than spotty contact . . .*

All this experience was new, while decades of growing up and getting educated in California were the true frame of his life. Yet that world was gone forever from him. In a moment, the entire prospect of his life—finding Beth, setting sail to Glory on *SunSeeker* to explore a world and make a whole new life for humanity—all collapsed around him. *Beth. God, I miss her.*

All his past life was a dream, one that had to be tossed aside now for a frank reality on an enormous construct. He sat, speechless.

"What's that grid?" Terry pointed at Irma's small flat display.

Cliff looked, trying to yank himself out of his reverie. Redwing had talked of "morale problems," but this was more like a moral problem. What did any of their grand plans matter, against this brute reality?

Irma was responding to Terry by refitting her map with keystrokes and voice commands, using elevations gotten from *SunSeeker*. As *SunSeeker* approached the Bowl, they had made

a clear mapping of the near-hemispherical crisscross weave on
the Bowl's outer skin. Those features stood out, a knitted bas-
ket that supported the enormous centrifugal forces caused by
the Bowl's spin. A miracle of mechanical engineering carried
out on the scale of a solar system.

She flipped the display over to view the living zone of the
Bowl's interior. These maps were much more complicated,
since huge continents, seas, and deserts overlaid everything.
But clearly, as Irma worked the analysis, a cross-mapping of
the outer grids had their parallels on the inward face.

"Ridgelines, that's it," she said. "There's a consistent matching of the support structures. The Bowl's ribs are big curved
tubes. We find them on both sides—the mechanical basis of
ridges here in the life zone."

Howard said, "Where's the nearest?"

"Ummm, hard to tell." This went back to the whole
problem of conformal mapping of the Bowl's curves and
slants that had bored Cliff on *SunSeeker* and did now, too.
When he came back to the Irma–Aybe–Howard conversation, they seemed to have resolved the issue and Irma said
adamantly, "I'm sure it's at least a thousand klicks, that way—"
and pointed.

Aybe had another objection and Cliff went back to watching the terrain. Aybe could fly the magcar around obstacles
with the surprisingly simple controls, and still keep up a
steady stream of disputation with Irma. Cliff got bored and
rode shotgun in the sense of watching for trouble to their
flanks. They were gently rising over terrain that got more bare
and stony.

While the three argued, they came upon some hills of
actual rock—cross sections of layers, some showing rippled
marks that bespoke the eddies of an ancient sea. There were
hollowed-out openings, some big enough to walk into. Parts
of the walls had the curved sheets that meant sand dunes,
each seam of differently colored red and tan grains sloping

smoothly, an echo of where ancient winds blew them. These rocks had to come from some planet's surface.

"Hey, I'd like to look at those," Cliff said. "Let's take a break."

The tech types broke off and Irma surged up. "Yes! Need to pee anyway."

They came behind as he scrambled up the slopes. Puffing, he scaled a climb into one of the caves. So the Bowl builders had kept some of their home world? Intriguing—

He blinked. Pink paintings marked the cave roof and walls. Simple line drawings showed lumpy animals. One was clearly a running stick figure like the Bird Folk, a slender long neck and arms carried forward. Before it ran smaller animals. The Bird carried a . . . spear? Hard to tell.

Something told him these were truly ancient. They reminded him of the aboriginal paintings he had seen in Australia. Those showed kangaroos and fish and human figures. Not as sophisticated as the French cave paintings, but very much older, dating back to fifty thousand years.

But these—these were alien artworks of . . . how long ago? Impossible to tell. The Bowl builders had brought this here, perhaps—these hills stuck out above the bland rolling terrain below. Probably this was an honored remnant of whatever world the Bird Folk came from. Their planetary origin, lost in time.

The others came up and all stood, silent before the strange artwork. There was a dry smell here, like a desiccated museum.

They left it silently, as if afraid to disturb the ghosts from far away in the abyss of time.

THIRTY-SEVEN

Memor made her clattering ritual steps and buzzing feather-rush display, bowing as she took her seat. Warm waters played down the walls of the huge chamber, tinkling and splattering on rocks, which calmed her for the duel to come. Though this was to be a small meeting—the better to get things done—the Minister had chosen to use this largely ceremonial hall, perhaps to stress the gravity of Memor's errors.

Her only friend here, Sarko, hurried forward, hips swaying. "Welcome, one-under-scrutiny. Let me help you."

Sarko was tall and elegant compared to the more pyramidally shaped Folk. Theirs was an unlikely friendship, since Memor was more the grave, solemn type. Yet both realized that the other had needed social skills. Sarko's willowy manner made her an excellent social guide. She made a point of knowing everyone and let Memor know just what intrigues were afoot. In return, Memor shielded Sarko from complaints that she seldom really contributed ideas to the general purpose. Social gadflies were useful, after all, to lubricate the grinding machinery of Folk hierarchy. Sarko's friendship with Memor went back to the ancient times when they had both been male. Such scandals they had narrowly averted! Gossip they had barely survived! The rich old days.

"Thanks, fond one," Memor said. "What can you tell me?"

"There'll be the usual minor business you'll sit through, of course. The Adopted—not that your primates are, ey?—fall under the Code, nominally. Especially if—" Here Sarko gave a flare-flutter of mirth. "—they are rampaging over the landscape."

"They are clever," Memor allowed herself.

"And hard to catch! We had abundant testimony to that last meeting. Pity you weren't here—exciting. I gather these primates are not like ours, not simpletons hanging around in trees. Anyway, no wonder they escaped, they seem quite clever. Tricky! I gather they got away from several large search parties, and now have—" Sarko paused in her usual head-long talking. "—have killed several Folk? . . . And captured a car? . . ."

Memor gave an assenting wave of feather-fan. "True enough. Word leaks out, I see. They have made the case against their kind quite well."

Sarko peered into Memor's face. "You do fathom that the best way to save your career is to agree that they must be exterminated."

"Oh, quite."

"So you will? Please."

"I think we play with fires we do not know here, and should be careful." Memor had planned that sentence; might as well try it out on a friend.

"That will not go well with the Profounds, old friend."

A slow side glance. "Friend, I can count on your support?"

A humble bow. "I have little power, alas."

"Use what you have. I have survived the Citadel of Remembrance, though not without scorn."

"May you do so well here!" Sarko said, her expression returning to her usual happy state, with blue eye-feathers furling.

Memor followed Sarko's guidance through the formal labyrinth, enjoying her quick, birdlike movements. Sarko was a quick but not deep intelligence, open to larger mental vistas but preferring the light joys of the social give-and-take.

As an Ecosystem Savant approached, Sarko fell back. "Would you have sustenance?" came the customary offer.

"Not before any other," Memor made the usual counter. The Ecosystem Savant ruffled colors of routine admiration and the introductions were complete.

At this formal moment, a Packmistress entered, seated herself, and nodded to all with a fluttering plumage neck-arc of authority. "We will commence." A flutter of acceptance ran round the moist chamber.

The first item was an anticlimax. An ecosystem engineer presented the latest problem. In Zone 28-94-4578, water temples controlled flow to terraces, preventing Folk tribes upstream from using it all, and so avoided impoverishing those below. Yet rainfall had slackened, despite the best Eco management. To prevent the highlands from withholding water without conflict demanded social cement. These Moist Temples used customary *subak* rituals to link the communities with full mingling ceremony and mandatory crossbreeding. Otherwise, they would be snatching at one another's feathers. Absent such community, crops would fail. Ancient forests would be overrun with loggers, potters, shepherds, and thieves, seeking what they could wrench forth. This evolving crisis challenged lands larger than whole planets.

The biology of all lands shifted in time, of course— nature's restless seekings making species that, in the evolutionary sense, pass by each other on their way to somewhere else. Adapt, evolve, or die—the eternal rule. But drought hastened nature here.

Memor watched as several Profounds tossed the problem among themselves. Much verbal artistry could not conceal the hard choices. There seemed no merciful solution. Accordingly, the Packmistress let each side play out, stating cases, pleading for more aid.

Then the Packmistress showed a crescent display of

resolute judgment—a bad sign. She said, "No extensions for longevity throughout the threatened domain. No appeals, no exceptions."

There it was. A hush fell upon the chamber. Memor could hear the gentle splashing of the calming waters on the walls. The Packmistress had condemned millions to their natural extinction. They could not claim special aging preventives.

The Packmistress ordered a recess for contemplation. Sarko immediately appeared at Memor's flank. "Perhaps such stern justice will be of help."

"Or set the tone," Memor said dryly.

"I have been circulating. . . ." Sarko always opened with a teasing promise, fluttering side feathers near her eyes. "Some say you know the most of these aliens, so should lead the hunt."

"Are you sure?"

"Yes, those who spoke at all seemed quite friendly to your cause."

"I do not seek to lead a hunt."

Feathers ringing Sarko's neck fluttered. "But you fathom these strange—"

"Has it occurred to you that I could *fail*?"

"Ah, no. You have such a sterling record—"

"This is the first alien invasion in countless twelve-cubed Cycles. We are inexperienced. As well, no one has ever dealt with such evil little creatures."

Sarko's elegant head jerked, weaved. Feathers fanned the astonished violet-rimmed eyes. "But you! Everyone says—"

"Everyone hasn't walked in my path. I do not wish to exchange one route to death for another. This hunt could fail, the aliens could do much damage—and there will be victims among us, then."

Sarko's joyful face collapsed. "Surely you can't—"

The summoning chimes sounded, reverberating in the

high chamber. Memor drew in the soft air, but tasted a bitter hint—her own bile?

Back in chambers, more Eco deliberations droned by. Movements of the Folk were not following the Design. Memor let her Undermind rove as she half listened.

All life was properly in movement, on the grand plains of the Bowl World. But the bigger, lower-grade-intelligence Folk, who lived as primitives and augmented their diet browsing shrubs and trees, were to move on—to give grazers a chance to live on the grasses that followed the loss of shrubs. These primitives were not crop-raising Folk, and should remain in their wild condition.

So populations had to be forced to move, and not set up camps and villages. The Packmistress made quick work of this matter, directing Suborns to destroy the primitive camps and force the subFolk to move on. They had their role in the Design, and should be reminded of it.

She reminded them all that the Originals had learned the Great Truth that governed all: that given vast new lands, the Folk then quickly invade these spaces, wreak destruction, and when resources grow short, fight with neighbors for more. Under the first rush of exploding populations in the Original Times, wildland had to pay or perish, to persist. Poachers and loggers turned lands into battlefields.

Only after much strife that threatened the Bowl itself did the Codes come, managed by the Savants. There was no alternative to a constant, assuring order. Another revelation was that death did not permit one to stay out of the Cycle. In some Bowl societies, the Folk tried to deny their own role, and so put their dead into coffins and mausoleums, burned themselves in pyres, even suspend themselves in cold for future resurrection. All were a wrongness, for the Bowl needed these bodies.

"Mites and worms *should* have us," the Packmistress said.

"This is the Cycle and it must be obeyed. Such is the Design. The Code does not protect lands and seas from the Folk, but rather *for* the Folk—by taking the long view. The Code teaches humility, because it engages us with Nature in the eternal dance with all other species."

Memor bowed her head at this obvious platitude and wondered how it would affect her—well, *trial* was not quite right, but the stern faces of those around her did not bode well.

At this moment Sarko piped forth, "I suppose the message here is, just remember that you can never predict the behavior of a system more complex than you. And if you want a project to stay on track after you're gone, you don't give control to anything that's guaranteed to develop its own agenda."

Ah, Memor thought. Sarko was drawing fire to defuse the tension in the room. And it worked. Those clustered around made derisive noises, though some just fluttered their feather-fans. "Surely that is too simple," an elderly Savant hooted. Others just laughed.

The Packmistress allowed a flicker of irritation to ripple through her feathered corona. "For we—Savants, Profounds, all those in the tier below Astronomers—corruption of purpose means simple bribery, graft, or nepotism. But for lower Folk who enjoy their lives in the unchanging state our Bowl ensures, corruption has an entirely different meaning. It is the failure to share any largesse you have received with those with whom you have formed ties of dependence."

Sarko said, "Surely that is predictable, my—"

"Our view of corruption makes sense in a culture of laws and impersonal institutions," the Packmistress rolled right over Sarko. "But theirs is a small world whose defining feature is the web of indebtedness, of obligations that ensure the social order. So to them, not to give a job to a cousin is corrupt, even if others are better qualified. Not to do deals with tribesFolk because better terms may be found elsewhere is

also corrupt. Reducing corruption of this sort demands—"
The Packmistress let her voice fall to a grave tone. "—resolve."

A sobered silence from those who saw what was going on.

"It is useful to recall the full brunt of our measures," she
began, displaying a somber arc-pattern of grays and pale blues.
"I remind us all that while such social dissension occurs on
occasion, there is a rogue element afoot, and not far from
these territories where the water temples are failing to make a
benign equilibrium."

With this she cast a significant long look at Memor. "Witness, I bid you, the current state of those we have condemned
for committing offenses of this type." With a great sway of her
body, she signaled the attendants. The dome over their heads
surged with popping energy, and a wide image played upon it.
Memor shivered with fear when she recognized the context.

The greatest preventive the Astronomers had, used against
only those whose actions threatened the Bowl's environment
and fate, was the Perpetual Hell. Mention of its very existence
could silence a crowd.

Those who violated the Code could face having their very
minds mapped, and their bodies then executed. They would
then awake suspended in a virtual, mental Hell from which
none escaped. Ever.

Memor had gone through the mandatory sampling of a
mere single Hell, and would never forget it. And now here it
came again, splashed across the ceiling.

A glowering sky, shot with red and amber. Beneath lay a
vast swamp flooded with fuming lava, the stench—the Packmistress had ordered the full sensorium to come into play
across the chamber—so strong, it now crawled into her nostrils and stung throughout her head.

"Attend!" the Packmistress commanded. Heads had already averted the images, eyes snatched away.

Memor looked up against her will. Rooted in this acrid
slime were . . . the doomed Folk. They writhed and screamed

in tiny shrill voices. Fires danced upon them as they twisted. A din of shrieking pain played across the bodies. They could not wrench free of the fires and so endured it like trees whipped by winds of agony. Eyes pleaded with them all—for those in this place knew they were watched; it was part of the torture—begging for release from agonies she could see but do nothing about. Rocks fell from the smoldering sky and smashed the fevered mud.

The first time she had to watch this, the intent was to educate her, and the lesson never left her mind for long. Now the Packmistress meant to instill discipline. Memor trembled, for the message was clearly focused on her.

At a nod, the image and scents fled. Sighs and worried murmurs laced the air as the Packmistress settled herself, looking satisfied.

All waited and the Packmistress let tension build. *She's toying with me,* Memor thought. At last the Packmistress said slowly, "The Bureau of the Adopted had as its Research Minister a Profound of the most high stratum. He will present their views now, and our guest, Memor, will answer. Attend— these are the firm results of our global staff, an analysis of the nature of these . . . aliens."

Memor watched as the Profound—a male, of course, since males push at the boundaries, as a rightful, youthful function—gave a rather hurried talk. He swept his great head about to stress his points, feathers ruffling constantly at his neck for emphasis. Masculine energy surged through his sentences.

"These are clever creatures, a form we never saw evolve in the Bowl." The Profound tipped his head at his audience, mirth playing in his eyes. "This may come from their tempting role as game—" This brought a storm of laughter, obviously a release from the tension of watching the Hell. "—but we can deduce aspects of their evolution from their surprising intelligence."

Memor knew where this was going. She was not so far from the male phase; she could still anticipate the channels of their thoughts; after all, that was a core female talent. Evolutionary theory would predict a clear pattern in the aliens, and males loved the mechanisms of theory. Selection pressure on some world had favored the climbers of trees, and then had somehow shifted, so the climbers came down to the ground. There they learned to hunt. As strategies go, hunting in groups compelled social communication, to find prey and coordinate attacks. That drove speech and language. In turn, intelligence acted on social cues so that group survival became enhanced, in conflict with other hunting groups of the same species. That drove cooperation. Particularly, selection would favor both the charismatic minds that could lead, and the analytical ones, which would see deeper. The social pyramid would have a bulge in the middle, of the variously competent.

"But this is a commonplace," Memor injected, a calculated move whose risk made her heart pound. She tasted in her breath the tang of her own sour apprehension. "We can all see where the argument goes. We ourselves evolved in something like this manner, in the Home."

Invoking the Home was a bold move, but she had to make it. Memor made a fan display of rattling colors. "But these creatures are tiny! They would lack the advantage of size, and so should not be very successful."

The Profound gave a jut of his head and a jaunty spray of derisive colors. "Size can become an instability, as surely even nonspecialists must know." This dig provoked a titter among some. "It is simple to grow large and dumb, yet remain secure. We—the Folk—found a balance. We became smart and yet our size let us develop the civilized arts. Our societies matured. We learned to sustain, the greatest of virtues. We learned to Adopt other species through modification of their genes, our great skill—though, of course, even the Adopted at times need recalibration."

Memor rose to her full height to challenge this. Rising was a risk, for it could offend. But her life was at stake here. Plainly, the Packmistress had chosen to subject them to the Perpetual Hell to make this point without speaking of it. "You speak of strategies we do not in fact know at all. Adopting is our method here, yes. But, I might remind the Profound, we do not know how *we* evolved!"

Memor had not expected this sally to deflect the Profound's argument, and it did not. He said, "Standard theory declares that this skill, plus our extraordinary social coherence, was decisive. I am not surprised you do not know this, for you are untutored in the evolutionary arts."

"Do *you* know what sort of world we came from?"

"Of course. The best parts of it were much like our Bowl."

"You like mean the Great Plain, the Knothole, the Zone of Reflectance, or—what?"

He shot back, "That is a specialist question, beyond the concerns of—"

"You do not know, do you?"

"I did not say that. I think it beside my point."

"Let us note the Profound did not answer the question."

"Halt!" the Packmistress ordered. "We are getting away from the reason for your appearance here, Memor, *and* I note you are using this diversion to delay our proper considerations."

Memor saw she had gone too far and so made the ritual bow with coronations of dutiful apology—three fan-trills and a rainbow display of self-dismay. The attendees nodded in approval and a few even sent quick fan-toasts at Memor's performance of a difficult salute. That seemed to calm everyone, but Memor knew it was mere polite manners.

The Profound said slowly, voice filled with deep sour notes, "Memor here has allowed to *escape* the *only* of these aliens our Security had captured! They are far away from the other primates, who escaped immediately when they entered."

"How did that occur?" a senior figure asked.

"Inexcusable oversight. I might add that the commanders responsible have been recycled."

"That seems brutal," a voice at the back called. "We are unaccustomed to invasion, and do not have anyone living who has experience."

The Profound said slowly, "As well it might, but word of recyclings spreads, and aids in discipline."

Silence. A senior member said, "We still cannot find those, the ones who got away at the air lock?"

"No, and that is the salient threat. These primates are vicious—they have killed some of us!—and at a demonstrably lower stage of evolution. But they are infernally hard to find, catch, and kill."

"We have *none* in captivity?" The senior figure rustled head feathers in surprise.

"Exactly so—" The Packmistress's head swiveled. "—due to Memor. The only dead primate we have found, left behind by his companions as they fled, apparently died from a large predator—which the other primates then killed. All this occurred during their escape from Memor." She ended with a long stare at Memor, aided by fan stirring of rebuke at her shoulders.

Memor disliked such smug orations but kept still.

The entire body turned and looked at Memor. She decided the best tactic was to stare right back.

The Profound did not hesitate. "There is a further issue. These are not truly rational minds. They cannot view the Underminds and so do not know themselves."

Gasps, frowns. Memor started to object to this intrusion into her own area. "Ah, I—"

The Profound waved her off. "For these primates, there is

always a silent partner riding along in the same mind. It can get in touch with their Foreselves. Yes—we do owe this discovery to Memor, I'll grant. But! Their Underminds can speak to them only through dreams during sleep. Memor showed that they have ideas that come to them out of 'nowhere.' Not words or exact thoughts, just images and sensations."

"Surely these cannot be significant ideas?" a senior asked. "They are unmotivated."

The Profound shook his head sadly, a theatrical move that made Memor grind her teeth. "Alas, I must report to you—again, due to Memor's work—that this primate 'silent partner' is the wellspring of their primitive creativity."

"But that is inefficient!" the senior Savant insisted.

"Apparently not, on whatever strange world these tree-swingers came from in their crude ship. Evolution must have preferred to keep their minds divided between the conscious self and the silent."

The Savant looked incredulous—eyes upcast, neck-fan puckered red, snout cocked at an angle. "Surely such disabled creatures, even if they have technologies, are no threat to us."

The Profound flicked a command, and the dome above them popped with an image—the alien primates gathered around a campfire. The audience rustled. "These look quite helpless," the Savant said.

"They are not," the Profound said, and cut to an image of three Folk sprawled, their bodies stripped of gear. Burns at their necks and heads had singed away many feathers. Brown blood stained the sand around them, and surprise lingered in their staring eyes.

"And now we turn to the cause of these events," the Profound said quietly.

Memor recognized the images she had sent in reports. Of course, the Profound had put his own interpretation on her brainscan data, slanting it to his pointed ends. Memor stood. "I am not the cause, my Profound. I am the discoverer."

"Of what?"

"The sobering implication that these primates undermine our understanding of our own minds."

"That is nonsense."

"You are a male, my dear Profound, and so should be more open to ideas, since you are young as well. These events imply a painfully fresh insight. These creatures somehow avoid the risks of an unfettered intelligence. The implications—"

"Are many, but the threat is clear," the Profound snapped. "*You* let them escape. The only concrete knowledge we have comes from the single corpse they left behind—being primitives, I would have expected them to at least try to bury it. Studying that body explains their archaic origins. They have organs that barely function, some clearly vestigial, particularly in their digestive tracts. Natural selection has not had time to edit out these simple flaws. And, tellingly, there is *no* sign of artificial selection."

Clucks of doubt greeted this news. An elder asked, "How could they become starfarers without tailoring their bodies?"

"They were in a hurry," Memor said dryly.

The Profound's eyes narrowed. "They must come from quite nearby, to reach us in such simple craft. Yet I checked with the Astronomers, and there are no habitable planets within several light-years."

Memor saw this digression was to mollify the crowd, by seeming reasonable. She said, "They caught up to us and slowed to board. They obviously do not come with an attitude of awe, as with prior aliens. Customarily we pass by a star, and any intelligent, technological life-form comes to us with great respect for the Bowl, its majesty. I doubt these, who apparently found us by accident, will join the Adopted without great trouble."

The Profound's eyes glistened as he saw an opportunity. "Then you agree they should be killed?"

"Of course. But the implications they bring—"

"Will not matter when they are dead, yes?"

"You speak of that as an easy thing. My point is that it will not be simple. They have resources I cannot fathom."

"But that is subject to demonstration, yes?" The Profound yawned elaborately, amused.

"If we muster—"

"I assure you we are receiving reports from varying Folk communities. I have not gotten reports from the party you let escape, alas." With this, he gave a derisive feather-flicker. "But other Folk do glimpse the primates who stole an aircar. They've been sighted as they pass in the distance."

"Then you— Wait, why do the Folk not attack them?"

"They proceed through a zone of low habitation. None who sighted them had weapons of such range, for obvious reasons."

The Folk communities had only low-power armaments. Large explosives could breach the shell and open the Bowl to vacuum. If such were used by the infrequent Adopted rebellions, disaster would follow.

Memor could sense the shift in the audience. A senior Savant said, "If you are correct, our Profound, we must use those who know these strange primates."

The Profound turned, puzzled. "I have made a case for extermination—"

"But only Memor knows how they think, yes?"

Memor said, "I cannot pretend to know, but I can at least sense how they respond."

The senior was puzzled and asked for explanation with a classic ruffle and coo.

"I can predict many actions of these primates, yet without understanding their motives."

The Profound sent his crown feathers into a circling pattern of blue and gold. "I think Memor has proved she does *not* know how—"

"She is what we have," the Packmistress said suddenly. "She studied these aliens."

"But the risk!" the Profound said, turning to make the strut-challenge to the entire room. "We know from prior eras that aliens drawn to us from planets arrive with a planetary view of life. This cripples them. Of course, once having seen and lived upon the Bowl of Heaven, they saw their errors and found a quiet equilibrium. The Adopted have been quite useful to us and, once rendered docile, improve the lives of us all. Yet inevitably such aliens suffer for reasons built deeply into their genes—a nostalgia for planets that necessarily suffer the pains of days and nights, of axial seasons, of uncontrolled, hammering weather. So the Adopted are susceptible to incitement. These Late Invaders could excite such nostalgia into rage, vast violence, and then—"

The Packmistress held up her arms, and the room fell silent. She did not react visibly, but turned to Memor and gazed steadily. "You will find a way to draw them out."

Memor hesitated. "But . . . how can I . . ."

"You know them. You have seen their ways of bonding, of talking with those curious faces of theirs. The idea of an intelligence that does not fully control expression, showing all to any who see—and so lets others know what emotions pass within! Use that! You have two bands of aliens moving across the majesty of the Bowl. They are communal animals, yes?"

"True, they daily meet and speak and—"

"Good. Use that."

"Lure them?"

"If you can devise a way, surely."

"May I have use of the Sky Command? I can cover territory quickly with the fliers. And especially the airfish."

"I suppose." A sniff.

Memor hesitated, then bowed. Her caution warned her not to go further, but—"What of their ship?"

"Eh?" A Packmistress is not used to being questioned.

"Their starship orbits about our star. Suppose it has some powers we do not know?"

"That is for the Astronomers, surely." The Packmistress stirred, as if she had not considered the issue. "I heard at Council that our mirror complexes probably cannot adjust quickly enough to focus on their ship. It has capacity to maneuver, and could evade a beam."

A senior Savant added, "No small ship could damage the Bowl, in any case."

"Ah, that is consoling," Memor said with a bow and a humble submission-flurry of crest feathers. Then, as she rose, she had an idea.

THIRTY-EIGHT

When they stopped for a rest after a long journey in the magcar, Cliff searched for food. It felt good to get out of the car and into the "sorta-natural," as Irma called it.

There was little of animal prints or scat here, he noticed automatically. He found ripe berries, spotting them from experience. Some large trees had fruit growing off their trunks, an oddity that he used. With Howard he shot several of them off the bark by laser. He had developed a small poison detector, using the gear he had brought. That time of their landing—going through the air lock and then on the run—seemed far in the past. He had expected a few days on the Bowl, mostly doing bio tests, then back to *SunSeeker*.

The fruit was a succulent purple and tested okay.

But the purple sap drew tiny flies that went for the fruit and then tried to suck the moisture off his eyeballs. They darted into his ears and dwelled there, prying deep inside. Dozens of them danced in the air, looking for suitable targets. Only running left them behind, and not for long.

This just led the flies to the others, who batted at the buzzing irritants. It got bad and they decided to fire up the magcar and flee. Aybe was irritable; they had stung him on the neck repeatedly. He took out his ire by "trying out the dynamics." This meant more acrobatics. Howard had measured the magnetic fields around the magcar and found it was an asymmetric dipole, with field squeezed tight under the car. With all aboard, the car sped faster by hugging the ground, so they skimmed along at only a meter in altitude. The more weight, the faster they could go. "Counterintuitive," Howard said. "Must be the fields grip the metal belowground better."

Aybe nodded. "I figure the Bowl underpinning is metal with magnetic fields already embedded."

Irma said, "Maybe those big grid lines we saw on the outer skin? Could be enormous superconductor lines. Howard, what's the magnetic field intensity at ground level?"

"Strong—so much, I can't measure it with my simple gear. At least a hundred times Earth's, maybe a lot more."

Soon a ridge of mountain loomed before them. Aybe took them straight at it and Irma said, "That's not far from the gridding I found. Maybe it's a city?"

"Then let's not go there," Howard said.

But under binocs, the rising ridge looked like bare rock and there were no signs of locals. Aybe worked them around the narrow canyons that led to the base.

"No signs of life," Aybe said. "Maybe it has some structural role?"

"We can get some perspective from up there," Cliff said mildly. He had wanted to see further around this immense place but until now could not think of a way to do it, short of capturing an aircraft. Yet they had seen few of those in the skies.

They started up the slope of the spire. It was mostly bare rock, but here and there they could see in the gullies some metal, as if the frame were showing through. The magcar handled well.

Howard said, "I think the magnetics are getting stronger."

Aybe nodded. "I'm feeling more grip now. We can go uphill pretty fast." He brought the magcar down even lower to the rock face and they lifted steadily.

Cliff watched the terrain fall away. Forest, grasslands,

rumpled hills. The spire steepened steadily but somehow the magcar held on, groaning, and propelled them up its flanks. He wondered what drove it—a compact fusion scheme? The oscillating rumble under his feet suggested that, but alien tech could—no, would—be alien.

As they rose he saw immense decks of clouds rising like mountains in the distance. The atmosphere was so deep, such stacks could form and drift like skyscrapers of cotton. The Bowl rotated around in about ten days, and this drove waves and eddies in the huge atmosphere. The clouds followed this rhythm in stately cadence. He had seen the effects on the thin film that capped the atmosphere, and in the deep air below— ripples that shaped the winds, tornados here and there spinning like vast purple storms, resembling a top on a distant table. How could anyone predict temperature and rainfall in something this big?

Aybe had taken them far up the spire now. It felt like climbing a building with no safety net. They were above the layer of air where small clouds hung, and now the view reached farther. Opposite the clouds was a clear zone. He was looking away from the rim of the Bowl, toward the Knothole. The Jet slowly wrapped and writhed, a slender red and orange snake. He followed its dim glow toward the Knothole but could not see past the foggy blur there. But nearer, beyond the vast mottled lands, lay a strange, huge curved zone—the mirrors.

He was about to turn away when he saw something new.

Glinting pixels struck his eye. The whole zone seemed to teem with activity—winks and stutters of light. Were the mirrors adjusting to tune the Jet, to stop the snarling waves that rode out on it?

"Let's go there." Cliff pointed. "That's got to be where whoever runs this place lives."

"Up to high latitudes?" Howard said. "We haven't any idea what's there!" .

"We haven't got *any* ideas!" Irma burst out.

"Then we need some," Aybe said.

. . .

They kept moving up the rocky flanks of the immense tower, then had another sleep stop. At their rest site were some of the helically coiled, willowy paper bark trees they had found before. These they used for toilet paper, but they also cooked fish wrapped in it. Terry discovered a local herb that, roasted inside the fish, gave a pleasant taste to the big slabs of white meat. Cliff gutted the fish they caught in the surprisingly rich streams and ponds, and kept notes on his slate about their guts. There were oddities to the usual tubular design, such as one that excreted to the sides, not at the tail, and another with a circular comb around its flanks. Disguise? Defense? Hard to know.

They all enjoyed the view. To one side, a gunmetal blue sheen of sea yawned in the distance. The seemingly flat horizon to either side disappeared into a haze; the water gave no impression of being concave, only vast. Here, Cliff mused, masts would not be the first sign of an approaching ship.

There were a few Earthly analogues to this place, he reflected. Earthside, deep sea creatures lived in constant darkness, the opposite of this steady daylight. Here the sun stayed put in the sky, so animals could navigate by it. They all hid away to sleep, except for some lizard carnivores he saw dozing in the eternal sun. Beyond those bare facts, Cliff could not see how to generalize.

Terry came and sat beside him to admire the views. They walked around a bluff to see the other side, silent. They had exhausted their small talk long ago. The unending days were wearing on them all. Their clothes, though of Enduro cloth, showed popped linings and ragged cuffs. They stopped whenever they found a stream or lake but often smelled rank. The men had ragged beards, and Irma's hair kept getting in her way. They didn't cut hair, though, because it kept their UV exposure down. Though everyone with a *SunSeeker* berth was exceptionally strong and tough, living in the open wore them down. Worst of all was the strong expectation that none of this was going to change soon.

"That way," Terry said, pointing, "that's up-Bowl, right?"

"You mean to higher latitudes?" Cliff tossed a rock onto the steep slate gray rock below them and watched it bounce and scatter until he lost track of it in mist below.

"Yeah, past the mirrors. Must be a hundred million klicks away from here."

"Pretty far, right," Cliff said, distracted by something he had glimpsed. He brought up his binocs and close-upped the mirror zone. It was flashing rainbow colors, tiny pixels of blue and white and pink rippling. He had seen that before, but this time whole regions of mirrors were forming the same color, making—*an image.*

He stared at it, mouth open.

"Look up close," he whispered to Terry. "What do you see?"

"Okay, I—good grief. It's . . . a face."

"Not just a face. A person—human."

"What?" Terry grew silent. "You're right! A woman."

"Moving, too—it's . . . it's Beth."

"My God . . . yes. It's her."

"And her lips are moving."

"Yeah. I used to lip-read, let me . . . She's saying 'come,' I think."

Cliff found he had been holding his breath. "Right."

"Come . . . to . . . me. Repeats. That's it."

The face on the mirrors repeated the words over and over. Her face rippled and snarled in spots where wave coherence failed.

Terry said, "Does that mean they have her?"

"These are aliens. Maybe their contexts are different. It

could mean they want her to go to them. Or it's directed to us, and me, and says, go to Beth."

"Damn," Terry said.

Cliff stared at the repeating pattern and frowned. He seemed to float on the shock of it, suspended, seeing a face he had longed for. He had dreamed of her so much through these desperate days, imagining her dead or in some alien hellhole. . . .

"Unless . . . it could be Beth sending the message."

THIRTY-NINE

For Cliff, dreams made it all worse. The next "day," he awoke with the scent of roast turkey in his mind. When he was a boy, his idea of heaven was Thanksgiving leftovers. He had loved chopping onions beside his mother, stuffing the bird with green cork tamales instead of regular stuffing, as Grandmother Martínez did. The other side of the family did ground lamb, rice, and pinyon nuts. Drifting up from sleep, he tasted the Arabic stuffing flavored with prickly spices and a little cinnamon. He blinked into the constant dappled sunlight, not wanting to leave the dream. His stomach growled in sympathy.

Food dreams . . . He had them every sleep now. They ate simply here, but his unconscious didn't have to like it.

He got up, yawning and reaching for some fragrant fruit they had found the day before. They managed to get enough small game, shooting from the magcar, and they all gathered berries and herbs to avoid hunger here—but his sleep turned to fragrant feasts nearly every "night." He suspected food stood in his dreams for some deeper yearning, but could not figure out what it might be.

He mentioned this to Irma as the "day" was drawing to a close, and she said immediately, looking him in the eye, "Beth. Obviously."

This made him blink because it was obvious and he had not seen it. "I . . . suppose so."

"Just as I miss and want Herb." Still the direct stare.

"Of course." That was his filler phrase while he tried to think, but Irma wasn't having any.

She shot back, "You don't remember Herb, do you?"

"Uh, engineer, right?"

"No, he's a systems man."

"Well, that sort of engin—"

"Redwing was going to revive him to work on the drive problem, but we got too busy."

"And you miss him. . . ." Cliff resorted to a leading phrase to get away from the Beth issue, but it didn't work.

She said, "We're helping each other through the hard stuff, Cliff. I want you to know that's all it is."

"Of course." Pause. "Not that I don't have, well, real feelings toward you."

She smiled. "I do, too, but they're—how to say?—not deep."

"Sex does have what the psychers call a 'utility function,' yes."

"As long as we both know that. And speaking of it, I'm not really tired . . . yet."

This was clearly a lead-in, so he smiled and said, "I've got to take a stroll before settling down."

The team followed a set procedure when they slept. Find a secure place, often one that surveyed the land around them but was in shadow. Be sure nothing could approach silently by rigging lines that would rattle some gear if tripped. Post a guard if the situation looked risky. Have a spot where people could retreat for a toilet, perhaps even fresh water.

Today—the term meant nothing more than their awake interval—they camped under a broad canopy of tall trees. Wildlife chattered and jeered above as they walked through dense vegetation. Cliff always kept aware of his flanks and regularly turned to look back, to recall the path. They kept silent, wary. What he called a smokebush bristled with its tiny branches, easing slowly toward them as it sensed their motion.

It could snare only insects and small birds, but a moving plant still gave him the creeps.

Irma checked above, head swiveling regularly, and they were a few hundred meters from camp when she abruptly turned and kissed him. He responded to her quick kisses and short, panting breath, and only when her clothes were mostly off did he notice that there was no comfortable place to lie down. "Maybe we should walk some more that—"

"There's a slanted tree, see?"

"Yeah, those zigzag trees. I think exploit the sun's constant position. See, they stage tiers of upward-facing limbs and leaves, to cup the sunlight. Each layer is staggered to the side, so a single tree, seen from above, makes a broad emerald area, captures more sun."

"Faaaa-scinating."

Her dry tone made him turn and she kissed him hard and deep. *Oh yeah, we came here to—*

She backed him onto the broad, slick-barked wood. He shucked his trousers down to his ankles, and she smiled when she saw he was ready.

"There." She settled on him. "That's better, isn't it?"

"Lots better."

"Stay still."

He wheezed with her weight as she moved. "Oh . . . kay."

"Hold me . . . here."

In the long moments he felt the breeze caress them with soft aromas and listened for any sound that might be a threat. Fidget birds that were always chattering and scattering chose this moment to go jumping through a nearby bush. He glanced to check, then focused on her eyes, which were drilling into him with concentration.

You're never off duty, he thought, and she whispered, "Slow. Don't rush it. Slow. Keep doing that. Oh yes. God, Herb, yes, that's it. Just like that."

He said nothing about the name, just concentrated. A

small tremor came from branches above, then stopped. Wind whistled, wood creaked. "Lift up a little."

"That?" he gasped out.

Then it got fast and intense and he lost all sense of place. When he came, it was hard and the scents of the woodland swarmed up into his nostrils.

"Ah . . . Okay." She exhaled a long, fluttery sigh and something fell on them.

"Snake!" she cried, and rolled away. So did the snake. It was long and fat and slithered away.

Cliff stood and snatched up his pants, which were caught in his boots. *Not smart*, he thought just before the second snake appeared. It paused, rearing up to a meter height on a fidgeting stand of short tails. The beady eyes jerked around, studying them. *It's smart*, he thought, and saw two more snakes come weaving out of the leafy background. They smelled like grease and ginger. Their eyes yawned wide in surprise.

Then they all paused. Cliff could now see all four snakes, taking their time as they studied Irma. He plucked his laser from his belt and said, "Just stay still. Don't look threatening."

"*Me* don't look threatening?"

This provoked some signals between the snakes, their slim heads jutting as they rasped out soft sounds. *Do they recognize that we're using a language?* Their sibilants also seemed like words, modulated with clicks and head-juts. He noticed suddenly that two snakes had a belt tightened near their heads, and small slim things like tools tucked into loops.

The moment hung in the soft air. The snakes eyed one another, heads jerked back to regard the humans, they rapped out a few more short bursts—and then darted away.

Cliff started after them and Irma called, "Let them go!"

He didn't fear them somehow. They hadn't bitten. Maybe this was just an accident.

They were just strange enough to make him follow the

wiggling shapes through the understory of thrashing green limbs, long stems with leaves, and flowering plants. After thirty meters he was going to give up, but the snakes, moving in parallel now and weaving in sequence like a wave, turned toward an out-jut of dirt. They went into a hole about twenty centimeters across, each taking a turn while the others turned to confront Cliff. The last one hissed something loudly, turned, and slipped quickly inside.

Irma came up beside him. "What the—?"

"I want to know more about those."

"Hell, they made me wet myself."

"They're tool users. I—"

"Snakes? Come on."

"And they're smart."

"Snakes!"

"They got away from us, didn't they?"

FORTY

They came down the spire easily, cushioned on magnetic fluxes that Aybe treated like a rubbery ski slope.

They got him to slow down, but he always took a slide when there was a catch basin below. Then he would fetch them up against the opposing slope, braking with the magnetic fields that were surprisingly strong within one meter of the rock.

Most of the catch basins held deep blue water. The look of mountain lakes rimmed by trees reminded Cliff of hiking in the Sierras, which were much the same as centuries ago, judging from the Ansel Adams photos he had studied.

After all, humans had restored the ancient world they destroyed in the twenty-first and twenty-second centuries, the Great Rewilding. In Siberia, people had even carried out a Pleistocene rewilding, bringing back wolves, lynx, cougars, wolverines, grizzlies, and sea otters—top carnivores driven nearly to extinction. Once the human population fell back to two billion, there was room.

Cliff had helped in that when a boy. Nothing biotech or major, just clearance of invasive species. He left near dawn in summers, wearing oiled pants to fend off chaparral scratches, carrying a big knife, a pick mattock, and binocs. *Who meets the dawn owns the day*, his father always said—and remembering this, he felt a pang that the father who had said goodbye to him with a firm handshake at their parting was now dead over a century.

In those bright summer days, he had killed invasive pampas grass, flamboyant blond plumes that sucked nutrients from the California soil and fed nothing. He cut and gouged down stands as big as his house. He was a bio-bigot supreme, angry at tough, foreign plants that took all and gave nothing. Far better than going after trout or deer, and better, rougher exercise. It felt good to yank pampas grass up. Then the chem death—spray the roots and dug-out ground with an herbicide sting.

The memory made him think of how any mind could build this Bowl and make it work. It was millions of times larger in area than the whole Earth. How did they deal with species and change?

Even California was hard to manage, demanding lots of gut labor. The golden hills where he grew up were in fact an outcome of invasive Spanish grasses. Those outcompeted the native bunchgrasses, whose deeper roots kept them green through the year. But the climate warming of the twenty-first and twenty-second centuries favored the feisty, talented travelers people called weeds—which just meant a plant someone didn't like—that were more robust compared to the local Spanish grasses. So change came again, and the Bowl would face such sweeping alterations, too.

Moodily mulling this over, he hardly noticed when Terry nudged him. "Something big."

Aybe saw it, too, and angled them over into shelter below a ledge. A long blue green tube was drifting high up across the sky. It was partway through a turn, coming around so the nose pointed their way.

"It's seen us," Terry said. "And coming down. Speeding up."

Aybe said, "Same old deal—you trade altitude for velocity."

"So they've got blimps," Terry said. "Makes sense, with this deep an atmosphere."

"Yeah," Aybe said. "Got no fossil fuels, hard to run a plane without 'em. Might as well float."

Irma pointed. "Not a blimp. Fins moving. Rowing in the sky? Look—" She close-upped with her binocs. "—it's got eyes."

"A living blimp," Cliff said. "That's one adaptation I didn't think of."

Through his binocs he close-upped the warty hide of the thing. Bumps and gouges expanded into turrets and sealed locks. Yet the thing had big eyes and ample fins like the sails of a fat ship. They canted to catch the wind and he saw other eyes toward the stern of it.

How could such a thing evolve? He had seen floating bird-like things with big, orange throats they could expand. But he'd guessed that was just a sexual display, not a navigational trick. There were odd slits in its side. At extreme magnification he saw things moving along there and abruptly knew he was seeing through a transparent window. The tiny shapes visible there looked like the Bird Folk. "Living, sure. With passengers."

Irma said, "I can see the tail as it comes around. Big! It's sure hard to judge distance here. From the detail, I can see it's a long way off, ten klicks at least."

Terry said, "So it's *really* large. . . ."

"We'd better run," Aybe said, and took the magcar whooshing down the slope. He popped up the field screen to deflect the wind.

Terry said, "Circle round, block their view so they can't see us as they approach."

"Right," Cliff said, thinking. "Run into those canyons and stay low. We'll be hidden then."

They continued down, Aybe deftly buffeting them against the magnetic fields. This took them frighteningly close to the sheets of rock that made up the spire. "Stay near the trees, at least!" shouted Terry. "If we smack those rocks at these speeds—"

"Don't bother me!" Aybe shouted, and narrowed his eyes, gripping the yoke tightly. Sweat ran down his brow and dripped off his chin.

They got into a narrow canyon just as something came arcing through the sky. It was a slim airplane with visible pilots. "Should've known they'd send something faster. Think they saw us?"

"We were visible only a few seconds—"

The canyon wall exploded. Shards and chunks of rock rained down. The windshield proved to be better than that. Cliff jerked his head up at the *wham* of impact and saw a rock larger than his head fall, tumbling, then sag into the field shield and bounce off.

Aybe threw the yoke forward and they accelerated, a meter above the rough ground. The car jittered as the magnetics dealt with the onrushing shelves of rock in the canyon floor.

Carl heard somebody's breath rasping in and out. He had heard it before. It was his. The others were hanging on as Aybe made a hard left into a narrow side cut. *What if this is a box canyon?* Cliff thought but decided not to say. It was too late. They rounded the sharp curve and another *wham* behind them threw rocks and gravel against the magcar. Cliff looked up but could not see the plane. Aybe took a hard right into a passage that angled steeply up so only a sliver of sky showed.

Irma said, "If we get trapped in here—"

"We're not running, we're hiding," Aybe said flatly. "I don't think they can see us this far down in a crevice."

Terry said, "You decided that without a word?"

"There wasn't time. They threw missiles at us so fast, I could barely stay out of their view. They'd catch us eventually."

Irma said, "You're right. Or anyway, we have to stick with this now."

Terry hunched down and twisted his mouth skeptically. "What if they just use bigger warheads?"

"I doubt they can. Punching away at the understructure of this Bowl is risky," Cliff said. "I'd bet they don't use heavy ordnance."

"Let's hope," Terry said.

So they sat. They kept the screen up, which in turn muffled outside sounds. They sat so they could watch in all four directions, including up at the crooked line of blue sky. That soon went white from clouds scudding in. They could hear no sounds of the plane or the colossal balloon creature, and neither crossed the crack of sky.

Purple clouds slid across the narrow slit above. For a moment they drew down the windscreen and listened. A breeze stirred the sand nearby but they could hear no odd sounds. "We'd better just stay here, lie still, draw no fire," Aybe said.

So they waited a long hour. Then another.

Terry got impatient. They dropped the screen again, and everyone got out to pee. Cliff squatted in a side passage and had just finished up using the paper tree bark to clean himself when suddenly big raindrops smacked his head. More spattered down as he ran back, getting soaked. By the time he got there, torrents were hammering on the magcar and bringing a prickly tinge of ozone as lightning forked and crackled. He was last and they all got more wet when Aybe dropped the screen to let Cliff in.

They sat and watched noisy water splash down the rock walls. Streams rushed by, gathering force and lapping at the car.

"We'd better get the hell out of here," Terry said.

Aybe scowled skeptically at the rushing water. "Okay. I'd rather get caught than drown."

"If water gets drawn up into our undercarriage—" Cliff

stopped. "Never mind, we don't really know how this thing works anyway."

This had been bothering him, but it did no good to say so now. *You learn more with your mouth shut,* he thought. *Amazing, how often that's the right way to go.* No one said anything as streams slid down the screen, blurring the view.

"Somebody could come up on us here and we'd never know," Terry mused. "But movement draws attention," Terry added.

Cliff recalled his father saying, *The early bird may get the worm, sure, but the second mouse gets the cheese.*

"We can't just sit here," Aybe said adamantly. "That living balloon will come looking, use a search grid."

Irma nodded, her hair bedraggled. Aybe tried the controls and got a comforting hum from the floor. He lifted them above the muddy, frothing waters. Gingerly he found a side channel and went up it. After cautiously following that for minutes, Aybe paused to see if any danger lurked. A broad canyon yawned ahead, ghostlike in the sleeting rain that blew by in gusts. "This is a real break," he said, looking back at the others, who were still wringing water out of their clothes. "Looks like a long valley. I think I'll make time up that canyon so that air whale can't find us."

"Unless they can look through rain in nonvisible wavelengths," Terry said. "Then we'll be a nice fat moving target."

Irma said, "And we *are* a target. Aybe, don't worry—you won't get caught. They're shooting to kill."

Silence as this sank in.

"Um," Aybe said. "I'll hug the walls, then."

"Might help," Terry said, "but—" He glanced up at an angle, saw nothing through the hammering downpour. "—we don't know where that sky whale is."

"And we won't know," Cliff said. "That's our problem."

Aybe grinned. "Indecision may or may not be my problem. . . ." They all laughed, breaking the tension.

Out they went. The canyon snaked a lot and through the screen looked like dim blobs. Without saying anything, Aybe turned up the speed, elevating another meter for safety. At a speed Cliff judged to be at least sixty klicks an hour, the driving rain seemed to miraculously go away. Water swept around the sides and Cliff realized this was from the speed, clearing the view far better than wipers could.

They sat and pretended not to worry, which only lengthened the silences between them. Cliff realized that while they had been running from aliens for long weeks now, the odds had changed. The birdlike aliens were trying to kill them now. If cornered, what should he do?

He knew he wouldn't beg. That would be an insult to all humanity. He felt this immediately, without thinking.

The others were probably thinking about this, too. He could see the strain in their averted eyes, the sagging lines of fatigue in Irma, who was still futilely trying to wring out her hair. How much longer could they take of this?

Aybe concentrated, flying them past rock walls, which zoomed by like ghosts that slid out of the storm, flashed by, and then fell away into mist. Cliff realized that rain was the only cover they or any living thing had here. No creature could take advantage of darkness, ever. He saw some animals running nearby and wondered if they, too, were repositioning themselves. Or using the rain as cover to mate?

"Y'know, maybe it's no accident that most people have sex at night," he said suddenly. "Or at least indoors." He had to get them out of this funk, if only because *he* had to get out of it.

"What?" Irma shot him a sharp warning look.

So he told them in roundabout fashion. Start with fear of attack while coupled, so do it in the dark and under shelter. Then frame it as really important to everyone. Give social signals, so nakedness implied you were willing to have sex— why else were people so embarrassed to be seen nude, as though they had revealed some deep secret? Set up tribal rules so couples don't get disturbed then. Make it important, not just a quick jump-on in the dark. It was a contrived theory, made up on the spot, but it did its job.

As he had guessed, Aybe made the first joke. It wasn't a very good one, but Terry followed that with a real groaner. They got to laugh and sport, and the lines in their faces faded. Talk came fast, short, punchy, delicious. Their group training came out unself-consciously—how to lift the mood, knit up the small abrasions of working together.

Cliff knew he had droned on during the long times they were sand sailing, and now in the mag car for days, so he made use of that history.

After the laughing, he went on just to distract them from the danger they were in and could take only so much of, and still stay steady and focused. So he told them what he thought about this strange huge place. He noticed that there were flowers, pretty unsurprising as a convergent evolution—but here they always bloomed. Trees didn't drop leaves unless they were dying, since no chill was coming, ever. Animals had no downtime—so burrows where they rested were large, and guarded. Small animals defended their nests ferociously since they had to have a sheltered spot in near darkness to rest, recuperate, and, of course, mate.

Irma gave him a skeptical look and he knew his little seminar was boring them again. When he paused, she said, "Why's this so big? And why's nobody here?"

Terry said, "You mean, why so much open land?"

Aybe said, "They don't like cities, maybe? We haven't seen anything more than towns."

Cliff nodded. "Even from *SunSeeker* we didn't see big metro areas."

"Maybe the Bird Folk like countryside, not cities," Irma said. "I know I do."

They came around a long curve and suddenly the rain died. Without prompting, they all stood and surveyed as far as they could. Terry called, "It's there!"

The balloon creature was a distant tube hanging above a rocky headland. Cliff hadn't thought till now that the balloon was subject to the winds that brought the storm. It was plain bad luck that the wind moved the creature to block their path.

Looking through his binocs, Terry called, "They just dispatched one of those silent planes. It's turning back toward us."

Only then did Cliff glance in the opposite direction and see that the spire lay behind them. "Damn!" he said. "We have to go back where we were." *So much for running away.*

Aybe expertly turned the magcar and took them away, using the canyon walls to keep them screened from the airplane's view. They ran hard for the spire canyons, which were deeper and afforded more shelter. They all sat in silence. Being hunted was now a gray fear they all carried at the back of their minds, with no letup.

Aybe slowed a bit and let out a yelp. "I got it! I've been wondering about that spire. Cliff, check me. We saw a pattern of them from *SunSeeker,* right?"

"Uh, yeah."

"I know why. They're in a grid because they're part of the construction. They're stress juncture points!"

They looked at him blankly. "They're like counterweights, see?" Aybe took his hands off the yoke and gestured, palms perpendicular to each other. "They draw support cables and pair them off against each other in bridges, see?"

Irma said vaguely, "This spinning bowl, it's like a bridge?"

"Yes," Aybe said eagerly, "one with both ends tied to each other."

"Why's it a spire?" Terry asked.

"I'll bet there's a counter-spire on the outside of the bowl, too. It's all about matching stress." To their hesitant looks, he added, "Think of it as like an arch, each side supporting the other."

"An arch works against gravity—," Terry began.

"And this place works against the centrifugal force— which we feel as gravity," Aybe said triumphantly.

Cliff liked Aybe's getting them out of their funk, but had to ask, "So what? I mean, that's cute but—"

"Don't you see?" Aybe asked, wide eyed. "The natural place to lay out a transit system is along the stress lines. That's where the heavy mechanics gets resolved. Plenty of support for rail lines, things like that."

Cliff thought he got it, but—"So some transport stops here? Like a train station?"

"Or elevator," Aybe said. "Same thing, really, in a damn weird contraption like this."

Cliff called up some pictures he had from the *SunSeeker* surveys. Under high resolution, he could make out the tiny needle points jutting off the back side, pointing at the stars. They formed a grid around the hemisphere and had seemed unimportant at the time. He had been overwhelmed with the whole idea then, just getting his head around it.

"So?" Terry asked. "We've got airplanes looking for us—"

"And we can hide, but who knows what kinds of detectors they have?" Aybe rushed on. "So we have to go to ground, get out of their view—"

"Into that subway system you think correlates with the spire, right?" Irma said brightly.

Aybe jerked a thumb up. "Yep! You're right, it's more like a subway, buried below us."

"And where is it?" Cliff said soberly.

"At the spire, of course. Makes engineering sense. I was stupid not to see it before."

They were all standing and Cliff slapped him on the shoulder. "Great! Sniff it out, then."

Irma hugged Aybe, and Terry shook his hand, but as he did so, they heard a distant whispering burr. Terry jerked his head. "The plane. It's coming."

"We'd better find this subway pretty damn soon," Cliff said.

They set off, moving fast.

PART VIII

ONE MAN'S MAGIC

One man's "magic" is another man's engineering.

—ROBERT A. HEINLEIN

FORTY-ONE

This alien technology had a strange effect on him. Cliff looked at it with foreboding as they approached.

The towering sides of great obsidian-dark slabs let intricate designs play out in the elongated perspectives. Bladelike sheaths of a gleaming yellow metal soared up the flat faces, ornamenting it with geometric shapes that tricked the eye into confusions of perspective. Or Cliff's eyes, anyway. Triple vertical vents like shark gills suggested a cooling channel.

It loomed above them as they dismounted from the magcar. In the last few hours, they had chased down innumerable narrow canyons, looking for Aybe's "train station" somewhere near the base of the stony spire. After several false leads into literal blind alleys, their nerves got frayed. Coming back out of a canyon they knew would serve as a perfect trap for their pursuers above, they wondered what waited in the sky. Airplanes swam like sharks in the pale blue and seemed to frighten big flocks of birds into flapping anxiously away. Aybe hugged the magcar to the stone walls, moving into the open only when they were low on the horizon.

Then the magcar nearly ground to a halt, strumming and grinding in its bowels. Aybe had a hard time getting it to inch forward. After a tense while, it surged again. Following a winding gorge that slowly widened, they came upon what Cliff now realized should have been obvious—a broad, steep canyon of what seemed to be a conglomerate blending into green sandstone, water cut and layered. This canyon spread out after a few kilometers into an enormous plaza of rough stone, baking beneath the constant sun. They circled this, still keeping to the walls, until across the expanse they saw a lofty construction sunk into the mass of the rising spire. Cliff judged it to be at least a kilometer high. It took them nearly an hour to circle around to near its base. Then they paused.

Irma said, "Look, tracks."

Wheeled transport had passed this way many times, leaving a spaghetti snarl of trails. Most were so faint, Cliff had to avert his eyes to see them.

Terry gestured. "Some gouged their way."

Deep ruts were spaced about ten meters apart. Whatever had come this way stressed the very rock it moved on. The rut rims were rounded, so it must have been long ago. "They go straight into that," Irma said, pointing to the open entrance at the center of the black façade.

They all hesitated. Aybe moved the magcar forward but again it slowed, muttered and snarled, and slowed even more.

"I hope it's not failing," Irma said.

"I can't figure what's up." Aybe shrugged. "Tried the registers in these funny displays, popped open what I could. Most of it's sealed tight, or has key slots I don't have tools for. Not like I have the operating manual."

"We've been driving it pretty hard now—" Terry glanced at his right, which meant he consulted his interior software. "—thirteen days. Maybe it needs an oil and lube."

Irma sniffed. "Smells like a lubricant coming to a boil."

Cliff let them talk it out, knowing there wasn't any real choice. He turned his e-gear toward the sun. Once inside, he suspected there would be no chance to get a recharge.

"It makes sense," Irma was saying. "And we're at the entrance of this place, so—"

"So we hide the car and see what's inside," Cliff said quietly. "Beat it if we find trouble."

. . .

It was big. Also empty.

More deep ruts in the flooring showed where the big weight had come from. They followed, eyes constantly moving.

In the middle of a huge, high-ceiling foyer stood stonework on a pedestal. It was the size of a big man and rotated slowly on a magnetic suspension. All surrounding light seemed to radiate out from it, sparkling as rich facets shifted up and down the color spectrum.

Cliff moved his head, and fresh detonations of blue and yellow lanced out. The stone did not seem to have a fixed shape. As facets shifted across its surface, the very boundaries of the thing seemed to alter. "It's hypnotic," Aybe said.

Its light came from within yet played on what light fell on it—brilliant, soothing, stunning in its sense of eternal hard beauty.

Irma took out her laser and down-tuned it to flashlight level. She played it over the stonework, fetching forth bright, coruscating waterfalls of spectral glows. "What an artwork," she said admiringly.

So it was, Cliff thought, but—"Turn your laser off. Maybe it's an alarm."

Irma blinked and backed away. The stonework subsided, its splintered light dimming. Plainly it fed on incoming light. "Let's move," she said.

They backed away from the stonework and followed the ruts toward a high arched entrance. Inside the next large cavern, they saw a huge door divided in two. "Looks like an elevator, all right," Terry said.

"No button on the side to summon it," Irma noted.

"Over millions of kilometers?" Aybe shook his head. "It'll have to work like a train to—"

Faint sounds from behind them. A rustling, then a clang.

Cliff looked around. "There, lower left on the far wall. Could be a door."

They scrambled for it. On close approach at a full run, Cliff saw it was much bigger than a human door and had a lumpy embedded ornament—maybe a lock?—in the middle.

As Cliff skidded to a halt, Aybe said, "Why run? Let's take them on."

"For what?" Irma spat out.

Cliff ignored them. The door didn't respond to a simple shove and it didn't look as though their lasers could quickly cut through the heavy metal around it—brass? Iron? He couldn't think. The thumping noises from behind them were louder now. The ornament had a complicated opening at its center. And now he heard clumping footsteps and rumblings of something heavier.

He fumbled with the collar around the center and then Irma said, "Let me." She took a tool kit out and tried several long slender instruments. It seemed incredible to Cliff that this could be an analog lock. He started to brush her aside but then thought, *What would last here?* Not digital nets, whose elements decay. No—simple hard metal.

Irma struggled and tried another tool. A third. A fourth. The sounds behind got stronger and now Cliff could hear some muffled jabber making sounds like words, but he was too frazzed out to think about them. Irma twisted hard— she had two levers in the complicated slot—and it gave.

The door was heavy and it squeaked as Irma and Terry shoved it open. Beyond lay darkness. They all stepped through and carefully tugged the door back. Irma turned her laser to illumination mode and they saw the rugged lock apparatus on the door's center. Terry shoved one of Irma's tools through the stay to stop it from locking them in, and they all pushed the door into its frame. No click.

"Is that smart?" Cliff whispered. "They can just push and know someone's come in through it."

Irma frowned. "Maybe so. They came so fast, as if they're answering that alarm—must be from nearby."

Aybe said, "If they're caretakers, they'll conduct a search. Maybe they can extract images from that stonework and know what we look like."

"Let's lock it behind us," Cliff said. "Now."

They did, releasing the rod and watching a big clamp take hold. "Now what?" Terry said.

They turned to peer through the gloom. Big machinery ran along one wall, secured with chains. Dust tickled his nostrils and coated his lips. It felt fine and acidic, the grime of millennia. Somehow this felt luxurious, as if he could fall into its soft domain. He had not realized how the silky texture of the restful dark felt like home.

"Cliff, come on," Terry called, and he went to explore.

They were in a framing room that apparently wrapped around the "railroad" and held repair equipment. Large transparent walls showed them the railroad itself. There were indeed two sets of rails in the middle of the large corridor, running flat on the ground and tapering away into blurred distance. A blue radiance showed collars lining the rail tunnel, pale frames with luminescent inner rims of white.

"Big rail cars, must be," Aybe said.

Cliff said, "Boxcars the size of a house."

"That white light is getting stronger," Irma pointed out.

"I feel a breeze," Terry said. Howard was coughing in the dust that swarmed up from the floor.

Cliff could see four of the collars brighten, and the breeze got stronger and suddenly the white collars flared. In the hard flash, a crackling came sharp as something shot by and a muffled *whump!*—with a quick flicker—told them the thing had passed at high velocity. The window rattled—

Then the true surge wrapped through the side rooms, and the heft of it knocked them down. It was quick and delayed just enough so that Cliff knew what had happened only when he found himself flat on his back, blinking up into the dimly lit dark. He got up, rubbing his head where it had hit the dusty floor. He sneezed.

The others were up and wandering. Irma stood, legs spread and head down, gasping in the low oxygen. Howard rubbed his head, cursing. Terry got to his feet and leaned on the wall beside the big window and breathed in and out in a systematic way, eyes ahead.

Aybe got unsteadily to his feet, slipped, caught himself. His eyes wandered and he shook his head, gasped. "See those?" he asked, pointing at slim, shiny fibers, electrical ribbons attached at all four sides. "They're dischargers. That flash— even through this thick window, my hair stood on end. This must be an electrodynamic system."

Cliff remembered e-lifts Earthside that worked by charging elevators and then handing the weight off to a steady wave of electrodynamic fields. This might be similar.

"Did you feel that tremor as it passed?" Aybe said. "It didn't just shake—the floor, it sank a bit. That 'train' is heavy."

Terry said, "How do we get on one?"

"Find out how to stop one, first," Cliff said.

Terry smiled. "Then—where do we go?"

The big question. "Away from here," Cliff said. "That's what we've been doing all this time—move, dodge, try to learn."

"What about finding Beth's team?" Irma asked.

Cliff paused and felt their eyes on him. "I'd like to, sure. As far as we know, they're in the hands of the Bird Folk. But where?"

"Maybe near the mirror zone?" Aybe asked.

"Because they sent that image from there?" Irma shook her head. "Could be just suckering us in."

Cliff held his tongue. He hadn't known when it happened how to discuss with the others the Beth image. He still didn't.

"Y'know," Terry said, "we're going way out on a limb here."

"Out on a limb," Irma said, "is where the fruit is."

Aybe said impatiently, "We need to get away! Why not take the first one we can get?"

They all looked at one another, as if realizing how little they knew and how few options they had—and nodded.

Cliff sensed a slight breeze. "Another one coming."

They braced themselves. But this time there was no gale, just an amiable breeze carrying a *whooooosh* that ebbed away. A long series of blocky cars passed, slowing, slowing—

That distracted them from seeing the black carapace of a machine that stood on three legs beside a side wall. Its slender arms manipulated controls on a panel. It made a final move and the train stopped.

Down a side alley of the vast alien platform came bulky gray robots. Soundless, swift, they ran on tracks and held their big arms up, as if saluting. A team of six opened the side of one car and started unloading capsules stacked within. They moved with surprising speed, all coordinated and specialized—lifting, loading, moving the capsules down the alley and into the distant reaches. None of the robot heads turned to look at the humans watching through the viewport nearby; they worked like monomaniacs, which of course they were.

"See that control box against the side wall?" Howard pointed. "That machine used it and the train stopped."

They studied the machines working, and Cliff felt a tremor beneath his feet. Again he had the sensation of something massive moving nearby. It seemed to pass perpendicular to the tracks he could see. "There's another level," he guessed. "The other axis of a grid, must be."

"Sure, longitude and latitude on the Bowl," Terry said.

"These tracks run to higher latitude," Aybe said.

Irma asked, "How can you tell?"

Aybe grinned, nodded to her. "I have an innate sense of direction. In basic, remember when they set us down in a forest and told us to find our way home?"

Cliff did. He had flunked. It had made him fear being dropped, though he did well in the other field tests. "So?"

Aybe's grin got wider. "I beat your asses, remember? I watched you straggle in."

It had been embarrassing. Cliff felt his face burn at the memory. The Georgia pine forest was utterly flat, the trees packed in tight to get the best yield for pulp paper, so the going was tough—and the sky cloudy, so he couldn't use the sun to navigate. He had finally paired up with a guy, then another, and they had found their way by using a search pattern, each staying within calling distance of the others. Not really a way to track in wilderness, when there might be predators or enemies, but it had worked. Sort of. Later he learned that he had nearly lost the cut for *SunSeeker* because of that. Even though he had been an Eagle Scout.

Irma's mouth twisted sardonically. "So?"

Aybe glared. "Just that these are the tracks we should take to higher latitude. This train is headed the right way. It's freight, no passengers we can see . . ."

"And?" Terry asked.

Aybe was making them wait for his wisdom. "Let's have it," Cliff said sharply.

"If we jump on this one, stay in the vacant cars, nobody will see us."

Hop a freight, Cliff remembered reading in a novel somewhere. A classical expression, apparently.

Irma looked dubious, eyebrows raised. Terry snorted. "We'd be stuck in a box!"

"Aren't we stuck right now?" Aybe shot back.

"These are freight cars—"

Aybe held up his phone, thumbed it to a slow replay. "I got

this while the first cars whizzed by." The lead car had windows, and through them they could see oddly shaped seats or couches. There were rectangular machines on the far walls. "Looks like passenger seats. Nobody in that one, as far as I can see."

Terry said, "Seems risky."

Cliff held up his hands. "How do we do it, anyway? I don't see a way—"

"There—" Aybe pointed down a side corridor. "I saw a doorway to the left, and I'll bet we can get to it that way."

Terry shook his head. "I doubt we—"

A clanking came at the big door they had come through. It was locked and secured with a metal bar Irma had found. They stared at the heavy door as the noise—rattles, bumps, jarring hits—got louder.

"They found us . . . ," Terry said. "Damn—"

The rattles stopped and so did Terry. Pause. A buzzing sound from the large door.

Cliff said, "They're cutting in."

Aybe said, "Let's get out of here."

Irma raised an eyebrow. "To . . . where?"

Cliff looked at the robots. They were nearly done unloading. He leaned against the hard, transparent window and saw in a long perspective other docking platforms, with milling robots. It was a long train.

He didn't like being forced into a move. *If you're on the run, though . . .*

"Let's do it," Cliff said. "Now."

Nods, some resigned sighs. They had brought most of their gear in backpacks and stuffed cargo pants. They ate some of their food as they watched the robots finishing up; less to carry. Cliff worried about getting on this train, but there seemed no other plausible option. How would they eat? When should they try to get off?

The robots were nearly done when they angled down the

left side corridor. There were periodic windows. Cliff could see similar robot teams unloading or loading other cars. They trotted along, looking for the passenger cars. "Let's pick it up," he called out. If the train left and they were trapped . . .

They ran for five minutes until they saw the sole passenger car, the leader of a long line that stretched far into the rear. This one was longer than the freight cars and had big windows. And it looked vacant.

No robots seemed to be around it. They went through a kind of lock with a pressure seal flexible frame, and onto the dock. Robots labored in the distance but took no notice of the humans. The car door slid easily aside, and they spread out to see if anyone was aboard. Nothing, though the place had a damp smell like a zoo. A forward-viewing window showed the tunnel ahead, lit every hundred meters or so by phosphor walls giving an ivory glow.

They tried the rectangular machines bolted to one wall and found that they yielded food—or what passed for it here. Punch and grab, an analog system. Some wrapped things fell into the hopper. They looked like dried cat litter but smelled not bad.

They stayed out of view of the windows. Cliff felt tired. Howard looked worse. There was blood in his scalp.

They watched carefully, but the machines that passed by outside seemed unaware of anything wrong. Just as he sat down, the train accelerated away without any warning. Irma had found a big door with pressure seals on it and was about to open it when the train started. She sat down hastily and they found the seats adjusted to their shape automatically, and warmed to a comfortable temperature as well. After so long in the magcar, Cliff let himself relax.

But the train kept accelerating. He sniffed the air and tasted the tang of ozone. The ride was smooth and he went forward to see. They were hurtling forward at a speed he estimated, from the rapid fluttering of the passing wall phosphors, at over a hundred kilometers an hour. Yet the acceleration increased still.

He sat next to Aybe and said, "We're still accelerating."

"This is a big place. This system is already better than any e-train I ever rode on. To move around it in, say, a week, means this thing has to get into the neighborhood of a hundred kilometers a *second*."

"Um. Maybe they take longer."

"I hope not. Those food machines can't—wait, maybe they *can* make food from scratch." Aybe blinked at the thought.

Cliff worried that he had led them not into a trap, but into a death voyage.

FORTY-TWO

Redwing watched the Bowl's enormous landscape slide by in the distance and reflected on how, decades ago, he had been something of a scientist, too. He'd become a spacer because of that.

And from that he'd won the habits of mind that led him to lead a band of scientists and engineers to a new world. This thing, the Bowl, was not a world, but a huge contrivance. It gave the appearance of being nearby, because he could see patterns resembling those he had watched for wonderful hours, in low Earth orbit. Yet it was tens of millions of kilometers away, its sealed-in atmosphere deep and strange.

The comparison deceived his eye. Here the atmospheric circulations he had studied as a young man were utterly different and vast beyond comprehension. The star's light fell uniformly, or nearly so, across the Bowl. But it never set, and so drove none of the night-day winds that shaped the movements he had studied, the stately currents of atmospheres on Mars, Earth, Titan, Venus. The Bowl always kept the same attitude toward its star, too. That meant no seasonal variations, no hard winters or hammering summers. He had savored long ago—centuries in real time!—crisp autumn skies, with their bright, blazing fall colors, and then after the cold months, the promise of spring. None of that happened here. Aliens had designed in the steady shine of a small star and its jet. No night. What would want *to live in endless day?*

So air currents did not flow up from the spot where the

star was directly above, since there were none. Or rather, it was the Knothole, where the Jet passed through. No Hadley cells, polar swirls, trade winds, or barren desert belts wrapping around the globe. Instead, here the effect of spin held sway.

He could see long streaming rivers of cloud begin above the ample dark blue seas, then arc over distances larger than the separation between the Earth and its moon, driven to higher latitudes of the immense Bowl. Purple anvils of sullen cumulonimbus towered up to seven kilometers above landscapes of mottled brown and red. The scale of all this violated his sense of what patterns could be possible. Clearly the whole vast contraption had been designed to hold everything constant—steady sunlight, no big differences of temperature to drive storms or trade winds. It left him with no intuitions at all of how weather got shaped.

Climate came from the spin, then. To pin its inhabitants to the ground, they spun it—and then got curious Coriolis effects.

Abruptly the name alone brought back his grad student days. That had been more than half a century ago, and there leaped to mind a drunken song of the climate modelers.

> On a merry-go-round in the night
> Coriolis was shaken with fright
> Despite how he walked
> 'Twas like he was stalked
> By some fiend always pushing him right!

Apparently Coriolis had been a mild man, but his force made hurricanes, tornadoes, jet streams, and assorted violences. Those should occur here—and as he thought it, he saw a brilliant white hurricane coming into view of the screen on his office wall. That slow churn of darkening clouds was the size of Earth itself, spinning its gravid whirl toward the shore of a huge sea. *Trouble for somebody*, he thought. *Or some thing.*

The knock on his door drew him back into the humdrum reality of *SunSeeker*.

Karl's lean face was all smiles, which could be good news. *There's a first time for everything*, Redwing thought. But the lean man folded himself into the guest chair and unloaded the bad news first.

"There's a progressive crazing of those transparent ceramic windows we use for the astronomy," he began. "Caused by mechanical stress or maybe some ions that get through the magnetic screen. Limits their working life."

"You can fix it?"

He waved a hand lazily, somehow sure of himself. "Sure, got the printer making new ones right now. The external robos can slap them on when done, and I'll feed the old ones in for materials stock. Not why I came to see you, Cap'n." The slow smile again, above dancing eyes. "I've got an idea."

"Good to hear," Redwing said automatically. This was maybe the twentieth notion Karl had delivered this way. The man did deserve some credit, for he had spruced up the ship and made it run better. But the man was so focused on his machines that he was not much further use as a deck officer. Redwing could see Karl was settling in to bask in the tech details, and it was more efficient to just let him work through it.

"I've been tuning our scoop fields for the plasma we're getting from that small star," Karl said. "It's not like protons incoming at a tenth of light speed, so I had to retune all the capture capacitors."

Redwing knew the big breakthrough that made starflight possible, though it relied on tech you never saw from the bridge. The method of catching the sleet of protons, slowing them down between charged grids for electrical power, then funneling them into the fusion chambers where a catalyst worked the nuclear magic—it all happened in the halo around the ship, and then the burn occurred in its guts, where no one could ever go. *We ride on miracles.*

He nodded, waiting for the idea.

"So we're flying with a scoop a thousand kilometers across now, all supported by nanotube mesh. Bigger funnel than we had before, 'cause the plasma's weaker. I tuned it all up—had to use the full complement of our external in-flight robos, too."

"I like the ride now," Redwing allowed. "It doesn't wake me up nights."

Karl beamed. "Glad to hear it. Lowers the structural stresses, too. Then I thought—this scoop arrangement we've got isn't optimal for where we are, so what would be better?"

Redwing wanted to ask him to just spit it out, but that didn't work well with tech crew. "I'll guess—the Jet?"

Karl's face fell. "How did you know? If—"

"What else do we have in this system?" Redwing asked with a grin. "Had to be the Jet. Plus, you know we flew in here through that Jet. What a ride!"

Karl looked surprised at Redwing's enthusiasm. The man was elaborately casual, but conservative to the bone. Useful in a deck officer, where a captain had to balance personality types against one another. A captain had to know when to take risks, not tech lieutenants.

Redwing had always thought that life's journey wasn't to get to your grave safely in a well-preserved body, but rather to tumble in, wrecked, shouting, *What a ride!* But he could see from Karl's puzzled expression that the man thought captains should be sober-minded authority figures, steady and sure, without a wild side.

"Well, sir, yes—I looked into that. The scoop settings we had then weren't as good at sailing up the Jet as the ones we have now, so . . ." Karl hesitated, as if his idea was too risky. "Why not use *SunSeeker* as a weapon?"

Now *this* was an idea. Not that he understood what it was, but the flavor of it quickened his pulse. "To . . ."

"Let me walk through it. Remember when we saw the mirror zone changing, painting a woman's face on it? I was outside with robot teams to repair the funnel struts. I could see it direct, right out my faceplate. Incredible! It was Elisabeth, the one they captured with her team, mouthing words."

Redwing gestured slightly to speed him up and Karl took the hint. "Even that—which lasted maybe an hour, then repeated every day or so—had an effect on the Jet. Gave it less sunlight, I guess, or just rippled the light over the Jet base. Big changes! A day or two later, I saw little snarls propagating out from the base of the Jet, at the star. They grew, too, moving out."

"We all did." It hadn't seemed much different from the variations Redwing had seen, over time—knots in the string. He was still amazed the bright scratch across the sky was so stable.

Karl leaned forward, eyes excited. "The mirrors focus on that spot, delivering the heat to blow plasma off the star's surface. Plus, there are stations circling the base of the Jet that must somehow generate magnetic fields. I'm guessing those big stations then shape and confine the Jet. So—" Karl cocked a jaunty grin. "—why not show them what we can do to the Jet?"

Redwing exhaled a skeptical breath. "To do what?"

"Screw it up!"

"So it—"

"Develops a kink instability. The disturbance grows as it advances out from the Jet base. It's like a fire hose—you have to hold it straight or it snarls up and fights you like an angry snake."

"Then when it gets to the Bowl . . ."

"I'm thinking we could force the kink amplitude to grow enough, it'll snake out sideways. If it hits the atmosphere containment layer—that sheet that sits on top of the ring section—then it can burn clean through it."

Redwing studied Karl's eager face. This was world destruction on a scale Redwing had never imagined. Should he have?

"Then there's the sausage instability—we get those sometimes in the funnel plasma, before it hits the capacitor sheets and slows down. A bulge starts in the flow, say, starting from turbulence. That bulge forces the magnetic fields out, and that can grow, too, just like the kink. You get a cylinder of fast plasma that looks like a snake that's eaten eggs, spaced out along it."

"So it gets fat and can—"

"Scorch the territories near the Knothole, where the Jet passes closest to the Bowl. Knock out their control installations there, I bet." The words came flooding out of the man. "I've studied them through our scopes, and they're huge coils all around the Knothole mouth. I bet they're magnets that keep the Jet away. Magnetic repulsion, gotta be."

Redwing was aghast, but he couldn't let Karl see that. "We do this by flying into the Jet?"

"More like tickling it. I can work out how we can zig across it, then zag back at the right time and place to drive an instability."

"Near the Jet base, by the star?"

"Okay, so it'll get a little hot in here, I grant you that."

Good to know he would grant something, at least. For a man proposing to kill the largest imaginable construct, he seemed unfazed.

"At no danger to *SunSeeker*?"

"I can tune the funnel parameters, do some robo work on the capacitor sheets. Fix 'em up." Karl smiled proudly. "I ran a simulation of running *SunSeeker* across the Jet already. There's a problem slicing through the hoops of magnetic stresses at the Jet boundary, sure. We cut through that and it's smooth sailing, looks like. Statistically, a Monte Carlo code shows we don't get bumped hard—"

"I recall a statistician who drowned in a lake that was on average fifty centimeters deep." Redwing smiled dryly.

Karl hastily retreated. "Well, we can just skim the Jet first, try it out."

"I'd like to see the detailed analysis, of course." He narrowed his eyes deliberately. "Written up in full."

If this crazy idea ever got anywhere, he wanted it documented to the hilt. Not that there would be any kind of superior review in his lifetime, Redwing mused, but it was good to leave a record, no matter what happened. Karl nodded and they went on to discuss some lesser tech issues.

After he left, Redwing stood and watched his wall screen show the unending slide of topography he still thought of as below, though of course *SunSeeker* was orbiting the star, not the Bowl. The hurricane was biting into the shoreline now, sowing havoc. Somebody was suffering.

He had seen that this Bowl, like a real planet, still had tropical wetlands, bleak deserts, thick green forests, and mellow, beautiful valleys. No mountain ranges worthy of the name, apparently because the mass loading would have thrown something out of kilter. But terrain and oceans galore, yes, of sizes no human had ever seen. But some minds had imagined, far back in ageless time.

The truly shocking aspect of Karl was not his idea, but the eager way he described ripping open the atmosphere cap. That would kill uncountable beings and might even destroy the Bowl itself. Redwing watched the Coriolis forces do their work. He tried to see how the global hydrologic cycle here could work—and then realized that this wasn't a globe, but a big dish, and all his education told him nearly nothing he could use.

Still, there were beings down there of unimaginable abilities. How could they survive a storm that lasted for weeks or months? That was the crucial difference here—scale. Everything was bigger and lasted longer. How long had the Bowl itself lasted? Somehow it had the look of antiquity about it.

And the creatures who made and ran it—they had both great experience and long history to guide them. Surely they would know what had just occurred to Karl.

Just as surely, they would have defenses against visitors such as Karl.

FORTY-THREE

The e-train zoomed on, at speeds Cliff estimated to be at least ten kilometers per second. Astronomical velocities, indeed. Maybe Aybe was right, arguing that to get around the Bowl in reasonable times demanded speeds of 100 km/s. The blur beyond their windows showed only the fast flickering of phosphor rings as they shot through them, until even those blended together to become a dim flickering glow.

They broke up to explore the long passenger car. There were roomy compartments with simple platforms for sitting and sleeping, and rough bedding supplied in slide shelving. Howard discovered the switches after the first hour aboard, while searching for more food. Cliff heard his shouts and came running.

"Look!" Howard said proudly when all five were there. He slid to the side a hinge switch near a compartment door. He slid a switch on the wall, and the compartment ceiling phosphors dimmed to utter dark.

They hooted, clapped, and Irma did a dance with Aybe. It was as though they had gained their freedom—freedom from sunlight.

Irma favored exploring the rest of the car, and they did. Compartments varied in size and style, mostly in the arrangement of platforms. Irma remarked, "These can accommodate passengers of varying sizes and needs. Fit to species, I guess."

Cliff nodded. "The Bird Folk are big, sure, but some of the forms we saw from a distance were smaller. Interesting, to have intelligence in a range of body types."

"But why is nobody here?" Terry insisted.

Aybe added, "And nobody at the station, 'cept robots."

"Maybe they don't travel much?" Irma wondered.

No answers, plenty of questions. The passenger car was over a hundred meters long and ended with a pressure door, where the car narrowed down. "Let's not go further," Irma said. "Great find, Howard, that light switch. Let's use them, huh?"

Aybe found something that sounded like a grinder in the tiled floor of an otherwise bare room. "That's gotta be the head," Terry said. Starships used nautical terms, and soon they were calling the train's nose the bow.

They ate before sleeping. All along, mealtimes had been important, just as they had been in their interplanetary training missions. On the Mars Cycler, Cliff had learned ship protocols and how to deal with short-arm centrifugal gravity (which made his head lurch the first week when he walked), but the most important lesson was the social congruence. Eating together promoted solidarity, teamwork, the crucial judgments of strengths and flaws they all needed to know. In a crisis, that knowledge let them respond intuitively. Here, where danger was never far away, those unspoken skills had quickly become crucial.

"What do we do when we pull into the next station?" Terry asked, munching one of the odd foods that he had squeezed out of a tube—which then evaporated into the air with a hiss, once emptied. How it knew to do this was a topic of puzzled discussion. Cliff watched them as they all pretty obviously—judging from expressions as they ate, each reflecting inwardly after the excitement of pursuit—wondered what they had gotten themselves into.

Too late, Cliff thought but did not say. He recalled another favorite phrase of his father's: *Life is just one damn thing after another.*

The train ran on in its silky way, electromagnetics handing off without a whisper of trouble. Cliff lay back and relaxed into the moody afterglow of eating more than one needed. The low hum of the train lulled him but he summoned up resolve to say, "We need to stand watches, same as before. Terry, you're up first."

Groans, rolled eyes, then the slow acceptance he had come to expect. Cliff made the most of it, standing up and trying to look severe. "We don't know anything here. We're not camping out anymore. This is a *train*, and it stops somewhere. When it does, we've got to be able to hide or run."

They nodded, logy with the meal, as he had planned.

Howard said, "We should break up, too. Don't clump up, so they can bag us all at once."

Cliff didn't like the pessimism behind that, but he said, "Good idea. But not alone."

Long silence. Terry glanced at Aybe, and Cliff suddenly remembered that one of them was gay. Which one? For the life of him, he could not remember. *Damn! All this time—*

Too late. Didn't matter anyway: Howard, Terry, and Aybe would be sharing. Nobody alone. Cliff and Irma—

Terry and Aybe looked at him, long steady gazes, and he realized that they knew. He would be with Irma and the compartments sealed off very nicely, thank you. Never mind who was gay, the big issue here was about him and Irma. He had been ignoring it. So consumed with his own emotions, he had not thought through what happened to a small band with cross-currents working below the surface. Now that they were inside again, back in a moving machine, somehow everything suppressed in the pseudo-wilderness of the Bowl melted away. It was about the old elementals—survival, sex, the splendor of the deep sensual accents. Life.

Realizing that left him speechless, which he also saw was a good idea. *Life is just one damn thing after another.*

"So what happens," Terry said evenly, "when we stop at a station?"

Irma said quickly, anxiously, "We need an exit."

All agreed. They trooped to the back end, *aft on the starboard side*, to consider the pressure door. "We've got to try it," Terry said.

The door opened with a shove. It led to a short lock chamber, and in the wall was a simple pressure gauge—long-lasting analog, of course—with release valves. Simple stuff, artifacts so clear they could serve generations without an instruction manual.

They factored through into a dark room that lit up slowly when they entered, phosphors brimming with sleepy glows.

"Freight," Terry said.

Dark lumps of webbed coverings secured units the size of Earthside freight cars at multiple points. It all looked mechanically secure and professional, robot work of a high order by Earthside standards.

Aybe said, "We fall back to here?"

"We don't have much choice," Terry said.

"If we start to slow down, send an all-alert," Irma said.

"Who's up on watch?" Terry asked innocently.

"You," Cliff said. He hadn't much hope the thin, angular man would stay awake more than five minutes beyond the rest. But it was good to set some standard, even if it was obviously not going to work. In their tired eyes he saw that they knew this, too.

So they went back, chose compartments, and cut the phosphors. For the first time in their new, strange lives here, blessed night descended.

. . .

Cliff sat up. A subtle long slow bass rumbling came through the floor. He blinked, thinking fuzzily that maybe he was under a tree, maybe some animal was nearby—and suddenly knew that this was real, solid darkness. Not shade. It wasn't going away.

He found the wall switch and powered up the phosphors. Irma jerked, shook her head, shot a palm up to block the light. "Uhh! Noooo . . ."

"Got to. We're slowing down."

Cliff clicked on his phone, sent an all-alert. Until this moment he hadn't thought if the walls of this train would block the signal. Well, too late—

"I'm up," Irma said unconvincingly. She got unsteadily to her feet, pulling on her gray underpants.

Cliff couldn't help himself. He started laughing, quick bursts of it. He bent over, tried to stop, couldn't. The laughs slowed, developed a hacking sound.

"What?" Irma said, struggling into her cargo pants.

He made himself stop. "I—I was thinking about . . . sex."

Skeptical frown. "Uh, yeah?"

"No, not now. I mean—just that—I worried about us and them, Terry and Howard and Aybe. Last night. Never realized that sleep was the big thing we all wanted."

She grimaced, yawned, stretched. "Well, yeah. This is a sleep high—feels *so good*."

"Wow, yes. I musta slept—" He glanced at his phone. "—oog . . . fourteen hours."

"And you thought about sex?" She tried to smile, failed, rubbed her eyes.

"Not really. Just thinking about the team, y'know—oh, hell. I'm not up to speed."

"Speaking of—"

Yes. *The train was slowing.* They had been so joyful, they'd ignored it. He hastened into his own pants, boots, backpack, field gear. All he had, now. Into battle, maybe.

He went out into the corridor, pulling up his backpack harness. He had run away from enough threats to know that you never can count on going back for your gear. Terry and Aybe were already there, standing warily as they looked out the windows at the dark sliding by.

"Y'know," Irma said, "we should've looked for underground places to sleep."

"We did. We ran into nothing like this train station, but yeah, we shoulda looked harder."

The phosphors were pulsing as the train passed by, their gray hoops fluttering so slow now, he could see the flicker. "I see a platform up ahead," Aybe said.

Cliff went forward. Harder glows showed the prospect ahead. He close-upped it with his binocs. There were teams of robots, standing in gray files. Beyond them . . . figures on the platform.

"Back into our rooms," Cliff said. Irma came up, still a little bleary eyed. "Seal the doors, too."

"What if some Bird Folk are assigned to our room?" Terry asked.

"Then we deal with it as it comes," Irma said, rolling her eyes.

The small surges of deceleration came slower now. Each segment of the rail line handed off to the next smoothly. Cliff went into the same compartment as Irma and they fell silent. This one had a window and they crouched down to be invisible from outside. The train slowed without any braking sound. Cliff felt hungry and fished out some of the salty food stock he had gotten from the machines. With plenty of water, it was bearable. They were long past the point of testing everything before eating now.

The train stopped. They waited. Distant clanks and rumbles. Irma and Cliff finally cast darting glances out the window. This went on and on. Robots trundled by, some as large as a car, their forward opticals never wavering. Irma put her hands on the floor, to feel any vibration from doors in their car.

"How do you feel?" she asked.

"Like a snowball in hell."

Footsteps outside, faint and hesitant. Stop, pause, then going on. Again. And again, closer.

The footsteps stopped outside. Cliff took out his laser and held his breath. The door had a mechanical lock that, despite their supposedly having secured it, now rotated. Cliff stepped forward and jerked it open.

A sleek, tawny creature held up its large, flat hands and said in slurred Anglish, "I share no harm."

Cliff glanced along the corridor, saw no one, gestured inward, and stepped back. The alien moved with grace, shifting its body to wedge into a corner, leaving the most space for the humans.

Irma said, "You speak . . . our language."

"Astronomers shared language with lessers, to make hunt easier. I loaded into my inwards. Please forgive my talk error. We were to seduce you into friendship giving out."

Cliff said, "Is anyone else coming on this train?"

The slim alien paused and consulted some internal link, Cliff judged, by the way it cast its gaze to the side. Cliff realized by standing they were visible to the platform and quickly squatted down. The alien mimicked this, bending as though it had no joints, only supple muscle.

"No. Distribute was to be, but I erased the possibility."

Its skull was highly domed, with high arches and a crest running along the top. Those and its short muzzle would give it strong jaw muscles, a classic predator feature. Yet it had no retractable claws, or maybe they were just relaxed. As he watched, the thick fingers extended sharp fingernails. *Ah!* Cliff thought. Binocular vision, too, with eyes that flicked restlessly from Irma to him.

"Erased?" Irma said cautiously.

It spoke with a low, silky growl that carefully enunciated vowels, as though they were strange. "Intersected controls so alone could greet you. And in keeping-with, deflected the pursuit team to the train orthogonal to this line."

"So we are safe here?" Irma persisted, focused intently on the alien.

"For short times."

"Why are you here?"

"To achieve consensus with you. We must bond to our joint cause."

"Which is?" Cliff said, bouncing quickly up from his squat to see the platform. Robots moving, no life-forms.

The alien made a short, soft, snorting sound. "Return to full sharing life."

To Irma's puzzled look—had it learned how to read human faces?—it said, "For all the Adopted."

"Which are—?" she asked.

"Many species, low and high. We are bonded here. We seek-wish to return-voyage our home worlds."

"You are from—?"

It made a sound like a soft shriek. In its large round eyes Cliff saw a kinship, an instant rapport that he did not need to think about. For one who dwelled in his head so much, this was a welcome rub of reality. The sensation of connection unsettled him. Why did he feel this way?

Then he had it—this was a smart cat.

"We will help you, if we can," Irma said. He saw at a glance that she felt the same as he.

"But we are only a few," Cliff hedged.

"You share-voyage with many in a ship that can damage-share the Astronomers." This came out as a fast, hissing statement, eyes widened.

A forward lurch came then, rocking them all on their

haunches. Cliff stood up with some relief. Nobody on the platform. The train surged into its heavy acceleration again, pressing at them.

"Oops! Let's get into some chairs," Irma said. "And tell Howard and Aybe and Terry. Breakfast!" She broke into a broad grin that cheered him up, out of his confusion.

FORTY-FOUR

Memor was glad she had not brought her friend, Sarko, for this was a rude and joyless place.

From their vantage here, she could see the long flanks of composite rock, carved by ancient rivers. This was bare country, left behind when topsoil had fled downhill in the far past. Now its canyons had a certain majestic uselessness for habitation, which made it perfect for an assembly of search parties. They could survey the low gravity forests that began at the canyon mouths below—a blue green ocean. Long, undulant waves marched across that plain of treetops, stretching into the distant dim oblivion. Those lofty reaches ranked among her favorite natural wonders, the gift of low gravity. There, one could "swim" in the trees, buoyed up by their fragrant multitude. The vast trees stood impossibly tall, swaying in the warm breezes that prevailed here at high latitudes. And the aliens lurked among them, surely.

"Do you have any amenities?" Memor asked the attendant, one of the lesser forms known as the Qualk, who sported an absurd headdress. Perhaps it was meant to impress her? That seemed unlikely, but one never knew.

The Qualk fluttered in tribute for the attention paid to him and gestured with an obliging neck-twirl toward the refreshments. Memor moved forward with grave energy, aware that all those in this field station watched her.

A Savant approached. "Astronomer, we have heard stories, ones we cannot believe—"

"Inability to believe is no insurance," Memor said, but laconic irony was lost on this small, squirming one with anxious eyes.

They were assembled for her. More fretful eyes, from a variety of the Bird Folk and some minor members of the Adopted. Memor allowed suspense to build as she quaffed a tangy drink and munched a crunchy thing.

"You are all here, leading your teams, to find the escaped aliens. How is that proceeding?"

Some restless shuffling, sidewise glances. The governing Savant moved to the fore. "The Packmistress sent us—"

"Never mind your prior instructions. What did you encounter?"

The Savant flicked looks around but could not avoid Memor's gaze. "Of course, we have not found the aliens. By the time we hear of them, they are gone. We could follow—after all, we have mobile troops, total air cover, local sensors—but they elude us."

"Why?"

"They seem able to move across terrain without regard for borders or the ancient constraints we all feel. They came over our regional boundaries, moving in natural terrain with concealment. We backtracked them and saw that they skirted our settlements and found ways around our checkpoints."

"You are not alone. There are two of their parties, far across our lands, and they both seem better at this than we."

The Savant nodded, said nothing.

They would come to her, this murderous band of Late Invaders, Memor thought. She had set upon the mirrors a portrait of the leader of the primary group, a face many worlds wide. "Come to me." The leader would certainly know that she had not sent that message, but the others would not. They had every motive to link somehow, and then they could all be caught.

But there was no certainty in this, and a worse danger loomed. So Memor persisted, "Is it the Adopted?"

"What—what do you imply?"

"Do they speedily report?"

"Well—" More furtive glances. No escape.

"I take it your reply is no?"

"Ah. Yes."

"You mean no?"

"Yes."

"And why is that?"

"The Adopted somehow—I have no idea why!—do not obey. They have heard of these aliens."

"And so?"

"They somehow . . ." The local Savant cast more anxious eyes. "These primates are unAdopted. Many ages have passed since the last invasive intelligences gained a foothold on the Bowl. This I truly do not understand—but many of the Adopted see them as . . . admirable."

A voice nearby said, "Improper genetic engineering, then. Or else there has been a slide in the Adopted's conditioning, occasioned by genetic drift."

An image from their Underminds, more likely, Memor thought. *An ancient archetype running free, from the times when the Adopted were on their own.* She huffed, worried, but gave no other sign of her true reaction. She had read and seen images of alien invasions, far back—many twelve-cubed Eras ago. No Astronomers now living were alive then. Though Astronomers were the longest-lived of all the Folk, even they faced a hard fact: The Bowl swam by life-rich worlds seldom. Still rarer were those planets inhabited by sentients—those who could perceive and know—which were of use to the Folk. Still more rare were aliens of sapience—entities who could act with appropriate judgment. The universe gave forth life reluctantly, and wisdom, far more so.

These alien primates, alas, had both—in quantities they surely did not deserve, given their primitive levels of development. Plainly some harsh world had shaped them, and cast them out into the vacuum, untutored.

But she was forgetting her role here. She snorted out anger, spat rebuke, and gave a reproaching feather display of brown and amber. "Admirable!"

"I regret to deliver such news."

"I had no such reports before."

"This was a regional problem, noble Astronomer."

"It is now a global one. These are dangerous aliens, afoot in our lands."

Murmurs of agreement erupted. But Memor did not want agreement; she wanted action. "We do not know what they want. We cannot allow them to remain loose."

The Savant caught her tone and lifted her head. "We shall redouble our efforts."

Memor supposed that was the best she could expect of these rural provinces. They slumbered, while mastering the Bowl fell to their betters. She sniffed, gave a flutter display, and was turning away when the Savant asked quietly, "We hear tales of the alien's excursions. . . ."

Obviously a leading question. How much did this minor Savant know? "You refer to—?"

"One of the alien bands, these tales say, discovered a Field of History."

"I believe the primary group stumbled upon one, yes. So?"

"Then they know our past. And can use it against us."

"I scarcely think they are so intelligent."

"They have eluded us." Short, to the point. This Savant was brighter than she looked.

"You worry that they will know we once passed by their world? These primates were not even *evolved* when we were nearby."

"We gather from the History that these invaders came from a world whose ancestors we once extracted."

Memor trembled but did not show it. These unsuspecting types were lurching toward a truth they should never glimpse. She stretched elaborately, looking a bit bored, and said carefully, "Yes. I researched that. They were without speech, had minimal culture, few tool-using skills. Scavengers, mostly, though they could hunt smaller animals in groups, and defend against other scavengers. Those primates, once Adopted, further evolved into game animals. Not particularly good ones, either."

This at least provoked a rippling laughter. Beneath it ran skittering anxiety in high notes. The Savant persisted, "They do not seem easy to Adopt. They may be angered to see what has become of their ancestors."

Memor did not let her feathers betray her true reaction. The Savant was right, but for reasons Savants were not privileged to know. Rely on cliché, then. No one remembered them even a moment later. "The essence of Adoption is self-knowledge."

The Savant nodded slightly, letting the matter pass when an Astronomer so indicated. Clichés, Memor reflected, were the most useful lubricant in conversation. Thus she missed the Savant's next statement, which was a question—and so soon had to give a summary of what she knew of the aliens. How this could help, she had no idea, but it deflected attention from the real, alarming issue.

She began, "These spacefaring primates have a linear view of life that extends forward and backwards in time. I discovered this while examining their minds while they functioned, and realize that some of what I say may seem implausible. It is not."

This provoked some tittering in the crowd, but Memor plowed on.

"They are very interested in the beginning of the universe,

despite the general uselessness of this information now. Even more oddly, they fix upon the long-term fate of the universe, and have strong views on these matters. Some are even religious! To Astronomers, these are matters subject to many unknowns, too many to lend a sense of urgency to the issue. Yet the Late Invaders feel urgently concerned."

A Savant asked, "How can that matter?"

"It has sent them out in their tiny, dangerous ship, yes?"

"To answer such vague questions?"

"Not entirely. Their deep drive, which they seldom know consciously, is to *expand their horizons*."

"Why? What use can that be?"

"An anxiety fills them, drives them out. I could see it simmering in their Underminds."

"I doubt such creatures could be Adopted," the Savant persisted.

"It is our task to enlighten them." Memor retreated into cliché again. "To erase this hunger for horizons, which evolution dealt them."

"Do we know their origins?"

Memor disguised her lie with a ruffle-display of purple guilt. "I fear we cannot say yet." It was truthful, in a way; she could not say.

"I meant, not what planet they are from, but why they have this anxiety?"

Memor had not considered that, and in a moment of guilty truth-telling, said so. Discussion wafted through the audience. She could see the teams who searched for the primates wondering why the discussion was so theoretical, but that was not crucial. The tone of this meeting was, though.

She took command again with, "We suspect they had to flee a hostile territory, and that crisis forced their evolution. Perhaps their numbers became too great for their environment, and the ambitious moved on to fruitful lands. This forced evolution of better tool-making and general, social in-telligence."

Now that she said it, the idea had some appeal. How *did* the primates get the urge to voyage forth in such frail ships? Because they were born on the move.

A Savant said, "They would flood our lands!"

Memor quieted their murmuring. "We can certainly con-tain that. We outnumber them by twenty orders of twelve-magnitude."

Until this moment she had not fully appreciated how strange the aliens were, even though she had seen into their minds. This was the nub of it: They loved novelty, excite-ment, and motion—even though it might mean death.

Whereas the Folk wisely lived in the perfect conditions for them, precisely to give life a constancy, a gliding sense of time that belied the issues of beginnings and endings. The reward was a place beyond the natural places, a machine for living that spun, as did worlds, and yet did so to maintain the con-stancy that was the point of the Folk. They froze time for the span of their species and perhaps beyond. Evolution of the Folk of course occurred. But the aim of artifice was to con-strain this, maintaining a close watch, so that the Folk could be in their exalted state. Thus they had thrived now through immense long tides of time, a fact well understood by each succeeding generation. The highest function of a species was surely to suspend the rude, blunt blow of happenstance, and control their own destiny. The Astronomers governed not just the relations between the Bowl and the heavens, but the Bowl Lifeshaping as well.

She thought on this, all the while letting the comments and open disputes work themselves through the assembly. When it had played out, she said with due gravity, "The pri-mates may know some of our history—but it is so vast! They cannot comprehend it."

This brought applause. The Adopted held as a matter of faith and history that the Bowl's serene constancy was the goal of all wise life. So did all the intellectual classes—Savants, Profounds, and Keepers. So what if primates knew a tiny fraction of the Saga?

Of course, her true mission here was to damp their fears. She reminded the audience of their resources, and let members of the search teams tell of their glancing contacts with the primates. None from the party who had lost their magcar, because the primates had killed them all. She mentioned this, to set the stage.

Now they would rehearse the enveloping movement planned to ensnare the roving primate band, the one that had found what they called the Field of History, which Astronomers termed the Past Worlds. A distant team would carry forward that hunt.

Memor asked, "So much for abstractions. I am here to direct your hunt for those who have already killed some of the Folk. I gather you recorded their entry at a Conveyance Station?"

Some of the Adopted nodded eagerly. "Yes, Astronomer! We have the sky creatures ready to depart."

"Most excellent. A long while has lapsed since I experienced the thrill of running down dangerous prey. Let us take to the air, then."

Nothing would get in their way now, since they had the primates located to a region. When captured, she forbade any questioning of them. A few chance remarks could wreck entire established structures of Bowl society. She could take no chance that anyone should come to know of the Great Shame.

FORTY-FIVE

The alien regarded them with its large eyes and made a curious squatting motion, its sinewy arms held out to the sides. With the large pancake hands and thick fingers, it formed a twisting architecture in the air. Its name was Quert, its Folk the Sil. Its graceful form moved restlessly, pacing among the odd chairs where the humans sat and ate. The train was moving fast now, and the staccato *snick-snick-snick* of the electromagnetic handoffs propelling it forward rang constantly in the background.

Quite deliberately it said, "*Bon voyage. Buon viaggio. Gute Reise. Buen viaje. Viagem boa. Goede reis. Ha en bra resa. God tur. Bonum iter. Καλό ταξίδι!*"

Silence. They all looked at one another.

Irma said brightly, "Those are words for parting. We are joining."

"Misalignment?" the alien said. "Then—" And silky words came from it, *good-bye* in several human languages.

Irma said slowly, carefully, "We are happy you have learned our languages. Very good. We all speak Anglish."

"I have compressor knowledge. Now can adjust."

Cliff said, "Where did you get such data on our languages?"

"Astronomers. They sent all to hunters."

"You are a hunter?"

"We Sils, true. Also others."

"What kind of others?"

"Others of Adopted."

"Who are—?"

"Those brought here. Not species made in Bowl."

"From other planets?"

"True." The big yellow eyes studied them all in turn. "Like you."

"We haven't been—"

"Now to be Adopted. That is goal Astronomers."

Irma asked, "Adopted . . . how?"

"Genes. Social rules. Status adjustment." This came out as hard, firm statements from the narrow mouth. Cliff wondered about inferring emotions from facial signatures in aliens, but this case at least seemed clear. The constricted face oozed resentment.

"What next?" Terry asked, puzzled.

"Large sharing comes soon," the catlike alien said. "Onto here I-we came to speak and share help. Have time now little."

"Why?" Aybe asked. They were having trouble understanding the slippery slide of Quert's words and the odd context.

"Stop soon, will. Others come."

"So we—?"

"Leave next stop. Must."

Quert flexed its hands. They had six fingers ending in sharp nails. The palm was broad and covered by fine hairs. Now that Cliff studied the creature, he saw it was clothed in a subtle woven fabric that mimicked the tan-colored fine hairs. Perhaps that helped camouflage it?

"How long do we have until the next stop?" Aybe asked, looking edgy.

"Short." Then Quert stopped prowling and looked at each of them in turn. "The Sky Rule will come."

"Those who are after us?" Aybe asked.

"I have fellows there. We may share violence."

"We all?" Irma asked.

"Must quick," Quert said with slippery vowels, and fished

from its clothes an oddly sloped cylinder with a transparent lens at one end. "You carry force?"

"You mean weapons?" Terry asked.

"Wea—yes. My vocabulary adjusting. Do I need of your tongues other?"

"Those languages?" Irma thought. "No. But—the Astronomers gave you all those?"

"They had from other primates, or so said."

"You can un-learn a language?"

Quert's eyes then did something startling. They elongated up and down, an expression with no human parallel. Cliff realized it must mean surprise or puzzlement. Quert said, "Must do. Am crowded and slow now."

Then the graceful creature sat at last and closed its eyes. Its eyelids vibrated as if shaken from behind and it did not move. Cliff noted the slowing of the *snick-snick-snicks*.

The electromagnetic handoffs now turned to braking. "Should we hide?" Howard asked. "If we're to get out—"

Quert abruptly sat up, shook its head. "Gone. Better." It looked around at them quizzically, as if coming out of a deep sleep. "Yes. Get down so they not see. Then leave we."

They went back into rooms and crouched below windows. A pale light rose in the walls outside, and they all brought out their lasers. These were nearly fully charged, since they had followed strict recharging rules in the magcar.

Quert crouched as the train slowed. Cliff sprang up as it stopped with a solid jolt and there were robots everywhere outside.

"Go time," Quert said, and they went.

Out onto the platform, identical to the one at which they'd boarded. Robots of gray and green worked steadily on the freight cars and ignored them as they passed. They ran.

After some dim corridors they came out into a broad high-arched plaza under the relentless sunlight. Cliff slowed, stunned.

Hundreds of howling creatures like Quert sent up a warbling, sonorous call. They carried tubes and packs and looked well organized, formed up into ranks. They greeted Quert with high-pitched shouts and words that came over more as shrieks to Cliff. In the eyes of these aliens he saw jittery vigor, anxious turns of heads, a fearful energy. They seemed oddly human, but made small dances that broke out among them, knots of spinning joy within rectangular ranks. This stirred and confused him. The smell was like a crisp, fragrant corral. The humans ran through a corridor of celebration.

They nearly made it. Outside in the raw sunlight, the surging bodies made an impressive display, but halfway across a big canyon floor some zipping pulses came down abruptly from the ramparts above.

Screams, loud hollow thumps, panic. Cliff stuck close to Quert and ran for the canyon walls.

They got into a cleft in an orange conglomerate rock and were working back through it, led by Quert, when a heavy rolling blast caught them and slammed them to the ground.

Quert got up unsteadily. "Come . . . they."

Strange whistling sounds came from the plain outside. Cliff glanced back as they jogged down the cleft. He could see a lancing green light surge down, a hard fizzing spark like a lightning flash you could see in full daylight. Answering deep explosions rocked the air. Pebbles and sand streaked by them with a *whoosh*. They ran harder.

They came out into a side canyon where more of Quert's kind clustered. They grouped around black angular snouts that thrust up into the air. *Guns*, Cliff thought. No matter how alien this place was, form followed function. They stopped and Quert said, "We show now."

The guns erupted in short, spatting flashes. Cliff ducked at the noise and tried to see what they were firing at. The narrow barrels recoiled like howitzers, but no spent shells ejected from their base. The barrels tracked slowly and the alien teams cheered.

"Get we over!" Quert yelled in a high, rasping voice.

"Where?" Irma shouted over the banging salvos.

Quert gestured to a rock bluff hundreds of meters away. There were at least a dozen of the long-barreled guns firing and aliens ran everywhere, shouting orders. *We're in a war,* Cliff thought. *And I thought we were getting away from trouble on the nice train. . . .*

"Better do what they say!" Aybe yelled. "We dunno what's up."

Understatement, Cliff thought, and nodded. They started running, weaving away from the gun crews.

They got about halfway across, led by the swift Quert, when suddenly horrible screeches rose from all sides. Quert barked out a congested howl and fell to the ground. But Cliff felt nothing.

The guns stopped. Screams of agony came from all around.

"It's some kind of pain gun!" Aybe yelled. "Gets them, not us."

They hesitated. He had once been the kid who stood at the top of the waterslide, overthinking it. Finally he had learned to do, not think, and navigate the chute as it came at you. A big moment, back when he was six years old. Now here it was again. Same answer: *down the chute.*

"Go!" He picked up Quert—surprisingly light, as if it had no bones—and sprinted forward. Where? With no guide, he just ran across the canyon. There was a tunnel in the canyon wall and the humans fled to it. Shrieks of terrifying pain came all around them. It was a long run through chaos, three hundred meters as fast as they could go. They made it, to the tunnel, leaping over writhing alien bodies, driven to hammer forward by barely controlled panic. He put the alien down.

Panting in the shadows, Irma gasped, "I couldn't see who was shooting."

"Up in the sky," Aybe said in a hoarse voice, winded. "A smaller version. Of that living blimp. We saw before."

Cliff looked down at Quert, who was sprawling, dazed. He edged out and looked up. A scaly brown football with fins was waltzing lazily across the sky. Big flat antennas hung down from it, probably the source of the pain ray. It moved like a fat, preying insect. The green beams cast down their burning lances.

He remembered feeling a pain flash once. His flesh had cried out, *I'm on fire!* He had looked down at his arm where the invisible beam was landing, and tried to say, *This is just my nerves getting jangled, I can take this*, but that didn't work. The body ignored his mind, which knew the 95-gigahertz radiation was stimulating the nerves in his skin. His skin just kept screaming, *I'm on fire!*

Same effect here, different frequency. The aliens had different wiring. If you wanted to hurt them, you tuned for the wavelengths that forked into the nervous system and didn't let go. Electromagnetics were the same everywhere; you just had to know the right frequency. Pain flowed into you on invisible wings.

The other aliens were running away. No, *herded* away.

The brown football was churning across the sky, angling its antennas toward the crowd it swept before it. He watched the hundreds of fleeing figures rush down the canyon. A rabble.

"Maybe they're rounding these up," Irma said at his side.

"Nope," Aybe said beside her. "Getting them out of the way, yes. They're after *us*. That was our reception committee, Quert's people. The ones up there are running them off. I think—"

Then there was no more thinking as the brown football forked down more of the green rays. This time the enormous hollow *whoosh* thundered on for endless moments. They ducked. Debris blew by them. Pebbles rattled against rock, and big orange, broad-winged birds fell from the sky, squawking as they died.

They stood and watched as the dust cleared. Cliff didn't want to acknowledge what had happened, resisting what his eyes told him, until at his elbow Quert said in its slow, sliding sibilants, "Know we share with you. They kill us."

"Where can we go?" Terry asked in a dry croak, eyes jittery.

Cliff felt the same—dozens of Quert's folk had died a few hundred meters away. Thin screams came from there. And the football was moving this way.

Quert, too, seemed shaken, its face a frozen stare. Slowly the alien drew its eyes away from infinity and said softly, slowly, "We share under ways. Must cross open spaces now."

"Why is that—" Terry groped for a word, failed. "—that thing in the sky shooting at you?"

"You they seek," Quert said simply, eyes still dazed.

"So they're after *us*?" Aybe asked, eyes wide.

"We heard you come. They know also."

Aybe eyed the living dirigible. "So they'll come after us."

"And we. Oppose Astronomers now."

"Then we have to nail them," Aybe said firmly.

Cliff saw the logic. Their pursuers knew the terrain; they didn't. "But we have no—"

"Use their guns. Can't be that hard."

The cries outside diminished. They looked out carefully and saw the big balloon was dealing with their victims, slamming down shots at them. "Distracted," Terry said. "Let's blow a hole in them. They're in range."

If the enemy's in range, so are you, Cliff thought but did not say.

• • •

Of course, the brown football turned and started beaming their pain gun again. The burst caught Quert while it was showing them how to aim and fire the auto-fed gun. Quert doubled up with the pain and went into thrashing jerks, head lolling back, eyes popping out as though pressure built inside its head. An awful sight.

With Terry, Cliff carried Quert into shelter. The pain gun cleared the area swiftly. Howard got a gun going and showed Terry how to manage another. They fired them intermittently as the brown football slowly made its way toward them. "Must be done killing the others," Terry said laconically. "We got maybe ten minutes before they can do that to us."

Cliff looked at the big lumbering thing in the sky, working its fins and—were those fans running under it? Yes, pushing the strange hybrid of life-form and engineering across the distance, maybe ten kilometers. Worse, the wind was with the thing.

They poured on the fire. The smart rounds burst into fragments as they neared the target, tearing into the wrinkled hide. Primitive weaponry, Cliff thought, and suddenly saw why. Quert's kind were unused to warfare, he gathered. No steady gun crew discipline, a lot of strange shouting. They had not done it before, and these guns were their first real try. Battlefields, Cliff reflected, are not the best place to learn your lessons.

Abruptly came the counterfire. He saw green stabs for an instant and then the cliff wall nearby shattered. He knew this only as he shook his head, on the ground. It had slammed him down and now he saw everything through a spatter of fractured light and clapping, hollow explosions. *Shock*, he thought. He drew in a big lungful of air, flavored with the tang of dirt. He got to his feet and helped Irma up. Dust clouds blew away in the wind and he saw that their artillery piece was shattered where a large rock had hit it. A few meters to the side, and it would have killed them all.

"Other . . . other guns still work," he croaked.

They limped to one nearby and Aybe jerked open the breech. "It's loaded. Let's give 'em hell."

They got it to firing, following shouted instructions from Quert. Cliff knew he was still dazed and stood aside as Aybe and Terry aimed it. There were systems that did sighting mounted on the gun deck, pictures that homed in and locked. Quert told them again how to work it, speaking patiently and slowly from shelter. The pain gun was still going, he could tell—the Sil who darted out to help others jerked and cried with the sheeting pain.

The gun slammed out shots at the approaching target. "Aim for the underside." Irma pointed. "There are portals there."

Aim changed. Shots exploded into shrapnel just short of the yellow ports lining the bottom seam of the big balloon creature. They could see the impact, kilometers away.

"That's a living thing," Aybe said. "It's gotta hurt."

The creature was unused to this. It flinched when the rounds struck—long waves broke across its skin, like slow-motion impacts of a huge fist on flesh. It began to turn.

At its side, a smaller craft burst from a green pod. It was a slim airplane and fell away in graceful arcs. All the action was smooth, slow. Then their guns ran dry and a silence fell on the canyon.

"Astronomer goes," Quert called weakly.

The huge creature hung in the air and small things began emerging from it. They crawled like spiders across the skin and covered the gaping red wounds with white layers.

"Fire some more?" Aybe asked. He had used up the ammo store.

"Don't think we have to," Irma said. She was getting her

composure back, patting the dust from her pants and blouse, and even brushing her hair into place.

Everyone quieted down. Faces human and alien alike were drawn, tired.

Apparently that meant the battle was over. Soon the pain gun antennas were out of view and the effect ended. The Sil who had stayed came out of shelter, and a great mournful dirge sounded. Their voices merged in a long, rolling chant. They moved among the fractured bodies, turning them to the perpetual sun. The song rose up and reverberated from canyon walls. Quert splayed arms to the sky and joined in the deep long notes. It was eerie and moving and Cliff let himself be drawn into it for a long while, despite his pounding heart.

But at last the feeling ebbed. The flapping balloon creature was moving languidly away across an empty sky as teams crawled over it, mending. Quietly the humans left their post and Quert seemed to revive, shaking itself in quick vibrations of arms and legs, as if shaking off a mood. Quert led them away and into a long, narrow passageway through the far side of the ruddy canyon.

They walked in silence, absorbing what had happened.

"May return," Quert warned. "Go."

They hurried through an underground passage. They spent five minutes of running, pounding down channels as the chants behind faded away. Quert showed them what looked like an air lock and they went through it fast. Beyond was a dimly lit tunnel. In this they ran for at least half an hour, just Quert and five other of the aliens—who ran with unhurried grace, their paces light, long, and quick—and following them came the humans, slogging on with thumping feet.

Like gazelles, Cliff thought, and then went back to pondering what might lie ahead. He had led them into this and for quite a while now he had not known where it was going.

Wandering and staying out of the hands of the Bird Folk had seemed obvious. Plus trying to learn—and those were the last things he had been certain of for a long time.

They reached a dock suddenly. But this was a vertical one with no-door elevators, chugging along at a speed that made it easy to step onto a descending plate. Quert showed them how and Howard jumped too heavily onto it, lost his balance, and fell to the floor. That made Terry laugh in a high-pitched way, while the others piled on.

Howard got his breath and they all looked at one another, aliens and humans alike. There was some odd commonality here he was too distracted to think about right now. Just assume it and see if it worked. Not a theory, but a plan.

Cliff staggered. His right leg went from a dull ache to a steadily building throb. *Adrenaline high is fading.* He felt the warmth from it flowing down into his boot. He sat down sloppily and breathed deep, sucking in air to calm his racing heart. Gingerly he felt the wound.

Irma said, "You're bleeding."

Cliff nodded, panting. "Flesh wound."

Howard said, "We're short of bandages."

"I'm not as badly hurt as we've seen," Cliff said. He tried a shrug. "I'll get by."

Irma had thought to take some of the clothing off the dead aliens. She handed him something shirtlike, cottony. With Irma's help, he tore it into lengths and folded one to make a pad. He tied that over the wound, pulling to get it tight, and the compress seemed to stop the bleeding. He did this automatically, recalling practice they had all gone through. *Centuries ago.*

They went on, Cliff limping.

They came down steadily in darkness and stepped off onto a metal frame in the rock. Beyond the elevator was no rock at all, just ceramics and fiber beams and even burnished metal. There were struts and the usual squared-off construction in a gravity well, but also curved arches and round hatches. Quert led them through support structures, and suddenly one wall was transparent and Cliff was looking into blackness pocked by tiny colored lights. *Stars.*

"It's . . . the backside of the Bowl," Aybe whispered.

Somehow the view was at an angle to vertical, not straight down through the floor. Local gravity was different here. Cliff watched a distant craft swim across this night sky, lit only by starlight. Then a nearer sphere came into view, with three small ships nosed against it. A fueling station? It slid by fast and Cliff realized they were the ones moving, spinning to maintain centrifugal grav at half a thousand kilometers per second. All you had to do to launch a ship was let go of it.

He pressed his face against the cold transparent window, just as the others did, and looked at long lanes of structures stretching away in all directions. Endless detail into the distance, with gray robot forms working over some towers nearby.

Quert's long vowels intruded on his thoughts. "Can see later. Now go."

It was hard to leave the view. The perspectives reminded him that they were never far from the vacuum of space, no matter how familiar some of the Bowl could seem.

"Come!" Quert took them onto another dock and then very fast into a narrow capsule. They fitted into horizontal slots with support straps, and as Cliff got his into place they took off to a swift sucking sound.

Cliff unwrapped the bulky bandage he had made, and the sight was not good. A dark stain had pasted his pants leg to the wound. It smelled bad and was suddenly popular with nasty little flies that came swirling out of nowhere. With Howard's help, Cliff shed the lower half of his peel-out trousers, unzipping to reveal the damage. There was an entrance wound on the right side of his calf and a matching, larger wound on the left. Water brought by the Sil washed off the crusted dark blood. The puckered openings were red and swollen.

Irma brought her first aid kit and pooled its resources with the kits of the others, each kit somewhat specialized. "Looks like some shrapnel went right through your calf muscle," she said calmly. "The leg's going to purple up."

"It's hard to walk on."

"Then don't."

She and Howard worked for a while, injecting him and putting clean compresses on the leg. Cliff watched the sky where puffy gray clouds raced one another.

Irma patted him. "You're not going to die."

"That's a relief. Don't have to call my insurance guy."

"You won't lose the leg."

"Even better. Hurts though. Got some fun drugs?"

That brought chuckles. "Ran out," Howard said. "My fault."

Irma said, "And your next question would be, 'Where are we?'"

"And the answer . . ."

"Going to a Sil refuge. Their casualties are in the cars ahead. They lost a lot of dead."

He didn't know what to say to that. And his head was feeling like a balloon that wanted to soar into the sky.

The trip lasted a long time amid bare dim lighting. He thought of talking to the others, but now he knew it was smarter to just rest when you could do nothing. He fell asleep, dreamed of discordant sights and sounds and colors, and just as on the train, came awake only to the tug of deceleration.

PART IX

I intend to live forever. So far, so good.

—STEVEN WRIGHT

FORTY-SIX

Beth stood in the entrance of the cave and listened as thunder forked down through immense, sullen cloud banks. They were stacked like a pyramid of anvils with purple bases. Down through them, leaping from anvil to anvil, came bright, sudden shafts of orange lightning. Fat raindrops smacked down, lit up by the flashes. Some of the glaring lances raced from one shadowy cloud to another and came down near them, exploding like bombs as they splintered trees.

"Majestic," Fred said at her side.

"Terrifying," she countered, but then admitted, "Beautiful, too."

"Look at those." Mayra pointed. In the milky daylight that filtered through the pyramid clouds, they watched moist plants move with a languid, articulating grace. Slowly they converged on the lightning damage. They came forth to extinguish the fires from those strikes.

"Protection, genetically ordained," Tananareve said.

"Sure they're not animals?" Fred asked.

"Do they look like animals?" Tananareve countered. "I checked, went out and lifted one. Roots on the end of those stalks. Roots that slip out easily from the soil when it rains."

"But the rain will put out the fires."

"Maybe they're healing something else. We really don't know how this ecology works, y'know," Tananareve said.

"And the ecology's only skin deep," Fred said. "Ten meters

or so down, there's raw open space. Maybe the lightning can screw up subsurface tech."

Beth listened to the full range of sounds rain makes in a high, dense forest. Pattering smacks at the top, gurgling rivulets lower, as the drops danced down the long columns of the immense canopy. The orchestrated sounds somehow encased her, lifted her up into a world utterly unnatural but somehow completely secure, while seeming still so strange.

Somewhere in this immense mechanism Cliff was . . . what? Still free? Captured and interrogated? Her skimpy communication with *SunSeeker* confirmed that he got through to them intermittently and was moving cross-country. That was all she knew, yet it would have to be enough.

The rain, wind, and lightning daggers swept her along in a sudden tide of emotions she had kept submerged. She longed for him, his touch, the low bass notes as he whispered in her ear of matters loving, delightful, often naughty. Lord, how she missed that. They liked making love while rain spattered on the windows, back there centuries ago. It gave them a warm, secure place to be themselves, while the world toiled on with its unending business. They had ignored the world for a while, and it ignored them.

Fair enough. But this whirling contrivance could not be ignored. It could kill you if you did not pay attention, and very probably would, she imagined. They would probably die here, and no one—Cliff, Redwing, Earth—would ever know, much less know why. Beth's small band certainly did not remotely understand this thing. Why was it cruising between the stars at all—driven forward by engineering that eclipsed into nothingness all that humanity had achieved? Why? . . .

"Fred, that idea of yours, where'd you get it?"

He shook himself from his reverie. "Just came to me."

"Straight out of your imagination?" Tananareve scowled at him. "Some imagination you got, to think dinosaurs—"

"I didn't *imagine* it, if you mean I concocted the idea. It just . . . came to me. Pieces all fit together. In a flash." As if in agreement, a big yellow bolt knifed down through the shimmering sky and slammed into the rock of the hill above them. Stones clattered down.

"There's no evidence for it," Lau Pin said.

"That globe we saw," Fred said. "It's like Earth, but the continents are wrong. All mushed together."

"Maybe the geologists got the continent details wrong," Beth said. "It's a long chain of reasoning, back seventy or so million years."

"Never mind that!" Mayra suddenly said. "What fossil evidence is there for any early civilization? Where are the ruins?"

"That much time?" Tananareve scoffed. "Nothing left. Subducted, rusted away, destroyed in a dinosaur war, maybe. Look, guys, the Cretaceous–Tertiary Boundary shows where the asteroid hit. It shows through in only a dozen places around the Earth. Why would you expect anything to be left at all?"

Lau Pin swept an arm out at the churning trees, the walking plants, lightning slicing down from towers of dark clouds. "What's the leap from some smart dinosaurs to *this*?"

"I don't know." Fred shrugged. "Depends on what the smart ones thought, how they saw their world."

"There's no fossil evidence for smart dinosaurs," Lau Pin said. He went back in the cave to turn their fire. It was cooking the last of the big carcass they had brought from the warehouse, and the yamlike roots. It had started smoking again, probably from rain blowing in, and they all had a coughing fit.

"You can't judge intelligence from the size of skulls," Beth said, "and anyway, dino skulls are plenty large. Look, they had grappler claws, a start toward hands. Later on, some dinosaurs had feathers—that's where birds came from. There's plenty we don't know about that era."

Fred nodded and then said quietly, "There was one clue.

When I saw that great holo of how they built this Bowl, I looked at the star in the distance. It looked a lot like the sun."

"That's it?" Lau Pin snorted dismissively.

Another shrug. "Started me thinking."

"They were really smart, built this—and got wiped out by a rock even we could deflect away centuries ago?" Mayra said. "Come *on*."

Fred shrugged yet again. "No answer. Maybe they got caught in a cultural phase where they stopped watching the skies. Look, it's an idea, not a complete theory."

As Mayra argued with Fred, Beth watched her. The deep furrows on Mayra's brow had gone away and the worry lines at the eyes, too. She seemed better about the death of her husband, and had even laughed a bit. But Beth was sure that Abduss was never far from her mind. Nor was Cliff from hers, of course. She would never forget the squashed Abduss she had seen, still breathing for a short while in milky spurts, frothy saliva dripping like cream down to his ears while his cracked skull leaked brown blood into his eyes.

Beth shook her head to sweep away the image. She left them to their discussion and sat down near the cave entrance to savor the scent of the rain. As a little girl, she had loved that smell—freshness enveloping her, fragrances boiling into the air. They weren't on Earth, but it *felt* the same. "This Bowl has a lot of similarities to Earth, yes? Maybe the really strange stuff, like those walking plants, are from other worlds."

Fred nodded eagerly. "Or tens of millions of years of directed evolution."

"Point is," Beth said, "even if Fred's right, *how do we use the theory*? How can it help us?"

Lau Pin stretched, drew in a clean lungful of moist air. "Sleep on it, I say. Fred, you get your ideas how? Dreaming?"

"No, but I have them when I wake up. I go to sleep thinking about things, problems—and when I wake up, there's an idea there. Maybe wrong, but . . . it's like getting a note from another part of myself."

Beth got up and patted Fred on the shoulder. "I suspect that's why you made *SunSeeker* crew, too. Didn't you figure out the high-voltage capacitors in the ramscoop?"

He smiled. "Yeah. That was fun. That was a neat puzzle."

"Sleep again, after you take the first watch. Maybe the part of you that never sleeps will come up with more ideas."

Beth unfolded her cushion from her backpack and inflated it with long, deep breaths. A part of her eyed Fred's lean stance framed by the cave's mouth. *Wait a bit, get it on with him? You're horny, alone—do something.* But she brushed the impulse away. *Don't complicate a team that's barely getting by.*

By the time she was ready to sleep, the rest were distributed back through the small cave, grateful for some shade and the storm's muting of the constant sunlight. She squinted through the clouds and could barely see the star's disk.

As she dropped off to sleep, she thought of Cliff again. He had always been better at fieldwork than she was, and she hoped maybe he understood this weird place better. Would she ever find him in this huge world-machine? "G'night, Cliffy. Wherever you are."

She hugged her blow-up pillow and smelled the rain and thought of places secure and warm and far away.

FORTY-SEVEN

Memor had always enjoyed the serene voyaging these living craft afforded. She looked down on the slow passage of rugged terrain and breathed in a luxurious sweet aroma. The mucus of this great beast had been engineered to carry a delicate fragrance unlike anything else. Its scent was a luxury and settled the mind, though chaos raged all about them. She allowed herself another lingering taste, then turned with an appropriately severe expression.

"This is truly absurd," Memor said. "We have dozens of airfish aloft and much airplane coverage. Yet the prey keeps ducking belowground, eluding us."

The Captain of this armed airfish gestured with indifference. "We will turn them up. They exited the Longline transport at the station below. They can surely not go far— Wait, see those Sils?"

The reed-thin male peered at a large wall display. Small life-forms filled narrow canyons of tan rock. More of the Adopted species, one Memor had not seen before, were coming into the crowds, arriving apparently by foot. Good—an agricultural culture, with low technologies and simple ways.

The Captain drawled thoughtfully, "They cluster in several canyons. No dancing, no parades or ceremony. This is not their usual communal gathering."

"You know well these . . . ?"

"Sils, we term them. Always an unruly lot. Not the first

time, my dear Astronomer, that I have taken to air to discipline these."

"The problem persists?"

"Yes, has worsened steadily. The Sils are among the worst of the Adopted. They are not much evolved beyond carnivores, so I suppose we should not be surprised. Herbivores—why did we not bring more of *those* aboard?" The Captain blinked, taken aback by his own outburst.

"Because herbivores are seldom intelligent," Memor said dryly. "Good eating, though—we do have some of those."

"Of course, of course." The Captain turned and barked out quick orders to his staff officers. They were taking more rattling fire. The great beast that carried them protested in long grumbling notes that rolled through the walls that ran with juice.

Memor watched the living opalescent walls run with anxiety dewdrops, shimmering moist jewels hanging and spattering with an acid odor. Skyfish expressed their deep selves through chemistry, an unreliable, or at least largely unreadable, medium. They were perhaps the most successful of the Adopted. Taken from the upper atmosphere of a gas giant world long ago, they found the deep atmosphere of the Bowl a similar paradise to cruise and mate and turn water into their life fluid, hydrogen. Somehow the great ones of the early Bowl had managed to make these living skyships merge into the blossoming Bowl ecosphere. To cruise the skies in them was a voyage into history.

She turned when the Captain, now quite distressed, was done. "Can we disperse this crowd? They hamper our finding these primates."

The Captain gave an efficient flutter of feather-arcs: agreement. "I can use standard suffering methods."

"Do so."

The Captain gave orders and the great belly of the skyfish

began its laborious turn. Memor circled the observation deck, scattering small crew before her, to see how the Sils were moving. Streams of them came from all directions. Such crowds! Many walked, some ran with a dogged pace, others rode animals. They looked up at the skyfish. Some stopped and shook themselves, their rage evident. At what? Their target was the Longline station.

"Captain! When might the primates arrive here?"

"They could get here soon, Astronomer. It is possible. But we do not expect them to follow a simple route, staying on the same line. That would be too obvious." This last sentence provoked an involuntary submission-flutter of amber and brown as the Captain saw the implications.

"They may realize we expect evasion."

"Our strategy command thinks that unlikely—"

"Humor me."

"These Sil have no way of knowing—"

"There are always betrayers, Captain. Information crosses patchwork boundaries, though we try to stop it."

"I wonder, Astronomer, why your esteemed presence came here. Surely the primate invaders would not take a simple route—"

"Do not presume to estimate the rationality of aliens. Nor their clever nature."

"Surely you do not expect them—"

"These Sils gather for a reason."

"But how could—? Of course, these Sils have given us trouble since my grandmother's time. They see this as another device to—"

"You are wasting time."

The Captain hurried off to alter his commands. The skyfish eased lower as it wallowed across the air, toward the stony ridges that marked the Longline here.

Memor took some moments to review on her private

mind-feed the background of these Adopted, the Sil. The Bowl had passed near their star as the Sil were still in hunter-gatherer stages. The Bird Folk found Sil promising, and brought many aboard. Those early Sil were long since left behind genetically—crafty they had been, yes, but not that smart. Something close to the far older Bowl primates, but with ambition, tool-making and better social skills, developed through group hunting. As usual, their first tools had been weapons. This always led to a spirited species, which could be positive—but not, alas, for the Sils. They made their periodic rebellions, and were periodically reinstructed, often genetically.

These Sils evolved first in trees—often a source of later troubles, for it gave them dexterous use of several limbs. Thus the Bird Folk bred quite deliberately for higher intelligence and tool use, by increasing artificial selection, testing the results, and directing their mating to enhance the effects. The Sil were domesticated and made smarter, suiting them better for the technological jobs needed to tend the Bowl. Troubles came when these wily ones rebelled, or worse, tried to expand their territory. The tragic solution was to be avoided, of course, but even that didn't always work.

"Crews! Begin firing!" the Captain called.

Memor braced herself. This was the inevitable problem with using living beings to fly in the Bowl's deep atmosphere. Of course, they could not use chemical fuels for every aircraft, as that would tax the farming regions beyond their endurance. Electrodynamic flight was preferred for long stays aloft, but was too delicate for the long skirmishes that regional patrol officers had to carry out. Skyfish, though, could bear up under the typically archaic weaponry Adopted species could bring to bear. Further, its immense vault of hydrogen made it ferocious in close air support.

As Memor watched, the crew used their flame guns on

scattered Sil groups on the ridgeline. These were apparently spotters, for they were armed with simple chemical explosive weapons. As the skyfish slewed slowly to the left, it brought its flame spouts to bear. Gouts of rich golden flame raked the ridge. They were so close, Memor could hear angry shouts from the burning ridge, often followed by shrieks and screams as their last agony came to them. Not a delicious sound, but reassuring, yes.

Then the pain projectors came into play. Memor watched as the Captain adroitly directed the assaults, driving the Sil. The running, struggling Sil looked like herd animals in a panic. Then the green laser pulses destroyed them in densely packed groups. It slashed down, annihilating in fire and ferment. The Sil broke into fleeing remnants.

But the skyfish was taking hits as well. The simple Sil had fixed artillery set up with surprisingly mischievous warheads that blew shredding blasts into the underbody. Memor felt the floor vibrate as the great beast reacted, flinching from the wounds. A deep bass note rang and the wall membranes fluttered. In answer the gun crews poured on more pain projector power. Soundless, this was the standard weapon to terrify opponents.

Yet the artillery fire did not abate, even under maximum power. "The Sil surely cannot withstand—" Memor broke off as she saw on the viewer the gun crews. Primates!

The Late Invaders had come. "Captain, use your lasers."

The male displayed a corona of dismay. "Their fire has disabled our forward batteries, Astronomer. I apologize for—"

The skyfish writhed as shrapnel struck it. Long rolling waves warped the moist walls. Equipment smashed down from their perches. Crew ran by, babbling of emergencies. Memor ignored this and said, "Your sting does not take with these primates. They have different neurons. You must use the gas-fed lasers."

"We will get them up and running. A few moments—"

A volley from below slammed into the great beast. Memor carefully descended, feet seeking a balance as the floor shifted—down a great curving stair and through a polished plate glass dilating door into the skyfish bridge. Chaos.

The Captain turned and bowed. "We have taken many hits, Astronomer. Perhaps we relied on the agony projectors too much—"

"Perhaps?" Memor scarcely thought it necessary to point out that the skyfish was floundering, spewing fluids from multiple wounds, losing altitude, veering erratically. "Perhaps?"

"I propose we withdraw—"

"If you can."

"We can mend and rearm at higher altitude—"

"If you can reach it."

Skyfish had all the advantages of living technologies, but they had their own life cycles as well. The marriage of life with material was a great ancient success that made the Bowl biosphere work, but of course with drawbacks. Life-forms needed rest and could self-repair, and even with help could reproduce—and all that took time. In battle, at times knowing the organism's limits meant having the wisdom to withdraw.

"This beast is badly damaged. It's frightened—feel it?" The floor and walls were vast lapidary membranes that now shook with a neurological spasm. Smoldering fumes rose amid the clanging discord.

"We relied too much perhaps on the agony projectors. In future—"

"You have no future. We are so close to these primates, yet they prevail."

"I can—"

"Get me to my pod."

"I believe we have the situation in hand, or soon will," the Captain persisted. "My crews can quickly bring the laser—"

"If the hydrogen vaults are breached, we shall have no further disputes. I will have my pod *now*."

Memor loved the moist, fragrant membranes of skyfish, but prudence demanded that she not risk herself while this great being floundered and perhaps even failed. She swiftly followed the running escorts, down a long ramp and to the side farthest away from the rattling battle. Here her pod waited, with crew looking anxious. "Depart," she said, "with speed."

As they dropped away from the great belly of the beast, Memor wondered what this reversal might mean. There had been regional revolts before, of course. These Sil fit the age-old pattern—an Adopted species suffers some cultural or even genetic shift, and becomes difficult to manage. Standard strategy was to contain the conflict, using reliable nearby territories. Such struggles set up larger scale rivalries, of course, and with adroit handling, these could lead to calm. Once the regional Profounds played factions off against each other, stability emerged.

That would have to be done here—unless the aliens upset the usual forces. These Sil were canny creatures, a fairly recent addition to the Adopted. A mere twelve-triple-cubed Annuals had passed since their genetic alteration had pacified them. Perhaps it was time for a more fundamental solution—pruning.

But the primates had now shown that they were too destabilizing. Their ship, which might hold technologies of some use, might as well be destroyed. Those at large would have to be exterminated. It was a pity, for their minds were a fount of oddities, and study might reveal some of the features of the Folk in far antiquity—even before the opening of the Undermind.

Well, perhaps Memor could conduct some research with them, before the executions. That would be a just reward for her, after all the annoying troubles they had brought.

FORTY-EIGHT

Sitting on a riverbank beside lounging aliens, Cliff recalled his father showing him how to cast for fish.

The rhythm, first—how to cast the line with his elbow doing the real work and his wrist firm while the left hand payed out the line. A quick rainbow trout had leaped for it in a silver flash. He had felt it tug back and forth as it fought. When he reeled it in, the gasping body was a sacred, beautiful thing. He had thrown it back, on impulse, and his dad had laughed, comprehending the wonder of it.

No such goal here. He landed a big, floppy thing that watched him with huge round yellow eyes when he dragged its bulk up onto the shoreline. Oddly, once out of the water it did not fight. Maybe it expected to be tossed back in? If aliens did catch-and-release, maybe so.

He fidgeted the hook out—the fish mouths were bony and complex here—and turned with the heavy body in his arms. The Sil danced their heads around and made a high, murmuring noise. Slowly it dawned on him that this was their way of applauding.

One Sil came forward, took the fish, and did an astonishing thing. It cast the fish up and with a flashing knife blade caught the skin, tossed the fish up using the leverage, and spooled the skin off. It was a miraculous trick, skinning the fish—and then the Sil sectioned the fish, too, in slashing cuts as it turned in air. One of the Sil offered Cliff a hand-sized slice of sashimi.

Cliff took a bite out of courtesy. It was near tasteless, something like tai.

These creatures were quicker than the eye could see.

Their lands were different, too: lush greenery, few rocky landscapes, odd trees and big-leafed plants rich in fruit. Plenty of scampering small game, too, which the Sil must relish hunting.

He sat and thought about the Sil for a while and then of Beth. He wondered where she was, what she had learned. He recalled the soft brush of her hair on his chest when she hovered over him, sighing in low, sliding notes. He longed to see her, share the eerie wonder of this place with her. There might be trouble over Irma, but . . . *but what?*

He had deliberately not thought about the problem. Irma had been a refuge from the increasing tensions that came from roving in hostile territory, yes. . . . But was there more to it? He didn't know.

Face problems as they come, he realized, had become his working rule. Irma sat down lazily beside him. "If you leave out these meaningful silences, I won't fall asleep."

Cliff shrugged. "No meaning at all. I'm just feeling good."

She yawned. "My dad always said—" She did a deep, boisterous male voice. "—it's never too late to have a happy childhood."

"I already had mine."

"Did you follow all that talk from Quert?"

"About being an 'Adopted' species?"

"Yeah, that whoever runs this place takes on board species from worlds they cruise by."

"They have the room for it."

"Not really a new idea, just bigger scale. I mean, we humans invented our own little niche evolution when we domesticated wolves."

"Sure, and when we turned bottle gourds into containers.

But equally, that let dogs and gourds colonize the human niches—catch a ride on an opportunity."

"The Bowl is an opportunity passing by, with land to spare."

"This is a clue to why they built this thing. It's impossibly big, sure, using materials so strong, they rival the subnuclear struts we have in *SunSeeker*. But they haven't let the smart species here overrun the natural environment."

She sat up and watched a Sil try Cliff's makeshift fishing rod. The Sil had their own, but were curious. It spun a line out a long distance with one liquid move. "You mean, they haven't done what we did to Earth."

"Right. And got to go star-hopping while they do it."

"We evolved to take short-term predictions and make snap decisions using them. Long term isn't our strong suit. Just look at the Age of Appetite—it ran more than two centuries!"

"Must have been fun."

He applauded as the Sil caught a fish, uglier and even bigger than his. His noise made Sils nearby turn, startled, and give them long looks. Cliff recalled that if humans stared at each other for long, it meant they would either fight or make love. With the Sil, staring was clearly more complex. Their graceful faces used the eyes as much as humans used their mouths for signaling. Apparently right eye squinting and left wide open meant puzzlement.

He contented himself with just waving. Their eyes widened in appreciation.

"The 2100s were about digging out from the damage, getting the climate stable. Only way to do it was with a big presence in space, metals and rare earths from asteroids, a solar system economy. Then we got hungry for the stars."

"They must've, too."

"Then why not just send out ramscoops, like us?"

"Maybe they did. Maybe came to Earth and left no trace."

"Haven't we seen Earth species here?"

He nodded. "I've seen plenty of things I recognized. It could be parallel evolution—function calls out form, the same shapes. Like that fish. It's god-awful ugly, but so are some fish I saw in the Caribbean."

"Bet it tastes good, though."

His stomach growled. "I'll start a fire. That's a good point—the twist of molecules, the chemical hookups here. They're close enough to ours so we don't starve."

Quert appeared from the rich foliage, carrying a pack. "Swimmer! Good." In one swift sweep, he took it from Cliff and said, "Cook we will."

Cliff sniffed the air. "Woodsmoke. They already knew I'd catch something."

"They're smart. I wonder why they took such losses just to pluck us off that train."

"They want out from under the boss who runs this."

"Well, we sure can't help them."

"Probably not. We're damned lucky to be alive."

"Did you think we'd last this long?"

"Not really." Cliff took a deep breath and plunged on, feeling awkward. "I . . . didn't think we'd become lovers, either."

She blinked and looked hard at the river flowing past, clear and cool. Avoiding his eyes. "We're not, really. At least, I don't love you."

"Me either. 'Utility sex,' wasn't that what you called it?"

She giggled nervously. "I did say that."

"You and your guy were going to have a standard contract marriage?" he said to be saying something.

"Yup, when we got settled at Glory. Then I'd bring out my stored eggs and have a family. We figured a twenty-five-year contract would do that nicely."

"Beth and me, we hadn't gotten that specific. In all the training, there wasn't time to . . ."

"To really think it through? Actually, it's feeling it through that does the trick."

"Um. 'Love is not love which alters when it alteration finds.' I suppose."

"What? Oh, Shakespeare. Well, this is alteration"—she waved a hand at the Bowl, which hung like a shimmering haze across the sky—"beyond anything I imagined."

"So . . ." He savored finally getting some use from his high school English, then sobered. He wanted to get something settled but didn't know how. "We keep up with the . . . utility?"

She shrugged. "It helps." Then she gave him a wicked grin. "That's my story for now."

"Might be trouble when we meet our mates."

"Face that when it comes."

He stood, stretching. He watched in the distance dust devils climb toward the roof of the sky, in an atmosphere so deep, he could see huge dark clouds that hung like mountains in the high, fuzzy distance. How were they ever going to figure out this place?

Aybe, Howard, and Terry arrived, carrying some plants they had harvested with the Sil. "Shoulda had you along, Cliff, so's you'd know what these things are, if we can eat 'em. Howard spotted a lot of this."

"My God, Terry, you're drunk!" Cliff took the plants and checked them; they looked reasonable. But he couldn't take his eyes from Terry and—yes, Aybe also had a bleary look.

"They gave us a drink, said it was refreshin'," Terry said.

Howard said, "Tastes a little like pineapple wine. Bland. I was not tricked, boss." He thumped his chest. "Alcohol."

"I'll say. The chemistry here really is similar." Cliff waved them to the riverside. *Might as well relieve the pressure when they can. . . .*

Was ethanol a universal? It appeared in low densities in star and planetary system forming regions: simple organic chemistry. It was just sugars turning bad, so they formed a hydroxyl with carbon. Chimpanzees used it, too. Maybe all higher intelligences sometimes needed to escape from the prison of reason?

"So," Aybe plopped down and said with the owlish manner of a drunk trying to pretend he's sober, "where do we go from here?"

"There's a price on our heads, boys," Irma said. "I say stay here, rest up, learn from these Sil."

"We can eat," Howard said. "Nev-ever a given."

"We need a plan," Aybe said.

"A goal without a plan is just a wish," Irma said. "But what's our goal?"

"There's enough room here," Terry said with leaden profundity, "for everybody cold sleepin' on *SunSeeker* to live."

"But this isn't a planet, it's a park!" Irma shot back.

"Seems big enough for a million planets. Strange aliens. Room to make somethin' new." Terry nodded to himself.

Irma's eyes and nostrils flared. "We didn't cast off everybody we knew to come to this place!"

"Well, we're here anyway," Aybe said solemnly. "We don't even know if we can get *SunSeeker* started up right again."

"There's damn plenty we don't know, right," Terry agreed.

Cliff eyed them and saw this was an idea brewing for some time among them. Carefully he said, "Look, we're in a crazy place. But don't let your preoccupation with reality stifle your imagination. We're bound for Glory."

In their pealing laughter he heard joy.

FORTY-NINE

The inhabited section of the Bowl, its vast ring-shaped rim, was what Redwing had come to call the Great Plain. Now *Sun-Seeker* crossed softly over the rim of the Bowl, and the Great Plain fell behind. Far below, the cellophane sky dropped to touch a rise in the Bowl's understructure, bulging outward by a few kilometers, as they crossed the Bowl rim. "Stay well clear," Redwing told Jam again. "We don't want to burn holes in their sky with our magnetics."

Jam grinned as if at a joke. "Yes, sir. Do your enemy no small injury." He added, "Machiavelli."

So the great ship floated past the rim with 100,000 kilometers to spare. Redwing watched, mesmerized, until Ayaan whacked his back with her fist. "Captain! I've got Fred Oyama!"

"Hot damn! Patch me through. Fred, need update on your condition."

Ayaan said, "Talk past him. You're twenty-three minutes apart at lightspeed, and all they can send us is text. Talk and I'll text-connect it."

"Yah. Fred, we're cruising around back of the Bowl to see what we can see. Our last contact with Beth's team had her in a cluster of caves. She's worried about what low gravity is doing to their bones and such. Otherwise they're safe. She should have at least a couple of months, but then they'll all need *SunSeeker*'s hospital section.

"We've solved the problem with *SunSeeker*'s motors," he

said, and decided not to give details. The ship had been delayed by the Bowl's head wind, just enough to matter. Maybe *SunSeeker* could have veered around the Bowl's wake and kept on to Glory, stretching their supplies to the max. But the Bowl was a bigger game, really, he decided. An unimaginable jackpot—if they survived it. Glory could wait.

Redwing watched Ayaan working their antenna system to keep him on target. Their technology was at its very limits, communicating over such vast, constantly moving ranges.

"We've fiddled some with the menu, including some biochem information, so I'll beam you an update, *now*." Ayaan nodded and pressed a key to send the prepared squirt.

"I'd like to pick you all up. We should at least plan to meet. It would be great if we could find a meet place. The trouble as I see it is that any site big enough to see from here would be like arranging to meet in Australia." Redwing laughed, then remembered that he wouldn't hear a response. "Too big. But if we could find something like a radio station, we could find each other there. We'll look for antennas of any kind while we're here."

He paced the deck, trying to wedge in every thought before they lost the connection. "Of course, there's no docking or refueling arrangements for us that we understand on the outer skin. Of course, we've lost one of our landers. Never mind, we still have the *Hawking* and *Chang* and *Dyson*. Your team has been without medical treatment for four months now. We need to debrief you."

Not the best time, a link just when they were coasting out over the rim. "I'm looking at the back of the Bowl, seeing quite a lot of structure. Blems, bubbles, angular structures, crisscrossed lines . . . I'm zooming on an intersection . . . those are tubes networking . . . maybe a transport system. Looks like spiderwebbing.

"Bigger, shorter tubes right at the rim. Knobby gray structures big as . . . well, little moons. Like Ceres. Several of 'em. I can see the nearest one in motion. Really big. Too big to be a weapon. Helical lines running round the inside—"

Redwing's internal alarm bells went off. "Karl, what do you think?"

Karl was standing alert, almost crouching. He said crisply, "Looks like they're encased in magnetic field coils. Maybe some sort of offensive weapon."

"Or telescope," Clare said.

Karl shook his head. "Astronomy? Nah. No need for that long cylinder. Could be a laser of a kind we don't know? Huge, in any case."

"Looks like old-style cannon," Redwing said. "Except bigger than makes any sense."

Clare Conway said, "Maybe they fight planets. *Big* cannon. Captain, we'll be looking right into that tube in maybe twenty minutes."

Karl said, "The nearest of them is swiveling to engage us, sir."

Redwing frowned. "Okay. Jam, start us turning. Stay away from the focus of that thing. Ayaan, do you still have Fred? Fred, give me some good news, will you?"

Jam said quickly, "With your permission, Captain, I'll bring us back above the Great Plain."

"Do that. Fred, we'll be out of touch in a few minutes. We have a message from Earth. I'll squirt it *now*."

. . .

They lost the Fred link. What Clare had called a cannon continued to follow them. Jam and Clare rolled the ship to escape. The magscoop flexed and fought as it reconfigured, seizing on whatever ionized solar wind it could grasp. They dropped down below the Bowl rim.

"No telescope could be that big," Clare said. "Right? Captain?"

"Jam, is she right?"

"I'm going lower," Jam said, concentrating on their trajectory. Long rolling waves hummed through the ship. "Scopes don't need to be long, just wide to capture light. But to emit light . . ."

They were over the Great Plain now, decelerating a little to bring them past the rim. Clare said, "That does it. That long tube isn't following us anymore."

"Doesn't want to fire on the Great Plain." Redwing made it a straight assertion based on his intuition. That hid some of his relief.

Jam said, "Maybe they can't. If it's a cannon, and if it could swivel down to fire on inhabited turf . . . a civil war could get really nasty, couldn't it?"

Redwing didn't know, so he didn't answer.

Ayaan said, "My lucky day. I've got fresh text from Cliff's team. Spotty and noisy, but the software cleaned it pretty well. Want to see it?"

She put the long message on all their screens. Cliff's team had discovered a tram system and learned to use it; had met aliens and fought a war with them as allies; those aliens had led them into the Bowl's structural undergrowth. There were low-res pictures. They were eating well enough, and grateful for Beth's menu instructions.

"Mostly they're staying alive and moving," Redwing said. There were smiles all around. "Great news."

"But even if they're not captured, they're getting nowhere," Ayaan added.

Redwing was getting near the end of his watch so handed off to Karl and went to his cramped quarters. They had snagged a cluster of messages from Sol system while beyond the Bowl's lip, and the AI had them crisply decoded on his private computer. He told it to speak the messages as he ate dinner alone—Sri Lankan rice and chicken in a deep tangy sauce. One of the biggest threats to stability in a spacecraft was sensory deprivation of a subtle sort, and tasty food helped a lot. So would sex, but that was a dead end for a captain. There was a certain lady he'd like to revive, but the circumstances had to call for it—probably, when he needed large ground teams. There was nothing official between them, no contract, no conditional agreement. And big ground teams didn't seem to be a good bet here anyway. He sighed, watched the great construct roll on below, and turned to the tightbeam communications.

There were some tech updates on the grav waves. He set them aside for Karl after a glance and read the executive summary. After centuries of study, Earthside didn't know a whole lot more. The wavelengths and wave packets still implied huge masses waltzing around each other in complex patterns. Yet large aperture studies of the Glory system showed no such masses at all. Maybe grav theory was wrong, one message said. Or they were watching a source accidentally in the same spot of the sky and much farther away.

He read that ". . . final merger of two black holes in a binary system releases more power than the combined light from all the stars in the visible Universe. This vast energy comes in the form of gravitational waves, bearing the waveform signature of the merger." Far too much power to be the Glory signature, but the waveforms were like those from the merger theory.

Or else, the summary said, ". . . the effect is fictional, made up somehow to deceive us." Fictional? Maybe the language had changed. Facts never had to be plausible; fiction did. He snorted.

The last century or so of messages had taken on an odd flavor of exhortations to the same refrain—the glories of their mission and urging them on. Sometimes these carried overt religious tones, but this one was an eco-sermon. He told his software to mine it for real information.

Most of the real news was on biosphere management: Earthside, the carbon sequestration that had worked well was having side effects. The warmed, expanded oceans were building up their carbonates, a product from the deployed farm waste carbon dropped into them. Now some was coming back out. Seeding the ocean to capture CO_2 by sweetening the ocean dead zones had also capped out, and the climate engineers couldn't stuff more in. Alarm bells . . .

All the things put off for a few centuries were now biting back. The only thing Earthside had truly planned for on a centuries-long timescale was the starships. . . .

He turned on his wall screen and looked at the distant landscapes drifting past—low mountains crested in snow, vast forests, river valleys the size of Earthly continents. How *did* these creatures run their Bowl? It had to be far more complex than managing a mere planet.

Could the Bowl teach Earth something crucial about terraforming? That alone would be worth stopping for.

He made himself run through the rest of the tightbeam signals. There were some updates on performance modes of their onboard AIs, some hardware issues, suggested upgrades here and there. Most likely these came as feedback from other starships. *SunSeeker*, too, had tightbeamed back such reports. He was pretty sure the summaries he had sent about the Bowl were the most bizarre ever transmitted.

He captained a starship, but this enormous thing was a star that drove a ship, was the propulsion, a star that was the essence of the ship itself. It ran on fusion, too, like *SunSeeker*. It was a . . . shipstar.

So . . . who captained it?

END OF VOLUME ONE

• • •

VOLUME TWO:

Shipstar

WILL FOLLOW SOON.

ACKNOWLEDGMENTS

We conferred on scientific and literary matters with many helpful people. Erik Max Francis, Joe Miller, and Joan Slonczewski gave detailed comments on the manuscript. Don Davis, Mark Martin, and Joe Miller and James Benford were of great help in technical issues. And of course, Olaf Stapledon and Freeman Dyson were first.